THE MARRIAGE
of
ELINOR

BY

MRS. OLIPHANT

First published in 1892

British Library Cataloguing-in-Publication Data
A catalogue record for this book is available
from the British Library

CONTENTS

Margaret Oliphant

Margaret Oliphant was born in Wallyford, Scotland in 1828. When she was ten years old, her family moved to Liverpool, where she began to experiment with writing. She had her first novel, *Passages in the Life of Mrs. Margaret Maitlan* (1849), published when she was just 21. It was a moderate commercial success, and following her second novel (*Caleb Field,* published in 1851) Oliphant became a regular contributor to the famous *Blackwood's Magazine.*

By the 1860s, Oliphant was a popular and recognized author, and in order to support her family (she had become a widow in 1959) she became an incredibly prolific author. Oliphant eventually went on to write more than 120 works, including novels travelogues, histories and volumes of literary criticism. Two of her better-known fictional works are *Miss Marjoribanks* (1866) and *Phoebe Junior* (1876). Towards the end of her life, she wrote a well-received series of supernatural short stories called *Tales of the Seen and Unseen* (1885), which remains popular to this day. Oliphant died in 1897, aged 69.

CHAPTER I.

John Tatham, barrister-at-law, received one summer morning as he sat at breakfast the following letter. It was written in what was once known distinctively as a lady's hand, in pointed characters, very fine and delicate, and was to this effect:—

"DEAR JOHN, Have you heard from Elinor of her new prospects and intentions? I suppose she must have written to you on the subject. Do you know anything of the man?... You know how hard it is to convince her against her will of anything, and also how poorly gifted I am with the power of convincing any one. And I don't know him, therefore can speak with no authority. If you can do anything to clear things up, come and do so. I am very anxious and more than doubtful; but her heart seems set upon it.

"Your affect.
"M. S. D."

Mr. Tatham was a well-built and vigorous man of five-and-thirty, with health, good behaviour, and well-being in every line of his cheerful countenance and every close curl of his brown hair. His hair was very curly, and helped to give him the cheerful look which was one of his chief characteristics. Nevertheless, when these innocent seeming words, "Do you know the man?" which was more certainly demonstrative of certain facts than had those facts been stated in the fullest detail, met his eye, Mr. Tatham paused and laid down the letter with a start. His ruddy colour paled for the moment, and he felt something which was like the push or poke of a blunt but heavy weapon somewhere in the regions of the heart. For the moment he felt that he could not read any more. "Do you know the man?" He did not even ask what man in the momentary sickness of his heart. Then he said to himself, almost angrily, "Well!" and took up the letter again and read to the end.

Well! of course it was a thing that he knew might happen any day, and which he had expected to happen for the last four or five years. It was nothing to him one way or another. Nothing could be more absurd than that a hearty and strong young man in the full tide of his life and with a good breakfast before him should receive a shock from that innocent little letter as if he had been a sentimental woman. But the fact is that he pushed his plate away with an exclamation of disgust and a feeling that everything was bad and uneatable. He drank his tea, though that also became suddenly bad too, full of tannin, like tea that has stood too long, a thing about which John was very particular. He had been half an hour later than usual this morning consequent on having been an hour or two later than usual last night. These things have their reward, and that very speedily; but as for the letter, what could that have to do with the bad toasting of the bacon and the tannin in the tea? "Do you know the man?" There was a sort of covert insult, too, in the phraseology, as if no explanation was needed, as if he must know by instinct what she meant—he who knew nothing about it, who did not know there was a man at all!

After a while he began to smile rather cynically to himself. He had got up from the breakfast table, where everything was so bad, and had gone to look out of one of the windows of his pleasant sitting-room. It was in one of the wider ways of the Temple, and looked out upon various houses with a pleasant misty light upon the redness of their old brickwork, and a stretch of green grass and trees, which were scanty in foliage, yet suited very well with the bright morning sun, which was not particularly warm, but looked as if it were a good deal for effect and not so very much for use. That thought floated across his mind with others, and was of the same cynical complexion. It was very well for the sun to shine, making the glistening poplars and plane-trees glow, and warming all the mellow redness of the old houses, but what did he mean by it? No warmth to speak of, only a fictitious gleam—a thing got up for effect. And so was the affectionateness of woman—meaning nothing, only an effect of warmth and geniality, nothing beyond that. As a matter of fact, he reminded himself after a while that he had never wanted anything beyond, neither asked for it, nor wished it. He had no desire to change the conditions of his life: women never rested till they had done so, manufacturing a new event, whatever it might be, pleased even when they were not pleased, to have a novelty to announce. That, no doubt, was the state of mind in which the lady who called herself his aunt was: pleased to have something to tell him, to fire off her big guns in his face, even though she was not at all pleased with the event itself. But John Tatham, on the other hand, had desired nothing to happen; things were very well as they were. He liked to have a place where he could run down from Saturday to Monday whenever he pleased, and where his visit was always a cheerful event for the womankind. He had liked to take them all the news, to carry the picture-papers, quite a load; to take down a new book for Elinor; to taste doubtfully his aunt's wine, and tell her she had better let him choose it for her. It was a very pleasant state of affairs: he wanted no change; not, certainly, above everything, the intrusion of a stranger whose very existence had been unknown to him until he was thus asked cynically, almost brutally, "Do you know the man?"

The hour came when John had to assume the costume of that order of workers whom a persistent popular joke nicknames the "Devil's Own:"—that is, he had to put on gown and wig and go off to the courts, where he was envied of all the briefless as a man who for his age had a great deal to do. He "devilled" for Mr. Asstewt, the great Chancery man, which was the most excellent beginning: and he was getting into a little practice of his own which was not to be sneezed at. But he did not find himself in a satisfactory frame of mind to-day. He found himself asking

9

the judge, "Do you know anything of the man?" when it was his special business so to bewilder that potentate with elaborate arguments that he should not have time to consider whether he had ever heard of the particular man before him. Thus it was evident that Mr. Tatham was completely *hors de son assiette*, as the French say; upset and "out of it," according to the equally vivid imagination of the English manufacturer of slang. John Tatham was a very capable young lawyer on ordinary occasions, and it was all the more remarkable that he should have been so confused in his mind to-day.

When he went back to his chambers in the evening, which was not until it was time to dress for dinner, he saw a bulky letter lying on his table, but avoided it as if it had been an overdue bill. He was engaged to dine out, and had not much time: yet all the way, as he drove along the streets, just as sunset was over and a subduing shade came over the light, and that half-holiday look that comes with evening—he kept thinking of the fat letter upon his table. Do you know anything of the man? That would no longer be the refrain of his correspondent, but some absurd strain of devotion and admiration of the man whom John knew nothing of, not even his name. He wondered as he went along in his hansom, and even between the courses at dinner, while he listened with a smile, but without hearing a word, to what the lady next him was saying—what she would tell him about this man? That he was everything that was delightful, no doubt; handsome, of course; probably clever; and that she was fond of him, confound the fellow! Elinor! to think that she should come to that—a girl like her—to tell him, as if she was saying that she had caught a cold or received a present, that she was in love with a man! Good heavens! when one had thought her so much above anything of that kind—a woman, above all women that ever were.

"Not so much as that," John said to himself as he walked home. He always preferred to walk home in the evening, and he was not going to change his habit now out of any curiosity about Elinor's

10

letter. Oh, not so much as that! not above all women, or better than the rest, perhaps—but different. He could not quite explain to himself how, except that he had always known her to be Elinor and not another, which was a quite sufficient explanation. And now it appeared that she was not different, although she would still profess to be Elinor—a curious puzzle, which his brain in its excited state was scarcely able to tackle. His thoughts got somewhat confused and broken as he approached his chambers. He was so near the letter now—a few minutes and he would no longer need to wonder or speculate about it, but would know exactly what she said. He turned and stood for a minute or so at the Temple gates, looking out upon the busy Strand. It was still as lovely as a summer night could be overhead, but down here it was—well, it was London, which is another thing. The usual crowd was streaming by, coming into bright light as it streamed past a brilliant shop window, then in the shade for another moment, and emerging again. The faces that were suddenly lit up as they passed—some handsome faces, pale in the light; some with heads hung down, either in bad health or bad humour; some full of cares and troubles, others airy and gay—caught his attention. Did any of them all know anything of this man, he wondered—knowing how absurd a question it was. Had any of them written to-day a letter full of explanations, of a matter that could not be explained? There were faces with far more tragic meaning in them than could be so easily explained as that—the faces of men, alas! and women too, who were going to destruction as fast as their hurrying feet could carry them; or else were languidly drifting no one knew where—out of life altogether, out of all that was good in life. John Tatham knew this very well too, and had it in him to do anything a man could to stop the wanderers in their downward career. But to-night he was thinking of none of these things. He was only wondering how she would explain it, how she could explain it, what she would say; and lingering to prolong his suspense, not to know too soon what it was.

At last, however, as there is no delay but must come to an end one time or another, he found himself at last in his room, in his smoking-coat and slippers, divested of his stiff collar—at his ease, the windows open upon the quiet of the Temple Gardens, a little fresh air breathing in. He had taken all this trouble to secure ease for himself, to put off a little the reading of the letter. Now the moment had come when it would be absurd to delay any longer. It was so natural to see her familiar handwriting— not a lady's hand, angular and pointed, like her mother's, but the handwriting of her generation, which looks as if it were full of character, until one perceives that it *is* the writing of the generation, and all the girls and boys write much the same. He took time for this reflection still as he tore open the envelope. There were two sheets very well filled, and written in at the corners, so that no available spot was lost. "My dear old John," were the first words he saw. He put down the letter and thought over the address. Well, she had always called him so. He was old John when he was fourteen, to little Elinor. They had always known each other like that—like brother and sister. But not particularly like brother and sister—like cousins twice removed, which is a more interesting tie in some particulars. And now for the letter.

"MY DEAR OLD JOHN: I want to tell you myself of a great thing that has happened to me—the very greatest thing that could happen in one's life. Oh, John, dear old John, I feel as if I had nobody else I could open my heart to; for mamma—well, mamma is mamma, a dear mother and a good one; but you know she has her own ways of thinking——"

He put down the letter again with a rueful little laugh. "And have not I my own ways of thinking, too?" he said to himself.

"Jack dear," continued the letter, "you must give me your sympathy, all your sympathy. You never were in love, I suppose (oh, what an odious way that is of putting it! but it spares one's feelings a little, for even in writing it is too tremendous a thing to say quite gravely and seriously, as one feels it). Dear John, I know you never were in love, or you would have told me; but still——"

"Oh," he said to himself, with the merest suspicion of a little quiver in his lip, which might, of course, have been a laugh, but, on the other hand, might have been something else, "I never was—or I would have told her—That's the way she looks at it." Then he took up the letter again.

"Because—I see nothing but persecution before me. It was only a week ago that it happened, and we wanted to keep it quiet for a time; but things get out in spite of all one can do—things of that sort, at least. And, oh, dear Jack, fancy! I have got three letters already, all warning me against him; raking up trifling things that have occurred long ago, long before he met me, and holding them up before me like scarecrows—telling me he is not worthy of me, and that I will be wretched if I marry him, and other dreadful lies like that, which show me quite plainly that they neither know him nor me, and that they haven't eyes to see what he really is, nor minds to understand. But though I see the folly of it and the wickedness of it, mamma does not. She is ready to take other people's words; indeed, there is this to be said for her, that she does not know him yet, and therefore cannot be expected to be ready to take his own word before all. Dear Jack, my heart is so full, and I have so much to tell you, and such perfect confidence in your sympathy, and also in your insight and capacity to see through all the lies and wicked stories which I foresee are going to be poured upon us like a flood that—I don't know how to begin, I have so many things to say. I know it is the heart of the season, and that you are asked out every night in the week, and are so popular everywhere; but if you could but come down from Saturday to Monday, and let me tell you everything and show you his picture, and read you parts of his letters, I know you would see how false and wrong it all is, and help me to face it out with all those horrid people, and to bring round mamma. You know her dreadful way of never giving an opinion, but just saying a great deal worse, and leaving you to your own responsibility, which nearly drives me mad even in little things—so you may suppose what it does in this. Of course, she must see him, which is all I want, for I know after she has had a half-hour's conversation with him that she will be like me and will not believe a word—not one word. Therefore, Jack dear, come, oh, come! I have always turned to you in my difficulties, since ever I have known what it was to have a difficulty, and you have done everything for me. I never remember any trouble I ever had but you found some means of clearing it away. Therefore my whole hope is in you. I know it is hard to give up all your parties and things; but it would only be two nights, after all— Saturday and Sunday. Oh, do come, do come, if you ever cared the least little bit for your poor cousin! Come, oh, come, dear old John!

"Your affect.
E———."

"Is that all?" he said to himself; but it was not all, for there followed a postscript all about the gifts and graces of the unknown lover, and how he was the victim of circumstances, and how, while other men might steal the horse, he dared not look over the wall, and other convincing pleadings such as these, till John's head began to go round. When he had got through this postscript John Tatham folded the letter and put it away. He had a smile on his face, but he had the air of a man who had been beaten about the head and was confused with the hurry and storm of the blows. She had always turned to him in all her difficulties, that was true: and he had always stood by her, and often, in the freemasonry of youth, had thought her right and vindicated her capacity to judge for herself. He had been called often on this errand, and he had never refused to obey. For Elinor was very wilful, she had always been wilful—"a rosebud

14

set about with wilful thorns, But sweet as English air could make her, she." He had come to her aid many a time. But he had never thought to be called upon by her in such a way as this. He folded the letter up carefully and put it in a drawer. Usually when he had a letter from Elinor he put it into his pocket, for the satisfaction of reading it over again: for she had a fantastic way of writing, adding little postscripts which escaped the eye at first, and which it was pleasant to find out afterwards. But with this letter he did not do so. He put it in a drawer of his writing-table, so that he might find it again when necessary, but he did not put it in his breast pocket. And then he sat for some time doing nothing, looking before him, with his legs stretched out and his hand beating a little tattoo upon the table. "Well: well? well!" That was about what he said to himself, but it meant a great deal: it meant a vague but great disappointment, a sort of blank and vacuum expressed by the first of these words—and then it meant a question of great importance and many divisions. How could it ever have come to anything? Am I a man to marry? What could I have done, just getting into practice, just getting a few pounds to spend for myself? And then came the conclusion. Since I can't do anything else for her; since she's done it for herself— shall I be a beast and not help her, because it puts my own nose out of joint? Not a bit of it! The reader must remember that in venturing to reflect a young man's sentiments a dignified style is scarcely possible; they express themselves sometimes with much force in their private moments, but not as Dr. Johnson would have approved, or with any sense of elegance; and one must try to be truthful to nature. He knew very well that Elinor was not responsible for his disappointment, and even he was aware that if she had been so foolish as to fix her hopes upon him, it would probably have been she who would have been disappointed, and left in the lurch. But still——

John had gone through an interminable amount of thinking, and a good deal of soda-water (with or without, how should I know, some other moderate ingredient), and a cigar or two—not to speak of certain hours when he ought to have been in bed to keep his head clear for the cases of to-morrow: when it suddenly flashed upon him all at once that he was not a step further on than when he had received Mrs. Dennistoun's letter in the morning, for Elinor, though she had said so much about him, had given no indication who her lover was. Who was the man?

CHAPTER II.

It was a blustering afternoon when John, with his bag in his hand, set out from the station at Hurrymere for Mrs. Dennistoun's cottage. Why that station should have had "mere" in its name I have never been able to divine, for there is no water to be seen for miles, scarcely so much as a duckpond: but, perhaps, there are two meanings to the words. It was a steep walk up a succession of slopes, and the name of the one upon which the cottage stood was Windyhill not an encouraging title on such a day, but true enough to the character of the place. The cottage lay, however, at the head of a combe or shelving irregular valley, just sheltered from the winds on a little platform of its own, and commanding a view which was delightful in its long sweeping distance, and varied enough to be called picturesque, especially by those who were familiar with nothing higher than the swelling slopes of the Surrey hills. It was wild, little cultivated, save in the emerald green of the bottom, a few fields which lay where a stream ought to have been. Nowadays there are red-roofed houses peeping out at every corner, but at that period fashion had not even heard of Hurrymere, and, save for a farm-house or two, a village alehouse and posting-house at a corner of the high-road, and one or two great houses within the circuit of six or seven miles, retired within their trees and parks, there were few habitations. Mrs. Dennistoun's cottage was red-roofed like the rest, but much subdued by lichens, and its walls were covered by climbing plants, so that it struck no bold note upon the wild landscape, yet was visible afar off in glimpses, from the much-winding road, for a mile or two before it could be come at. There was, indeed, a nearer way, necessitating a sharp scramble, but when

John came just in sight of the house his heart failed him a little, and, notwithstanding that his bag had come to feel very heavy by this time, he deliberately chose the longer round to gain a little time—as we all do sometimes, when we are most anxious to be at our journey's end, and hear what has to be told us. It looked very peaceful seated in that fold of the hill, no tossing of trees about it, though a little higher up the slim oaks and beeches of the copse were flinging themselves about against the grey sky in a kind of agonised appeal. John liked the sound of the wind sweeping over the hills, rending the trees, and filling the horizon as with a crowd of shadows in pain, twisting and bending with every fresh sweep of the breeze. Sometimes such sounds and sights give a relief to the mind. He liked it better than if all had been undisturbed, lying in afternoon quiet as might have been expected at the crown of the year—but the winds had always to be taken into account at Windyhill.

When he came in sight of the gate, John was aware of some one waiting for him, walking up and down the sandy road into which it opened. Her face was turned the other way, and she evidently looked for him by way of the combe, the scrambling steep road which he had avoided in despite: for why should he scramble and make himself hot in order to hear ten minutes sooner what he did not wish to hear at all? She turned round suddenly as he knocked his foot against a stone upon the rough, but otherwise noiseless road, presenting a countenance flushed with sudden relief and pleasure to John's remorseful eye. "Oh, there you are!" she said; "I am so glad. I thought you could not be coming. You might have been here a quarter of an hour ago by the short road."

"I did not think there was any hurry," said John, ungraciously. "The wind is enough to carry one off one's feet; though, to be sure, it's quiet enough here."

"It's always quiet here," she said, reading his face with her eyes after the manner of women, and wondering what the harassed look meant that was so unusual in John's cheerful face. She jumped at the idea that he was tired, that his bag was heavy, that he had been beaten about by the wind till he had lost his temper, always a possible thing to happen to a man. Elinor flung herself upon the bag and tried to take possession of it. "Why didn't you get a boy at the station to carry it? Let me carry it," she said.

"That is so likely," said John, with a hard laugh, shifting it to his other hand.

Elinor caught his arm with both her hands, and looked up with wistful eyes into his face. "Oh, John, you are angry," she said.

"Nonsense. I am tired, buffeting about with this wind." Here the gardener and man-of-all-work about the cottage came up and took the bag, which John parted with with angry reluctance, as if it had been a sort of weapon of offence. After it was gone there was nothing for it but to walk quietly to the house through the flowers with that girl hanging on his arm, begging a hundred pardons with her eyes. The folly of it! as if she had not a right to do as she pleased, or he would try to prevent her; but finally, the soft, silent apology of that clinging, and the look full of petitions touched his surly heart. "Well—Nelly," he said, with involuntary softening.

"Oh, if you call me that I am not afraid!" she cried, with an instant upleaping of pleasure and confidence in her changeable face, which (John tried to say to himself) was not really pretty at all, only so full of expression, changing with every breath of feeling. The eyes, which had only been brown a moment before, leaped up into globes of light, yet not too dazzling, with some liquid medium to soften their shining. Even though you know that a girl is in love with another man, that she thinks of you no more than of the old gardener who has just hobbled round the corner, it is pleasant to be able to change the whole aspect of affairs to her and make her light up like that, solely by a little unwilling softening of your gruff and surly tone.

"You know, John," she said, holding his arm tight with her two hands, "that nobody ever calls me Nelly—except you."

19

"Possibly I shall call you Nelly no longer. Why? Why, because that fellow will object."

"That fellow! Oh, *he*!" Elinor's face grew very red all over, from the chin, which almost touched John's arm, to the forehead, bent back a little over those eyes suffused with light which were intent upon all the changes of John's face. This one was, like the landscape, swept by all the vicissitudes of sun and shade. It was radiant now with the unexpected splendour of the sudden gleam.

"Oh, John, John, I have so much to say to you! He will object to nothing. He knows very well you are like my brother—almost more than my brother—for you could help it, John. You almost chose me for your friend, which a brother would not. He says, 'Get him to be our friend and all will be well!'"

He had not said this, but Elinor had said it to him, and he had assented, which was almost the same—in the way of reckoning of a girl, at least.

"He is very kind, I am sure," said John, gulping down something which had almost made him throw off Elinor's arm, and fling away from her in indignation. Her brother——!! But there was no use making any row, he said to himself. If anything were to be done for her he must put up with all that. There had suddenly come upon John, he knew not how, as he scanned her anxious face, a conviction that the man was a scamp, from whom at all hazards she should be free.

Said Elinor, unsuspecting, "That is just what he is, John! I knew you would divine his character at once. You can't think how kind he is—kind to everybody. He never judges anyone, or throws a stone, or makes an insinuation." ("Probably because he knows he cannot bear investigation himself," John said, in his heart.) "That was the thing that took my heart first. Everybody is so censorious—always something to say against their neighbours; he, never a word."

"That's a very good quality," said John, reluctantly, "if it doesn't mean confounding good with bad, and thinking nothing matters."

Elinor gave him a grieved, reproachful look, and loosened the clasping of her hands. "It is not like you to imagine that, John!"

"Well, what is a man to say? Don't you see, if you do nothing but blow his trumpet, the only thing left for me to do is to insinuate something against him? I don't know the man from Adam. He may be an angel, for anything I can say."

"No; I do not pretend he is that," said Elinor, with impartiality. "He has his faults, like others, but they are *nice* faults. He doesn't know how to take care of his money (but he hasn't got very much, which makes it the less matter), and he is sometimes taken in about his friends. Anybody almost that appeals to his kindness is treated like a friend, which makes precise people think——but, of course, I don't share that opinion in the very least."

("A very wasteful beggar, with a disreputable set," was John's practical comment within himself upon this speech.)

"And he doesn't know how to curry favour with people who can help him on; so that though he has been for years promised something, it never turns up. Oh, I know his faults very well indeed," said Elinor; "but a woman can do so much to make up for faults like that. We're naturally saving, you know, and we always keep those unnecessary friends that were made before our time at a distance; and it's part of our nature to coax a patron—that is what Mariamne says."

"Mariamne?" said John.

"His sister, who first introduced him to me; and I am very fond of her, so you need not say anything against her, John. I know she is—fashionable, but that's no harm."

"Mariamne," he repeated; "it is a very uncommon name. You don't mean Lady Mariamne Prestwich, do you? and not— not——Elinor! not Phil Compton, for goodness' sake? Don't tell me he's the man?"

Elinor's hands dropped from his arm. She drew herself up until she seemed to tower over him. "And why should I say it is not Mr. Compton," she asked, with a scarlet flush of anger, so different from that rosy red of love and happiness, covering her face.

"Phil Compton! the *dis*-Honourable Phil! Why, Elinor! you cannot mean it! you must not mean it!" he cried.

Elinor said not a word. She turned from him with a look of pathetic reproach but with the air of a queen, and walked into the house, he following in a ferment of wrath and trouble, yet humbled and miserable more than words could say. Oh, the flowery, peaceful house! jasmine and rose overleaping each other upon the porch, honeysuckle scenting the air, all manner of feminine contrivances to continue the greenness and the sweetness into the little bright hall, into the open drawing-room, where flowers stood on every table amid the hundred pretty trifles of a woman's house. There was no one in this room where she led him, and then turned round confronting him, taller than he had ever seen her before, pale, with her nostrils dilating and her lips trembling. "I never thought it possible that you of all people in the world, you, John—my stand-by since ever I was a baby—my—— Oh! what a horrid thing it is to be a woman," cried Elinor, stamping her foot, "to be ready to cry for everything!— you, John! that I always put my trust in—that you should turn against me—and at the very first word!"

"Elinor," he said, "my dear girl! not against you, not against you, for all the world!"

"And what is *me*?" she said, with that sudden turning of the tables and high scorn of her previous argument which is common with women; "do I care what you do to *me*? Oh, nothing, nothing! I am of no account, you can trample me down under your feet if you like. But what I will not bear," she said, clenching her hands, "is injustice to him: that I will not bear, neither from you, Cousin John, who are only my distant cousin, after all, and have no right to thrust your advice upon me—or from any one in the world."

"What you say is quite true, Elinor, I am only a distant cousin—after all: but——"

"Oh, no, no," she cried, flying to him, seizing once more his arm with her clinging hands, "I did not mean that—you know I did not mean that, my more than brother, my good, good John, whom I have trusted all my life!"

And then the poor girl broke out into passionate weeping with her head upon his shoulder, as she might have leant upon the handy trunk of a tree, or on the nearest door or window, as John Tatham said in his heart. He soothed her as best he could, and put her in a chair and stood with his hand upon the back of it, looking down upon her as the fit of crying wore itself out. Poor little girl! he had seen her cry often enough before. A girl cries for anything, for a thorn in her finger, for a twist of her foot. He had seen her cry and laugh, and dash the tears out of her eyes on such occasions, oh! often and often: there was that time when he rushed out of the bushes unexpectedly and frightened her pony, and she fell among the grass and vowed, sobbing and laughing, it was her fault! and once when she was a little tot, not old enough for boy's play, when she fell upon her little nose and cut it and disfigured herself, and held up that wounded little knob of a feature to have it kissed and made well. Oh, why did he think of that now! the little thing all trust and simple confidence! There was that time too when she jumped up to get a gun and shoot the tramps who had hurt somebody, if John would but give her his hand! These things came rushing into his mind as he stood watching Elinor cry, with his hand upon the back of her chair.

She wanted John's hand now when she was going forth to far greater dangers. Oh, poor little Nelly! poor little thing! but he could not put her on his shoulder and carry her out to face the foe now.

She jumped up suddenly while he was thinking, with the tears still wet upon her cheeks, but the paroxysm mastered, and the light of her eyes coming out doubly bright like the sun from the clouds. "We poor women," she said with a laugh, "are so badly off, we are so handicapped, as you call it! We can't help crying like fools! We can't help caring for what other people think, trying to conciliate and bring them round to approve us—when we ought to stand by our own conscience and judgment, and sense of what

23

is right, like independent beings."

"If that means taking your own way, Elinor, whatever any one may say to you, I think women do it at least as much as men."

"No, it does not mean taking our own way," she cried, "and if you do not understand any better than that, why should I—— But you do understand better, John," she said, her countenance again softening: "you know I want, above everything in the world, that you should approve of me and see that I am right. That is what I want! I will do what I think right; but, oh, if I could only have you with me in doing it, and know that you saw with me that it was the best, the only thing to do! Happiness lies in that, not in having one's own way."

"My dear Elinor," he said, "isn't that asking a great deal? To prevent you from doing what you think right is in nobody's power. You are of age, and I am sure my aunt will force nothing; but how can we change our opinions, our convictions, our entire points of view? There is nobody in the world I would do so much for as you, Elinor: but I cannot do that, even for you."

The hot tears were dried from her cheeks, the passion was over. She looked at him, her efforts to gain him at an end, on the equal footing of an independent individual agreeing to differ, and as strong in her own view as he could be.

"There is one thing you can do for me," she said. "Mamma knows nothing about—fashionable gossip. She is not acquainted with the wicked things that are said. If she disapproves it is only because—— Oh, I suppose because one's mother always disapproves a thing that is done without her, that she has no hand in, what she calls pledging one's self to a stranger, and not knowing his antecedents, his circumstances, and so forth! But she hasn't any definite ground for it as you—think you have, judging in the uncharitable way of the world—not remembering that if we love one another the more there is against him the more need he has of me! But all I have to ask of you, John, is not to prejudice my mother. I know you can do it if you please—a hint would be enough, an uncertain word, even hesitating when you answer a question—that would be quite enough! John, if you put things into her head——"

"You ask most extraordinary things of me," said John, turning to bay. "To tell her lies about a man whom everybody knows—to pretend I think one thing when I think quite another. Not to say that my duty is to inform her exactly what things are said, so that she may judge for herself, not let her go forth in ignorance—that is my plain duty, Elinor."

"But you won't do it; oh, you won't do it!" she said. "Oh, John, for the sake of all the time that you have been so good to Nelly—your own little Nelly, nobody else's! Remember that I and everybody who loves him know these stories to be lies—and don't, don't put things into my mother's head! Let her judge for herself—don't, don't prejudice her, John. It can be no one's duty to repeat malicious stories when there is no possibility of proving or disproving them. Don't make her think—— Oh, mamma! we couldn't think where you had gone to. Yes, here is John."

"So I perceive," said Mrs. Dennistoun. It was getting towards evening, and the room was not very light. She could not distinguish their looks or the agitation that scarcely could have been hidden but for the dusk. "You seem to have been having a very animated conversation. I heard your voices all along the garden walk. Let me have the benefit of it, if there is anything to tell."

"You know well enough, mamma, what we must have been talking about," said Elinor, turning half angrily away.

"To be sure," said the mother, "I ought to have known. There is nothing so interesting as that sort of thing. I thought, however, you would probably have put it off a little, Elinor."

"Put it off a little—when it is the thing that concerns us more than anything else in the world!"

"That is true," said Mrs. Dennistoun, with a sigh. "Did you walk all the way, John? I meant to have sent the pony-cart for you, but the man was too late. It is a nice evening though, and coming out of town it is a good thing for you to have a good

25

walk."

"Yes, I like it more than anything," said John, "but the evening is not so very fine. The wind is high, and I shouldn't wonder if we had rain."

"The wind is always high here," said Mrs. Dennistoun. "We don't have our view for nothing; but the sky is quite clear in the west, and all the clouds blowing away. I don't think we shall have more than a shower."

Elinor stood listening to this talk with restrained impatience, as if waiting for the moment when they should come to something worth talking about. Then she gave herself a sort of shake—half weary, half indignant—and left the room. There was a moment's silence, until her quick step was heard going to the other end of the house and up-stairs, and the shutting of a door.

"Oh, John, I am very uneasy, very uneasy," said Mrs. Dennistoun. "I scarcely thought she would have begun to you about it at once; but then I am doing the very same. We can't think of anything else. I am not going to worry you before dinner, for you must be tired with your walk, and want to refresh yourself before we enter upon that weary, weary business. But my heart misgives me dreadfully about it all. If I only had gone with her! It was not for want of an invitation, but just my laziness. I could not be troubled to leave my own house."

"I don't see what difference it would have made had you been with her, aunt."

"Oh, I should have seen the man: and been able to judge what he was and his motive, John."

"Elinor is not rich. He could scarcely have had an interested motive."

"There is some comfort in that. I have said that to myself again and again. He could not have an interested motive. But, oh! I am uneasy! There is the dressing-bell. I will not keep you any longer, John; but in the evening, or to-morrow, when we can get a quiet moment——"

The dusk, was now pervading all the house—that summer

dusk which there is a natural prejudice everywhere against cutting short by lights. He could not see her face, nor she his, as they went out of the drawing-room together and along the long passage, which led by several arched doorways to the stairs. John had a room on the ground floor which was kept for gentlemen visitors, and in which the candles were twinkling on the dressing-table. He was more than ever thankful as he caught a glimpse of himself in the vague reflected world of the mirror, with its lights standing up reflected too, like inquisitors spying upon him, that there had not been light enough to show how he was looking: for though he was both a lawyer and a man of the world, John Tatham had not been able to keep the trouble which his interview with Elinor had caused him out of his face.

CHAPTER III.

The drawing-room of the cottage was large and low, and had that *faux air* of being old-fashioned which is dear to the hearts of superior people generally. Mrs. Dennistoun and her daughter scarcely belonged to that class, yet they were, as ladies of leisure with a little taste for the arts are bound to be, touched by all the fancies of their time, which was just beginning to adore Queen Anne. There was still, however, a mixture of luxury with the square settees and spindle-legged cabinets which were "the fashion:" and partly because that was also "the fashion," and partly because on Windyhill even a July evening was sometimes a little chill, or looked so by reason of the great darkness of the silent, little-inhabited country outside—there was a log burning on the fire-dogs (the newest thing in furnishing in those days though now so common) on the hearth. The log burned as little as possible, being, perhaps, not quite so thoroughly dry and serviceable as it would have been in its proper period, and made a faint hissing sound in the silence as it burned, and diffused its pungent odour through the house. The bow window was open behind its white curtains, and it was there that the little party gathered out of reach of the unnecessary heat and the smoke. There was a low sofa on either side of this recess, and in the centre the French window opened into the garden, where all the scents were balmy in the stillness which had fallen upon the night.

Mrs. Dennistoun was tall and slim, a woman with a presence, and sat with a sort of dignity on her side of the window, with a little table beside her covered with her little requirements, the properties, so to speak, without which she was never known to be—a book for moments when there was nothing else to interest

her, a case for work should there arise any necessity for putting
in a stitch in time, a bottle of salts should she or any one else
become suddenly faint, a paper cutter in cases of emergency, and
finally, for mere ornament, two roses, a red and a white, in one
of those tall old-fashioned glasses which are so pretty for flowers.
I do wrong to dismiss the roses with such vulgar qualifications
as white and red—the one was a *Souvenir de Malmaison*, the
other a *General* —— something or other. If you spoke to Mrs.
Dennistoun about her flowers she said, "Oh, the Malmaison," or
"Oh, the General So-and-so." Rose was only the family name,
but happily, as we all know, under the other appellation they
smelt just as sweet. Mrs. Dennistoun kept up all this little state
because she had been used to do so; because it was part of a lady's
accoutrements, so to speak. She had also a cushion, which was
necessary, if not for comfort, yet for her sense of being fully
equipped, placed behind her back when she sat down. But with
all this she was not a formal or prim person. She was a woman
who had not produced a great deal of effect in life; one of those
who are not accustomed to have their advice taken, or to find
that their opinion has much weight upon others. Perhaps it
was because Elinor resembled her father that this peculiarity
which had affected all Mrs. Dennistoun's married life should
have continued into a sphere where she ought to have been
paramount. But she was with her daughter as she had been with
her husband, a person of an ineffective character, taking refuge
from the sensation of being unable to influence those about
her whose wills were stronger than her own, by relinquishing
authority, and in her most decided moments offering an opinion
only, no more. This was not because she was really undecided,
for on the contrary she knew her own mind well enough; but it
had become a matter of habit with her to insist upon no opinion,
knowing, as she did, how little chance she had of imposing her
opinion upon the stronger wills about her. She had two other
children older than Elinor: one, the eldest of all, married in India,
a woman with many children of her own, practically altogether

severed from the maternal nest; the other an adventurous son, who was generally understood to be at the ends of the earth, but seldom or never had any more definite address. This lady had naturally gone through many pangs and anxieties on behalf of these children, who had dropped away from her side into the unknown; but it belonged to her character to have said very little about this, so that she was generally supposed to take things very easily, and other mothers were apt to admire the composure of Mrs. Dennistoun, whose son might be being murdered by savages at any moment, for anything she knew—or minded, apparently. "Now it would have driven *me* out of my senses!" the other ladies said. Mrs. Dennistoun perhaps did not feel the back so well fitted to the burden as appeared—but she kept her own sentiments on this subject entirely to herself.

(I may say too—but this, the young reader may skip without disadvantage—by way of explanation of a peculiarity which has lately been much remarked as characteristic of those records of human history contemptuously called fiction, *i.e.*, the unimportance, or ill-report, or unjust disapproval of the mother in records of this description—that it is almost impossible to maintain her due rank and character in a piece of history, which has to be kept within certain limits—and where her daughter the heroine must have the first place. To lessen *her* pre-eminence by dwelling at length upon the mother, unless that mother is a fool, or a termagant, or something thoroughly contrasting with the beauty and virtues of the daughter—would in most cases be a mistake in art. For one thing the necessary incidents are wanting, for I strongly object, and so I think do most people, to mothers who fall in love, or think of marriage, or any such vanity in their own person, and unless she is to interfere mischievously with the young lady's prospects, or take more or less the part of the villain, how is she to be permitted any importance at all? For there cannot be two suns in one sphere, or two centres to one world. Thus the mother has to be sacrificed to the daughter: which is a parable; or else it is the other way, which is against all the principles and prepossessions of life.)

Elinor did not sit up like her mother. She had flung herself upon the opposite sofa, with her arms flung behind her head, supporting it with her fingers half buried in the twists of her hair. She was not tall like Mrs. Dennistoun, and there was far more vivid colour than had ever been the mother's in her brown eyes and bright complexion, which was milk-white and rose-red after an old-fashioned rule of colour, too crude perhaps for modern artistic taste. Sometimes these delightful tints go with a placid soul which never varies, but in Elinor's case there was a demon in the hazel of the eyes, not dark enough for placidity, all fire at the best of times, and ready in a moment to burst into flame. She it was who had to be in the forefront of the interest, and not her mother, though for metaphysical, or what I suppose should now be called psychological interests, the elder lady was probably the most interesting of the two. Elinor beat her foot upon the carpet, out of sheer impatience, while John lingered alone in the dining-room. What did he stay there for? When there are several men together, and they drink wine, the thing is comprehensible; but one man alone who takes his claret with his dinner, and cares for nothing more, why should he stay behind when there was so much to say to him, and not one minute too much time till Monday morning, should the house be given up to talk not only by day but by night? But it was no use beating one's foot, for John did not come.

"You spoke to your cousin, Elinor, before dinner?" her mother said.

"Oh, yes, I spoke to him before dinner. What did he come here for but that? I sent for him on purpose, you know, mamma, to hear what he would say."

"And what did he say?"

This most natural question produced a small convulsion once more on Elinor's side. She loosed the hands that had been supporting her head and flung them out in front of her. "Oh, mamma, how can you be so exasperating! What did he say?

31

What was he likely to say? If the beggar maid that married King Cophetua had a family it would have been exactly the same thing—though in that case surely the advantage was all on the gentleman's side."

"We know none of the particulars in that case," said Mrs. Dennistoun, calmly. "I have always thought it quite possible that the beggar maid was a princess of an old dynasty and King Cophetua a *parvenu*. But in your case, Elinor——"

"You know just as little," said the girl, impetuously.

"That is what I say. I don't know the man who has possessed himself of my child's fancy and heart. I want to know more about him. I want——"

"For goodness' sake, whatever you want, don't be sentimental, mamma!"

"Was I sentimental? I didn't mean it. He has got your heart, my dear, whatever words may be used."

"Yes—and for ever!" said the girl, turning round upon herself. "I know you think I don't know my own mind; but there will never be any change in me. Oh, what does John mean, sitting all by himself in that stuffy room? He has had time to smoke a hundred cigarettes!"

"Elinor, you must not forget it is rather hard upon John to be brought down to settle your difficulties for you. What do you want with him? Only that he should advise you to do what you have settled upon doing. If he took the other side, how much attention would you give him? You must be reasonable, my dear."

"I would give him every attention," said Elinor, "if he said what was reasonable. You don't think mere blind opposition is reasonable, I hope, mamma. To say Don't, merely, without saying why, what reason is there in that?"

"My dear, when you argue I am lost. I am not clever at making out my ground. Mine is not mere blind opposition, or indeed opposition at all. You have been always trained to use your own faculties, and I have never made any stand against you."

"Why not? why not?" said the girl, springing to her feet. "That is just the dreadful, dreadful part of it! Why don't you say straight out what I am to do and keep to it, and not tell me I must make use of my own faculties? When I do, you put on a face and object. Either don't object, or tell me point-blank what I am to do."

"Do you think for one moment if I did, you would obey me, Elinor?"

"Oh, I don't know what I might do in that case, for it will never happen. You will never take that responsibility. For my part, if you locked me up in my room and kept me on bread and water I should think *that* reasonable; but not this kind of letting I dare not wait upon I would, saying I am to exercise my own faculties, and then hesitating and finding fault."

"I daresay, my dear," said Mrs. Dennistoun, with great tolerance, "that this may be provoking to your impatient mind: but you must put yourself in my place a little, as I try to put myself in yours. I have never seen Mr. Compton. It is probable, or at least quite possible, that if I knew him I might look upon him with your eyes——"

"Probable! Possible! What words to use! when all my happiness, all my life, everything I care for is in it: and my own mother thinks it just possible that she might be able to tolerate the man that—the man who——"

She flung herself down on her seat again, panting and excited. "Did you wear out Adelaide like that," she cried, "before she married, papa and you——"

"Adelaide was very different, Elinor. She married *salon les règles* a man whom we all knew. There was no trouble about it. Your father was the one who was impatient then. He thought it too well arranged, too commonplace and satisfactory. You may believe he did not object to that in words, but he laughed at them and it worried him. It has done very well on the whole," said Mrs. Dennistoun, with a faint sigh.

"You say that—and then you sigh. There is always a little reserve. You are never wholly satisfied."

"One seldom is in this world," said Mrs. Dennistoun, this time with a soft laugh. "This world is not very satisfactory. One makes the best one can of it."

"And that is just what I hate to hear," said Elinor, "what I have always heard. Oh, yes, when you don't say it you mean it, mamma. One can read it in the turn of your head. You put up with things. You think perhaps they might have been worse. In every way that's your philosophy. And it's killing, killing to all life! I would rather far you said out, 'Adelaide's husband is a prig and I hate him.'"

"There is only one drawback, that it would not be true. I don't in the least hate him. I am glad I was not called upon to marry him myself, I don't think I should have liked it. But he makes Adelaide a very good husband, and she is quite happy with him—as far as I know."

"The same thing again—never more. I wonder, I wonder after I have been married a dozen years what you will say of me?"

"I wonder, too: if we could but know that it would solve the question," the mother said. Elinor looked at her with a provoked and impatient air, which softened off after a moment—partly because she heard the door of the dining-room open—into a smile.

"I try you in every way," she said, half laughing. "I do everything to beguile you into a pleasanter speech. I thought you must at least have said then that you hoped you would have nothing to say but happiness. No! you are not to be caught, however one tries, mamma."

John came in at this moment, not without a whiff about him of the cigarette over which he had lingered so. It relieved him to see the two ladies seated opposite each other in the bow window, and to hear something like a laugh in the air. Perhaps they were discussing other things, and not this momentous marriage question, in which certainly no laughter was.

"You have your usual fire," he said, "but the wind has quite gone down, and I am sure it is not wanted to-night."

"It looks cheerful always, John."

"Which is the reason, I suppose, why you carefully place yourself out of sight of it—one of the prejudices of English life."

And then he came forward into the recess of the window, which was partly separated from the room by a table with flowers on it, and a great bush in a pot, of delicate maiden-hair fern. It was perhaps significant, though he did not mean it for any demonstration of partisanship, that he sat down on Elinor's side. Both the ladies felt it so instinctively, although, on the contrary, had the truth been known, all John's real agreement was with the mother; but in such a conjuncture it is not truth but personal sympathy that carries the day. "You are almost in the dark here," he said.

"Neither of us is doing anything. One is lazy on a summer night."

"There is a great deal more in it than that," said Elinor, in a voice which faltered a little. "You talk about summer nights, and the weather, and all manner of indifferent things, but you know all the time there is but one real subject to talk of, and that we are all thinking of that."

"That is my line, aunt," said John. "Elinor is right. We might sit and make conversation, but of course this is the only subject we are thinking of. It's very kind of you to take me into the consultation. Of course I am in a kind of way the nearest in relation, and the only man in the family—except my father—and I know a little about law, and all that. Now let me hear formally, as if I knew nothing about it (and, in fact, I know very little), what the question is. Elinor has met someone who—who has proposed to her—not to put too fine a point upon it," said John, with a smile that was somewhat ghastly—"and she has accepted him. Congratulations are understood, but here there arises a hitch."

"There arises no hitch. Mamma is dissatisfied (which mamma generally is) chiefly because she does not know Mr. Compton; and some wretched old woman, who doesn't know him either, has written to her—to her and also to me—telling us a pack of lies," said Elinor, indignantly, "to which I do not give the least credence for a moment—not for a moment!"

"That's all very well for you," said John, "it's quite simple; but for us, Elinor—that is, for your mother and me, as you are good enough to allow me to have a say in the matter—it's not so simple. We feel, you know, that, like Cæsar's wife, our Elinor's—husband"—he could not help making a grimace as he said that word, but no one saw or suspected it—"should be above suspicion."

"That is exactly what I feel, John."

"Well, we must do something about it, don't you see? Probably it will be as easy as possible for him to clear himself." (The dis-Honourable Phil! Good heavens! to think it was a man branded with such a name that was to marry Elinor! For a moment he was silenced by the thought, as if some one had given him a blow.)

"To clear himself!" said Elinor. "And do you think I will permit him to be asked to clear himself? Do you think I will allow him to believe for a moment that *I* believed anything against him? Do you think I will take the word of a spiteful old woman?"

"Old women are not always spiteful, and they are sometimes right." John put out his hand to prevent Mrs. Dennistoun from speaking, which, indeed, she had no intention of doing. "I don't mean so, of course, in Mr. Compton's case—and I don't know what has been said."

"Things that are very uncomfortable—very inconsistent with a happy life and a comfortable establishment," said Mrs. Dennistoun.

"Oh, if you could only hear yourself, mamma! You are not generally a Philistine, I must say that for you; but if you only heard the tone in which you said 'comfortable establishment!' the most conventional match-making in existence could not have done it better; and as for what has been said, there has nothing been said but what is said about everybody—what, probably, would be said of you yourself, John, for you play whist sometimes, I hear, and often billiards, at the club."

A half-audible "God forbid!" had come from John's lips when she said, "What would probably be said of yourself"—audible that is to Elinor, not to the mother. She sprang up as this murmur came to her ear: "Oh, if you are going to prejudge the case, there is nothing for me to say!"

"I should be very sorry to prejudge the case, or to judge it all," said John. "I am too closely interested to be judicial. Let somebody who knows nothing about it be your judge. Let the accusations be submitted—to your Rector, say; he's a sensible man enough, and knows the world. He won't be scared by a rubber at the club, or that sort of thing. Let him inquire, and then your mind will be at rest."

"There is only one difficulty, John," said Mrs. Dennistoun. "Mr. Hudson would be the best man in the world, only for one thing—that it is from his sister and his wife that the warning came."

"Oh!" said John. This fact seemed to take him aback in the most ludicrous way. He sat and gazed at them, and had not another word to say. Perhaps the fact that he himself who suggested the inquiry was still better informed of the true state of the case, and of the truth of the accusation, than were those to whom he might have submitted it, gave him a sense of the hopelessness and also absurdity of the attempt more than anything else could have done.

"And that proves, if there was nothing else," said Elinor, "how false it is: for how could Mrs. Hudson and Mary Dale know? They are not fashionable people, they are not in society. How could they or any one like them know anything of Phil"—she stopped quickly, drew herself up, and added—"of Mr. Compton, I mean?"

"They might not know, but they might state their authority," Mrs. Dennistoun said; "and if the Rector cannot be used to help us, surely, John, you are a man of the world, you are not like a woman, unacquainted with evidence. Why should not you do it, though you are, as you kindly say, an interested party?"

"He shall not do it. I forbid him to do it. If he takes in hand anything of the kind he must say good-by to me."

"You hear?" said John; "but I could not do it in any case, my dear Elinor. I am too near. I never could see this thing all round. Why not your lawyer, old Lynch, a decent old fellow——"

"I will tell him the same," cried Elinor; "I will never speak to him again."

"My dear," said her mother, "you will give everybody the idea that you don't want to know the truth."

"I know the truth already," said Elinor, rising with great dignity. "Do you think that any slander would for a moment shake my faith in you—or you? You don't deserve it, John, for you turn against me—you that I thought were going to take my part; but do you think if all the people in London set up one story that I would believe it against you? And how should I against *him*?" she added, with an emphasis upon the word, as expressing something immeasurably more to be loved and trusted than either mother or cousin, by which, after having raised John up to a sort of heaven of gratified affection, she let him down again to the ground like a stone. Oh, yes! trusted in with perfect faith, nothing believed against him, whom she had known all her life—but yet not to be mentioned in the same breath with the ineffable trust she reposed in the man she loved—whom she did not know at all. The first made John's countenance beam with emotion and pleasure, the second brought a cold shade over his face. For a moment he could scarcely speak.

"She bribes us," he said at last, forcing a smile. "She flatters us, but only to let us drop again, Mrs. Dennistoun; it is as good as saying, 'What are we to *him*?'"

"They all do so," said the elder lady, calmly; "I am used to it."

"But, perhaps, I am not quite—used to it," said John, with something in his voice which made them both look at him—Elinor only for a moment, carelessly, before she swept away—Mrs. Dennistoun with a more warmly awakened sensation, as if she had made some discovery. "Ah!" she said, with a tone of pain. But Elinor did not wait for any further disclosures. She waved her hand, and went off with her head high, carrying, as she felt, the honours of war. They might plot, indeed, behind her back, and try to invent some tribunal before which her future husband might be arraigned; but John, at least, would say nothing to make things worse. John would be true to her—he would not injure Phil Compton. Elinor, perhaps, guessed a little of what John was thinking, and felt, though she could scarcely have told how, that it would be a point of honour with him not to betray her love.

He sat with Mrs. Dennistoun in partial silence for some time after this. He felt as if he had been partially discovered—partially, and yet more would be discovered than there was to discover; for if either of them believed that he was in love with Elinor, they were mistaken, he said to himself. He had been annoyed by her engagement, but he had never come to the point of asking her that question in his own person. No, nor would not, he said to himself—certainly would not—not even to save her from the clutches of this gambler and adventurer. No; they might think what they liked, but this was the case. He never should have done it—never would have exposed himself to refusal—never besought this high-tempered girl to have the control of his life. Poor Nelly all the same! poor little thing! To think she had so little judgment as to ignore what might have been a great deal better, and to pin her faith to the dis-Honourable Phil.

CHAPTER IV.

In the morning John accompanied Elinor to church. Mrs. Dennistoun had found an excuse for not going, which I am sorry to say was a way she had. She expressed (and felt) much sorrow for it herself, saying, which was quite true, that not to go was a great distress to her, and put the household out, and was a custom she did not approve of. But somehow it had grown upon her. She regretted this, but did it, saying that everybody was illogical, and that when Elinor had some one to go with she thought herself justified at her age in this little indulgence. Neither Elinor nor John objected to the arrangement. There are things that can be said in a walk while both parties are in motion, and when it is not necessary to face each other and to be subjected each to the other's examination of feature and expression. It is easier in this way to say many things, to ask questions which might be embarrassing, to receive the fire of an examination which it might be otherwise difficult to meet. Thus the two had not walked above half the way to church, which was on the other edge of the combe, and stood, a lovely old place—but not the trim and restored and well-decorated edifice it is nowadays—tinkling its little bells into the sweet moorland air, amid such a hum of innumerable bees as seemed to make the very sunshine a vehicle for sound—before John began to perceive that he was being ingeniously driven to revelations which he had never intended, by a process for which he was not at all prepared. She who had been so indignant last night and determined not to allow a word to be said against the immaculate honour of the man she loved, was now—was it possible?—straining all her faculties to obtain from him, whom she would not permit to be Phil Compton's judge, such unguarded admissions as would enlighten her as to what Phil Compton was accused of. It was some time before John perceived her aim; he did not even grasp the idea at first that this girl whose whole heart was set upon marrying Phil Compton, and defying for his sake every prophecy of evil and all the teachings of prudence, did not indeed at all know what it was which Phil had been supposed to have done. Had she been a girl in society she could scarcely have avoided some glimmerings of knowledge. She would have heard an unguarded word here and there, a broken phrase, an expression of scorn or dislike, she might even have heard that most unforgettable of nicknames, the dis-Honourable Phil. But Elinor, who was not in society, heard none of these things. She had been warned in the first fervour of her betrothal that he was not a man she ought to marry, but why? nobody had told her; how was she to know?

"You don't like Lady Mariamne, John?"

"It matters very little whether I like her or not: we don't meet once in a year."

"It will matter if you are to be in a kind of way connected. What has she ever done that you shouldn't like her? She is very nice at home; she has three nice little children. It's quite pretty to see her with them."

"Ah, I daresay; it's pretty to see a tiger with her cubs, I don't doubt."

"What do you mean, John? What has she ever done?"

"I cannot tell you, Elinor; nothing perhaps. She does not take my fancy: that's all."

"That's not all; you could never be so unjust and so absurd. How dreadful you good people are! Pretending to mean kindness," she cried, "you put the mark of your dislike upon people, and then you won't say why. What have *they* done?"

It was this "they" that put John upon his guard. Hitherto she had only been asking about the sister, who did not matter so very much. If a man was to be judged by his sister! but "they" gave him a new light.

41

"Can't you understand, Elinor," he said, "that without doing anything that can be built upon, a woman may set herself in a position of enmity to the world, her hand against every one, and every one's hand against her?"

"I know that well enough—generally because she does not comply with every conventional rule, but does and thinks what commends itself to her; I do that myself—so far as I can with mamma behind me."

"You! the question has nothing to do with you."

"Why not with me as much as with another of my family?" said Elinor, throwing back her head.

He turned round upon her with something like a snort of indignation: she to be compared—but Elinor met his eyes with scornful composure and defiance, and John was obliged to calm himself. "There's no analogy," he said; "Lady Mariamne is an old campaigner. She's up to everything. Besides, a sister-in-law—if it comes to that—is not a very near relation. No one will judge you by her." He would not be led into any discussion of the other, whose name, alas! Elinor intended to bear.

"If it comes to that. Perhaps you think," said Elinor, with a smile of fine scorn, "that you will prevent it ever coming to that?"

"Oh, no," he said, "I'm very humble; I don't think much of my own powers in that way: nothing that I can do will affect it, if Providence doesn't take it in hand."

"You really think it's a big enough thing to invoke Providence about?"

"If Providence looks after the sparrows as we are told," said John, "it certainly may be expected to step in to save a nice girl like you, Nelly, from—from connections you'll soon get to hate—and—and a shady man!"

She turned upon him with sparkling eyes in a sudden blaze of indignation. "How dare you! how dare you!"

"I dare a great deal more than that to save you. You must hear me, Nelly: they're all badly spoken of, not one, but all. They are a shady lot—excuse a man's way of talking. I don't know what

other words to use—partly from misfortune, but more from——
Nelly, Nelly, how could you, a high-minded, well-brought-up girl
like you, tolerate that?"

She turned upon him again, breathing hard with restrained
rage and desperation; evidently she was at a loss for words to
convey her indignant wrath: and at last in sheer inability to
express the vehemence of her feelings she fastened on one word
and repeated "well-brought-up!" in accents of scorn.

"Yes," said John, "my aunt and you may not always understand
each other, but she's proved her case to every fair mind by yourself,
Elinor. A girl could not be better brought up than you've been:
and you could not put up with it, not unless you changed your
nature as well as your name."

"With what?" she said, "with what?" They had gone up and
down the sloping sides of the combe, through the rustling copse,
sometimes where there was a path, sometimes where there was
none, treading over the big bushes of ling and the bell-heather,
all bursting into bloom, past groups of primeval firs and seedling
beeches, self-sown, over little hillocks and hollows formed of
rocks or big old roots of trees covered with the close glittering
green foliage and dark blue clusters of the dewberry, with the
hum of bees filling the air, the twittering of the birds, the sound
of the church bells—nothing more like the heart of summer,
more peaceful, genial, happy than that brooding calm of nature
amid all the harmonious sounds, could be.

But as Elinor put this impatient question, her countenance
all ablaze with anger and vehemence and resolution, yet with
a gleam of anxiety in the puckers of her forehead and the eyes
which shone from beneath them, they stepped out upon the
road by which other groups were passing, all bound towards
the centre of the church and its tinkling bells. Elinor stopped,
and drew a longer panting breath, and gave him a look of fierce
reproach, as if this too were his fault: and then she smoothed
her ruffled plumes, after the manner of women, and replied to
the Sunday-morning salutations, with the smiles and nods of use

and wont. She knew everybody, both the rich and the poor, or rather I should say the well-off and the less-well-off, for there were neither rich nor poor, formally speaking, on Windyhill. John did not find it so easy to put his emotions in his pocket. He cast an admiring glance upon her as with heightened colour and a little panting of the breath, but no other sign of disturbance, she made her inquiries after this one's mother and that one's child. It was wonderful to him to see how the storm was got under in a moment. An occasional glance aside at himself from the corner of her eye, a sort of dart of defiance as if to bid him remember that she was not done with him, was shot at John from time to time over the heads of the innocent country people in whom she pretended to be so much interested. Pretended!—was it pretence, or was the one as real as the other? He heard her promising to come to-morrow to see an invalid, to send certain articles as soon as she got home, to look up certain books. Would she do so? or was all this a mere veil to cover the other which engaged all her soul?

And then there came the service—that soothing routine of familiar prayers, which the lips of men and women absorbed in the violence and urgency of life murmur over almost without knowing, with now and then an awakening to something that touches their own aspirations, to something that offers or that asks for help. "Because there is none other that fighteth for us but only Thou, O God." That seems to the careless soul such a *non sequitur*, as if peace was asked for, only because there was none other to fight; but to the man heavily laden, what a cry out of the depths! Because there is none other—all resources gone, all possibilities: but one that fighteth for us, standing fast, always the champion of the perplexed, the overborne, the weak. John was a little careless in this respect, as so many young men are. He thought most of the music when he joined the fashionable throng in the Temple Church. But there was no music to speak of at Windyhill. There was more sound of the bees outside, and the birds and the sighing bass of the fir-trees than of anything more

44

carefully concerted. The organ was played with a curious drone in it, almost like that of the primitive bagpipe. But there was that one phrase, a strong strain of human appeal, enough to lift the world, nay, to let itself go straight to the blue heavens: "Because there is none other that fighteth for us but only Thou, O God."

Mr. Hudson preached his little sermon like a discord in the midst. What should he have preached it for, that little sermon, which was only composed because he could not help himself, which was about nothing in heaven or earth? John gave it a sort of partial attention because he could not help it, partly in wonder to think how a sensible man like Mr. Hudson could account to himself for such strange little interruption of the natural sequence of high human emotion. What theory had he in his mind? This was a question John was fond of putting to himself, with perhaps an idea peculiar to a lawyer, that every man must be thinking what he is about, and be able to produce a clear reason, and, as it were, some theory of the meaning of his own actions—which everybody must know is nonsense. For the Rector of course preached just because it was in his day's work, and the people would have been much surprised, though possibly much relieved, had he not done so—feeling that to listen was in the day's work too, and to be gone through doggedly as a duty. John thought how much better it would be to have some man who could preach now and then when he had something to say, instead of troubling the Rector, who, good man, had nothing. But it is not to be supposed that he was thinking this consecutively while the morning went on. It flitted through his mind from time to time among his many thinkings about the Compton family and Elinor; poor Nelly, standing upon the edge of that precipice and the helplessness of every one to save her, and the great refrain like the peal of an organ going through everything, "None other that fighteth for us but only Thou, O God." Surely, surely to prevent this sacrifice He would interfere.

She turned to him the moment they were out of the church doors with that same look of eager defiance yet demand, and as soon as they left the road, the first step into the copse, putting out her hand to call his attention: "You said I could not put up with it, a girl so well-brought-up as I am. What is it a well-brought-up girl can't put up with? A disorderly house, late hours, and so forth, hateful to the well-brought-up? What is it, what is it, John?"

"Have you been thinking of that all through the morning prayers?" he said.

"Yes, I have been thinking about it. What did you expect me to think about? Is there anything else so important? Mr. Hudson's sermon, perhaps, which I have heard before, which I suppose *you* listened to," she said, with a troubled laugh.

"I did a little, wondering how a good man like that could go on doing it; and there were other things——" John did not like to say what it was which was still throbbing through the air to him, and through his own being.

"Nothing that is of so much moment to me: come back, John, to the well-brought-up girl."

"You think that's a poor sort of description, Elinor; so it is. You are of course a great deal more than that. Still it's what one can turn to most easily. You don't know what life is in a sort of fast house, where there is nothing thought of but amusement or where it's a constant round of race meetings, yachting, steeplechases—I don't know if men still ride steeplechases—I mean that sort of thing: Monte Carlo in the winter: betting all the year round—if not on one thing then on another; expedients to raise money, for money's always wanted. You don't know—how can you know?—what goes on in a fast life."

"Don't you see, John," she cried, eagerly, "that all that, if put in a different way not to their prejudice, if put in the right way would sound delightful? There is no harm in these things at all. Betting's not a sin in the Bible any more than races are. Don't you see it's only the abuse of them that's wrong? One might ruin one's health, I believe, with tea, which is the most righteous thing! I should like above all things a yacht, say in the Mediterranean, and to go to Monte Carlo, which is a beautiful place, and where there is the best music in the world, besides the gambling. I should like even to see the gambling once in a way, for the fun of the thing. You don't frighten me at all. I have been a fortnight at Lady Mariamne's, and the continual 'go' was delightful; there was never a dull moment. As for expedients to raise money, there——"

"To be sure—old Prestwich is as rich as Crœsus—or was," said John, with significance, "but you are not going to live with Lady Mariamne, I suppose."

"Oh, John!" she cried, "oh, John!" suddenly seizing him by the arm, clasping her hands on it in the pretty way of earnestness she had, though one hand held her parasol, which was inconvenient. The soft face was suffused with rosy colour, so different from the angry red, the flush of love and tenderness—her eyes swam in liquid light, looking up with mingled happiness and entreaty to John's face. "Fancy what he says, that he will not object to come here for half the year to let me be with my mother! Remember what he is, a man of fashion, and fond of the world, and of going out and all that. He has consented to come, nay, he almost offered to come for six months in the year to be with mamma."

"Good heavens," cried John to himself, "he must indeed be down on his luck!" but what he said was, "Does your mother know of this, Elinor?"

"I have not told her yet. I have reserved it to hear first what you had to say: and so far as I can make out you have nothing at all to say, only general things, disapproval in the general. What should you say if I told you that he disapproves too? He said himself that there had been too much of all that—that he had backed something—isn't that what you say?—backed it at odds, and stood to win what he calls a pot of money. But after that was decided—for he said he could not be off bets that were made— never any more. Now that I know you have nothing more to say my heart is free, and I can tell you. He has never really liked that sort of life, but was led into it when he was very young. And now as soon as—we are together, you know"—she looked so bright, so sweet in the happiness of her love, that John could have flung her from his arms, and felt that she insulted him by that clinging hold—"he means to turn entirely to serious things, and to go into politics, John."

"Oh, he is going into politics!"

"Of course, on the people's side—to do everything for them—Home Rule, and all that is best: to see that they are heard in Parliament, and have their wants attended to, instead of jobs and corruption everywhere. So you will see, John, that if he has been fast, and gone a little too far, and been very much mixed up in the Turf, and all that, it was only in the exuberance of youth, liking the fun of it, as I feel I should myself. But that now, now all that is to be changed when he steps into settled, responsible life. I should not have told you if you had repeated the lies that people say. But as you did not, but only found fault with him for being fast——"

"Then you have heard—what people say?" He shifted his arm a little, so that she instinctively perceived that the affectionate clasp of her hands was no longer agreeable to him, and his face seemed suddenly to have become a blank page, absolutely devoid of all expression. He kicked vigorously at one of the hillocks he had stumbled against, as if he thought he could dislodge it and get it out of his way.

"Mariamne told me there was a lot of lies—that people said—I am so glad, John, oh! so thankful, that you have not repeated any of them; for now I can feel you are my own good John, as you always were, not a slanderer of any one, and we can go on being fond of each other like brother and sister. I have told him you have been the best of brothers to me."

"Oh," said John, without a sign of wonder or admiration in him, with a dead blank in his face.

"And what do you think he said? 'Then I know he must be a capital fellow, Ne——'"

"Not Nelly," said poor John, with a foolish pang that seemed to rend his heart. Oh, if that scamp, that cheat, that low betting, card-playing rascal were but here! he would capital-fellow him. To take not herself only, but the dear pet name that she had said was only John's——

"He says Nell sometimes, John. Oh, not Nelly—Nelly is for you only. I would never let him call me that. But they are all for short names, one syllable—he is Phil, and Mariamne, well at home they call her Jew—horrible, isn't it?—because she was called after some Jewess; but somehow it seems queer when you see her, so fair and frizzy, like anything but a Jew."

"So I have got one letter to myself," said John. "I don't know that I think that worth very much, however. And so far as I can see, you seem to think everything very fine—the bets, perhaps, and the rows and all."

"Well they are, you know," said Elinor, with a laugh, "to a little country mouse like me that has never seen anything. There is always something going on, and their slang way of speaking is certainly very amusing if it is not at all dignified, and they have such droll ways of looking at things. All so entirely different! Don't you know, John, sometimes in one's life one longs for something to be quite different. A complete change, anything new."

"If that is what you long for, no doubt you will get it, Elinor."

"Well!" she cried, "I have had the other for three-and-twenty years, long enough to have exhausted it, don't you think? but I don't mean to throw it over, oh, no! Coming back to mamma makes the arrangement perfect. Probably in the end it is the old life, the life I was brought up in that I shall like best in the long run. That is one thing of being well brought up. Phil will laugh till he cries when I tell him of your description of me as a well-brought-up girl."

John set his teeth as he walked or rather stumbled along by her side, catching in the roots of the trees as he had never done before, and swearing under his breath. Her flutter of talk running on, delighted, full of laughter and softness, as if he had fully declared his satisfaction and was interested in every detail, kept

John in a state of suppressed fury which made his countenance dark, and almost took the sight from his eyes. He did not know how to escape from that false position, nor did she give him time, she had so much to say. Mrs. Dennistoun looked anxiously at the pair as they came up through the copse to the level of the cottage. There were no enclosures in that primitive place. From the copse you came straight into the garden with its banks of flowers. She was seated near the cottage door in a corner sheltered from the sun, with a number of books about her. But I don't think she had read anything except some portions of the lessons in the morning service. She had been sitting with her eyes vaguely fixed upon the horizon and her hands clasped in her lap, and a heavy shadow like an overhanging cloud upon her mind. But when she heard Elinor's voice approaching so gay and tuneful her heart rose a little. John evidently could have had nothing very bad to say. Elinor had been satisfied with the morning. Mrs. Dennistoun had expected to see them come back estranged and silent. The conclusion she drew was entirely satisfactory. After all John must have been moved solely by general disapproval, which is so very different from the dreadful hints and warnings that might mean any criminality. Elinor was talking to him as freely as she had done before this spectre rose. It must, Mrs. Dennistoun concluded, be all right.

It was not till he was going away that she had an opportunity of talking with him alone. Her satisfaction, it must be allowed, had been a little subdued by John's demeanour during the afternoon and evening. But Mrs. Dennistoun had said to herself that there might be other ways of accounting for this. She had long had a fancy that John was more interested in Elinor than he had confessed himself to be. It had been her conviction that as soon as he felt it warrantable, as soon as he was sufficiently well-established, and his practice secured, he would probably declare himself, with, she feared, no particular issue so far as Elinor was concerned. And perhaps he was disappointed, poor fellow, which was a very natural explanation of his glum looks.

But at breakfast on Monday Elinor announced her intention of driving her cousin to the station, and went out to see that the pony was harnessed, an operation which took some time, for the pony was out in the field and had to be caught, and the man of all work, who had a hundred affairs to look after, had to be caught too to perform this duty; which sometimes, however, Elinor performed herself, but always with some expenditure of time. Mrs. Dennistoun seized the opportunity, plunging at once into the all-important subject.

"You seemed to get on all right together yesterday, John, so I suppose you found that after all there was not very much to say."

"I was not allowed to say——anything. You mean——"

"Oh, John, John, do you mean to tell me after all——"

"Aunt Ellen," he said, "stop it if you can; if there is any means in the world by which you can stop it, do so. I can't bring accusations against the man, for I couldn't prove them. I only know what everybody knows. He is not a man fit for Elinor to marry. He is not fit to touch the tie of her shoe."

"Oh, don't trouble me with your superlatives, John. Elinor is a good girl and a clever girl, but not a lady of romance. Is there anything really against him? Tell me, for goodness' sake! Even with these few words you have made me very unhappy," Mrs. Dennistoun said, in a half resentful tone.

"I can't help it," said the unfortunate man, "I can't bring accusations, as I tell you. He is simply a scamp—that is all I know."

"A scamp!" said Mrs. Dennistoun, with a look of alarm. "But then that is a word that has so many meanings. A scamp may be only a careless fellow, nice in his way. That is not enough to break off a marriage for. And, John, as you have said so much, you must say more."

"I have no more to say, that's all I know. Inquire what the Hudsons have heard. Stop it if you can."

"Oh, dear, dear, here is Elinor back already," Mrs. Dennistoun said.

CHAPTER V.

The next time that John's presence was required at the cottage was for the signing of the very simple settlements; which, as there was nothing or next to nothing in the power of the man to settle upon his wife, were easy enough. He met Mr. Lynch, who was Mrs. Dennistoun's "man of business," and a sharp London solicitor, who was for the husband. Elinor's fortune was five thousand pounds, no more, not counting her expectations from him, which were left out of the question. It was a very small matter altogether, and one which the smart solicitor who was in Mr. Compton's interest spoke of with a certain contempt, as who should say he was not in the habit of being disturbed and brought to the country for any such trifle. It was now August— not a time when any man was supposed to be available for matters like these. Mr. Lynch was just about starting for his annual holiday, but came, at no small personal inconvenience, to do his duty by the poor girl whom he had known all his life. John and he travelled to the cottage together, and their aspect was not cheerful. "Did you ever hear," said Mr. Lynch, "such a piece of folly as this—a man with no character at all? This is what it is to leave a girl in the sole care of her mother. What does a woman know about such things?"

"I don't think it was her mother's fault," said John, anxious to do justice all round. "Elinor is very head-strong, and when she has made up her mind to a thing——"

"A bit of a girl!" said Mr. Lynch, contemptuously. He was an old bachelor and knew nothing about the subject, as the reader will perceive. "Her mother ought never to have permitted it for a moment. She should have put down her foot: and then Miss

Elinor would soon have come to reason. What I wonder is the ruffian's own motives? for it can't be a little bit of money like that. Five thousand's a mere mouthful to such a man as he is. He'll get rid of it all in a week."

"It must be tied up as tight as possible," said John.

Here Mr. Lynch faltered a little. "She has got an idea into her head, with the intention, I don't doubt, of defrauding herself if she can. He has got some investment for it, it appears. He is on the board of some company—a pretty board to take in such a fellow? But the Honourable is always something, I suppose."

John did not say the *dis*-Honourable, though it trembled on the edge of his tongue. "But you will not permit that?" he said.

"No, no; we will not permit it," said Mr. Lynch, with an emphasis on the negative which sounded like failing resolution.

"That would be giving the lamb to the wolf with a vengeance."

"Exactly what I said; exactly what I said. I am very glad, Mr. Tatham, that you take the same view."

"There is but one view to be taken," said John. "He must not have the slightest power over her money. It must be tied up as tight as the law can do it; not that I think it of the least consequence," he added. "Of course, he will get it all from her one way or another. Law's but a poor barrier against a determined man."

"I'm glad you see that too," said Mr. Lynch, "and you might say a determined woman: for she has set her mind on this, and we'll have a nice business with her, I can see."

"A bit of a girl!" said John, with a laugh, echoing the previous sentiment.

"That's very true," said the old lawyer; "and still I think her mother—but I don't put any great confidence in my own power to resist Elinor. Poor little thing, I've known her since she was *that* high; indeed, I may say I knew her before she was born. And you are a relation, Mr. Tatham?"

"Third or fourth cousin."

"But still, more intimate than a person unconnected with them, and able to speak your mind more freely. I wonder now that you never said anything. But in family matters sometimes one is very reluctant to interfere."

"I said everything I could say, not to offend them mortally; but I could only tell them the common talk of society. I told my aunt he was a scamp: but after the first shock I am not sure that she thought that was any such bad thing. It depended upon the sense you put upon the word, she said."

"Oh, women, women!" said Mr. Lynch. "That's their way—a reformed rake makes the best husband. It's an old-fashioned sentiment, but it's in the background of their minds, a sort of tradition that they can't shake off—or else the poor fellow has had so many disadvantages, and they think they can make it all right. It's partly ignorance and partly vanity. But they are all the same, and their ways in the matter of marriage are not to be made out."

"You have a great deal of experience."

"Experience—oh, don't speak of it!" said the old gentleman. "A man has a certain idea of the value of money, however great a fool he may be, but the women——"

"And yet they are said to stick to money, and to be respectful of it beyond anything but a miser. I have myself remarked——"

"In small matters," said Mr. Lynch, "in detail—sixpences to railway porters and that sort of thing—so people say at least. But a sum of money on paper has no effect on a woman, she will sign it away with a wave of her hand. It doesn't touch their imagination. Five pounds in her pocket is far more than five thousand on paper, to Elinor, for instance. I wish," cried the old gentleman, with a little spitefulness, "that this Married Women's Property Bill would push on and get itself made law. It would save us a great deal of trouble, and perhaps convince the world at the last how little able they are to be trusted with property. A nice mess they will make of it, and plenty of employment for young solicitors," he said, rubbing his hands.

For this was before that important bill was passed, which has not had (like so many other bills) the disastrous consequences which Mr. Lynch foresaw.

They were met at the station by the pony carriage, and at the door by Elinor herself, who came flying out to meet them. She seized Mr. Lynch by both arms, for he was a little old man, and she was bigger than he was.

"Now you will remember what I said," she cried in his ear, yet not so low but that John heard it too.

"You are a little witch; you mustn't insist upon anything so foolish. Leave all that to me, my dear," said Mr. Lynch. "What do you know about business? You must leave it to me and the other gentleman, who I suppose is here, or coming."

"He is here, but I don't care for him. I care only for you. There are such advantages: and I do know a great deal about business; and," she said, with her mouth close to the old lawyer's ear, "it will please Phil so much if I show my confidence in him, and in the things with which he has to do."

"It will not please him so much if the thing bursts, and you are left without a penny, my dear."

Elinor laughed. "I don't suppose he will mind a bit: he cares nothing for money. But I do," she said. "You know you always say women love acquisition. I want good interest, and of course with Phil on it, it must be safe for me."

"Oh, that makes it like the Bank of England, you think! but I don't share your confidence, my pretty Elinor. I'm an old fellow. No Phil in the world has any charm for me. You must trust me to do what I feel is best for you. And Mr. Tatham here is quite of my opinion."

"Oh, John! he is sure to be against me," said Elinor, with an angry glimmer in her eyes. She had not as yet taken any notice of him while she welcomed with such warmth his old companion. And John had stood by offering no greeting, with his bag in his hand. But when she said this the quick feeling girl was seized with compunction. She turned from Mr. Lynch and held out both her hands to her cousin. "John, I didn't mean that; it is only that I am excited and cross. And don't, oh, don't go against me," she cried.

"I never did, and never will, Elinor," he said gravely. Then he asked, after a moment, "Is Mr. Compton here?"

"No; how could he be here? Three gentlemen in the cottage is enough to overwhelm us already. Mr. Sharp, fortunately, can't stay," she added, lowering her voice; "he has to be driven back to the station to catch the last express. And it is August," she said with a laugh; "you forget the 15th. Now, could Phil be anywhere but where there is grouse? You shall have some to dinner to-night that fell by his gun. That should mollify you, for I am sure you never got grouse at the cottage before in August. Mamma would as soon think of buying manna for you to eat."

"I think it would have been more respectful, Elinor, if he had been here. What is grouse to you?"

"Then I don't think anything of the kind," cried Elinor. "He is much better away. And I assure you, John, I never mean to put myself in competition with the grouse."

The old lawyer had gone into the drawing-room, where Mrs. Dennistoun was holding parley with Mr. Sharp. Elinor and John were standing alone in the half light of the summer evening, the sun down, the depths of the combe below falling into faint mist, but the sunset-tinted clouds still floating like a vapour made of roses upon the clearness of the blue above. "Come and take a turn through the copse," said John. "They don't want either of us indoors."

She went with a momentary reluctance and a glance back at the bow-window of the drawing-room, from which the sound of voices issued. "Don't you think I should be there to keep them up to the mark?" she said, half laughing. And then, "Well, yes—as you are going to Switzerland too. I think you might have stayed and seen me married after all, and made acquaintance with Phil."

"I thought I should have met him here to-day, Elinor."

"Now, how could you? You know the accommodation of the cottage just as well as I do. We have two spare rooms, and no more."

"You could have sent me out somewhere to sleep. That has been done before now."

"Oh, John, how persistent you are, and worrying! When I tell you that Phil is shooting, as everybody of his kind is—do you think I want him to give up all the habits of his life? He is not like us: we adapt ourselves: but these people parcel out their time as if they were in a trade, don't you know? So long in London, so long abroad, and in the Highlands for the grouse, and somewhere else for the partridges, or they would die."

"I think he might have departed from that routine once in a way, Elinor, for you."

"I tell you again, John, I shall never put myself in competition"— Elinor stopped abruptly, with perhaps, he thought, a little glimmer of indignation in her eyes. "I hate women who do that sort of thing," she cried. "'Give up your cigar—or me,' as I've heard girls say. Such an unworthy thing! When one accepts a man one accepts him as he stands, with all his habits. What should I think of him if he said, 'Give up your tea—or me!' I should laugh in his face and throw him overboard without a pause."

"You would never look at tea again as long as you lived if he did not like it; I suppose that is what you mean, Elinor?"

"Perhaps if I found that out, afterwards; but to be given the choice beforehand, never! After all, you don't half know me, John."

"Perhaps not," he said, gravely. They had left the garden behind in its blaze of flowers, and strayed off into the subdued twilight of the copse, where everything was in a half tone of greenness and shadow and waning light. "There are always new lights arising on a many-sided creature like you—and that makes one think. Do you know you are not at all the person to take a great disappointment quietly, if that should happen to come to you in your life?"

"A great disappointment?" she said, looking up at him with a wondering glance. Then he thought the colour paled a little in her face. "No," she said, "I don't suppose I should take it quietly.

Who does?"

"Oh, many people—people with less determination and more patience than you. You are not very patient by nature, Elinor."

"I never said I was."

"And though no one would give up more generously, as a voluntary matter, you could not bear being made a nonentity of, or put in a secondary place."

"I should not like it, I suppose."

"You would give everything, flinging it away; but to have all your sacrifices taken for granted, your tastes made of no account——"

There was no doubt now that she had grown pale. "May I ask what all these investigations into my character mean? I never was so anatomized before."

"It was only to say that you are not a good subject for this kind of experiment, Elinor. I don't see you putting up with things, making the best of everything, submitting to have your sense of right and wrong outraged perhaps. Some women would not be much disturbed by that. They would put off the responsibility and feel it their duty to accept whatever was put before them. But you—it would be a different matter with you."

"I should hope so, if I was ever exposed to such dangers. But now may I know what you are driving at, John, for you have some meaning in what you say!"

He took her hand and drew it through his arm. He was in more moved than he wished to show. "Only this, Elinor,"—he said.

"Oh, John, will you never call me Nelly any more?"

"Only this, Nelly, my little Nelly, never mine again—and that never was mine, except in my silly thought. Only this: that if you have the least doubt, the smallest flutter of an uncertainty, just enough to make you hold your breath for a moment, oh, my dear girl, stop! Don't go on with it; pause until you can make sure."

"John!" she forced her arm from his with an indignant movement. "Oh, how do you dare to say it?" she said. "Doubt of

Mr. Compton! Uncertainty about Phil!" She laughed out, and the echo seemed to ring into all the recesses of the trees. "I would be much more ready to doubt myself," she said.

"Doubt yourself; that is what I mean. Think if you are not deceiving yourself. I don't think you are so very sure as you believe you are, Nelly. You don't feel so certain——"

"Do you know that you are insulting me, John? You say as much as that I am a fool carried away by a momentary enthusiasm, with no real love, no true feeling in me, tempted, perhaps, as Mrs. Hudson thinks, by the Honourable!" Her lip quivered, and the fading colour came back in a rush to her face. "It is hard enough to have a woman like that think it, who ought to know better, who has always known me—but you, John!"

"You may be sure, Elinor, that I did not put it on that ground."

"No, perhaps: but on ground not much more respectful to me—perhaps that I have been fascinated by a handsome man, which is not considered derogatory. Oh, John, a girl does not give herself away on an argument like that. I may be hasty and self-willed and impatient, as you say; but when you—love!" Her face flushed like a rose, so that even in the grey of the evening it shone out like one of the clouds full of sunset that still lingered on the sky. A few quick tears followed, the natural consequence of her emotion. And then she turned to him with the ineffable condescension of one farther advanced in life stooping sweetly to his ignorance. "You have not yet come to the moment in your experience when you can understand that, dear John."

Oh, the insight and the ignorance, the knowledge and the absence of all perception! He, too, laughed out, as she had done, with a sense of the intolerable ridicule and folly and mistake. "Perhaps that's how it is," he said.

Elinor looked at him gravely, in an elder-sisterly, profoundly-investigating way, and then she took his arm quietly and turned towards home. "I shall forget what you have said, and you will forget that you ever said it; and now we will go home, John, and be just the same dear friends as before."

"Will you promise me," he said, "that whatever happens, without pride, or recollection of what I've been so foolish as to say, in any need or emergency, or whenever you want anything, or if you should be in trouble—trouble comes to everybody in this life—you will remember what you have said just now, and send for your cousin John?"

Her whole face beamed out in one smile, she clasped her other hand round his arm; "I should have done it without being asked, without ever doubting for a moment, because it was the most natural thing in the world. Whom should I turn to else if not to my dear old—— But call me Nelly, John."

"Dear little Nelly!" he said with faltering voice, "then that is a bargain."

She held up her cheek to him, and he kissed it solemnly in the shadow of the little young oak that fluttered its leaves wistfully in the breeze that was getting up—and then very soberly, saying little, they walked back to the cottage. He was going abroad for his vacation, not saying to himself even that he preferred not to be present at the wedding, but resigning himself to the necessity, for it was not to be till the middle of September, and it would be breaking up his holiday had he to come back at that time. So this little interview was a leave-taking as well as a solemn engagement for all the risks and dangers of life. The pain in it, after that very sharp moment in the copse, was softened down into a sadness not unsweet, as they came silently together from out of the shadow into the quiet hemisphere of sky and space, which was over the little centre of the cottage with its human glimmer of fire and lights. The sky was unusually clear, and among those soft, rose-tinted clouds of the sunset, which were no clouds at all, had risen a young crescent of a moon, just about to disappear, too, in the short course of one of her earliest nights. They lingered for a moment before they went indoors. The depth of the combe was filled with the growing darkness, but the ridges above were still light and softly edged with the silver of the moon, and the distant road, like a long, white line, came conspicuously into sight, winding for a little way along the hill-top unsheltered, before it plunged into the shadow of the trees—the road that led into the world, by which they should both depart presently to stray into such different ways.

CHAPTER VI.

The drawing-room after dinner always looked cheerful. Perhaps the fact that it was a sort of little oasis in the desert, and that the light from those windows shone into three counties, made the interior more cosy and bright. (There are houses now upon every knoll, and the wind cannot blow on Windyhill for the quantity of obstructions it meets with.) There was the usual log burning on the hearth, and the party in general kept away from it, for the night was warm. Only Mr. Sharp, the London lawyer, was equal to bearing the heat. He stood with his back to it, and his long legs showing against the glow behind, a sharp-nosed, long man in black, who had immediately suggested Mephistopheles to Elinor, even though he was on the Compton side. He had taken his coffee after dinner, and now he stood over the fire slowly sipping a cup of tea. There was a look of acquisitiveness about him which suggested an inclination to appropriate anything from the unnecessary heat of the fire to the equally unnecessary tea. But Mr. Sharp had been on the winning side. He had demonstrated the superior sense of making the money—which was not large enough sum to settle—of real use to the young pair by an investment which would increase Mr. Compton's importance in his company, besides producing very good dividends—much better dividends than would be possible if it were treated in the old-fashioned way by trustees. This was how the bride wished it, which was the most telling of arguments: and surely, to insure good interest and an increase of capital to her, through her husband's hands, was better than to secure some beggarly hundred and fifty pounds a year for her portion, though without any risks at all.

Mr. Sharp had also taken great pains to point out that there were only three brothers—one an invalid and the other two soldiers—between Mr. Phil and the title, and that even to be the Honourable Mrs. Compton was something for a young lady, who was, if he might venture to say so, nobody—not to say a word against her charms. Lord St. Serf was hourly getting an old man, and the chances that his client might step over a hecatomb of dead relations to the height of fortune was a thing quite worth taking into account. It was a much better argument, however, to return to the analogy of other poor young people, where the bride's little fortune would be put into the husband's business, and thus their joint advantage considered. Mr. Sharp, at the same time, did not hesitate to express politely his opinion that to call him down to the country for a discussion which could have been carried on much better in one or other of their respective offices was a most uncalled for proceeding, especially as even now the other side was wavering, and would not consent to conclude matters, and make the signatures that were necessary at once. Mr. Lynch, it must be allowed, was of the same opinion too.

"Your country is a little bleak at night," said Mr. Sharp, partially mollified by a good dinner, but beginning to remember unpleasantly the cold drive in a rattletrap of a little rustic pony carriage over the hills and hollows. "Do you really remain here all the year? How wonderful! Not even a glimpse of the world in summer, or a little escape from the chills in winter? How brave of you! What patience and powers of endurance must be cultivated in that way!"

"One would think Windyhill was Siberia at least," said Mrs. Dennistoun, laughing; "we do not give ourselves credit for all these fine qualities."

"Some people are heroes—or heroines—without knowing it," said Mr. Sharp, with a bow.

"And yet," said the mother, with a little indignation, "there was some talk of Mr. Compton doing me the honour to share my hermitage for a part of the year."

"Mr. Compton! my dear lady! Mr. Compton would die of it in a week," said Mr. Sharp.

"I am quite well aware of it," said Mrs. Dennistoun; and she added, after a pause, "so should I."

"What a change it will be for your daughter," said Mr. Sharp. "She will see everything that is worth seeing. More in a month than she would see here in a dozen years. Trust Mr. Compton for knowing all that's worth going after. They have all an instinct for life that is quite remarkable. There's Lady Mariamne, who has society at her feet, and the old lord is a most remarkable old gentleman. Your daughter, Mrs. Dennistoun, is a very fortunate young lady. She has my best congratulations, I am sure."

"Sharp," said Mr. Lynch from the background, "you had better be thinking of starting, if you want to catch that train."

"I'll see if the pony is there," said John.

Mr. Sharp put down his teacup with precipitation. "Is it as late as that?" he cried.

"It is the last train," said Mrs. Dennistoun, with great satisfaction. "And I am afraid, if you missed it, as the house is full, there would be nothing but a bed at the public-house to offer——"

"Oh, not another word," the lawyer said: and fortunately he never knew how near that rising young man at the bar, John Tatham, who had every object in conciliating a solicitor, was to a charge of manslaughter, if killing an attorney can thus be called. But the feelings of the party were expressed only in actions of the greatest kindness. They helped him on with his coat, and covered him with rugs as he got in, shivering, to the little pony carriage. It was a beautiful night, but the wind is always a thing to be considered on Windyhill.

"Well, that's a good thing over," said Mr. Lynch, going to the fire as he came in from the night air at the door and rubbing his hands.

"It would have been a relief to one's feeling to have kicked that fellow all the way down and up the other side of the combe, and kept him warm," said John, with a laugh of wrath.

"It is a pity a man should have so little taste," said Mrs. Dennistoun.

Elinor still stood where she had been standing, with every feeling in her breast in commotion. She had not taken any part in the insidious kindnesses of speeding the parting guest; and now she remembered that he was her Phil's representative: whatever she might herself think of the man, how could she join in abuse of one who represented Phil?

"He is no worse, I suppose, than others," she said. "He was bound to stand up for those in whose interest he was. Mr. Lynch would have made himself quite as disagreeable for me."

"Not I," said the old gentleman; "for what is the good of standing up for you? You would throw me over on the first opportunity. You have taken all the force out of my sword-arm, my dear, as it is. How can I make myself disagreeable for those who won't stand up for themselves? I suppose you must have it your own way."

"Yes, I suppose it will be the best," said Mrs. Dennistoun, in subdued tones.

"It would come to about the same thing, however you settled it," said John.

Elinor looked from one to another with eyes that began to glow. "You are a cheerful company," she said. "You speak as if you were arranging my funeral. On the whole I think I like Mr. Sharp best; for if he was contemptuous of me and my little bit of money, he was at all events cheerful about the future, and that is always something; whereas you all——"

There was a little pause, no one responding. There was no pleasant jest, no bright augury for Elinor. The girl's heart rose against this gloom that surrounded her. "I think," she said, with an angry laugh, "that I had better run after Mr. Sharp and bring him back, for he had at least a little sympathy with me!"

"Don't be too sure of that," said Mr. Lynch, "for if we think you are throwing yourself away, Elinor, so does he on his side. He thinks the Honourable Mr. Compton is going dreadfully cheap for five thousand pounds."

"Elinor need not take any of us *au pied de la lettre*—of course we are all firm for our own side," said John.

Elinor turned her head from one to another, growing pale and red by turns. There was a certain surprise in her look, as she found herself thus at bay. The triumph of having got the better of their opposition was lost in the sense of isolation with which the girl, so long the first object of everybody about her, felt herself thus placed alone. And the tears were very ready to start, but were kept back by jealous pride which rose to her help. Well! if they put her outside the circle she would remain so; if they talked to her as one no longer of them, but belonging to another life, so be it! Elinor determined that she would make no further appeal. She would not even show how much it hurt her. After that pale look round upon them all, she went into the corner of the room where the piano stood, and where there was little light. She was too proud to go out of the room, lest they should think she was going to cry. She went with a sudden, quick movement to the piano instead, where perhaps she might cry too, but where nobody should see. Poor Elinor! they had made her feel alone by their words, and she made herself more alone by this little instinctive withdrawal. She began to play softly one thing after another. She was not a great performer. Her little "tunes" were of the simplest—no better indeed than tunes, things that every musician despises: they made a little atmosphere round her, a voluntary hermitage which separated her as if she had been a hundred miles away.

"I wish you could have stayed for the marriage," Mrs. Dennistoun said.

"My dear lady, it would spoil my holiday—the middle of September. You'll have nobody except, of course, the people you have always. To tell the truth," John added. "I don't care tuppence for my holiday. I'd have come—like a shot: but I don't think I could stand it. She has always been such a pet of mine. I don't think I could bear it, to tell the truth."

"I shall have to bear it, though she is more than a pet of mine," said Mrs. Dennistoun.

"I know, I know! the relatives cannot be let off—especially the mother, who must put up with everything. I trust," said Mr. Lynch, with a sigh, "that it may all turn out a great deal better than we hope. Where are they going after the marriage?"

"Some one has lent them a place—a very pretty place—on the Thames, where they can have boating and all that—Lord Sudbury, I think. And later they are going on a round of visits, to his father, Lord St. Serf, and to Lady Mariamne, and to his aunt, who is Countess of—something or other." Mrs. Dennistoun's voice was not untouched by a certain vague pleasure in these fine names.

"Ah," said the old lawyer, nodding his head at each, "all among the aristocracy, I see. Well, my dear lady, I hope you will be able to find some satisfaction in that; it is better than to fall among—nobodies at least."

"I hope so," said Mrs. Dennistoun, with a sigh.

They were speaking low, and fondly hoped that they were not heard; but Elinor's ears and every faculty were quickened and almost every word reached her. But she was too proud to take any notice. And perhaps these dreary anticipations, on the whole, did her good, for her heart rose against them, and any little possible doubts in her own mind were put to sudden flight by the opposition and determination which flooded her heart. This made her playing a little more unsteady than usual, and she broke down several times in the middle of a "tune;" but nobody remarked this: they were all fully occupied with their own thoughts.

All, at least, except John, who wandered uneasily about the room, now studying the names of the books on the bookshelves—which he knew by heart, now pulling the curtain aside to look out at the moonlight, now pulling at the fronds of the great maidenhair in his distraction till the table round was scattered with little broken leaves. He wanted to keep out of that atmosphere of emotion which surrounded Elinor at the piano. But it attracted him, all the same, as the light attracts a moth. To get away from that, to make the severance which so soon must be a perfect severance, was the only true policy he knew; for what was he to her, and what could she be to him? He had already said everything which a man in his position ought to say. He took out a book at last, and sat down doggedly by the table to read, thus making another circle of atmosphere, so to speak, another globe of isolated being in the little room, while the two elder people talked low in the centre, conventionally inaudible to the girl who was playing and the young man who was reading. But John might as well have tried to solve some tremendous problem as to read that book. He too heard every word the elders were saying. He heard them with his own ears, and also he heard them through the ears of Elinor, gauging the effect which every word would have upon her. At last he could bear it no longer. He was driven to her side to bear a part of her burden, even to prevent her from hearing, which would be something. He resisted the impulse to throw down his book, and only placed it very quietly on the table, and even in a deliberate way, that there might be no appearance of feeling about him—and made his way by degrees, pausing now and then to look at a picture, though he knew them all by heart. Thus he arrived at last at the piano, in what he flattered himself was an accidental way.

"Elinor, the stars are so bright over the combe, do come out. It is not often they are so clear."

"No," she said, more with the movement of her lips than with any sound.

"Why not? You can't want to play those old pieces just at this moment. You will have plenty of time to play them to-morrow."

She said "No" again, with a little impatient movement of her hands on the keys and a look towards the others.

"You are listening to what they are saying? Why should you? They don't want you to hear. Come along, Elinor. It's far better for you not to listen to what is not intended——"

"Oh, go away, John."

"I must say no in my turn. Leave the tunes till to-morrow, and come out with me."

"I thought," she said, roused a little, "that you were fond of music, John."

This brought John up suddenly in an unexpected way. "Oh, as for that,"—he said, in a dubious tone. Poor Elinor's tunes were not music in his sense, as she very well knew.

She laughed in a forlorn way. "I know what you mean; but this is quite good enough for what I shall want. I am going down, you know, to a different level altogether. Oh, you can hear for yourself what mamma and Mr. Lynch are saying."

"Going up you mean, Elinor. I thought them both very complaisant over all those titles."

"Ah," she said, "they say that mocking. They think I am going down; so do you, too, to the land of mere fast people, people with no sense. Well; there is nothing but the trial will teach any of us. We shall see."

"It is rather a dreadful risk to run, if it's only a trial, Elinor."

"A trial—for you, not for me—I am not the one that thinks so, except so far as the tunes are concerned," she said with a laugh. "I confess so far as that Lady Mariamne is fond of a comic song. I don't think she goes any further. I shall be good enough for them in the way of music."

"I should be content never to hear another note of music all my life, Elinor, if——"

"Ah, there you begin again. Not you, John, not you! I can't bear any more. Neither stars, nor walks, nor listening; no more! This rather," and she brought down her hands with a great crash upon the piano, making every one start. Then Elinor rose, having produced her effect. "I think it must be time to go to bed, mamma. John is talking of the stars, which means that he wants his cigar, and Mr. Lynch must want just to look at the tray in the dining-room. And you are tired by all this fuss, all this unnatural fuss about me, that am not worth—— Come, mother, to bed."

CHAPTER VII.

The days in the cottage were full of excitement and of occupation during the blazing August weather, not so much indeed as is common in many houses in which the expectant bridegroom is always coming and going; though perhaps the place of that exhilarating commotion was more or less filled by the ever-present diversity of opinion, the excitement of a subdued but never-ended conflict in which one was always on the defensive, and the other covertly or openly attacking, or at least believed to be so doing, the distant and unseen object to which all their thoughts turned. Mrs. Dennistoun, indeed, was not always aggressive, her opposition was but in fits and starts. Often her feelings of pain and alarm were quiescent in that unfeigned and salutary interest in clothes and necessities of preparation which is almost always a resource to a woman's mind. It is wrong to undervalue this possibility which compensates a woman in a small degree for some of her special troubles. When the mother's heart was very heavy, it was often diverted a little by the discussion of a dinner dress, or made to forget itself for the moment in a question about the cut of a sleeve, or which would be most becoming to Elinor of two colours for a ball gown. But though Mrs. Dennistoun forgot often, Elinor never forgot. The dresses and "things" generally occupied her a great deal, but not in the form of the anodyne which they supplied to her mother. Her mind was always on the alert, looking out for those flying arrows of warfare which your true fighter lets fly in the most innocent conversation at the most unexpected moments. Elinor thus flung her shield in her mother's face a hundred times when that poor lady was thinking no evil, when she was altogether occupied by the question of frills and laces, or whether tucks or flounces were best, and she was startled many times by that unnecessary rattle of Elinor's arms. "I was not thinking of Mr. Compton," she would sometimes be driven to say; "he was not in my head at all. I was thinking of nothing more important than that walking dress, and what you had best wear in the afternoon when you are on those grand visits."

There was one thing which occasioned a little discussion between them, and that was the necessary civility of asking the neighbours to inspect these "things" when they were finally ready. It was only the argument that these neighbours would be Mrs. Dennistoun's sole resource when she was left alone that made Elinor assent at last. Perhaps, however, as she walked quickly along towards the moorland Rectory, a certain satisfaction in showing them how little their hints had been taken, mingled with the reluctance to admit those people who had breathed a doubt upon the sacred name of Phil, to such a sign of intimacy.

"I have been watching you along the side of the combe, and wondering if it was you such a threatening day," said Alice Hudson, coming to the door to meet her. "How nice of you to come, Elinor, when you must be so busy, and you have not been here since—I don't know how long ago!"

"No, I have not been here," said Elinor with a gravity worthy the bride of a maligned man. "But the time is so near when I shall not be able to come at all that I thought it was best. Mamma wishes you to come over to-morrow, if you will, to see my things."

"Oh!" the three ladies said together; and Mrs. Hudson came forward and gave Elinor a kiss. "My dear," she said, "I take it very kind you coming yourself to ask us. Many would not have done it after what we felt it our duty—— But you always had a beautiful spirit, Elinor, bearing no malice, and I hope with all my heart that it will have its reward."

"Well, mother," said Alice, "I don't see how Elinor could do anything less, seeing we have been such friends all our lives as girls, she and I, and I am sure I have always been ready to give her patterns, or to show her how a thing was done. I should have been very much disappointed if she had not asked me to see her things."

Mary Dale, who was Mrs. Hudson's sister, said nothing at all, but accepted the visit as in the course of nature. Mary was the one who really knew something about Phil Compton: but she had been against the remonstrance which Mrs. Hudson thought it her duty to make. What was the good? Miss Dale had said; and she had refrained from telling two or three stories about the Comptons which would have made the hair stand upright on the heads of the Rector and the Rectoress. She did not even now say that it was kind, but met Elinor in silence, as, in her position as the not important member of the family, it was quite becoming for her to do.

Then the Rector came in and took her by both hands, and gave her the most friendly greeting. "I heard Elinor's voice, and I stopped in the middle of my sermon," he said. "You will remark in church on Sunday a jerky piece, which shows how I stopped to reflect whether it could be you—and then went on for another sentence, and then decided that it must be you. There is a big Elinor written across my sermon paper." He laughed, but he was a little moved, to see, after the "coolness," the little girl whom he had christened come back to her old friends again.

"She has come to ask us to go and see her things, papa," said Mrs. Hudson, twinkling an eye to get rid of a suspicion of a tear.

"Am I to come, too?" said the Rector; and thus the little incident of the reconciliation was got over, to the great content of all.

Elinor reflected to herself that they were really kind people, as she went out again into the grey afternoon where everything was getting up for rain. She made up her mind she would just have time to run into the Hills', at the Hurst, and leave her message, and so get home before the storm began. The clouds lay low like a dark grey hood over the fir-trees and moorland shaggy tops of the downs all round. There was not a break anywhere in the consistent grey, and the air, always so brisk, had fallen still with

73

that ominous lull that comes over everything before a convulsion of nature. Some birds were still hurrying home into the depths of the copses with a frightened straightness of flight, as if they were afraid they would not get back in time, and all the insects that are so gay with their humming and booming had disappeared under leaves and stones and grasses. Elinor saw a bee burrowing deep in the waxen trumpet of a foxglove, as if taking shelter, as she walked quickly past. The Hills—there were two middle-aged sisters of them, with an old mother, too old for such diversion as the inspection of wedding-clothes, in the background—would scarcely let Elinor go out again after they had accepted her invitation with rapture. "I was just wondering where I should see the new fashions," said Miss Hill, "for though we are not going to be married we must begin to think about our winter things——" "And this will be such an opportunity," said Miss Susan, "and so good of you to come yourself to ask us."

"What has she come to ask you to," said old Mrs. Hill; "the wedding? I told you girls, I was sure you would not be left out. Why, I knew her mother before she was married. I have known them all, man and boy, for nearer sixty than fifty years—before her mother was born! To have left you out would have been ridiculous. Yes, yes, Elinor, my dear; tell your mother they will come—delighted! They have been thinking for the last fortnight what bonnets they would wear——"

"Oh, mother!" and "Oh, Elinor!" said the "girls," "you must not mind what mother says. We know very well that you must have worlds of people to ask. Don't think, among all your new connections, of such little country mice as us. We shall always just take the same interest in you, dear child, whether you find you can ask us or not."

"But of course you are asked," said Elinor, in *gaieté de cœur*, not reflecting that her mother had begun to be in despair about the number of people who could be entertained in the cottage dining-room, "and you must not talk about my new grand connections, for nobody will ever be like my old friends."

"Dear child!" they said, and "I always knew that dear Elinor's heart was in the right place." But it was all that Elinor could do to get free of their eager affection and alarm lest she should be caught in the rain. Both of the ladies produced waterproofs, and one a large pair of goloshes to fortify her, when it was found that she would go; and they stood in the porch watching her as she went along into the darkening afternoon, without any of their covers and shelters. The Miss Hills were apt to cling together, after the manner of those pairs of sweet sisters in the "Books of Beauty" which had been the delight of their youth; they stood, with arms intertwined, in their porch, watching Elinor as she hurried home, with her light half-flying step, like the belated birds. "Did you hear what she said about old friends, poor little thing?" "I wonder if she is finding out already that her new grand connections are but vanity!" they said, shaking their heads. The middle-aged sisters looked out of the sheltered home, which perhaps they had not chosen for themselves, with a sort of wistful feeling, half pity, perhaps half envy, upon the "poor little thing" who was running out so light-hearted into the storm. They had long ago retired into waterproofs and goloshes, and had much unwillingness to wet their feet—which things are a parable. They went back and closed the door, only when the first flash of lightning dazzled them, and they remembered that an open door is dangerous during a thunderstorm.

Elinor quickened her pace as the storm began and got home breathless with running, shaking off the first big drops of thunder-rain from her dress. But she did not think of any danger, and sat out in the porch watching how the darkness came down on the combe; how it was met with the jagged gleam of the great white flash, and how the thunderous explosion shook the earth. The combe, with its hill-tops on either side, became like the scene of a battle, great armies, invisible in the sharp torrents of rain, meeting each other with a fierce shock and recoil, with now and then a trumpet-blast, and now the gleam that lit up tree and copse, and anon the tremendous artillery. When the lightning came she caught a glimpse of the winding line of the white road leading away out of all this—leading into the world where she was going—and for a moment escaped by it, even amid the roar of all the elements: then came back, alighting again with a start in the familiar porch, amid all the surroundings of the familiar life, to feel her mother's hand upon her shoulder, and her mother's voice saying, "Have you got wet, my darling? Did you get much of it? Come in, come in from the storm!"

"It is so glorious, mamma!" Mrs. Dennistoun stood for a few minutes looking at it, then, with a shudder, withdrew into the drawing-room. "I think I have seen too many storms to like it," she said. But Elinor had not seen too many storms. She sat and watched it, now rolling away towards the south, and bursting again as though one army or the other had got reinforcements; while the flash of the explosions and the roar of the guns, and the white blast of the rain, falling like a sheet from the leaden skies, wrapped everything in mystery. The only thing that was to be identified from time to time was that bit of road leading out of it—leading her thoughts away, as it should one day lead her eager feet, from all the storm and turmoil out into the bright and shining world. Elinor never asked herself, as she sat there, a spectator of this great conflict of nature, whether that one human thing, by which her swift thoughts traversed the storm, carried any other suggestion as of coming back.

Perhaps it is betraying feminine counsels too much to the modest public to narrate how Elinor's things were all laid out for the inspection of the ladies of the parish, the dresses in one room, the "under things" in another, and in the dining-room the presents, which everybody was doubly curious to see, to compare their own offerings with those of other people, or else to note with anxious eye what was wanting, in order, if their present had not yet been procured, to supply the gap. How to get something that would look well among the others, and yet not be too expensive, was a problem which the country neighbours had much and painfully considered. The Hudsons had given

Elinor a little tea-kettle upon a stand, which they were painfully conscious was only plated, and sadly afraid would not look well among all the gorgeous articles with which no doubt her grand new connections had loaded her. The Rector came himself, with his ladies to see how the kettle looked, with a great line of anxiety between his brows; but when they saw that the revolving dishes beside it, which were the gift of the wealthy Lady Mariamne, were plated too, and not nearly such a pretty design, their hearts went up in instant exhilaration, followed a moment after by such indignation as they could scarcely restrain. "That rich sister, the woman who married the Jew" (which was their very natural explanation of the lady's nickname), "a woman who is rolling in wealth, and who actually made up the match!" This was crescendo, a height of scorn impossible to describe upon a mere printed page. "One would have thought she would have given a diamond necklace or something of consequence," said Mrs. Hudson in her husband's ear. "Or, at least silver," said the Rector. "These fashionable people, though they give themselves every luxury, have sometimes not very much money to spend; but silver, at least, she might have been expected to give silver." "It is simply disgraceful," said the Rector's wife. "I am glad, at all events, my dear," said he, "that our little thing looks just as well as any." "It is one of the prettiest things she has got," said Mrs. Hudson, with a proud heart. Lord St. Serf sent an old-fashioned little ring in a much worn velvet case, and the elder brother, Lord Lomond, an album for photographs. The Rector's wife indicated these gifts to her husband with little shrugs of her shoulders. "If that's all the family can do!" she said: "why Alice's cushion, which was worked with floss silks upon satin, was a more creditable present than that." The Miss Hills, who as yet had not had an opportunity, as they said, of giving their present, roamed about, curious, inspecting everything. "What is the child to do with a kettle, a thing so difficult to pack, and requiring spirit for the lamp, and all that—and only plated!" the Hills said to each other. "Now, that little teapot of ours," said Jane to Susan, "if mother would only consent to it, is no use to us, and would look very handsome here." "Real silver, and old silver, which is so much the rage, and a thing she could use every day when she has her visitors for afternoon tea," said Susan to Jane. "It is rather small," said Miss Hill, doubtfully. "But quite enough for two people," said the other, forgetting that she had just declared that the teapot would be serviceable when Elinor had visitors. But that was a small matter. Elinor, however, had other things better than these—a necklace, worth half a year's income, from John Tatham, which he had pinched himself to get for her that she might hold up her head among those great friends; and almost all that her mother possessed in the way of jewellery, which was enough to make a show among these simple people. "Her own family at least have done Elinor justice," said the Rector, going again to have a look at the kettle, which was the chief of the display to him. Thus the visitors made their remarks. The Hills did nothing but stand apart and discuss their teapot and the means by which "mother" could be got to assent.

The Rector took his cup of tea, always with a side glance at the kettle, and cut his cake, and made his gentle jest. "If Alick and I come over in the night and carry them all off you must not be surprised," he said; "such valuable things as these in a little poor parish are a dreadful temptation, and I don't suppose you have much in the way of bolts and bars. Alick is as nimble as a cat, he can get in at any crevice, and I'll bring over the box for the collections to carry off the little things." This harmless wit pleased the good clergyman much, and he repeated it to all the ladies. "I am coming over with Alick one of these dark nights to make a sweep of everything," he said. Mr. Hudson retired in the gentle laughter that followed this, feeling that he had acquitted himself as a man ought who is the only gentleman present, as well as the Rector of the parish. "I am afraid I would not be a good judge of the 'things,'" he said, "and for anything I know there may be mysteries not intended for men's eyes. I like to see your pretty dresses when you are wearing them, but I can't judge of their effect in the gross." He was a man who had a pleasant wit. The ladies all agreed that the Rector was sure to make you laugh whatever was the occasion, and he walked home very briskly, pleased with the effect of the kettle, and saying to himself that from the moment he saw it in Mappin's window he had felt sure it was the very thing.

The other ladies were sufficiently impressed with the number and splendour of Elinor's gowns. Mrs. Dennistoun explained, with a humility which was not, I fear, untinctured by pride, that both number and variety were rendered necessary by the fact that Elinor was going upon a series of visits among her future husband's great relations, and would have to be much in society and among fine people who dressed very much, and would expect a great deal from a bride. "Of course, in ordinary circumstances the half of them would have been enough: for I don't approve of too many dresses."

"They get old-fashioned," said Mrs. Hudson, gravely, "before they are half worn out."

"And to do them up again is quite as expensive as getting new ones, and not so satisfactory," said the Miss Hills.

The proud mother allowed both of these drawbacks, "But what could I do?" she said. "I cannot have my child go away into such a different sphere unprovided. It is a sacrifice, but we had to make it. I wish," she said, looking round to see that Elinor was out of hearing, "it was the only sacrifice that had to be made."

"Let us hope," said the Rector's wife, solemnly, "that it will all turn out for the best."

"It will do that however it turns out," said Miss Dale, who was even more serious than it was incumbent on a member of a clerical household to be, "for we all know that troubles are sent for our advantage as well as blessings, and poor dear Elinor may require much discipline——"

"Oh, goodness, don't talk as if the poor child was going to be executed," said Susan Hill.

"I am not at all alarmed," said Mrs. Dennistoun. It was unwise of her to have left an opening for any such remark. "My Elinor has always been surrounded by love wherever she has been. Her future husband's family are already very fond of her. I am not at all alarmed on Elinor's account."

She laid the covering wrapper over the dresses with an air of pride and confidence which was remembered long afterwards— as the pride that goeth before a fall by some, but by others with more sympathy, who guessed the secret workings of the mother's heart.

CHAPTER VIII.

Time went on quickly enough amid all these preparations and the little attendant excitements of letters, congratulations, and presents which came in on every side. Elinor complained mildly of the fuss, but it was a new and far from unpleasant experience. She liked to have the packets brought in by the post, or the bigger boxes that arrived from the station, and to open them and produce out of the wadding or the saw-dust one pretty thing after another. At first it was altogether fresh and amusing, this new kind of existence, though after a while she grew *blasée*, as may be supposed. Lady Mariamne's present she was a little ashamed of: not that she cared much, but because of the look on her mother's face when those inferior articles were unpacked; and at the ring which old Lord St. Serf sent her she laughed freely.

"I will put it with my own little old baby rings in this little silver tray, and they will all look as if they were antiques, or something worth looking at," said Elinor. Happily there were other people who endowed her more richly with rings fit for a bride to wear. The relations at a distance were more or less pleased with Elinor's prospects. A few, indeed, from different parts of the world wrote in the vein of Elinor's home-advisers, hoping that it was not the Mr. Compton who was so well known as a betting man whom she was going to marry; but the fact that she was marrying into a noble family, and would henceforward be known as the Honourable Mrs. Compton, mollified even these critics. Only three brothers—one a great invalid, and two soldiers—between him and the title. Elinor's relations promptly inaugurated in their imaginations a great war, in which two noble regiments were cut to pieces, to dispose of the two Captains Compton; and as for the invalid, that he would obligingly die off was a contingency which nobody doubted—and behold Elinor Dennistoun Lady St. Serf! This greatly calmed criticism among her relations, who were all at a distance, and whose approval or disapproval did not much affect her spirits anyhow. John Tatham's father, Mrs. Dennistoun's cousin, was of more consequence, chiefly as being John's father, but also a little for himself, and it was remarked that he said not a word against the marriage, but sent a very handsome present, and many congratulations—chiefly inspired (but this Elinor did not divine) by an unfeigned satisfaction that it was not his son who was the bridegroom. Mr. Tatham, senr., did not approve of early marriages for young men pushing their way at the bar, unless the bride was, so to speak, in the profession and could be of use to her husband. Even in such cases, the young man was better off without a wife, he was of opinion. How could he get up his cases properly if he had to drag about in society at the tail of a gay young woman? Therefore he sent Elinor a very nice present in gratitude to her and providence. She was a danger removed out of his boy's way.

All this kept a cheerful little commotion about the house, and often kept the mother and daughter from thinking more than was good for them. These extraneous matters did not indeed preserve Elinor altogether from the consciousness that her *fiancé's* letters were very short and a little uncertain in their arrival, sometimes missing several days together, and generally written in a hurry to catch the post. But they kept Mrs. Dennistoun from remarking that fact, as otherwise she would have been sure to do. If any chill of disappointment was in Elinor's mind, she said to herself that men were generally bad correspondents, not like girls, who had nothing else to do, and other consolations of this kind, which to begin with beg the question, and show the beginning of that disenchantment which ought to be reserved at least for a later period. Elinor had already given up a good deal of her own ideal. She would not, as she said, put herself in competition with the grouse, she would not give him the choice between her and a cigar; but already the consciousness that he preferred the grouse, and even a cigar, to her society, had come an unwilling intruder into Elinor's mind. She would not allow to herself that she felt it in either case. She said to herself that she was proud of it, that it showed the freedom and strength of a man, and that love was only one of many things which occupied his life. She rebelled against the other deduction that "'tis woman's sole existence," protesting loudly (to herself) that she too had a hundred things to do, and did not want him always at her apron-strings like a tame curate. But as a matter of fact, no doubt the girl would have been flattered and happy had he been more with her. The time was coming very quickly in which they should be together always, even when there was grouse in hand, when his wife would be invited with him, and all things would be in common between them; so what did it matter for a few days? The marriage was fixed for the 16th of September, and that great date was now scarcely a fortnight off. The excitement quickened as everything grew towards this central point. Arrangements had to be made about the wedding breakfast and where the guests were to be placed. The Hudsons had put their spare rooms at the disposition of the Cottage, and so had the Hills. The bridegroom was to stay at the Rectory. Lady Mariamne must of course, Mrs. Dennistoun felt, be put up at the Cottage, where the two rooms on the ground floor—what were called the gentlemen's rooms—had to be prepared to receive her. It was with a little awe indeed that the ladies of the Cottage endeavoured, by the aid of Elinor's recollections, to come to an understanding of what a fine lady would want even for a single night. Mrs. Dennistoun's experiences were all old-fashioned, and of a period when even great ladies were less luxurious than now; and it made her a little angry to think how much more was required for her daughter's future sister-in-law than had been necessary to herself. But after all, what had herself to do with it? The thing was to do Elinor credit, and make the future sister-in-law perceive that the Cottage was no rustic establishment, but one in which it was known what was what, and all the requirements of the most refined life. Elinor's bridesmaid, Mary Tatham, was to have the spare room up-stairs, and some other cousins, who were what Mrs. Dennistoun called "quiet people," were to receive the hospitalities of the Hills, whose house was roomy and old-fashioned. Thus the arrangements of the crisis were more or less settled and everything made smooth.

Elinor and her mother were seated together in the drawing-room on one of those evenings of which Mrs. Dennistoun desired to make the most, as they would be the last, but which, as they actually passed, were—if not occupied with discussions of how everything was to be arranged, which they went over again and again by instinct as a safe subject—heavy, almost dull, and dragged sadly over the poor ladies whose hearts were so full, but to whom to be separated, though it would be bitter, would also at the same time almost be a relief. They had been silent for some time, not because they had not plenty to say, but because it was so difficult to say it without awaking too much feeling. How could they talk of the future in which one of them would be away in strange places, exposed to the risks and vicissitudes of a new life, and one of them be left alone in the unbroken silence, sitting over the fire, with nothing but that blaze to give her any comfort? It was too much to think of, much more to talk about, though it need not be said that it was in the minds of both—with a difference, for Elinor's imagination was most employed upon the brilliant canvas where she herself held necessarily the first place, with a sketch of her mother's lonely life, giving her heart a pang, in the distance; while Mrs. Dennistoun could not help but see the lonely figure in her own foreground, against the brightness of all the entertainments in which Elinor should appear as a queen. They were sitting thus, the mother employed at some fine needlework for the daughter, the daughter doing little, as is usual nowadays. They had been talking over Lady Mariamne and her requirements again, and had come to an end of that subject. What a pity that it was so hard to open the door of their two hearts, which were so close together, so that each might see all the tenderness and compunction in the other; the shame and sorrow of the mother to grudge her child's happiness, the remorse and trouble of the child to be leaving that mother out in all her calculations for the future! How were they to do it on either side? They could not talk, these poor loving women, so they were mostly silent, saying a word or two at intervals about Mrs. Dennistoun's work (which of course, was for Elinor), or of Elinor's village class for sewing, which was to be transferred to her mother, skirting the edges of the great separation which could neither be dismissed nor ignored.

Suddenly Elinor looked up, holding up her finger. "What was that?" she said. "A step upon the gravel?"

"Nonsense, child. If we were to listen to all these noises of the night there would always be a step upon—— Oh! I think I did hear something."

"It is someone coming to the door," said Elinor, rising up with that sudden prevision of trouble which is so seldom deceived.

"Don't go, Elinor; don't go. It might be a tramp; wait at least till they knock at the door."

"I don't think it can be a tramp, mamma. It may be a telegram. It is coming straight up to the door."

"It will be the parcel porter from the station. He is always coming and going, though I never knew him so late. Pearson is in the house, you know. There is not any cause to be alarmed."

"Alarmed!" said Elinor, with a laugh of excitement; "but I put more confidence in myself than in Pearson, whoever it may be."

She stood listening with a face full of expectation, and Mrs. Dennistoun put down her work and listened too. The step advanced lightly, scattering the gravel, and then there was a pause as if the stranger had stopped to reconnoitre. Then came a knock at the window, which could only have been done by a tall man, and the hearts of the ladies jumped up, and then seemed to stop beating. To be sure, there were bolts and bars, but Pearson was not much good, and the house was full of valuables and very lonely. Mrs. Dennistoun rose up, trembling a little, and went forward to the window, bidding Elinor go back and keep quite quiet. But here they were interrupted by a voice which called from without, with another knock on the window, "Nell! Nell!"

"It is Phil," said Elinor, flying to the door.

Mrs. Dennistoun sat down again and said nothing. Her heart sank in her breast. She did not know what she feared; perhaps that he had come to break off the marriage, perhaps to hurry it and carry her child away. There was a pause as was natural at the door, a murmur of voices, a fond confusion of words, which made it clear that no breach was likely, and presently after that interval, Elinor came back beaming, leading her lover. "Here is Phil," she said, in such liquid tones of happiness as filled her mother with mingled pleasure, gratitude, and despite. "He has found he had a day or two to spare, and he has rushed down here, fancy, with an apology for not letting us know!"

"She thinks everyone is like herself, Mrs. Dennistoun, but I am aware that I am not such a popular personage as she thinks me, and you have least reason of all to approve of the man who is coming to carry her away."

"I am glad to see you, Mr. Compton," she said, gravely, giving him her hand.

The Hon. Philip Compton was a very tall man, with very black hair. He had fine but rather hawk-like features, a large nose, a complexion too white to be agreeable, though it added to his romantic appearance. There was a furtive look in his big dark eyes, which had a way of surveying the country, so to speak, before making a reply to any question, like a man whose response depended upon what he saw. He surveyed Mrs. Dennistoun in this way while she spoke; but then he took her hand, stooped his head over it, and kissed it, not without grace. "Thank you very much for that," he said, as if there had been some doubt on his mind about his reception. "I was glad enough to get the opportunity, I can tell you. I've brought you some birds, Mrs. Dennistoun, and I hope you'll give me some supper, for I'm as hungry as a hawk. And now, Nell, let's have a look at you," the

86

lover said. He was troubled by no false modesty. As soon as he had paid the required toll of courtesy to the mother, who naturally ought to have at once proceeded to give orders about his supper, he held Elinor at arm's length before the lamp, then, having fully inspected her appearance, and expressed by a "Charming, by Jove!" his opinion of it, proceeded to demonstrations which the presence of the mother standing by did not moderate. There are few mothers to whom it would be agreeable to see their child engulfed in the arms of a large and strong man, and covered with his bold kisses. Mrs. Dennistoun was more fastidious even than most mothers, and to her this embrace was a sort of profanation. The Elinor who had been guarded like a flower from every contact—to see her gripped in his arms by this stranger, made her mother glow with an indignation which she knew was out of the question, yet felt to the bottom of her soul. Elinor was abashed before her mother, but she was not angry. She forced herself from his embrace, but her blushing countenance was full of happiness. What a revolution had thus taken place in a few minutes! They had been so dull sitting there alone; alone, though each with the other who had filled her life for more than twenty years; and now all was lightened, palpitating with life. "Be good, sir," said Elinor, pushing him into a chair as if he had been a great dog, "and quiet and well-behaved; and then you shall have some supper. But tell us first where you have come from, and what put it into your head to come here."

"I came up direct from my brother Lomond's shooting-box. Reply No. 1. What put it into my head to come? Love, I suppose, and the bright eyes of a certain little witch called Nell. I ought to have been in Ireland for a sort of a farewell visit there; but when I found I could steal two days, you may imagine I knew very well what to do with them. Eh? Oh, it's mamma that frightens you, I see."

"It is kind of you to give Elinor two days when you have so many other engagements," said Mrs. Dennistoun, turning away.

But he was not in the least abashed. "Yes isn't it?" he said;

"my last few days of freedom. I consider I deserve the prize for virtue—to cut short my very last rampage; and she will not as much as give me a kiss! I think she is ashamed before you, Mrs. Dennistoun."

"It would not be surprising if she were," said Mrs. Dennistoun, gravely. "I am old-fashioned, as you may perceive."

"Oh, you don't need to tell me that," said he; "one can see it with half an eye. Come here, Nell, you little coquette: or I shall tell the Jew you were afraid of mamma, and you will never hear an end of it as long as you live."

"Elinor, I think you had better see, perhaps, what there is to make up as good a meal as possible for Mr. Compton," said her mother, sitting down opposite to the stranger, whose long limbs were stretched over half the floor, with the intention of tripping up Elinor, it seemed; but she glided past him and went on her way—not offended, oh, not at all—waving her hand to him as she avoided the very choice joke of his stretched-out foot.

"Mr. Compton," said Mrs. Dennistoun, "you will be Elinor's husband in less than a fortnight."

"I hope so," he said, displaying the large cavern of a yawn under his black moustache as he looked her in the face.

"And after that I will have no right to interfere; but, in the meantime, this is my house, and I hope you will remember that these ways are not mine, and that I am too old-fashioned to like them. I prefer a little more respect to your betrothed."

"Oh, respect," he said. "I have never found that girls like too much respect. But as you please. Well, look here, Nell," he said, catching her by the arm as she came back and swinging her towards him, "your mother thinks I'm too rough with you, my little dear."

"Do you, mamma?" said Elinor, faltering a little; but she had the sweetest rose-flush on her cheeks and the moisture of joy in her eyes. In all her twenty-three years she had never looked as she looked now. Her life had been a happy one, but not like this. She had been always beloved, and never had known for a day what it was to be neglected; yet love had never appeared to her as it did now, so sweet, nor life so beautiful. What strange delusion! what a wonderful incomprehensible mistake! or so at least the mother thought, looking at her beautiful girl with a pang at her heart.

"It is only his bad manners," said Elinor, in a voice which sounded like a caress. "He knows very well how to behave. He can be as nice as any one, and as pretty spoken, and careful not to offend. It is only arriving so suddenly, and not being expected—or that he has forgotten his nice manners to-night. Phil, do you hear what I say?"

Phil made himself into the semblance of a dog, and sat up and begged for pardon. It was a trick which made people "shriek with laughing;" but Mrs. Dennistoun's gravity remained unbroken. Perhaps her extreme seriousness had something in it that was rather ridiculous too. It was a relief when he went off to his supper, attended by Elinor, and Mrs. Dennistoun was left alone over her fire. She had a slight sense that she had been absurd, as well as that Philip Compton had lacked breeding, which did not make her more comfortable. Was it possible that she would be glad when it was all over, and her child gone—her child gone, and with that man! Her child, her little delicately bred, finely nurtured girl, who had been wrapped in all the refinements of life from her cradle, and had never heard a rough word, never been allowed to know anything that would disturb her virginal calm!—yet now in a moment passed away beyond her mother to the unceremonious wooer who had no reverence for her, none of the worship her mother expected. How strange it was! Yet a thing that happened every day. Mrs. Dennistoun sat over the fire, though it was not cold, and listened to the voices and laughter in the next room. How happy they were to be together! She did not, however, dwell upon the fact that she was alone and deserted, as many women would have done. She knew that she would have plenty of time to dwell on this in the lonely days to come. What occupied her was the want of more than manners, of any delicate feeling in the lover who had seized with rude caresses upon Elinor in her mother's presence, and the fact that Elinor did not object, nor dislike that it should be so. That she should feel forlorn was no wonderful thing; that did not disturb her mind. It was the other matter about Elinor that pained and horrified her, she could not tell why; which, perhaps, was fantastic, which, indeed, she felt sure must be so.

They were so long in the dining-room, where Compton had his supper, that when that was over it was time to go to bed. Still talking and laughing as if they could never exhaust either the fountain of talk or the mirth, which was probably much more sheer pleasure in their meeting than genuine laughter produced by any wit or *bon mot*, they came out into the passage, and stood by Mrs. Dennistoun and the housemaid, who had brought her the keys and was now fastening the hall door. A little calendar hung on the wall beneath the lamp, and Phil Compton walked up to it and with a laugh read out the date. "Sixth September," he said, and turned round to Elinor. "Only ten days more, Nell." The housemaid stooping down over the bolt blushed and laughed too under her breath in sympathy; but Mrs. Dennistoun turning suddenly round caught Compton's eye. Why had he given that keen glance about him? There was nothing to call for his usual survey of the company in that sentiment. He might have known well enough what were the feelings he was likely to call forth. A keen suspicion shot through her mind. Suspicion of what? She could not tell. There was nothing that was not most natural in his sudden arrival, the delightful surprise of his coming, his certainty of a good reception. The wonder was that he had come so little, not that he should come now.

The next morning the visitor made himself very agreeable: his raptures were a little calmed. He talked over all the arrangements, and entered into everything with the interest of a man to whom that great day approaching was indeed the greatest day in his life. And it turned out that he had something to tell which was of practical importance. "I may relieve your mind about Nell's money," he said, "for I believe my company is going to be wound up. We'll look out for another investment which will pay as well and be less risky. It has been found not to be doing quite so well as was thought, so we're going to wind up."

"I hope you have not lost anything," said Mrs. Dennistoun.

"Oh, nothing to speak of," he said, carelessly.

"I am not fond of speculative companies. I am glad you are done with it," Mrs. Dennistoun said.

"And I'm glad to be done with it. I shall look out for something permanent and decline joint-stock companies. I thought you would like to know. But that is the last word I shall say about business. Come, Nell, I have only one day; let's spend it in the woods."

Elinor, who felt that the day in the woods was far more important than any business, hurried to get her hat and follow him to the door. It chanced to her to glance at the calendar as she passed hastily out to where he stood awaiting her in the porch. Why that should have happened to anyone in the Cottage twice in the twenty-four hours is a coincidence which I cannot explain, but so it was. Her eye caught the little white plaque in passing, and perceived with surprise that it had moved up two numbers, and that it was the figure 8 which was marked upon it now.

"We cannot have slept through a day and night," she said, laughing as she joined him. "The calendar says the eighth September now."

"But I arrived on the sixth," he said. "Mind that, Nell, whatever happens. You saw it with your own eyes. It may be of consequence to remember."

"Of what consequence could it be?" said Elinor, wondering.

"One can never tell. The only thing is I arrived on the sixth— that you know. And, Nell, my darling, supposing any fellow should inquire too closely into my movements, you'll back me up, won't you, and agree in everything I say?"

"Who should inquire into your movements? There is no one here who would be so impertinent, Phil."

91

"Oh," he said, "there is never any telling how impertinent people may be."

"And what is there in your movements that any one dare inquire about? I hope you are not ashamed of coming to see me."

"That is just what is the saving of me, Nell. I can't explain what I mean now, but I will later on. Only mind you don't contradict me if we should meet any inquisitive person. I arrived on the sixth, and you'll back me like my true love in everything I say."

"As far as—as I know, Phil."

"Oh, we must have no conditions. You must stand by me in everything I say."

CHAPTER IX.

This day in the copse was one that Elinor never forgot. At the moment it seemed to her the most blissful period of all her life. There had been times in which she had longed that Phil knew more and cared more for the objects which had always been most familiar, and told for most in her own existence—although it is true that at first his very ignorance, real or assumed, his careless way of treating all intellectual subjects, his indifference to books and pictures, and even nature, had amused and pleased her, giving a piquancy to the physical strength and enjoying manhood, the perpetual activity and state of doing something in which he was. It was not a kind of life which she had ever known before, and it dazzled her with its apparent freedom and fulness, the variety in it, the constant movement, the crowd of occupations and people. To her who had been used to finding a great deal of her amusement in reading, in sketching (not very well), in playing (tunes), and generally practising with very moderate success arts for which she had no individual enthusiasm, it had seemed like a new life to be plunged into the society of horses and dogs, into the active world which was made up of a round of amusements, race meetings, days on the river, follies of every conceivable kind, exercise, and air, and movement. The ignorance of all these people dazzled her as if it had been a new science. It had seemed something wonderful and piquant to Elinor to find people who knew so much of subjects she had never heard of, and nothing at all of those she had been trained to know. And then there had come a moment when she had begun to sigh under her breath, as it were, and wish that Phil would sometimes open a book, that when he took up the newspaper he would look at something more than the sporting news and the bits of gossip, that he would talk now and then of something different from the racings and the startings, and the odds, and the scrapes other men got into, and the astonishing "frocks" of the Jew—those things, so wonderful at first, like a new language, absurd, yet amusing, came to be a little tiresome, especially when scraps of them made up the bulk of the very brief letters which Phil scribbled to his betrothed. But during this day, after his unexpected arrival, the joy of seeing him suddenly, the pleasure of feeling that he had broken through all his engagements to come to her, and the fervour of his satisfaction in being with her again (that very fervour which shocked her mother), Elinor's first glow of delight in her love came fully back. And as they wandered through the pleasant paths of the copse, his very talk seemed somehow changed, and to have gained just that little mingling of perception of her tastes and wishes which she had desired. There was a little autumnal mist about the softening haze which was not decay, but only the "mellow fruitfulness" of the poet; and the day, notwithstanding this, was as warm as June, the sky blue, with only a little white puff of cloud here and there. Phil paused to look down the combe, with all the folds of the downs that wrapped it about, going off in blue outlines into the distance, and said it was "a jolly view"—which amused Elinor more than if he had used the finest language, and showed that he was beginning (she thought) to care a little for the things which pleased her. "And I suppose you could see a man coming by that bit of road."

"Yes," said Elinor, "you could see a man coming—or going: but, unless you were to make believe very strong, like the Marchioness, you could not make out who the man was."

"What Marchioness?" said Phil. "I didn't know you had anybody with a title about here. I say, Nell, it's a very jolly view, but hideously dull for you, my pet, to have lived so long here."

"I never found it in the least dull," she said.

"Why, there is nothing to do! I suppose you read books, eh? That's what you call amusing yourself. You ought to have made the old lady take you about a deal, abroad, and all over the place: but I expect you have never stood up for yourself a bit, Nell."

"Don't call mamma the old lady, Phil. She is not old, and far prettier than most people I know."

"Well, she should have done it for herself. Might have picked up a good match, eh? a father-in-law that would have left you a pot of money. You don't mean to say you wouldn't have liked that?"

"Oh, Phil, Phil! I wish you could understand."

"Well, well, I'll let the old girl alone." And then came the point at which Phil improved so much. "Tell me what you've been reading last," he said. "I should like to know what you are thinking about, even if I don't understand it myself. I say, Nell, who do you think that can be dashing so fast along the road?"

"It is the people at Reddown," she said. "I know their white horses. They always dash along as if they were in the greatest hurry. Do you really want to know what I have been reading, Phil? though it is very little, I fear, because of the dressmakers and—all the other things."

"You see," he said, "when you have lots to do you can't keep up with your books: which is the reason why I never pretend to read—I have no time."

"You might find a little time. I have seen you look very much bored, and complain that there was nothing to do."

"Never when you were there, Nell, that I'll answer for—but of course there are times when a fellow isn't doing anything much. What would you have me read? There's always the *Sporting and Dramatic*, you know, the *Pink 'un*, and a few more."

"Oh, Phil! you don't call them literature, I hope."

"I don't know much about what you call literature. There's Ruff, and Hoyle, and—I say, Nell, there's a dog-cart going a pace! Who can that be, do you suppose?"

"I don't know all the dog-carts about. I should think it was some one coming from the station."

"Oh!" he said, and made a long pause. "Driving like that, if they don't break their necks, they should be here in ten minutes or so."

"Oh, not for twice that time—the road makes such a round—but there is no reason to suppose that any dog-cart from the station should be coming here."

"Well, to return to the literature, as you call it. I suppose I shall have to get a lot of books for you to keep you amused—eh, Nell? even in the honeymoon."

"We shall not have time to read very much if we are moving about all the time."

"Not me, but you. I know what you'll do. You'll go and leave me planted, and run up-stairs to read your book. I've seen the Jew do it with some of her confounded novels that she's always wanting to turn over to me."

"But there are some novels that you would like to read, Phil."

"Not a bit. Why, Nell, I know far better stories of fellows in our own set than any novel these writing men ever can put on paper: fellows, and women, too—stories that would make your hair stand on end, and that would make you die with laughing. You can't think what lots I know. That cart would have been here by this time if it had been coming here, eh?"

"Oh, no, not yet—the road makes such a long round. Do you expect any one, Phil?"

"I don't quite know; there's something on at that confounded office of ours; everything, you know, has gone to smash. I didn't think it well to say too much to the old lady last night. There's been a regular row, and the manager's absconded, and all turns on whether they can find some books. I shouldn't wonder if one of the fellows came down here, if they find out where I am. I say, Nell, mind you back me up whatever I say."

"But I can't possibly know anything about it," said Elinor, astonished.

"Never mind—about dates and that—if you don't stand by me, there may be a fuss, and the wedding delayed. Remember that, my pet, the wedding delayed—that's what I want to avoid. Now, come, Nell, let's have another go about the books. All English, mind you. I won't buy you any of the French rot. They're too spicy for a little girl like you."

"I don't know what you mean, Phil. I hope you don't think that I read nothing but novels," Elinor said.

"Nothing but novels! Oh, if you go in for mathematics and that sort of thing, Nell! the novels are too deep for me. Don't say poetry, if you love me. I could stand most things from you, Nell, you little darling—but, Nell, if you come spouting verses all the time——"

His look of horror made Elinor laugh. "You need not be afraid. I never spout verses," she said.

"Come along this way a little, where we can see the road. All women seem to like poetry. There's a few fellows I don't mind myself. Ingoldsby, now that's something fine. We had him at school, and perhaps it was the contrast from one's lessons. Do you know Ingoldsby, Nell?"

"A—little—I have read some——"

"Ah, you like the sentimental best. There's Whyte Melville, then, there's always something melancholy about him—'When the old horse died,' and that sort of thing—makes you cry, don't you know. You all like that. Certainly, if that dog-cart had been coming here it must have come by this time."

"Yes, it must have come," Elinor admitted, with a little wonder at the importance which he gave to this possible incident. "But there is another train at two if you are very anxious to see this man."

"Oh, I'm not anxious to see him," said Mr. Compton, with a laugh, "but probably he will want to see me. No, Nell, you will not expect me to read poetry to you while we're away. There's quite a library at Lomond's place. You can amuse yourself there when I'm shooting; not that I shall shoot much, or anything that takes me away from my Nell. But you must come out with us. There is no such fun as stumping over the moors—the Jew has got all the turn-out for that sort of thing—short frocks and knickerbockers, and a duck of a little breech-loader. She thinks she's a great shot, poor thing, and men are civil and let her imagine that she's knocked over a pheasant or a hare, now and then. As for the partridges, she lets fly, of course, but to say she hits anything——"

"I should not want to hit anything," said Elinor. "Oh, please Phil! I will try anything else you like, but don't make me shoot."

"You little humbug! See what you'll say when you get quite clear of the old lady. But I don't want you to shoot, Nell. If you don't get tired sitting at home, with all of us out on the hill, I like to come in for my part and find a little duck all tidy, not blowzy and blown about by the wind, like the Jew with her ridiculous bag, that all the fellows snigger at behind her back."

"You should not let any fellow laugh at your sister, Phil——"

"Oh, as for that! they are all as thick with her as I am, and why should I interfere? But I promise you nobody shall cut a joke upon my Nell."

"I should hope not, indeed," said Elinor, indignant; "but as for your 'fellows,' Phil, as you call them, you mustn't be angry with me, but I don't much like those gentlemen; they are a little rude and rough. They shall not call me by my Christian name, or anything but my own formal——"

"Mrs. Compton," he said, seizing her in his arms, "you little duck! they'll be as frightened of you as if you were fifty. But you mustn't spoil good company, Nell. I shall like you to keep them at a distance, but you mustn't go too far; and, above all, my pet, you mustn't put out the Jew. I calculate on being a lot there; they have a nice house and a good table, and all that, and Prestwich is glad of somebody to help about his horses. You mustn't set up any of your airs with the Jew."

"I don't know what you mean by my airs, Phil."

"Oh, but I do, and they're delicious, Nell: half like a little girl and half like a queen: but it will never do to make the Jew feel small in her own set. Hallo! there's some one tumbling alone over the stones on that precious road of yours. I believe it's that cart from the station after all."

"No," said Elinor, "it is only one of the tradespeople. You certainly are anxious about those carts from the station, Phil."

"Not a bit!" he said, and then, after a moment, he added, "Yes, on the whole, I'd much rather the man came, if he's coming while I'm here, and while you are with me, Nell; for I want you to stick to me, and back me up. They might think I ought to go after that manager fellow and spoil the wedding. Therefore mind you back me up."

"I can't think, dear Phil, what there is for me to do. I know nothing about the business nor what has happened. You never told me anything, and how can I back you up about things I don't know?"

"Oh, yes, you can," he said, "you'll soon see if the fellow comes; just you stand by me, whatever I say. You mayn't know—or even I may seem to make a mistake; but you know me if you don't know the circumstances, and I hope you can trust me, Nell, that it will be all right."

"But——" said Elinor, confused.

"Don't go on with your buts; there's a darling, don't contradict me. There is nothing looks so silly to strangers as a woman contradicting every word a fellow says. I only want you to stand by me, don't you know, that's all; and I'll tell you everything about it after, when there's time."

"Tell me about it now," said Elinor; "you may be sure I shall be interested; there's plenty of time now."

"Talk about business to you! when I've only a single day, and not half time enough, you little duck, to tell you what a darling you are, and how I count every hour till I can have you all to myself. Ah, Nell, Nell, if that day were only here——"

And then Phil turned to those subjects and those methods which cast so much confusion into the mind of Mrs. Dennistoun, when practised under her sedate and middle-aged eyes. But Elinor, as has been said, did not take exactly the same view.

Presently they went to luncheon, and Phil secured himself a

place at table commanding the road. "I never knew before how jolly it was," he said, "though everything is jolly here. And that peep of the road must give you warning when any invasion is coming."

"It is too far off for that," said Mrs. Dennistoun.

"Oh, no, not for sharp eyes. Nell there told me who several people were—those white horses—the people at—where did you say, Nell?"

"Reddown, mamma—the Philistines, as you call them, that are always dashing about the country—*nouveaux riches*, with the finest horses in the county."

"I like the *nouveaux riches* for that," said Phil (he did not go wrong in his French, which was a great consolation to Elinor), "they like to have the best of everything. Your poor swell has to take what he can get, but the *parvenu's* the man in these days; and then there was a dog-cart, which she pronounced to be from the station, but which turned out to be the butcher, or the baker, or the candle-stick maker——"

"It is really too far off to make sure of anything, except white horses."

"Ah, there's no mistaking them. I see something sweeping along, but that's a country wagon, I suppose. It gives me a great deal of diversion to see the people on the road—which perhaps you will think a vulgar amusement."

"Not at all," said Mrs. Dennistoun, politely, but she thought within herself how empty the brain must be which sought diversion from the distant carriages passing two miles off: to be sure across the combe, as the crow flies, it was not a quarter part so far as that.

"Phil thinks some one may possibly come to him on business—to explain things," said Elinor, anxious on her part to make it clear that it was not out of mere vacancy that her lover had watched so closely the carriages on the road.

"Unfortunately, there is something like a smash," he said; "they'll keep it out of the papers if they can, but you may see it in the papers; the manager has run away, and there's a question about some books. I don't suppose you would understand—they may come to me here about it, or they may wait till I go back to town."

"I thought you were going to Ireland, Phil."

"So I shall, probably, just for three days—to fill up the time. One wants to be doing something to keep one's self down. You can't keep quiet and behave yourself when you are going to be married in a week: unless you're a little chit of a girl without any feelings," he said with a laugh. And Elinor laughed too; while Mrs. Dennistoun sat as grave as a judge at the head of the table. But Phil was not daunted by her serious face: so long as the road was quite clear he had all the appearance of a perfectly easy mind.

"We have been talking about literature," he said. "I am a stupid fellow, as perhaps you know, for that sort of thing. But Nell is to indoctrinate me. We mean to take a big box of books, and I'm to be made to read poetry and all sorts of fine things in my honeymoon."

"That is a new idea," said Mrs. Dennistoun. "I thought Elinor meant to give up reading, on the other hand, to make things square."

There was a little breath of a protest from Elinor. "Oh, mamma!" but she left the talk (he could do it so much better) in Compton's hand.

"I expect to figure as a sort of prodigy in my family," he said; "we're not bookish. The Jew goes in for French novels, but I don't intend to let Nell touch them, so you may be easy in your mind."

"I have no doubt Lady Mariamne makes a good selection," said Mrs. Dennistoun.

"Not she! she reads whatever comes, and the more salt the better. The Jew is quite an emancipated person. Don't you think she'll bore you rather in this little house? She carries bales of rubbish with her wherever she goes, and her maid, and her dog, and I don't know what. If I were you I'd write, or better wire, and tell her there's a capital train from Victoria will bring her here in time for the wedding, and that it's a thousand pities she should disturb herself to come for the night."

"If your sister can put up with my small accommodation, I shall of course be happy to have her, whatever she brings with her," Mrs. Dennistoun said.

"Oh! it's not a question of putting up—she'd be delighted, I'm sure: but I think you'll find her a great bore. She is exceedingly fussy when she has not all her things about her. However, you must judge for yourself. But if you think better of it, wire a few words, and it'll be all right. I'm to go to the old Rectory, Nell says."

"It is not a particularly old Rectory; it is a very nice, pleasant house. I think you will find yourself quite comfortable—you and the gentleman——"

"Dick Bolsover, who is going to see me through it: and I daresay I should not sleep much, if I were in the most luxurious bed in the world. They say a man who is going to be hanged sleeps like a top, but I don't think I shall; what do you say, Nell?"

"Elinor, I should think, could have no opinion on the subject," said Mrs. Dennistoun, pale with anger. "You will all dine here, of course. Some other friends are coming, and a cousin, Mr. Tatham, of Tatham's Cross."

"Is that," said Phil, "the Cousin John?"

"John, I am sorry to say, is abroad; the long vacation is the worst time. It is his father who is coming, and his sister, Mary Tatham, who is Elinor's bridesmaid—she and Miss Hudson at the Rectory."

"Only two; and very sensible, instead of the train one sees, all thinking how best to show themselves off. Dick Bolsover is man enough to tackle them both. He expects some fun, I can tell you. What is there to be after we are gone, Nell?" He stopped and looked round with a laugh. "Rather close quarters for a ball," he said.

"There will be no ball. You forget that when you take Elinor away I shall be alone. A solitary woman living in a cottage, as you remark, does not give balls. I am much afraid that there will be very little fun for your friend."

"Oh, he'll amuse himself well enough; he's the sort of fellow who always makes himself at home. A Rectory will be great fun for him; I don't suppose he was ever in one before, unless perhaps when he was a boy at school. Yes, as you say—what a lot of trouble it will be for you to be sure: not as if Nell had a sister to enjoy the fun after. It's a thousand pities you did not decide to bring her up to town, and get us shuffled off there. You might have got a little house for next to nothing at this time of the year, and saved all the row, turning everything upside down in this nice little place, and troubling yourself with visitors and so forth. But one always thinks of that sort of thing too late."

"I should not have adopted such an expedient in any case. Elinor must be married among her own people, wherever her lot may be cast afterwards. Everybody here has known her ever since she was born."

"Ah, that's a thing ladies think of, I suppose," said Compton. He had stuck his glass into his eye and was gazing out of the window. "Very jolly view," he continued. "And what's that, Nell, raising clouds of dust? I haven't such quick eyes as you."

"I should think it must be a circus or a menagerie, or something, mamma."

"Very likely," said Mrs. Dennistoun. "They sometimes come this way on the road to Portsmouth, and give little representations in all the villages, to the great excitement of the country folk."

"We are the country folk, and I feel quite excited," said Phil, dropping his glass. "Nell, if there's a representation, you and I will go to-night."

"Oh, Phil, what——" Elinor was about to say folly: but she paused, seeing a look in his eye which she had already learned to know, and added "fun," in a voice which sounded almost like an echo of his own.

"There is nothing like being out in the wilderness like this to make one relish a little fun, eh? I daresay you always go. The Jew is the one for every village fair within ten miles when she is in the country. She says they're better than any play. Hallo! what is that?"

"It is some one coming round the gravel path."

A more simple statement could not be, but it made Compton strangely uneasy. He rose up hastily from the table. "It is, perhaps, the man I am looking for. If you'll permit me, I'll go and see."

He went out of the room, calling Elinor by a look and slight movement of his head, but when he came out into the hall was met by a trim clerical figure and genial countenance, the benign yet self-assured looks of the Rector of the Parish: none other could this smiling yet important personage be.

CHAPTER X.

The Rector came in with his smiling and rosy face. He was, as many of his parishioners thought, a picture of a country clergyman. Such a healthy colour, as clear as a girl's, limpid blue eyes, with very light eyelashes and eyebrows; a nice round face, "beautifully modelled," according to Miss Sarah Hill, who did a little in that way herself, and knew how to approve of a Higher Sculptor's work. And then the neatest and blackest of coats, and the whitest and stiffest of collars. Mr. Hudson, I need scarcely say, was not so left to himself as to permit his clerical character to be divined by means of a white tie. He came in, as was natural among country neighbours, without thinking of any bell or knocker on the easily opened door, and was about to peep into the drawing-room with "Anybody in?" upon his smiling lips, when he saw a gentleman approaching, picking up his hat as he advanced. Mr. Hudson paused a moment in uncertainty. "Mr. Compton, I am sure," he said, holding out both of his plump pink hands. "Ah, Elinor too! I was sure I could not be mistaken. And I am exceedingly glad to make your acquaintance." He shook Phil's hand up and down in a sort of see-saw. "Very glad to make your acquaintance! though you are the worst enemy Windyhill has had for many a day—carrying off the finest lamb in all the fold."

"Yes, I'm a wolf, I suppose," said Phil. He went to the door and took a long look out while Elinor led the Rector into the drawing-room. Then Mr. Compton lounged in after them, with his hands in his pockets, and placed himself in the bow-window, where he could still see the white line across the combe of the distant road.

105

"They'll think I have stolen a march upon them all, Elinor," said the Rector, "chancing upon Mr. Compton like this, a quite unexpected pleasure. I shall keep them on the tenterhooks, asking them whom they suppose I have met? and they will give everybody but the right person. What a thing for me to have been the first person to see your intended, my dear! and I congratulate you, Elinor," said the Rector, dropping his voice; "a fine handsome fellow, and such an air! You are a lucky girl—" he paused a little and said, with a slight hesitation, in a whisper, "so far as meets the eye."

"Oh, Mr. Hudson, don't spoil everything," said Elinor, in the same tone.

"Well, I cannot tell, can I, my dear?—the first peep I have had." He cleaved his throat and raised his voice. "I believe we are to have the pleasure of entertaining you, Mr. Compton, on a certain joyful occasion (joyful to you, not to us). I need not say how pleased my wife and I and the other members of the family will be. There are not very many of us—we are only five in number—my son, and my daughter, and Miss Dale, my wife's sister, but much younger than Mrs. Hudson—who has done us the pleasure of staying with us for part of the year. I think she has met you somewhere, or knows some of your family, or—something. She is a great authority on noble families. I don't know whether it is because she has been a good deal in society, or whether it is out of Debrett——"

"Nell, come and tell me what this is," Compton said.

"Oh, Phil! it is nothing, it is a carriage. I don't know what it is. Be civil to the Rector, please."

"So I am, perfectly civil."

"You have not answered a single word, and he has been talking to you for ten minutes."

"Well, but he hasn't said anything that I can answer. He says Miss Something or other knows my family. Perhaps she does. Well, much good may it do her! but what can I say to that? I am sure I don't know hers. I didn't come here to be talked to by the

Rector. Could we slip out and leave him with your mother? That would suit his book a great deal better. Come, let's go."

"Oh! he is speaking to you, Phil."

Compton turned round and eyed the Rector. "Yes?" he said in so marked an interrogative that Mr. Hudson stopped short and flushed. He had been talking for some time.

"Oh! I was not precisely asking a question," he said, in his quiet tones. "I was saying that we believe and hope that another gentleman is coming with you—for the occasion."

"Dick Bolsover," said Compton, "a son of Lord Freshfield's; perhaps Miss ——, the lady you were talking of, may know his family too. His brother got a little talked of in that affair about Fille d'Or, don't you know, at Newmarket. But Dick is a rattling good fellow, doesn't race, and has no vices. He is coming to stand by me and see that all's right."

"We shall be happy to see Mr. Bolsover, I am sure." The Rector rubbed his hands and said to himself with pleasure that two Honourables in his quiet house was something to think of, and that he hoped it would not turn the heads of the ladies, and make Alice expect—one couldn't tell what. And then he said, by way of changing yet continuing the subject, "I suppose you've been looking at the presents. Elinor must have shown you her presents."

"By Jove, I never thought of the presents. Have you got a lot, Nell?"

"She has got, if I may be allowed to answer for her, having known her all her life, a great many pretty things, Mr. Compton. We are not rich, to be sure, her old friends here. We have to content ourselves with but a small token of a great deal of affection; but still there are a number of pretty things. Elinor, what were you thinking of, my dear, not to show Mr. Compton the little set out which you showed us? Come, I should myself like to look them over again."

Phil gave another long look at the distant road, and then he thrust his arm into Elinor's and said, "To be sure, come along,

Nell. It will be something to do." He did not wait for the Rector to pass first, which Elinor thought would have been better manners, but thrust her before him quite regardless of the older people. "Let's see the trumpery," he said.

"Don't use such a word, Phil: the Rector will be so hurt."

"Oh, will he? did he work you an—antimacassar or something?"

"Phil, speak low at least. No, but his daughter did; and they gave me——"

"I know: a cardcase or a button-hook, or something. And how many biscuit-boxes have you got, and clocks, and that sort of thing? I advise you to have an auction as soon as we get away. Hallo! that's a nice little thing; look pretty on your pretty white neck I should say, Nell. Who gave you that?" He took John's necklace out of its box where it had lain undisturbed until now, and pulled it through his fingers. "Cost a pretty bit of money that, I should say. You can raise the wind on it when we're down on our luck, Nell."

"My cousin John, whom you have heard me speak of, gave me that, Phil," said Elinor, with great gravity. She thought it necessary, she could scarcely tell why, to make a stand for her cousin John.

"Ah, I thought it was one of the disappointed ones," said Phil, flinging it back carelessly onto the bed of white velvet where it had been fitted so exactly. "That's how they show their spite; for of course I can't give you anything half as good as that."

"There was no disappointment in the matter," said Elinor, almost angry with the misconceptions of her lover.

"You are a nice one," said Compton, taking her by the chin, "to tell me! as if I didn't know the world a long sight better than you do, my little Nell."

The Rector, who was following slowly, for he did not like to go up-stairs in a hurry, saw this attitude and drew back, a little scandalized. "Perhaps we were indiscreet to—to follow them too closely," he said, disconcerted. "Please to go in first, Mrs. Dennistoun—the young couple will not mind you."

Mr. Hudson was prim; but he was rather pleased to see that "the young couple" were, as he said, so fond of each other. He went into the room under the protection of the mother—blushing a little. It reminded him, as he said afterwards, of his own young days; but it was only natural that he should walk up direct to the place where his kettle stood conspicuous, waiting only the spark of a match to begin to boil the water for the first conjugal tea. It appeared to him a beautiful idea as he put his head on one side and looked at it. It was like the inauguration of the true British fireside, the cosy privacy in which, after the man had done his work, the lady awaited him at home, with the tea-kettle steaming. A generation before Mr. Hudson there would have been a pair of slippers airing beside the fire. But neither of these preparations supply the ideal of perfect happiness now.

"I say, where did you get these hideous things?" said Compton, approaching the table on which "the silver" was laid out. By a special dispensation it was Lady Mariamne's dishes which caught Phil's attention. "Some old grandmother, I suppose, that had 'em in the house. Hallo! if it isn't the Jew! Nell, you don't mean to tell me you got these horrors from the Jew?"

"They are supposed to be—quite handsome," said Elinor, with a suppressed laugh. "We must not criticise. It is very kind of people to send presents at all. We all know it is a very severe tax—to those who have a great many friends——"

"The stingy old miser," said Compton. "Rolling in money, and to send you these! By Jove! there's a neat little thing now that looks what it is; probably one of your nice country friends, Nell——" (It was the kettle, as a kind Providence decreed; and both the ladies breathed an internal thanksgiving.) "Shows like a little gem beside that old, thundering, mean-spirited Jew!"

"That," said the Rector, bridling a little and pink with pleasure, "is our little offering: and I'm delighted to think that it should please so good a judge. It was chosen with great care. I saw it first myself, and the idea flashed upon me—quite an inspiration—that it was the very thing for Elinor; and when I went home I told my wife—the very thing—for her boudoir, should she not be seeing company—or just for your little teas when you are by yourselves. I could at once imagine the dear girl looking so pretty in one of those wonderful white garments that are in the next room."

"Hallo!" said Compton, with a laugh, "do you show off your things in this abandoned way, Nell, to the killingest old cov——"

She put her hand up to his mouth with a cry of dismay and laughter, but the Rector, with a smile and another little blush, discreetly turned his back. He was truly glad to see that they were so fond of each other, and thought it was pretty and innocent that they should not mind showing it—but it was a little embarrassing for an old and prim clergyman to look on.

"What a pleasure it must be to you, my dear lady," he said when the young couple had gone: which took place very soon, for Phil soon grew tired of the presents, and he was ill at ease when there was no window from which he could watch the road— "what a pleasure to see them so much attached! Of course, family advantage and position is always of importance—but when you get devoted affection, too——"

"I hope there is devoted affection," said Mrs. Dennistoun; "at all events, there is what we are all united in calling 'love,' for the present. He is in love with Elinor—I don't think there can be much doubt of that."

"I did not of course know that he was here," said the Rector, with some hesitation. "I came with the intention of speaking—I am very sorry to see in the papers to-day something about that Joint-Stock Company of which Mr. Compton was a director. It's rather a mysterious paragraph: but it's something about the manager having absconded, and that some of the directors are said to be involved."

"Do you mean my future son-in-law?" she said, turning quickly upon him.

"Good heavens, no! I wouldn't for the world insinuate—— It was only that one felt a desire to know. Just upon the eve of a marriage it's—it's alarming to hear of a business the bridegroom is involved in being—what you may call broken up."

"That was one of the things Mr. Compton came to tell us about," said Mrs. Dennistoun. "He said he hoped it might be kept out of the papers, but that some of the books have got lost or destroyed. I am afraid I know very little about business. But he has lost very little—nothing to speak of—which was all that concerned me."

"To be sure," said the Rector, but in a tone not so assured as his words. "It is not perhaps quite a nice thing to be director of a company that—that collapses in this way. I fear some poor people will lose their money. I fear there will be things in the papers."

"On what ground?" she said. "Oh, I don't deny there may be some one to blame; but Mr. Compton was, I suspect, only on the board for the sake of his name. He is not a business man. He did it, as so many do, for the sake of a pretence of being in something. And then, I believe, the directors got a little by it; they had a few hundreds a year."

"To be sure," said Mr. Hudson, but still doubtfully; and then he brightened up. "For my part, I don't believe there is a word of truth in it. Since I have seen him, indeed, I have quite changed my opinion—a fine figure of a man, looking an aristocrat every inch of him. Such a contrast and complement to our dear Elinor—and so fond of her. A man like that would never have a hand in any sham concern. If it was really a bogus company, as people say, he must be one of the sufferers. That is quite my decided opinion; only the ladies, you know—the ladies who have not seen him, and who are so much more suspicious by nature (I don't know that you are, my dear Mrs. Dennistoun), would give me no rest. They thought it was my duty to interfere. But I am sure they are quite wrong."

To think that it was the ladies of the Rector's family who were interfering made Mrs. Dennistoun very wroth. "Next time they have anything to say, you should make them come themselves," she said.

"Oh, they would not do that. They say it is the clergyman's

business, not theirs. Besides, you know, I have not time to read all the papers. We get the *Times*, and Mary Dale has the *Morning Post*, and another thing that is all about stocks and shares. She has such a head for business—far more than I can pretend to. She thought——"

"Mr. Hudson, I fear I do not wish to know what was thought by Miss Dale."

"Well, you are, perhaps, right, Mrs. Dennistoun. She is only a woman, of course, and she may make mistakes. It is astonishing, though, how often she is right. She has a head for business that might do for a Chancellor of the Exchequer. She made me sell out my shares in that Red Gulch—those American investments have most horrible names—just a week before the smash came, all from what she had read in the papers. She knows how to put things together, you see. So I have reason to be grateful to her, for my part."

"And what persuaded you, here at Windyhill, a quiet clergyman, to put money in any Red Gulch? It is a horrible name!"

"Oh, it was Mary, I suppose," said Mr. Hudson. "She is always looking out for new investments. She said we should all make our fortunes. We did not, unfortunately. But she is so clever, she got us out of it with only a very small loss indeed."

"No doubt she is very clever. I wish, though, that she would let us know definitely on what ground——"

"Oh, there is no ground," cried the Rector. "Now that I have seen Mr. Compton I am certain of it. I said to her before I left the Rectory, 'Now, my dear Mary, I am going like a lamb to the slaughter. I have no reason to give if Mrs. Dennistoun should ask me, and you have no reason to give. And she will probably put me to the door.' If I said that before I started, you may fancy how much more I feel it now, when I have made Mr. Compton's acquaintance. A fine aristocratic face, and all the ease of high breeding. There are only three lives—and those not very good ones—between him and the title, I believe?"

"Two robust brothers, and an invalid who will probably outlive them all; that is, I believe, the state of the case."

"Dear me, what a pity!" said the Rector, "for our little Elinor would have made a sweet little Countess. She would grow a noble lady, like the one in Mr. Tennyson's poem. Well, now I must be going, and I am extremely glad to have been so lucky as to come in just in time. It has been the greatest pleasure to me to see them together—such a loving couple. Dear me, like what one reads about, or remembers in old days, not like the commonplace pairs one has to do with now."

Mrs. Dennistoun accompanied the Rector to the garden gate. She was half inclined to laugh and half to be angry, and in neither mood did Mr. Hudson's insinuations which he made so innocently have much effect upon her mind. But when she took leave of him at the gate and came slowly back among her brilliant flower-beds, pausing here and there mechanically to pick off a withered leaf or prop up the too heavy head of a late rose; her mind began to take another turn. She had always been conscious of an instinctive suspicion in respect to her daughter's lover. Probably only, she said to herself, because he was her daughter's lover, and she was jealous of the new devotion that withdrew from her so completely the young creature who had been so fully her own. That is a hard trial for a woman to undergo. It is only to be borne when she, too, is fascinated by her future son-in-law, as happens in some fortunate cases. Otherwise, a woman with an only child is an alarming critic to encounter. She was not fascinated at all by Phil. She was disappointed in Elinor, and almost thought her child not so perfect as she had believed, when it proved that she could be fascinated by this man. She disliked almost everything about him—his looks, the very air which the Rector thought so aristocratic, his fondness for Elinor, which was not reverential enough to please the mother, and his indifference, nay, contempt, for herself, which was not calculated to please any woman. She had been roused into defence of him in anger at the interference, and at the insinuation which had no proof; but as that anger died away, other thoughts came into her mind. She began to put the broken facts together which already had roused her to suspicion: his sudden arrival, so unexpected; walking from the station—a long, very long walk—carrying his own bag, which was a thing John Tatham did, but not like Phil Compton. And then she remembered, suddenly, his anxiety about the carriage on the distant road, his care to place himself where he could see it. She had thought with a little scorn that this was a proof of his frivolity, of the necessity of seeing people, whoever these people might be. But now there began to be in it something that could have a deeper meaning. For whom was he looking? Who might be coming? Stories she had heard of fugitives from justice, of swindlers taking refuge in the innocence of their families, came up into her mind. Could it be possible that Elinor's pure name could be entangled in such a guilty web as this?

CHAPTER XI.

"Funny old poop!" said Compton. "And that is your Rector, Nell. I shall tell Dick there's rare fun to be had in that house: but not for me. I know what I shall be thinking of all the time I'm there. Odious little Nell! to interfere like this with a fellow's fun. But I say, who's that woman who knows me or my family?— much good may it do her, as I said before. Tell me, Nell, did she speak ill of me?"

"Oh, Phil, how could you ask? or what would it matter if she spoke ever so ill?"

"She did then," he said with a graver face. "Somebody was bound to do it. And what did she say?"

"Oh, what does it matter, Phil? I don't remember; nothing of any consequence. We paid no attention, of course, neither mamma nor I."

"That was plucky of the old girl," said Compton. "I didn't suppose you would give ear, my Nell. Ain't so sure about her. If I'd been your father, my pet, I should never have given you to Phil Compton. And that's the fact: I wonder if the old lady would like to reconsider the situation now."

"Phil!" said Elinor, clinging to his arm.

"Perhaps it would be best for you if you were to do so, Nell, or if she were to insist upon it. Eh! You don't know me, my darling, that's the fact. You're too good to understand us. We're all the same, from the old governor downwards—a bad lot. I feel a kind of remorseful over you, child, to-day. That rosy old bloke, though he's a snob, makes a man think of innocence somehow. I do believe you oughtn't to marry me, Nell."

"Oh, Phil! what do you mean? You cannot mean what you say."

"I suppose I don't, or I shouldn't say it, Nell. I shouldn't certainly, if I thought you were likely to take my advice. It's a kind of luxury to tell you we're a bad lot, and bid you throw me over, when I know all along you won't."

"I should think not indeed," she said, clinging to him and looking up in his face. "Do you know what my cous—I mean a friend, said to me on that subject?"

"You mean your cousin John, whom you are always quoting. Let's hear what the fellow said."

"He said—that I wasn't a girl to put up with much, Phil. That I wasn't one of the patient kind, that I would not bear—— I don't know what it was I would not bear; but you see you must consider my defects, which you can understand well enough, whether I can understand yours or not."

"That you could not put up with—that you could not bear? that meant me, Nell. He had been talking to you on the same subject, me and my faults. Why didn't you listen to him? I suppose he wanted you to have him instead of me."

"Phil! how dare you even think of such a thing? It is not true."

"Wasn't it? Then he is a greater fool than I took him for, and his opinion's no good. So you're a spitfire, are you? Can't put up with anything that doesn't suit you? I don't know that I should have found that out."

"I am afraid though that it is true," she said, half-laughingly looking up at him. "Perhaps you will want to reconsider too."

"If you don't want it any more than I want it, Nell—— What's that?" he cried hastily, changing his expression and attitude in a moment. "Is that one of your neighbours at the gate?"

Elinor looked round, starting away a little from his side, and saw some one—a man she had never seen before—approaching along the path. She was just about to say she did not know who it was when Phil, to her astonishment, stepped past her, advancing to meet the newcomer. But as he did so he put out his hand and caught her as he passed, leading her along with him.

"Mind what I said, and stick to me," he said, in a whisper;

116

then—

"Stanfield!" he cried with an air of perfect ease and cordiality, yet astonishment. "I thought it looked like you, but I could not believe my eyes."

"Mr. Compton!" said the other. "So you are here. I have been hunting after you all over the place. I heard only this morning this was a likely spot."

"A very likely spot!" said Phil. "I suppose you know the good reason I have for being in these parts. Elinor, this is Mr. Stanfield, who has to do with our company, don't you know. But I say, Stanfield, what's all this row in the papers? Is it true that Brown's bolted? I should have taken the first train to see if I could help; but my private affairs are most urgent just at this moment, as I suppose you know."

"I wish you had come," said the other; "it would have looked well, and pleased the rest of the directors. There has been some queer business—some of the books abstracted or destroyed, we can't tell which, and no means of knowing how we stand."

"Good Heavens!" said Phil, "to cover that fellow's retreat."

"It you mean Brown, it was not he. They were all there safe enough after he was gone; somebody must have got in by night and made off with them, some one that knew all about the place; the watchman saw a light, but that's all. It's supposed there must have been something compromising others besides Brown. He could not have cheated the company to such an extent by himself."

"Good Heavens!" cried Phil again in natural horror; "I wish I had followed my impulse and gone up to town straight: but it was very vague what was in the papers; I hoped it might not have been our place at all. And I say, Stanfield—who's the fellow they suspect?" Elinor had disengaged herself from Compton's arm; she perceived vaguely that the stranger paused before he replied, and that Phil, facing him with a certain square attitude of opposition which affected her imagination vaguely, though she did not understand why—was waiting with keen attention

117

for his reply. She said, a little oppressed by the situation, "Phil, perhaps I had better go."

"Don't go," he said; "there's nothing secret to say. If there's anyone suspected it must very soon be known."

"It's difficult to say who is suspected," said the stranger, confused. "I don't know that there's much evidence. You've been in Scotland?"

"Yes, till the other day, when I came down here to see——" He paused and turned upon Elinor a look which gave the girl the most curious incomprehensible pang. It was a look of love; but, oh! heaven, was it a look called up that the other man might see? He took her hand in his, and said lightly yet tenderly, "Let's see, what day was it? the sixth, wasn't it the sixth, Nell?"

A flood of conflicting thoughts poured through Elinor's mind. What did it mean? It was yesterday, she was about to say, but something stopped her, something in Phil's eye—in the touch of his hand. There was something warning, almost threatening, in his eye. Stand by me; mind you don't contradict me; say what I say. All these things which he had repeated again and again were said once more in the look he gave her. "Yes," she said timidly, with a hesitation very unlike Elinor, "it was the sixth." She seemed to see suddenly as she said the words that calendar with the date hanging in the hall: the big 6 seemed to hang suspended in the air. It was true, though she could not tell how it could be so.

"Oh," said Stanfield, in a tone which betrayed a little surprise, and something like disappointment, "the sixth? I knew you had left Scotland, but we did not know where you had gone."

"That's not to be wondered at," said Phil, with a laugh, "for I should have gone to Ireland, to tell the truth; I ought to have been there now. I'm going to-morrow, ain't I, Nell? I had not a bit of business to be here. Winding up affairs in the bachelor line, don't you know; but I had to come on my way west to see this young lady first. It plays the deuce and all with one's plans when there's such a temptation in the way."

"You could have gone from Scotland to Ireland," said Stanfield, gravely, "without coming to town at all."

"Very true, old man. You speak like a book. But, as you perceive, I have not gone to Ireland at all; I am here. Depends upon your motive, I suppose, which way you go."

"It is a good way roundabout," said the other, without relaxing the intent look on his face.

"Well," said Phil, "that's as one feels. I go by Holyhead wherever I may be—even if I had nowhere else to go to on the way."

"And Mr. Compton got here on the sixth?—this is the eighth," said the stranger, pointedly. He turned to Elinor, and it seemed to the girl that his eyes, though they were not remarkable eyes, went through and through her. He spoke very slowly, with a curious meaning. "But it was on the sixth, you say, that he got here?"

That big 6 on the calendar stood out before her eyes; it seemed to cover all the man's figure that stood before her. Elinor's heart and mind went through the strangest convulsion. Was it false—was it true? What was she saying? What did it all mean? She repeated mechanically, "It was on the sixth," and then she recovered a kind of desperate courage, and throwing off the strange spell that seemed to be upon her, "Is there any reason," she asked, suddenly, with a little burst of impatience, looking from one to another, "why it should not be the sixth, that you repeat it so?"

"I beg your pardon," said the stranger, visibly startled. "I did not mean to imply—only thought——Pray, Mr. Compton, tell the lady I had no intention of offending. I never supposed——"

Phil's laugh, loud and clear, rang through the stillness of the afternoon. "He's so used to fibs, he thinks everybody's in a tale," said Phil, "but I can assure you he is a very good fellow, and a great friend of mine, and he means no harm, Nell."

Elinor made Mr. Stanfield an extremely dignified bow. "I ought to have gone away at once, and left you to talk over your business," she said, turning away, and Phil did not attempt to detain her. Then the natural rural sense of hospitality came over Elinor. She turned back to find the two men looking after her, standing where she had left them. "I am sure," she said, "that mamma would wish me to ask the gentleman if he would stay to dinner—or at least come in with you, Phil, to tea."

Mr. Stanfield took off his hat with anxious politeness, and exclaimed hastily that he must go back to town by the next train, and that the cab from the station was waiting to take him. And then she left them, and walked quietly away. She was almost out of hearing before they resumed their conversation; that is, she was beyond the sound, not of their voices, but of what they said. The murmur of the voices was still audible when she got to her favourite seat on the side of the copse looking down the combe. It was a very retired and silent place, not visible from either the cottage or the garden. And there Elinor took refuge in the quiet and hush of the declining day. She was in a great tremor of agitation and excitement as she sat down upon the rustic seat— so great a tremor that she had scarcely been able to walk steadily down the roughly-made steps—a tremor which had grown with every step she took. She did not in the least understand the transaction in which she had been engaged. It was something altogether strange to her experiences, without any precedent in her life. What was it she had been called upon to do? What had she said, and why had she been made to say it? Her heart beat so that she put her two hands upon it crossed over her breast to keep it down, lest it should burst away. She had the sensation of having been brought before some tribunal, put suddenly to the last shift, made to say—what, what? She was so bewildered that she could not tell. Was it the truth, said with the intention to deceive—was it——? She could not tell. There was that great numeral wavering in the air, stalking along with her like a ghost. 6—. She had read it in all innocence, they had all read it, and nobody had said it was wrong. No one was very careful about the date in the cottage. If it was right, if it was wrong, Elinor could not tell. But yet somehow she was conscious that the man to whom she had spoken had been deceived. And Phil! and Phil! what had he meant, adjuring her to stick to him, to stand by him, not to contradict him? Elinor's mind was in such a wild commotion that she could not answer these inquiries. She could not feel that she had one solid step of ground to place herself upon in the whirlwind which swept her about and about. Had she—lied? And why had he asked her to lie? And what, oh, what did it all mean?

One thing that at last appeared to her in the chaos which seemed like something solid that she could grasp at was that Phil had never changed in his aspect. The other man had been very serious, staring at her as if to intimidate her, like a man who had something to find out; but Phil had been as careless, as indifferent, as he appeared always to be. He had not changed his expression. It is true there was that look in which there was at once an entreaty and a command—but only she had seen that, and perhaps it was merely the emotion, the excitement, the strange feeling of having to face the world for him, and say—— what, what? Was it simply, the truth, nothing but the truth, or was it—— Again Elinor's mind began to whirl. It was the truth: she could see now that big 6 on the calendar distinct as the sunshine. And yet it was only yesterday—and there was 8 this morning. Had she gone through an intervening dream for a whole day without knowing it; or had she, Elinor—she who would not have done it to save her life—told—a lie for Phil? And why should he want her to tell a lie?

Elinor got up from her seat, and stood uncertain, with a cold dew on her forehead, and her hands clasping and holding each other. Should she go back to them and say there must be some mistake—that though she had said the truth it was not true, that there was some mistake, some dreadful mistake! There was no longer any sound of voices where she was. The whole incident seemed to have died out. The sudden commotion of Phil's visit and everything connected with it had passed away. She was alone in the afternoon, in the hush of nature, looking over the combe, listening to the rustle of the trees, hearing the bees drone homeward. Had Phil ever been here at all? Had he watched the distant road winding over the slopes for some one whom he had expected to come after him all the time? Had he ever told her to stand by him? to say what he said, to back him up? Had there ever been another man standing with that big 6 wavering between her and him like a ghost? Had all that been at all, or was it merely a foolish dream? And ought she to go back now, and find the man before he disappeared, and tell him it was all true, yet somehow a dreadful, dreadful mistake?

Elinor sat down again abruptly on her seat, and put her handkerchief to her forehead and pushed back the damp clusters of her hair, turning her face to the wind to get a little refreshment and calm, if that were possible. She heard in the sunny distance behind her, where the garden and the peaceful house lay in the light, the clang of the gate, a sound which could not be mistaken. The man then had gone—if there was anything to rectify in what she said it certainly could not be rectified now—he was gone. The certainty came to her with a feeling of relief. It had been horrible to think of standing before the two men again and saying—what could she have said? She remembered now that it was not her assertion alone, but that it all hung together, a whole structure of incidents, which would be put wrong if she had said it was a mistake—a whole account of Phil's time, how it had been passed—which was quite true, which he had told them on his arrival; how he had been going to Ireland, and had stopped, longing for a glimpse of her, his bride, feeling that he must have her by him, see her once again before he came for her to fetch her away. He had told the ladies at the cottage the very same, and of course it was true. Had he not come straight from Scotland with his big bundle of game, the grouse and partridges which had already been shared with all the friends about? Was he not going off to Ireland to-morrow to fulfil his first intention? It was all quite right, quite true, hanging perfectly together—except that curious falling out of a day. And then again Elinor's brain swam round and round. Had he been two days at the cottage instead of one, as he said? Was it there that the mistake lay? Had she been in such a fool's paradise having him there, that she had not marked the passage of time—had it all been one hour of happiness flying like the wind? A blush, partly of sweet shame to think that this was possible, that she might have been such a happy fool as to ignore the divisions of night and day, and partly of stimulating hope that such might be the case, a wild snatch at justification of herself and him flushed over her from head to foot, wrapping her in warmth and delight; and then this all faded away again and left her as in ashes—black and cold. No! everything, she saw, now depended upon what she had been impelled to say; the whole construction, Phil's account of his time, his story of his doings— all would have fallen to pieces had she said otherwise. Body and soul, Elinor felt herself become like a machine full of clanging wheels and beating pistons, her heart, her pulses, her breath, all panting, beating, bursting. What did it mean? What did it mean? And then everything stood still in a horrible suspense and pause.

She began to hear voices again in the distance and raised her head, which she had buried in her hands—voices that sounded so calmly in the westering sunshine, one answering another, everything softened in the golden outdoor light. At first as she raised herself up she thought with horror that it was the man, the visitor whom she had supposed to be gone, returning with Phil to give her the opportunity of contradicting herself, of bringing back that whirlwind of doubt and possibility. But presently her excited senses perceived that it was her mother who was walking calmly through the garden talking with Phil. There was not a tone of excitement in the quiet voices that came gradually nearer and nearer, till she could hear what they were saying. It was Phil who was speaking, while her mother now and then put in a word. Elinor did not wish on ordinary occasions for too many private talks between her mother and Phil. They rubbed each other the wrong way, they did not understand each other, words seemed to mean different things in their comprehension of them. She knew that her lover would laugh at "the old girl," which was a phrase which offended Elinor deeply, and Mrs. Dennistoun would become stiffer and stiffer, declaring that the very language of the younger generation had become unintelligible to her. But to hear them now together was a kind of anodyne to Elinor, it stayed and calmed her. The cold moisture dried from her forehead. She smoothed her hair instinctively with her hand, and put herself straight in mind as she did with that involuntary action in outward appearance, feeling that no sign of agitation, no trouble of demeanour must meet her mother's eye. And then the voices came so near that she could hear what they were saying. They were coming amicably together to her favourite retreat.

"It's a very queer thing," said Phil, "if it is as they think, that somebody went there the night before last and cleared off the books. Well, not all the books, some that are supposed to contain the secret transactions. Deucedly cleverly done it must have been, if it was done at all, for nobody saw the fellow, or fellows, if there were more than one——"

"Why do you doubt?" said Mrs. Dennistoun. "Is there any way of accounting for it otherwise?"

"Oh, a very good way—that Brown, the manager, simply took them with him, as he would naturally do, if he wasn't a fool. Why should he go off and leave papers that would convict him, for the pleasure of involving other fellows, and ruining them too?"

"Are there others, then, involved with him?" Oh, how calm, how inconceivably calm, was Mrs. Dennistoun's voice! Had she been asking the gardener about the slugs that eat the young plants it would have been more disturbed.

"Well, Stanfield seemed to think so. He's a sort of head clerk, a fellow enormously trusted. I shouldn't wonder if he was at the bottom of it himself, they're so sure of him," said Phil, with a laugh. "He says there's a kind of suspicion of two or three. Clumsy wretches they must be if they let themselves be found out like that. But I don't believe it. I believe Brown's alone in it, and that it's him that's taken everything away. I believe it's far the safest way in those kind of dodges to be alone. You get all the swag, and you're in no danger of being rounded on, don't you know—till you find things are getting too hot, and you cut away."

"I don't understand the words you use, but I think I know what you mean," said Mrs. Dennistoun. "How dreadful it is to think that in business, where honesty is the very first principle, there should be such terrible plots and plans as those!"

"'Tis awful, isn't it?" said Phil, with a laugh that seemed to ring all down the combe, and came back in echoes from the opposite slope, where in the distance the cab from the station was seen hastening back towards the railway in a cloud of dust. The laugh was like a trumpet of triumph flung across the distance at the discomfited enemy thus going off drooping in the hurry of defeat. He added, "But you may imagine, even if I had known anything, he wouldn't have got much out of me. I didn't know anything, however, I'm very glad to say."

"That is always the best," said Mrs. Dennistoun, with a certain grave didactic tone. "And here is Elinor, as I thought. When one cannot find her anywhere else she's sure to be found here."

CHAPTER XII.

"Well," said Compton, placing himself beside her, "here you are, Nell; kind of the old lady to bring me, wasn't it? I should never have found you out by myself."

"Has he gone, Phil?" Elinor raised her scared face from her hands, and gave him a piteous look.

"Why, Nell! you are trembling like a leaf. Was it frightened, my pretty pet, for Stanny? Stanny's gone off with his tail between his legs. Not a bit of starch left in him. As limp a lawyer as ever you saw."

"Was he a lawyer?" she said, not knowing why she said it, for it mattered nothing at all to Elinor what the man was.

"Not exactly; and yet, I suppose, something of the kind. He is the one that knows about law points, and such things. But now he's as quiet as a lamb, thanks to you."

"Phil," she cried, "what did you make me say? I don't know what I have done. I have done something dreadful—deceived the man, as good as told him a lie."

"You told him the truth," said Phil, with a laugh, "in the most judgmatical way. You stuck to it like a—woman. There's nothing like a woman for sticking to a text. You didn't say a word too much. And I say, Nell, that little defiant bit of yours—'Was there any reason why it shouldn't be the sixth?' was grand. That was quite magnificent, my pet. I never thought you had such spirit in you."

"Oh, Phil," she cried, "why did you make me say it? What was it I said? I don't know; I don't understand a bit. Whatever it was, I know that it was wrong. I deceived the man."

"That's not so great a sin," he said. "I've known worse things done. Put an old reynard off the scent to save his prey. I don't see what's wrong in that, especially as the innocent chicken to be saved was your own poor old Phil."

"Phil, Phil," she cried, "what could that man have done to you? What had put you in his power? You have made me lose all my innocence. I have got horrible things in my head. What could he have done to you that you made me tell a lie?"

"What lie did I make you tell? be reasonable; I did arrive on the sixth, you know that just as well as I do. Don't you really remember the calendar in the hall? You saw it, Nell, as well as I."

"I know, I know," she cried, putting her hands up to her eyes, "I see it everywhere staring at me, that big, dreadful 6. But how is it the 8th now? There is something in it—something I don't understand."

He laughed loudly and long: one of those boisterous laughs which always jarred upon Elinor. "I don't in the least mind how it was," he said. "It was, and that's quite enough for me; and let it be for you too, Nell. I hope you're not going to search into the origin of things like this; we've quite enough to do in this world to take things as they come."

"Oh, Phil! if at least I could understand—I don't understand: or if I had not been made to say what is so mysterious—what must be false."

"Hush, Nell; how could it be false when you saw with your own eyes it was true? Now let us be done with this, my darling. The incident is terminated, as the French say. I came here as fast as I could come to have a good laugh with you over it, and lo! you're nearer crying. Why should you have Stanny on your conscience, Nell? a fellow that would like no better than to hang me if he could get the chance."

"But Phil, Phil—oh, tell me, what could this man have done to you? Why are you afraid of him? Why, why have you made me tell him——"

"Now, Nell, no exaggerated expression. It was a fact you told him, according to the best of evidence; and what he could have done to me is just this—he might have given me a deal of trouble, and put off our marriage. I should have had to go back to town, and my time would have been taken up with finding out about those books, and our marriage would have been put off; that's what he could have done."

"Is that all?" cried Elinor, "was that all?"

"All!" he said, with that loud laugh again; "you don't mind a bit how you hurt a fellow's pride, and his affections, and all that. Do you mean to say, you hard-hearted little coquette, that you wouldn't mind? I don't believe you would mind! Here am I counting the hours, and you, you little cold puss, you aggravating little——"

"Oh, Phil, don't talk such nonsense. If we were to be separated, for a week or a month, what could that matter, in comparison with saying what wasn't——"

"Hush," he said, putting his hand to her mouth. "It's not nice of you to take it so easily, Nell. I'd tell as many what-d'ye-call-'ems as you like, rather than put it off an hour. Why, feeling apart (and I don't think you've any feeling, you little piece of ice), think how inconvenient it would have been; the people all arriving; the breakfast all ready; the Rector with his surplice on; and no wedding! Fancy the Jew with all her fallals, on the old lady's hands, and your cousin John——"

"I have told you already, Phil, my cousin John will not be there."

"So much the better," he said, with a laugh, "I don't want him to be there—shows his sense, when his nose is put out of joint, to keep out of the way."

"I wish you would understand," she said, with a little vexation, "that John is not put out of joint, as you say in that odious way. He has never been anything more to me, nor I to him, than we are now—like brother and sister."

"The more fool he," said Compton, "to have the chance of a nice girl like you, Nell, and not to go in for it. But I don't believe a bit in the brother and sister dodge."

"We will be just the same all our lives," cried Elinor.

"Not if I know it," said Phil. "I'm an easy-going fellow in most ways, but you'll find I'm an old Turk about you, my little duck of a Nell. No amateur brother for me. If you can't get along with your old Phil, without other adorers——"

"Phil! as if I should ever think or care whether there was another man in the world!"

"Oh, that's going too far," he said, laughing. "I shan't mind a little flirtation. You may have a man or two in your train to fetch and carry, get your shawl for you, and call your carriage, and so forth; but no serious old hand, Nell—nothing to remind you that there was a time when you didn't know Phil Compton." His laugh died away at this point, and for a moment his face assumed that grave look which changed its character so much. "If you don't come to repent before then that you ever saw that fellow's ugly face, Nell——"

"Phil, how could I ever repent? Nobody but you should dare to say such a thing to me!"

"I believe that," he said. "If that old John of yours tried it on—— Well, my pet, he is your old John. You can't change facts, even if you do throw the poor fellow over. Now, here's a new chance for all of them, Nell. I shouldn't wonder a bit if you had another crop of letters bidding you look before you leap. That Rectory woman, what's her name? that knows my family. You'll see she'll have some new story before we're clear of her. They'll never stop blackguarding me, I know, until you're Phil Compton yourself, my beauty. I wish that day was come. I'm afraid to go off again and leave you, Nell. They'll be putting something into your head, or the old lady's. Let's get it over to-morrow morning, and come to Ireland with me; you've never been there."

"Phil, what nonsense! mamma would go out of her senses."

"My pet, what does it matter? She'd come back to them again as soon as we were gone, and think what a botheration spared her! All the row of receiving people, turning the house upside down. And here I am on the spot. And what do you want with bridesmaids and so forth? You've got all your things. Suppose we walk out to church to-morrow before breakfast, Nell——"

"Phil, you are mad, I think; and why should we do such a thing, scandalizing everybody? But of course you don't mean it. You are excited after seeing that man."

"Excited about Stanny!—not such a fool; Stanny is all square, thanks to—— But what I want is just to take you up in my arms, like this, and run off with you, Nell. Why we should call the whole world to watch us while we take that swing off—into space."

"Phil!"

"So it is, for you, Nell. You don't know a bit what's going to happen. You don't know where I'm going to take you, and what I'm going to do with you, you little innocent lamb in the wolf's grip. I want to eat you up, straight off. I shall be afraid up to the last moment that you'll escape me, Nell."

"I did not know that you were so fond of innocence," said Elinor, half afraid of her lover's vehemence, and trying to dispel his gravity with a laugh. "You used to say you did not believe in the *ingénue*."

"I believe in you," he said, with an almost fierce pressure of her arm; then, after a pause, "No, I don't believe in women at all, Nell, only you. They're rather worse than men, which is saying a good deal. What would the Jew care if we were all drawn and quartered; so long as she had all her paraphernalia about her and got everything she wanted? For right-down selfishness commend me to a woman. A fellow may have gleams of something better about him, like me, warning you against myself."

"It is a droll way of warning me against yourself to want to carry me off to-morrow."

"It's all the same thing," he said. "I've warned you that those old hags are right, and I'm not good enough for you, not fit to come near you, Nell. But if the sacrifice is to be, let's get it over at once, don't let us stand and think of it. I'm capable of jilting you," he said, "leaving you *planté là*, all out of remorse of conscience;

or else just catching you up in my arms, like this, and carrying you off, never to be seen more."

"You are very alarming," said Elinor. "I don't know what you mean. You can be off with your bargain if you please, Phil; but you had better make up your mind at once, so that mamma may countermand her invitations, and stop Gunter from sending the cake."

(It was Gunter who was the man in those days. I believe people go to Buszard now.)

He gave her again a vehement hug, and burst into a laugh. "I might jilt you, Nell; such a thing is on the cards. I might leave you in the lurch at the church door; but when you talk of countermanding the cake, I can't face that situation. Society would naturally be up in arms about that. So you must take your chance like the other innocents. I'll eat you up as gently as I can, and hide my tusks as long as it's possible. Come on, Nell, don't let us sit here and get the mopes, and think of our consciences. Come and see if that show is in the village. Life's better than thinking, old girl."

"Do you call the show in the village, life?" she said, half pleased to rouse him, half sorry to be thus carried away.

"Every show is life," said Phil, "and everywhere that people meet is better than anywhere where you're alone. Mind you take in that axiom, Nell. It's our rule of life, you know, among the set you're marrying into. That's how the Jew gets on. That's how we all get on. By this time next year you'll be well inured into it like all the rest. That's what your Rector never taught you, I'll be bound; but you'll see the old fellow practises it whenever he has a chance. Why, there they begin, tootle-te-too. Come on, Nell, and don't let us lose the fun."

He drew her along hastily, hurrying while the flute and the drum began to perform their parts. Sound spreads far in that tranquil country, where no railway was visible, and where the winds for the moment were still. It was Pan's pipes that were being played, attracting a few stragglers from the scattered houses. Within a hundred yards from the church, at the corner of four roads, stood the Bull's Head, with a cottage or two linked on to its long straggling front. And this was all that did duty for a village at Windyhill. The Rectory stood back in its own copse, surrounded by a growth of young birches and oak near the church. The Hills dwelt intermediate between the Bull's Head and the ecclesiastical establishment. The school and schoolmaster's house were behind the Bull. The show was surrounded by the children of the place, who looked on silent with ecstasy, while a burly showman piped his pipes and beat his drum. A couple of ostlers, with their shirt-sleeves rolled up to their shoulders, and one of them with a pail in his hand, stood arrested in their work. And in the front of the spectators was Alick Hudson, a sleepy-looking youth of twenty, who started and took his hands out of his pockets at sight of Elinor. Mr. Hudson himself came walking briskly round the corner, swinging his cane with the air of a man who was afraid of being too late.

"Didn't I tell you?" said Compton, pressing Elinor's arm.

As the tootle-te-too went on, other spectators appeared—the two Miss Hills, one putting on her hat, the other hastily buttoning her jacket as they hurried up. "Oh, you here, Elinor! What fun! We all run as if we were six years old. I'm going to engage the man to come round and do it opposite Rosebank to amuse mother. She likes it as much as any of us, though she doesn't see very well, poor dear, nor hear either. But we must always consider that the old have not many amusements," said the elder Miss Hill.

"Though mother amuses herself wonderfully with her knitting," said Miss Sarah. "There's a sofa-cover on the stocks for you, Elinor."

It appeared to be only at this moment that the sisters became aware of the presence of "the gentleman" by whom Elinor stood. They had been too busy with their uncompleted toilettes to observe him at first. But now that Miss Hill's hat was settled to her satisfaction, and the blue veil tied over her face as she liked it to be, and Miss Sarah had at last succeeded, after two false starts, in buttoning her jacket straight, their attention was released for other details. They both gave a glance over Elinor at the tall figure on the other side, and then looked at each other with a mutual little "Oh!" and nod of recognition. Then Miss Hill took the initiative as became her dignity. "I hope you are going to introduce us to your companion, Elinor," she said. "Oh, Mr. Compton, how do you do? We are delighted to make your acquaintance, I am sure. It is charming to have an opportunity of seeing a person of so much importance to us all, our dear Elinor's intended. I hope you know what a prize you are getting. You might have sought the whole country over and you wouldn't have found a girl like her. I don't know how we shall endure your name when you carry her away."

"Except, indeed," said Miss Sarah, "that it will be Elinor's name too."

"So here we all are again," said the Rector, gazing down tranquilly upon his flock, "not able to resist a little histrionic exhibition—and Mr. Compton too, fresh from the great world. I daresay our good friend Mrs. Basset would hand us out some chairs. No Englishman can resist Punch. Alick, my boy, you ought to be at your work. It will not do to neglect your lessons when you are so near your exam."

"No Englishman, father, can resist Punch," said the lad: at which the two ostlers and the landlord of the Bull's Head, who was standing with his hands in his pockets in his own doorway, laughed loud.

"Had the old fellow there," said Compton, which was the first observation he had made. The ladies looked at him with some horror, and Alick a little flustered, half pleased, half horrified, by this support, while the Rector laughed, but stiffly *au bout des lèvres*. He was not accustomed to be called an old fellow in his own parish.

"The old fellows, as you elegantly say, Mr. Compton, have always the worst of it in a popular assembly. Elinor, here is a chair for you, my love. Another one please, Mrs. Basset, for I see Miss Dale coming up this way."

"By Jove," said Compton, under his breath. "Elinor, here's the one that knows society. I hope she isn't such an old guy as the rest."

"Oh, Phil, be good!" said Elinor, "or let us go away, which would be the best."

"Not a bit," he said. "Let's see the show. I say, old man, where are you from last?"

"Down from Guildford ways, guv'nor—awful bad trade; not taken a bob, s' help me, not for three days, and bed and board to get off o' that, me and my mate."

"Well, here is a nice little party for you, my man," said the Rector, "it is not often you have such an audience—nor would I encourage it, indeed, if it were not so purely English an exhibition."

"Master," said the showman, "worst of it is, nobody pays till we've done the show, and then they goes away, and they've got it, don't you see, and we can't have it back once it's in their insides, and there ain't nothink then, neither for my mate nor me."

"Here's for you, old fellow," said Phil. He took a sovereign from his waistcoat pocket and chucked it with his thumbnail into the man's hand, who looked at it with astonished delight, tossed it into the air with a grin, a "thank'ee, gentleman!" and a call to his "mate" who immediately began the ever-exciting, ever-amusing drama. The thrill of sensation which ran through the little assembly at this incident was wonderful. The children all turned from Punch to regard with large open eyes and mouths the gentleman who had given a gold sovereign to the showman. Alick Hudson looked at him with a grin of pleasure, a blush of envy on his face; the Rector, with an expression of horror, slightly shaking his head; the Miss Hills with admiration yet dismay. "Goodness, Sarah, they'll never come now and do it for a shilling to amuse mother!" the elder of the sisters said.

Miss Dale came hurrying up while still the sensation lasted.

"Here is a chair for you, Mary," said her brother-in-law, "and the play is just going to begin. I can't help shaking my head when I think of it, but still you must hear what has just happened. Mr. Compton, let me present you to my sister-in-law, Miss Dale. Mr. Compton has made the widow's heart, nay, not the widow's, but the showman's heart to sing. He has presented our friend with a——"

"Mind you," said Phil, from behind Elinor's shoulders, "I've paid the fellow only for two."

At which the showman turned and winked at the Rector. To think that such a piece of audacity could be! A dingy fellow in a velveteen coat, with a spotted handkerchief round his neck, and a battered hat on his unkempt locks, with Pan's pipes at his mouth and a drum tied round his waist—winked at the Rector! Mr. Hudson fell back a step, and his very lips were livid with the indignity. He had to support himself on the back of the chair he had just given to Miss Dale.

"I think we are all forgetting our different positions in this world," he said.

"I ain't," said the showman, "not taking no advantage through the gentleman's noble ways. He's a lord, he is, I don't make no doubt. And we're paid. Take the good of it, Guv'nor, and welcome; all them as is here is welcome. My mate and I are too well paid. A gentleman like that good gentleman, as is sweet upon a pretty young lady, and an open 'eart a-cause of her, I just wish we could find one at every station; don't you, Joe?"

Joe assented, in the person of Mr. Punch, with a horrible squeak from within the tent.

The sensations of Elinor during this episode were peculiar and full of mingled emotion. It is impossible to deny that she was proud of the effect produced by her lover. The sovereign chucked into the showman's hand was a cheap way of purchasing a little success, and yet it dazzled Elinor, and made her eyelids droop and her cheek light up with the glow of pleasure. Amid all the people who would search for pennies, or perhaps painfully

135

and not without reluctance produce a sixpence to reward the humble artists, there was something in the careless familiarity and indifference which tossed a gold coin at them which was calculated to charm the youthful observer. Elinor felt the same mixture of pleasure and envy which had moved Alick Hudson; yet it was not envy, for was not he her own who did this thing which she would have liked to have done herself, overwhelming the poor tramps with delight? Elinor knew, as Alick also did, that it would never have occurred to her to do it. She would have been glad to be kind to the poor men, to give them a good meal, to speak to Basset at the Bull's Head in their favour that they might be taken in for the night and made comfortable, but to open her purse and take a real sovereign from it, a whole potential pound, would not have come into her head. Had such a thing been done, for instance, by the united subscriptions of the party, in case of some peculiarly touching situation, the illness of a wife, the loss of a child, it would have been done solemnly, the Rector calling the men up, making a little speech to them, telling them how all the ladies and gentlemen had united to make up this, and how they must be careful not to spend it unworthily. Elinor thought she could see the little scene, and the Rector improving the occasion. Whereas Phil spun the money through the air into the man's ready hand as if it had been a joke, a trick of agility. Elinor saw that everybody was much impressed with the incident, and her heart went forth upon a flood of satisfaction and content. And it was no premeditated triumph. It was so noble, so accidental, so entirely out of his good heart!

When he hurried her home at the end of the performance, that Mrs. Dennistoun might not be kept waiting, the previous events of the afternoon, and all that happened in the copse and garden, had faded out of Elinor's mind. She forgot Stanfield and the 6th and everything about it. Her embarrassment and trouble were gone. She went in gayly and told her mother all about this wonderful incident. "The Rector was trying for a sixpence. But, mamma, Phil must not be so ready with his sovereigns, must he?

We shall have nothing to live upon if he goes chucking sovereigns at every Punch and Judy he may meet."

CHAPTER XIII.

Phil Compton went off next morning by an early train, having in the meanwhile improved the impression of him left upon the family in general, and specially upon Mrs. Dennistoun, to whom he had talked with enthusiasm about Elinor, expressed indeed in terms unusual to her ears, but perhaps only more piquant on that account, which greatly conciliated the mother. "Don't you think," said the Honourable Phil, "because I speak a little free and am not one for tall talk, that I don't know what she is. I've got no poetry in me, but for the freest goer and the highest spirit, without a bit of vice in her, there never was one like Nell. The girls of my set, they're not worthy to tie her shoes—thing I most regret is taking her among a lot that are not half good enough for her. But you can't help your relations, can you? and you have to stick to them for dozens of reasons. There's the Jew, when you know her she's not such a bad sort—not generous, as you may see from what she's given Nell, the old screw: but yet in her own way she stands by a fellow, and we'll need it, not having just the Bank of England behind us. Her husband, old Prestwich, isn't bad for a man that has made his own money, and they've got a jolly house, always something going on."

"But I hope," said Mrs. Dennistoun, "that as soon as these autumn visits are over you will have a house of your own."

"Oh, that!" said Compton, with a wave of his hand, which left it in some doubt whether he was simply throwing off the suggestion, or treating it as a foregone conclusion of which there could be no doubt. "Nell," he went on, "gets on with the Jew like a house on fire—you see they don't clash. Nell ain't one of the mannish sort, and she doesn't flirt—at least not as far as I've seen——"

"I should hope not, indeed," said Mrs. Dennistoun.

"Oh, I'm not one of your curmudgeons. Where's the harm? But she don't, and there's an end of it. She keeps herself to herself, and lets the Jew go ahead, and think she's the attraction. And she'll please the old lord down to the ground. For he's an old-fashioned old coon, and likes what he calls *tenue*, don't you know: but the end is, there ain't one of them that can hold a candle to Nell. And I should not wonder a bit if she made a change in the lot of us. Conversion of a family by the influence of a pious wife, don't you know. Sort of thing that they make tracts out of. Capital thing, it would be," said Phil, philosophically, "for some of us have been going a pace——"

"Mr. Compton," said Mrs. Dennistoun, solemnly, "I don't understand very well what you mean by these phrases. They may be much more innocent than they seem to a country lady's ears. But I implore you to keep my Elinor clear of anything that you call going the pace. It must mean something very unlike her, whatever it means. She has been used to a very quiet, orderly life. Don't hurry her off into a whirl of society, or among noisy gay people. Indeed I can assure you that the more you have her to herself the more you will be happy in her. She is the brightest companion, the most entertaining—— Oh, Mr. Compton!"

"I think it's about time, now, mater, to call me Phil."

She smiled, with the tears in her eyes, and held out her hand. "Philip, then," she said, "to make a little difference. Now remember what I say. It is only in the sacredness of her home that you will know what is in Elinor. One is never dull with her. She has her own opinions—her bright way of looking at things—as you know. It is, perhaps, a strange thing for a mother to say, but she will amuse you, Philip; she is such company. You will never be dull with Elinor: she has so much in her, which will come out in society, it is true, but never so brightly as between you two alone."

This did not seem to have quite the effect upon the almost-bridegroom which the mother intended. "Perhaps" (she said to herself), "he was a little affected by the thought" (which she kept so completely out of the conversation) "of the loss she herself was about to undergo." At all events, his face was not so bright as in the vision of that sweet prospect held before him it ought to have been.

"The fact is," he said, "she knows a great deal more than I do, or ever will. It's she that will be the one to look blue when she finds herself alone with a fool of a follow that doesn't know a book from a brick. That's the thing I'm most afraid—— As for society, she can have her pick of that," he added, brightening up, "I'll not bind her down."

"You may be sure she'll prefer you to all the world."

He shrugged his shoulders a little.

"They say it's always a leap in the dark," he said, "for how's she to know the sort of fellow I am with what she sees of me here? But I promise you I'll do my best to take her in, and keep her in that delusion, for her good—making believe to be all that's virtuous: and perhaps not a bad way—some of it may stick. Come, mater, don't look so horrified. I'm not of the Cousin John sort, but there may be something decent in me after all."

"I am sure," said Mrs. Dennistoun, "that you will try to make her happy, Philip." She was crying by this time, which was a thing very odious to Phil. He took her by both hands and gave her a hearty kiss, which was a thing for which she was not at all prepared.

"I'll do by her——" he said, with a murmur which sounded like an oath, "as well as I know how."

Perhaps this was not the very greatest comfort to her mother, but it was the best she was at all likely to get from a man so entirely different in all ways from her own species. She had her cry out quietly while he went off to get his bag. The pony carriage was at the door in which Elinor was to drive him to the station, and a minute after Mrs. Dennistoun heard his voice in the hall calling to his Nell, his old girl, in terms which went against all the mother's prejudices of soft and reverent speech. To have her carefully-trained child, her Elinor, whom every one had praised and honoured, her maiden-princess so high apart from all such familiarity, addressed so, gave the old-fashioned lady a pang. It meant nothing but love and kindness, she said to herself. He reverenced Elinor as much as it was in such a man to do. He meant with all his heart to do by her as well as he knew how. It was as fantastic to object to his natural language as it would be to object to a Frenchman speaking French. That was his tongue, the only utterance he knew—— She dried her eyes and went out to the door to see them start. The sun was blazing over all the brilliant autumnal colours Of the garden, though it was still full and brilliant summer in the September morning, and only the asters and dahlias replacing the roses betrayed the turn of the season. And nothing could be more bright than the face of Elinor as she sat in the homely little carriage, with the reins gathered up in her hand. He was going away, indeed, but in a week he was coming back. Philip, as Mrs. Dennistoun now called him with dignity, yet a little beginning of affection, packed up his long limbs as well as he could in the small space. "I believe she'll spill us on the road," he said, "or bring back the shandrydan with a hole in it."

"There is too much of you, Phil," said Elinor, giving the staid pony a quiet touch.

"I should like some of those fellows to see me," he said, "joggled off to market like a basket of eggs; but don't smash me, Nell, on the way."

Mrs. Dennistoun stood on the steps looking after them, or rather, listening after them, for they had soon turned the corner of the house and were gone. She heard them jogging over the stony road, and the sound of their voices in the air for a long time after they were out of sight—the air was so still and so close, nothing in it to break the sound. The atmosphere was all sunshine, not a cloud upon the sky, scarcely a breath stirring over those hill-tops, which had almost the effect of a mountainous landscape, being the highest ground in all the visible space. Along the other side of the combe, where the road became visible, there were gleams of heather brilliant under the dark foliage of the firs. She sat down in the porch and waited to see them pass; there was a sorrowful background to her thoughts, but for the moment she was not actually sad, if perhaps a little forlorn. They had gone away leaving her alone, but yet in an hour or two Elinor was coming back. Time enough to think of the final parting. Next week Elinor would go and would not return. Mrs. Dennistoun held on by both hands to to-day and would not think of that future, near as it was. She waited in a hush of feeling, so near to great commotions of the heart and mind, but holding them at a distance in a suspense of all thought, till the shandrydan appeared in the opening of the road. They were thinking of her, for she saw a gleam of white, the waving of a handkerchief, as the little carriage trundled along the road, and for a moment the tears again blinded her eyes. But Mrs. Dennistoun was very reasonable. She got up from the cottage porch after the pony carriage had passed in the distance, with that determination to make the best of it, which is the inspiration of so many women's lives.

And what a drive the others had through the sunshine—or at least Elinor! You can never tell by what shadows a man's thoughts may be haunted, who is a man of the world, and has had many other things to occupy him besides this vision of love. But the girl had no shadows. The parting which was before her was not near enough to harm as yet, and she was still able to think, in her ignorance of the world, that even parting was much more in appearance than in reality, and that she would always be running home, always going upon long visits brightening everything, instead of saddening. But even had she been going to the end of the world with her husband next week, Elinor would still have been happy to-day. The sunshine itself was enough to go to any one's head, and the pony stepped out so that Phil had the grace to be ashamed of his reflections upon "the old girl." They got to the station too early for the train, and had half an hour's stroll together, with all the railway porters looking on admiring. They all knew Miss Dennistoun from her childhood, and they were interested in her "young man."

"And to think you will be in Ireland to-morrow," said Elinor, "over the sea, with the Channel between us—in another island!"

"I don't see much that's wonderful in that," said Phil, "the boat goes every day."

"Oh, there's nothing wonderful about the boat. Hundreds might go, and I shouldn't mind, but you—— It's strange to think of your going off into a world I don't know at all—and then coming back."

"To take you off to that world you don't know, Nell; and then the time will come when you will know it as well as I do, and more, too; and be able to set me down in my proper place."

"What is your proper place? Your place will always be the same. Phil, you've been so good to me this time; you've made everybody like you so. Mamma—that's the best of all. She was a little—I can't say jealous, that is not the right word, but uncertain and frightened—which just means that she did not know you, Phil; now you've condescended to let yourself be known."

"Have I, Nell? I've had more luck than meaning if that's so."

"'Tis that you've condescended to let yourself be known. A man has such odious pride. He likes to show himself all on the wrong side, to brave people's opinions—as if it was better to be liked for the badness in you than for the goodness in you!"

"What's the goodness in me, Nell? I'd like to know, and then I can have it ready in other emergencies and serve it out as it is wanted."

"Oh, Phil! the goodness in you is—yourself. You can't help being nice when you throw off those society airs. When you are talking with Mariamne and all that set of people——"

"Why can't you call her Jew? life is too short to say all those syllables."

"I don't like you to call her Jew. It's unkind. I don't think she deserves it. It's a sort of an insult."

"Shut up, Nell. It's her name and that's enough. Mar-ry-am-ne! It's a beast of a name to begin with. And do you think any of us has got time to say as much as that for one woman? Oh, I suppose I'm fond of her—as men are of their sisters. She is not a bad sort—mean as her name, and never fond of parting with her money—but stands by a fellow in a kind of a way all the same."

"I'll never call her Jew," said Elinor; "and, Phil, all this wonderful amount of things you have to do is simply—nothing. What do you ever do? It is the people who do things that have time to spare. I know one——"

"Don't come down on me, Nell, again with that eternal Cousin John."

"Phil! I never think of him till you put him into my head. I was thinking of a gentleman who writes——"

"Rubbish, Nell! What have I to do with men that write, or you either? We are none of us of that sort. I do what my set do, and more—for there was this director business; and I should never mind a bit of work that was well paid, like attending Board meetings and so forth, or signing my name to papers."

"What, without reading them, Phil?"

"Don't come over a fellow with your cleverness, Nell! I am not a reader; but I should take good care I knew what was in the papers before I signed them, I can tell you. Eh! you'd like me to slave, to get you luxuries, you little exacting Nell."

"Yes, Phil," she said, "I'd like to think you were working for our living. I should indeed. It seems somehow so much finer—so real a life. And I should work at home."

"A great deal you would work," he said, laughing, "with those scraps of fingers! Let's hear what you would do—bits of little pictures, or impossible things in pincushions, or so forth—and walk out in your most becoming bonnet to force them down some poor shop-keeper's throat?"

"Phil!" she said, "how contemptuous you are of my efforts. But I never thought of either sketches or pincushions. I should work at home to keep the house nice—to look after the servants, and guide the cook, and see that you had nice dinners."

"And warm my slippers by the parlour fire," said Phil. "That's too domestic, Nell, for you and me."

"But we are going to be very domestic, Phil."

"Are we? Not if I knows it; yawn our heads off, and get to hate one another. Not for me, Nell. You'll find yourself up to the eyes in engagements before you know where you are. No, no, old girl, you may do a deal with me, but you don't make a domestic man of Phil Compton. Time enough for that when we've had our fling."

"I don't want any fling, Phil," she said, clinging a little closer to his arm.

"But I do, my pet, in the person of Benedick the married man. Don't you think I want to show all the fellows what a stunning little wife I've got? and all the women I used to flirt with——"

"Did you use to flirt much with them, Phil?"

"You didn't think I flirted with the men, did you? like you did," said Phil, who was not particular about his grammar. "I want to show you off a bit. Nell. When we go down to the governor's, there you can be as domestic as you like. That's the line to take with him, and pays too if you do it well."

"Oh, don't talk as if you were always calculating for your advantage," she said, "for you are not, Phil. You are not a prudent person, but a horrid, extravagant spendthrift; if you go on chucking sovereigns about as you did yesterday."

"Well," he said, laughing, "wasn't it well spent? Didn't I make your Rector open his old eyes, and stop the mouths of the old maids? I don't throw away sovereigns in a general way, Nell, only when there's a purpose in it. But I think I did them all finely that time—had them on toast, eh?"

"You made an impression, if that is what you mean; but I confess I thought you did it out of kindness, Phil."

"To the Punch and Judy? catch me! Sovereigns ain't plentiful enough for that. You little exacting thing, ain't you pleased, when I did it to please you, and get you credit among your friends?"

"It was very kind of you, I'm sure, Phil," she said, very soberly, "but I should so much rather you had not thought of that. A shilling would have done just as well and they would have got a bed at the Bull's Head, and been quite kindly treated. Is this your train coming? It's a little too soon, I think."

"Thanks for the compliment, Nell. It is really late," he said, looking at his watch, "but the time flies, don't it, pet, when you and I are together? Here, you fellow, put my bag in a smoking carriage. And now, you darling, we've got to part; only for a little time, Nell."

"Only for a week," she said, with a smile and a tear.

"Not so long—a rush along the rail, a blow on the sea, and then back again; I shall only be a day over there, and then—bless you, Nell. Good-bye—take care of yourself, my little duck: take care of yourself for me."

"Good-bye," said Elinor, with a little quiver of her lip. A parting at a roadside station is a very abrupt affair. The train stops, the passenger is shoved in, there is a clanging of the doors, and in a moment it is gone. She had scarcely realized that the hour had come before he was whirled off from her, and the swinging line of carriages disappeared round the next curve. She stood looking vaguely after it till the old porter came up, who had known her ever since she was a child.

"Beg your pardon, miss, but the pony is a-waiting," he said. And then he uttered his sympathy in the form of a question:— "Coming back very soon, miss, ain't the gentleman?" he said.

"Oh, yes; very soon," she said, rousing herself up.

"And if I may make bold to say it, miss," said the porter, "an open-hearted gentleman as ever I see. There's many as gives us a threepenny for more than I've done for 'im. And look at what he's give me," he said, showing the half-crown in his hand.

Did he do that from calculation to please her, ungracious girl as she was, who was so hard to please? But he never could have known that she would see it. She walked through the little station to the pony carriage, feeling that all the eyes of the people about were upon her. They were all sympathetic, all equally aware that she had just parted with her lover: all ready to cheer her, if she had given them an opportunity, by reminding her of his early return. The old porter followed her out, and assisted at her ascent into the pony carriage. He said, solemnly, "And an 'andsome gentleman, miss, as ever I see," as he fastened the apron over her feet. She gave him a friendly nod as she drove away.

How dreadful it is to be so sensitive, to receive a wound so easily! Elinor was vexed more than she could say by her lover's denial of the reckless generosity with which she had credited him. To think that he had done it in order to produce the effect which had given her so distinct a sensation of pleasure changed that effect into absolute pain. And yet in the fantastic susceptibility of her nature, there was something in old Judkin's half-crown which soothed her again. A shilling would have been generous, Elinor said to herself, with a feminine appreciation of the difference of small things as well as great, whereas half-a-crown was lavish— ergo, he gave the sovereign also out of natural prodigality, as she had hoped, not out of calculation as he said. She drove soberly home, thinking over all these things in a mood very different from that triumphant happiness with which she started from the cottage with Phil by her side. The sunshine was still as bright, but it had taken an air of routine and commonplace to Elinor. It had come to be only the common day, not the glory and freshness of the morning. She felt herself, as she had never done before, on the edge of a world unknown, where everything would be new to her, where—it was possible—that which awaited her might not be unmixed happiness, might even be the reverse. It is seldom that a girl on the eve of marriage either thinks this or acknowledges to herself that she thinks it. Elinor did so involuntarily, without thinking upon her thought. Perhaps it would not be unmixed happiness. Strange clouds seemed to hang upon the horizon, ready to roll up in tragic darkness and gloom. Oh, no, not tragic, only commonplace, she said to herself; opaqueness, not blackness. But yet it was ominous and lowering, that distant sky.

CHAPTER XIV.

———————

The days of the last week hurried along like the grains of sand out of an hour-glass when they are nearly gone. It is true that almost everything was done—a few little bits of stitching, a few things still to be "got up" alone remaining, a handkerchief to mark with Elinor's name, a bit of lace to arrange, just enough to keep up a possibility of something to do for Mrs. Dennistoun in the blank of all other possibilities—for to interest herself or to occupy herself about anything that should be wanted beyond that awful limit of the wedding-day was of course out of the question. Life seemed to stop there for the mother, as it was virtually to begin for the child; though indeed to Elinor also, notwithstanding her love, it was visible more in the light of a point at which all the known and certain ended, and where the unknown and almost inconceivable began. The curious thing was that this barrier which was placed across life for them both, got somehow between them in those last days which should have been the most tender climax of their intercourse. They had a thousand things to say to each other, but they said very little. In the evening after dinner, whether they went out into the garden together to watch the setting of the young moon, or whether they sat together in that room which had witnessed all Elinor's commencements of life, free to talk as no one else in the world could ever talk to either of them, they said very little to each other, and what they said was of the most commonplace kind. "It is a lovely night; how clear one can see the road on the other side of the combe!" "And what a bright star that is close to the moon! I wish I knew a little more about the stars." "They are just as beautiful," Mrs. Dennistoun would say, "as if you knew everything about them, Elinor." "Are you cold, mamma? I am sure I can see you shiver. Shall I run and get you a shawl?" "It is a little chilly: but perhaps it will be as well to go in now," the mother said. And then indoors: "Do you think you will like this lace made up as a jabot, Elinor?" "You are giving me all your pretty things, though you know you understand lace much better than I do." "Oh, that doesn't matter," Mrs. Dennistoun said hurriedly; "that is a taste which comes with time. You will like it as well as I do when you are as old as I am." "You are not so dreadfully old, mamma." "No, that's the worst of it," Mrs. Dennistoun would say, and then break out into a laugh. "Look at the shadow that handkerchief makes—how fantastic it is!" she cried. She neither cared for the moon, nor for the quaintness of the shadows, nor for the lace which she was pulling into dainty folds to show its delicate pattern—for none of all these things, but for her only child, who was going from her, and to whom she had a hundred, and yet a hundred, things to say: but none of them ever came from her lips.

"Mary Dale has not seen your things, Elinor: she asked if she might come to-morrow."

"I think we might have had to-morrow to ourselves, mamma—the last day all by ourselves before those people begin to arrive."

"Yes, I think so too; but it is difficult to say no, and as she was not here when the others came—— She is the greatest critic in the parish. She will have so much to say."

"I daresay it may be fun," said Elinor, brightening up a little, "and of course anyhow Alice must have come to talk about her dress. I am tired of those bride's-maids' dresses; they are really of so little consequence." Elinor was not vain, to speak of, but she thought it improbable that when she was there any one would look much at the bride's-maids' dresses. For one thing, to be sure, the bride is always the central figure, and there were but two bride's-maids, which diminished the interest; and then—well, it had to be allowed at the end of all, that, though her closest friends, neither Alice Hudson nor Mary Tatham were, to look at, very interesting girls.

"They are of great consequence to them," said Mrs. Dennistoun, with the faintest smile.

"I didn't mean that, of course," said Elinor, with a blush; "only I never should have worried about my own dress, which after all is the most important, as Alice does about hers."

"Which nobody will look at," Mrs. Dennistoun said.

"I did not say that: but to tell the truth, it is a pity for the girls that the men will not quite be, just of their world, you know. Oh, mamma, you know it is not that I think anything of that, but I am sorry for Alice and Mary. Mr. Bolsover and the other gentlemen will not take that trouble which country neighbours, or—or John's friends from the Temple might have done."

"Why do you speak of John's friends from the Temple, Elinor?"

"Mamma! for no reason at all. Why should I? They were the only other men I could think of."

"Elinor, did John ever give you any reason to think——"

"Mamma," cried Elinor again, with double vehemence, her countenance all ablaze, "of course he never did! how could you think such foolish things?"

"Well, my dear," said her mother, "I am very glad he did not; it will prevent any embarrassment between him and you—for I must always believe——"

"Don't, please, oh, don't! it would make me miserable; it would take all my happiness away."

Mrs. Dennistoun said nothing, but she sighed—a very small, infinitesimal sigh—and there was a moment's silence, during which perhaps that sigh pervaded the atmosphere with a sort of breath of what might have been. After a moment she spoke again:

"I hope you have not packed up your ornaments yet, Elinor. You must leave them to the very last, for Mary would like to see that beautiful necklace. What do you think you shall wear on the day?"

"Nothing," said Elinor, promptly. She was about to add, "I have nothing good enough," but paused in time.

"Not my little star? It would look very well, my darling, to fix your veil on. The diamonds are very good, though perhaps a little old-fashioned; you might get them reset. But—your father gave it me like that."

"I would not change it a bit, mamma, for anything in the world."

"Thanks, my dearest. I thought that was how you would feel about it. It is not very big, of course, but it really is very good."

"Then I will wear it, mamma, if it will please you, but nothing else."

"It would please me: it would be like having something from your father. I think we had less idea of ornaments in my day. I cannot tell you how proud I was of my diamond star. I should like to put it in for you myself, Elinor."

"Oh, mamma!" This was the nearest point they had come to that outburst of two full hearts which both of them would have called breaking down. Mrs. Dennistoun saw it and was frightened. She thought it would be betraying to Elinor what she wished her never to know, the unspeakable desolation to which she was looking forward when her child was taken from her. Elinor's exclamation, too, was a protest against the imminent breaking down. They both came back with a hurry, with a panting breath, to safer ground.

"Yes, that's what I regret," she said. "Mr. Bolsover and Harry Compton will laugh a little at the Rectory. They will not be so— nice as young men of their own kind."

"The Rectory people are just as well born as any of us, Elinor."

"Oh, precisely, mamma: I know that; but we too—— It is what they call a different *monde*. I don't think it is half so nice a *monde*," said the girl, feeling that she had gone further than she intended to do; "but you know, mamma——"

"I know, Elinor: but I scarcely expected from you——"

"Oh," cried Elinor again, in exasperation, "if you think that I share that feeling! I think it odious, I think their *monde* is vulgar, nasty, miserable! I think——"

"Don't go too far the other way, Elinor. Your husband will be of it, and you must learn to like it. You think, perhaps, all that is new to me?"

"No," said Elinor, her bright eyes, all the brighter for tears, falling before her mother's look. "I know, of course, that you have seen—all kinds——"

But she faltered a little, for she did not believe that her mother was acquainted with Phil's circle and their wonderful ways.

"They will be civil enough," she went on, hurriedly, "and as everybody chaffs so much nowadays they will, perhaps, never be found out. But I don't like it for my friends."

"They will chaff me also, no doubt," Mrs. Dennistoun said.

"Oh, *you*, mamma! they are not such fools as that," cried poor Elinor; but in her own mind she did not feel confident that there was any such limitation to their folly. Mrs. Dennistoun laughed a little to herself, which was, perhaps, more alarming than that other moment when she was almost ready to cry.

"You had better wear Lord St. Serf's ring," she said, after a moment, with a tone of faint derision which Elinor knew.

"You might as well tell me," cried the bride, "to wear Lady Mariamne's revolving dishes. No, I will wear nothing, nothing but your star."

"You have got nothing half so nice," said the mother. Oh yes, it was a little revenge upon those people who were taking her daughter from her, and who thought themselves at liberty to jeer at all her friends: but as was perhaps inevitable it touched Elinor a little too. She restrained herself from some retort with a sense of extreme and almost indignant self-control: though what retort Elinor could have made I cannot tell. It was much "nicer" than anything else she had. None of Phil Compton's great friends, who were not of the same *monde* as the people at Windyhill, had offered his bride anything to compare with the diamonds which her father had given to her mother before she was born. And Elinor was quite aware of the truth of what her mother said. But she would have liked to make a retort—to say something smart and piquant and witty in return.

And thus the evening was lost, the evening in which there was so much to say, one of the three only, no more, that were left.

Miss Dale came next day to see "the things," and was very amiable: but the only thing in this visit which affected Elinor's mind was a curious little unexpected assault this lady made upon her when she was going away. Elinor had gone out with her to the porch, according to the courteous usage of the house. But when they had reached that shady place, from which the green combe and the blue distance were visible, stretching far into the soft autumnal mists of the evening, Mary Dale turned upon her and asked her suddenly, "What night was it that Mr. Compton came here?"

Elinor was much startled, but she did not lose her self-possession. All the trouble about that date had disappeared out of her mind in the stress and urgency of other things. She cast back her mind with an effort and asked herself what the conflict and uncertainty of which she was dimly conscious, had been? It came back to her dimly without any of the pain that had been in it. "It was on the sixth," she said quietly, without excitement. She could scarcely recall to her mind what it was that had moved her so much in respect to this date only a little time ago.

"Oh, you must be mistaken, Elinor, I saw him coming up from the station. It was later than that. It was, if I were to give my life for it, Thursday night."

This was four or five nights before and a haze of uncertainty had fallen on all things so remote. But Elinor cast her eyes upon the calendar in the hall and calm possessed her breast. "It was the sixth," she said with composed tones, as certain as of anything she had ever known in the course of her life.

"Well, I suppose you must know," said Mary Dale.

CHAPTER XV.

"Look at that, Elinor," said Mrs. Dennistoun, next day, when she had read, twice over, a letter, large and emblazoned with a very big monogram, which Elinor, well perceiving from whom it came, had furtively watched the effect of from behind an exceeding small letter of her own. Phil was not remarkable as a correspondent: his style was that of the primitive mind which hopes its correspondent is well, "as this leaves me." He had never much more to say.

"From Mariamne, mamma?"

"She takes great pains to make us certain of that fact at least," Mrs. Dennistoun said; which indeed was very true, for the name of the writer was sprawled in gilt letters half over the sheet. And this was how it ran:—

"DEAR   MRS.   DENNISTOUN,—
"I have been thinking what a great pity it would be to bore you with me, and my maid, and all my belongings. I am so silly that I can never be happy without dragging a lot of things about with me—dogs, and people, and so forth. Going to town in September is dreadful, but it is rather *chic* to do a thing that is quite out of the way, and one may perhaps pick up a little fun in the evening. So if you don't mind, instead of inflicting Fifine and Bijou and Leocadie, not to mention some people that might be with me, upon you, and putting your house all out of order, as these odious little dogs do when people are not used to them—I will come down by the train, which I hope arrives quite punctually, in time to see poor Phil turned off. I am sure you will be so kind as to send a carriage for me to the railway. We shall be probably a

party of four, and I hear from Phil you are so hospitable and kind that I need not hesitate to bring my friends to breakfast after it's all over. I hope Phil will go through it like a man, and I wouldn't for worlds deprive him of the support of his family. Love to Nell. I am,

"Yours truly,
"MARIAMNE PRESTWICH."

"The first name very big and the second very small," said Mrs. Dennistoun, as she received the letter back.

"I am sure we are much obliged to her for not coming, mamma!"

"Perhaps—but not for this announcement of her not coming. I don't wish to say anything against your new relations, Elinor——"

"You need not put any restraint upon yourself in consideration of my feelings," said Elinor, with a flush of annoyance.

And this made Mrs. Dennistoun pause. They ate their breakfast, which was a very light meal, in silence. It was the day before the wedding. The rooms down-stairs had been carefully prepared for Phil's sister. Though Mrs. Dennistoun was too proud to say anything about it, she had taken great pains to make these pretty rooms as much like a fine lady's chamber as had been possible. She had put up new curtains, and a Persian carpet, and looked out of her stores all the pretty things she could find to decorate the two rooms of the little apartment. She had gone in on the way down-stairs to take a final survey, and it seemed to her that they were very pretty. No picture could have been more beautiful than the view from the long low lattice window, in which, as in a frame, was set the foreground of the copse with its glimpses of ruddy heather and the long sweep of the heights beyond, which stretched away into the infinite. That at least could not be surpassed anywhere; and the Persian carpet was like moss under foot, and the chairs luxurious—and there was a collection of old china in some open shelves which would have made the mouth of an amateur water. Well! it was Lady

Mariamne's own loss if she preferred the chance of picking up a little fun in the evening, to spending the night decorously in that pretty apartment, and making further acquaintance with her new sister. It was entirely, Mrs. Dennistoun said to herself, a matter for her own choice. But she was much affronted all the same.

"It will be very inconvenient indeed sending a carriage for her, Elinor. Except the carriage that is to take you to church there is none good enough for this fine lady. I had concluded she would go in your uncle Tatham's carriage. It may be very fine to have a Lady Mariamne in one's party, but it is a great nuisance to have to change all one's arrangements at the last moment."

"If you were to send the wagonette from the Bull's Head, as rough as possible, with two of the farm horses, she would think it *genre*, if not *chic*——"

"I cannot put up with all this nonsense!" cried Mrs. Dennistoun, with a flush on her cheek. "You are just as bad as they are, Elinor, to suggest such a thing! I have held my own place in society wherever I have been, and I don't choose to be condescended to or laughed at, in fact, by any visitor in the world!"

"Mamma! do you think any one would ever compare you with Mariamne—the Jew?"

"Don't exasperate me with those abominable nicknames. They will give you one next. She is an exceedingly ill-bred and ill-mannered woman. Picking up a little fun in the evening! What does she mean by picking up a little fun——"

"They will perhaps go to the theatre—a number of them; and as nobody is in town they will laugh very much at the kind of people, and perhaps the kind of play—and it will be a great joke ever after among themselves—for of course there will be a number of them together," said Elinor, disclosing her acquaintance with the habits of her new family with downcast eyes.

"How can well-born people be so vulgar and ill-bred?" cried Mrs. Dennistoun. "I must say for Philip that though he is careless and not nearly so particular as I should like, still he is not like that. He has something of the politeness of the heart."

Elinor did not raise her downcast eyes. Phil had been on his very good behaviour on the occasion of his last hurried visit, but she did not feel that she could answer even for Phil. "I am very glad anyhow, that she is not coming, mamma: at least we shall have the last night and the last morning to ourselves."

Mrs. Dennistoun shook her head. "The Tathams will be here," she said; "and everybody, to dinner—all the party. We must go now and see how we can enlarge the table. To-night's party will be the largest we have ever had in the cottage." She sighed a little and paused, restraining herself. "We shall have no quiet evening—nor morning either—again; it will be a bustle and a rush. You and I will never have any more quiet evenings, Elinor: for when you come back it will be another thing."

"Oh, mother!" cried Elinor, throwing herself into her mother's arms: and for a moment they stood closely clasped, feeling as if their hearts would burst, yet very well aware, too, underneath, that any number of quiet evenings would be as the last, when, with hearts full of a thousand things to say to each other, they said almost nothing—which in some respects was worse than having no quiet evenings evermore.

In the afternoon Phil arrived, having returned from Ireland that morning, and paused only to refresh himself in the chambers which he still retained in town. He had met all his hunting friends during the three days he had been away; and though he retained a gallant appearance, and looked, as Alice Hudson thought, "very aristocratic," Mrs. Dennistoun caught with anxiety a worn-out look—the look of excitement, of nights without sleep, much smoke, and, perhaps, much wine, in his eyes. What a woman feels who has to hand over her spotless child, the most dear and pure thing upon earth, to a man fresh from those indulgences and dissipations which never seem harmless, and always are repellent to a woman, is not to be described. Fortunately the bride herself, in invincible ignorance and unconsciousness, seldom feels in that way. To Elinor her lover looked tired about the eyes, which was very well explained by his night journey, and by the agitation of the moment. And, indeed, she did not see very much of Phil, who had his friends with him—his aide-de-camp, Bolsover, and his brother Harry. These three gentlemen carried an atmosphere of smoke and other scents with them into the lavender of the Rectory, which was too amazing in that hemisphere for words, and talked their own talk in the midst of the fringe of rustics who were their hosts, with a calm which was extraordinary, breaking into the midst of the Rector's long-winded, amiable sentences, and talking to each other over Mrs. Hudson's head. "I say, Dick, don't you remember?" "By Jove, Phil, you are too bad!" sounded, with many other such expressions and reminders, over the Rectory party, strictly silent round their own table, trying to make a courteous remark now and then, but confounded, in their simple country good manners, by the fine gentlemen. And then there was the dinner-party at the cottage in the evening, to which Mr. and Mrs. Hudson were invited. Such a dinner-party! Old Mr. Tatham, who was a country gentleman from Dorsetshire, with his nice daughter, Mary Tatham, a quiet country young lady, accustomed, when she went into the world at all, to the serious young men of the Temple, and John's much-occupied friends, who had their own asides about cases, and what So-and-So had said in court, but were much too well-bred before ladies to fall into "shop;" and Mr. and Mrs. Hudson, who were such as we know them; and the bride's mother, a little anxious, but always debonair; and Elinor herself, in all the haze and sweet confusion of the great era which approached so closely. The three men made the strangest addition that can be conceived to the quiet guests; but things went better under the discipline of the dinner, especially as Sir John Huntingtower, who was a Master of the hounds and an old friend of the Dennistouns, was of the party, and Lady Huntingtower, who was an impressive person, and knew the world. This lady was very warm in her congratulations to Mrs. Dennistoun after dinner on the absence of Lady Mariamne. "I think you are the luckiest woman that ever was to have got clear of that dreadful creature," she said. "Oh, there is nothing wrong about her that I know. She goes everywhere with her dogs and her *cavaliers servantes*. There's safety in numbers, my dear. She has always two of them at least hanging about her to fetch and carry, and she thinks a great deal more of her dogs; but I can't think what you could have done with her here."

"And what will my Elinor do in such a sphere?" the troubled mother permitted herself to say.

"Oh, if that were all," said Lady Huntingtower, lifting up her fat hands—she was one of those who had protested against the marriage, but now that it had come to this point, and could not be broken off, the judicious woman thought it right to make the best of it—"Elinor need not be any the worse," she said. "Thank heaven, you are not obliged to be mixed up with your husband's sister. Elinor must take a line of her own. You should come to town yourself her first season, and help her on. You used to know plenty of people."

"But they say," said Mrs. Dennistoun, "that it is so much better to leave a young couple to themselves, and that a mother is always in the way."

"If I were you I would not pay the least attention to what they say. If you hold back too much they will say, 'There was her own mother, knowing numbers of nice people, that never took the trouble to lend her a hand.'"

"I hope," said Mrs. Dennistoun, turning round immediately to this other aspect of affairs, "that it never will be necessary for the world to interest itself at all in my child's affairs."

"Well, of course, that is the best," Lady Huntingtower allowed, "if she just goes softly for a year or two till she feels her way."

"But then she is so young, and so little accustomed to act for herself," said the mother, with another change of flank.

"Oh, Elinor has a great deal of spirit. She must just make a stand against the Compton set and take her own line."

Mrs. Hudson and Alice and Miss Tatham were at the other end

of the room exchanging a few criticisms under their breath, and disposed to think that they were neglected by their hostess for the greater personage with whom she was in such close conversation. And Lady Mariamne's defection was a great disappointment to them all. "I should like to have seen a fine lady quite close," said Mary (it was not, I think, usual to speak of "smart" people in those days), "one there could be no doubt about, a little fast and all that. I have seen them in town at a distance, but all the people we know are sure country people."

"My dear," said Mrs. Hudson, primly, "I don't like to hear you talk of any other kind. An English lady, I hope, whatever is her rank, can only be of one kind."

"Oh, mamma, you know very well Lady Mariamne is as different from Lady Huntingtower as——"

"Don't mention names, my dear; it is not well-bred. The one is young, and naturally fond of gayety; the other—well, is not quite so young, and stout, and all that."

"Oh, that is all very well," said Alice; "but Aunt Mary says——"

Miss Dale was coming in the evening, and the Miss Hills, and the curate, and the doctor, and various other people, who could not be asked to dinner, to whom it had been carefully explained (which, indeed, was a fact they knew) that to dine twelve people in the little dining-room of the cottage was a feat which was accomplished with difficulty, and that more was impossible. Society at Windyhill was very tolerant and understanding on this point, for all the dining-rooms were small, except, indeed, when you come to talk of such places as Huntingtower—and they were very glad to be permitted to have a peep at the bridegroom on these terms, or rather, if truth were told, of the bride, and how she was bearing herself so near the crisis of her fate. The bridegroom is seldom very interesting on such occasions. On the present occasion he was more interesting than usual, because he was the Honourable Philip, and because he had a reputation of which most people had heard something. There was a mixture of alarm and suspicion in respect to him which increased the excitement; and many remarks of varied kinds were made. "I think the fellow's face quite bears out his character," said the doctor to the Rector. "What a man to trust a nice girl to!" Mr. Hudson felt that as the bridegroom was living under his roof he was partially responsible, and discouraged this pessimistic view. "Mr. Compton has not, perhaps, had all the advantages one tries to secure for one's own son," he said, "but I have reason to believe that the things that have been said of him are much exaggerated." "Oh, advantages!" said the doctor, thinking of Alick, of whom it was his strongly expressed opinion that the fellow should be turned out to rough it, and not coddled up and spoiled at home. But while these remarks were going on, Miss Hill had been expressing to the curate an entirely different view. "I think he has a *beautiful* face," she said with the emphasis some ladies use; "a little worn, perhaps, with being too much in the world, and I wish he had a better colour. To me he looks delicate: but what delightful features, Mr. Whitebands, and what an aristocratic air!"

"He looks tremendously up to everything," the curate said, with a faint tone of envy in his voice.

"Don't he just?" cried Alick Hudson. "I should think there wasn't a thing he couldn't do—of things that men *do* do, don't you know," cried that carefully trained boy, whose style was confused, though his meaning was good. But probably there were almost as many opinions about Phil as there were people in the room. His two backers-up stood in a corner—half intimidated, half contemptuous of the country people. "Queer lot for Phil to fall among," said Dick Bolsover. "Que diable allait-il faire dans cette galère?" said Harry Compton, who had been about the world. "Oh, bosh with your French, that nobody understands," said the best man.

But in the meantime Phil was not there at all to be seen of men. He had stolen out into the garden, where there was a white vision awaiting him in the milky moonlight. The autumn haze had come early this season, and the moon was misty, veiled with

161

white amid a jumble of soft floating vapours in the sky. Elinor stood among the flowers, which showed some strange subdued tints of colours in the flooding of the white light, like a bit of consolidated moonlight in her white dress. She had a white shawl covering her from head to foot, with a corner thrown over her hair. What had they to say to each other that last night? Not much; nothing at all that had any information in it—whispers inaudible almost to each other. There was something in being together for this stolen moment, just on the eve of their being together for always, which had a charm of its own. After to-night, no stealing away, no escape to the garden, no little conspiracy to attain a meeting—the last of all those delightful schemings and devices. They started when they heard a sound from the house, and sped along the paths into the shadow like the conspirators they were—but never to conspire more after this last enthralling time.

"You're not frightened, Nell?"

"No—except a little. There is one thing——"

"What is it, my pet? If it's to the half of my kingdom, it shall be done."

"Phil, we are going to be very good when we are together? don't laugh—to help each other?"

He did laugh low, not to be heard, but long. "I shall have no temptation," he said, "to be anything but good, you little goose of a Nell," taking it for a warning of possible jealousy to come.

"Oh, but I mean both of us—to help each other."

"Why, Nell, I know you'll never go wrong——"

She gave him a little impatient shake. "You will not understand me, Phil. We will try to be better than we've ever been. To be good—don't you know what that means?—in every way, before God."

Her voice dropped very low, and he was for a moment overawed. "You mean going to church, Nell?"

"I mean—yes, that for one thing; and many other things."

"That's dropping rather strong upon a fellow," he said, "just at this moment, don't you think, when I must say yes to everything you say."

"Oh, I don't mean it in that way; and I was not thinking of church particularly; but to be good, very good, true and kind, in our hearts."

"You are all that already, Nell."

"Oh, no, not what I mean. When there are two of us instead of one we can do so much more."

"Well, my pet, it's for you to make out the much more. I'm quite content with you as you are; it's me that you want to improve, and heaven knows there's plenty of room for that."

"No, Phil, not you more than me," she said.

"We'll choose a place where the sermon's short, and we'll see about it. You mean little minx, to bind a man down to go to church, the night before his wedding day!"

And then there was a sound of movement indoors, and after a little while the bride appeared among the guests with a little more colour than usual, and an anxiously explanatory description of something she had been obliged to do; and the confused hour flew on with much sound of talking and very little understanding of what was said. And then all the visitors streamed away group after group into the moonlight, disappearing like ghosts under the shadow of the trees. Finally, the Rectory party went too, the three mild ladies surrounded by an exciting circle of cigars; for Alick, of course, had broken all bonds, and even the Rector accepted that rare indulgence. Alice Hudson half deplored, half exulted for years after in the scent that would cling round one particular evening dress. Five gentlemen, all with cigars, and papa as bad as any of them! There had never been such an extraordinary experience in her life.

And then the Tathams, too, withdrew, and the mother and daughter stood alone on their own hearth. Oh, so much, so much as there was to say! but how were they to say it?—the last moment, which was so precious and so intolerable—the moment that would never come again.

"You were a long time with Philip, Elinor, in the garden. I think all your old friends —— the last night."

"I wanted to say something to him, mamma, that I had never had the courage to say."

Mrs. Dennistoun had been looking dully into the dim mirror over the mantelpiece. She turned half round to her daughter with an inquiring look.

"Oh, mamma, I wanted to say to him that we must be good! We're so happy. God is so kind to us; and you—if you suppose I don't think of you! It was to say to him—building our house upon all this, God's mercy and your loss, and all—that we are doubly, doubly bound to serve—and to love—and to be good people before God; and like you, mother, like you!"

"My darling!" Mrs. Dennistoun said. And that was all. She asked no questions as to how it was to be done, or what he replied. Elinor had broken down hysterically, and sobbed out the words one at a time, as they would come through the choking in her throat. Needless to say that she ended in her mother's arms, her head upon the bosom which had nursed her, her slight weight dependent upon the supporter and protector of all her life.

That was the last evening. There remained the last morning to come; and after that—what? The great sea of an unknown life, a new pilot, and a ship untried.

CHAPTER XVI.

And now the last morning had come.

The morning of a wedding-day is a flying and precarious moment which seems at once as if it never would end, and as if it were a hurried preliminary interval in which the necessary preparations never could be done. Elinor was not allowed to come down-stairs to help, as she felt it would be natural to do. It was Mary Tatham who arranged the flowers on the table, and helped Dennistoun to superintend everything. All the women in the house, though they were so busy, were devoted at every spare moment to the service of Elinor. They brought her simple breakfast up-stairs, one maid carrying the tray and another the teapot, that each might have their share. The cook, though she was overwhelmed with work, had made some cakes for breakfast, such us Elinor liked. "Most like as we'll never have her no more—to mind," she said. The gardener sent up an untidy bundle of white flowers. And Mrs. Dennistoun came herself to pour out the tea. "As if I had been ill, or had turned into a baby again," Elinor said. But there was not much said. Mary Tatham was there for one thing, and for another and the most important they had said all they had to say; the rest which remained could not be said. The wedding was to be at a quarter to twelve, in order to give Lady Mariamne time to come from town. It was not the fashion then to delay marriages to the afternoon, which no doubt would have been much more convenient for her ladyship; but the best that could be done was done. Mr. Tatham's carriage, which he had brought with him to grace the ceremony, was despatched to the station to meet Lady Mariamne, while he, good man, had to get to church as he could in one of the flys. And then came the important moment, when the dressing of the bride had to be begun. The wedding-breakfast was not yet all set out in perfect order, and there were many things to do. Yet every woman in the house had a little share in the dressing of the bride. They all came to see how it fitted when the wedding-dress was put on. It fitted like a glove! The long glossy folds of the satin were a wonder to see. Cook stood just within the door in a white apron, and wept, and could not say a word to Miss Elinor; but the younger maids sent forth a murmur of admiration. And the Missis they thought was almost as beautiful as the bride, though her satin was grey. Mrs. Dennistoun herself threw the veil over her child's head, and put in the diamond star, the old-fashioned ornament, which had been her husband's present to herself. And then again she had meant to say something to Elinor—a last word—but the word would not come. They were both of them glad that somebody should be there all the time, that they should not be left alone. And after that the strange, hurried, everlasting morning was over, and the carriage was at the door.

Then again it was a relief that old Mr. Tatham had missed his proper place in the fly, and had to go on the front seat with the bride and her mother. It was far better so. If they had been left even for ten minutes alone, who could have answered that one or the other would not have cried, and discomposed the bouquet and the veil? It seemed a great danger and responsibility over when they arrived at last safely at the church door. Lady Mariamne was just then arriving from the station. She drew up before them in poor Mr. Tatham's carriage, keeping them back. Harry Compton and Mr. Bolsover sprang to the carriage window to talk to her, and there was a loud explosion of mirth and laughter in the midst of the village people, and the children with their baskets of flowers who were already gathered. Lady Mariamne's voice burst out so shrill that it overmastered the church bells. "Here I am," she cried, "out in the wilderness. And Algy has come with me to take care of me. And how are you, dear boys; and how is poor Phil?" "Phil is all ready to be turned off, with the halter round his neck," said Dick Bolsover; and Harry Compton said, "Hurry up, hurry up, Jew, the bride is behind you, waiting to get out." "She must wait, then," said Lady Mariamne, and there came leisurely out of the carriage, first, her ladyship's companion, by name, Algy, a tall person with an eye-glass, then a little pug, which was carefully handed into his arms, and then lightly jumping down to the ground, a little figure in black—in black of all things in the world! a sight that curdled the blood of the village people, and of Mrs. Hudson, who had walked across from the Rectory in a gown of pigeon's-breast silk which scattered prismatic reflections as she walked. In black! Mrs. Hudson bethought herself that she had a white China crape shawl in her cupboard, and wondered if she could offer it to conceal this ill omened gown. But if Lady Mariamne's dress was dark, she herself was fair enough, with an endless fluff of light hair under her little black lace bonnet. Her gloves were off, and her hands were white and glistening with rings. "Give me my puggy darling," she said in her loud, shrill tone. "I can go nowhere, can I, pet, without my little pug!"

"A Jew and a pug, both in church. It is enough," said her brother, "to get the poor parson into trouble with his bishop."

"Oh, the bishop's a great friend of mine," said the lady; "he will say nothing to me, not if I put Pug in a surplice and make him lead the choir." At this speech there was a great laugh of the assembled party, which stood in the centre of the path, while Mr. Tatham's carriage edged away, and the others made efforts to get forward. The noise of their talk disturbed the curious abstraction in which Elinor had been going through the morning hours. Mariamne's jarring voice seemed louder than the bells. Was this the first voice sent out to greet her by the new life which was about to begin? She glanced at her mother, and then at old Uncle Tatham, who sat immovable, prevented by decorum from apostrophising the coachman who was not his own, but fuming inwardly at the interruption. Mrs. Dennistoun did not move at all, but her daughter knew very well what was meant by that look straight before her, in which her mother seemed to ignore all obstacles in the way.

"I got here very well," Lady Mariamne went on; "we started in the middle of the night, of course, before the lamps were out. Wasn't it good of Algy to get himself out of bed at such an unearthly hour! But he snapped at Puggy as we came down, which was a sign he felt it. Why aren't you with the poor victim at the altar, you boys?"

"Phil will be in blue funk," said Harry; "go in and stand by your man, Dick: the Jew has enough with two fellows to see her into her place."

The bride's carriage by this time pushed forward, making Lady Mariamne start in confusion. "Oh! look here; they have splashed my pretty toilette, and upset my nerves," she cried, springing back into her supporter's arms.

That gentleman regarded the stain of the damp gravel on the lady's skirt through his eye-glass with deep but helpless anxiety. "It's a pity for the pretty frock!" he said with much seriousness. And the group gathered round and gazed in dismay, as if they expected it to disappear of itself—until Mrs. Hudson bustled up. "It will rub off; it will not make any mark. If one of you gentlemen will lend me a handkerchief," she said. And Algy and Harry and Dick Bolsover, not to speak of Lady Mariamne herself, watched with great gravity while the gravel was swept off. "I make no doubt," said the Rector's wife, "that I have the pleasure of speaking to Lady Mariamne: and I don't doubt that black is the fashion and your dress is beautiful: but if you would just throw on a white shawl for the sake of the wedding—it's so unlucky to come in black——"

"A white shawl!" said Lady Mariamne in dismay.

"The Jew in a white shawl!" echoed the others with a burst of laughter which rang into the church itself and made Phil before the altar, alone and very anxious, ask himself what was up.

"It's China crape, I assure you, and very nice," Mrs. Hudson said.

Lady Mariamne gave the good Samaritan a stony stare, and

took Algy's arm and sailed into the church before the Rector's wife, without a word said; while all the women from the village looked at each other and said, "Well, I never!" under their breath.

"Let me give you my arm, Mrs. Hudson," said Harry Compton, "and please pardon me that I did not introduce my sister to you. She is dreadfully shy, don't you know, and never does speak to anyone when she has not been introduced."

"My observation was a very simple one," said Mrs. Hudson, very angry, yet pleased to lean upon an Honourable arm.

"My dear lady!" cried the good-natured Harry, "the Jew never wore a shawl in her life——"

And all this time the organ had been pealing, the white vision passing up the aisle, the simple villagers chanting forth their song about the breath that breathed o'er Eden. Alas! Eden had not much to do with it, except perhaps in the trembling heart of the white maiden roused out of her virginal dream by the jarring voices of the new life. The laughter outside was a dreadful offence to all the people, great and small, who had collected to see Elinor married.

"What could you expect? It's that woman whom they call the Jew," whispered Lady Huntingtower to her next neighbour.

"She should be put into the stocks," said Sir John, scarcely under his breath, which, to be sure, was also an interruption to the decorum of the place.

And then there ensued a pause broken by the voice, a little lugubrious in tone, of the Rector within the altar rails, and the tremulous answers of the pair outside. The audience held its breath to hear Elinor make her responses, and faltered off into suppressed weeping as the low tones ceased. Sir John Huntingtower, who was very tall and big, and stood out like a pillar among the ladies round, kept nodding his head all the time she spoke, nodding as you might do in forced assent to any dreadful vow. Poor little thing, poor little thing, he was saying in his heart. His face was more like the face of a man at a funeral than a man at a wedding. "Blessed are the dead that die in the

Lord"—he might have been nodding assent to that instead of to Elinor's low-spoken vow. Phil Compton's voice, to tell the truth, was even more tremulous than Elinor's. To investigate the thoughts of a bridegroom would be too much curiosity at such a moment. But I think if the secrets of the hearts could be revealed, Phil for a moment was sorry for poor little Elinor too.

And then the solemnity was all over in a moment, and the flutter of voices and congratulations began.

I do not mean to follow the proceedings through all the routine of the wedding-day. Attempts were made on the part of the bridegroom's party to get Lady Mariamne dismissed by the next train, an endeavour into which Harry Compton threw himself— for he was always a good-hearted fellow—with his whole soul. But the Jew declared that she was dying of hunger, and whatever sort of place it was, must have something to eat; a remark which naturally endeared her still more to Mrs. Dennistoun, who was waiting by the door of Mr. Tatham's carriage, which that anxious old gentleman had managed to recover control of, till her ladyship had taken her place. Her ladyship stared with undisguised amazement when she was followed into the carriage by the bride's mother, and when the neat little old gentleman took his seat opposite. "But where is Algy? I want Algy," she cried, in dismay. "Absolutely I can't go without Algy, who came to take care of me."

"You will be perfectly safe, my dear lady, with Mrs. Dennistoun and me. The gentlemen will walk," said Mr. Tatham, waving his hand to the coachman.

And thus it was that the forlorn lady found herself without her cavalier and without her pug, absolutely stranded among savages, notwithstanding her strong protest almost carried the length of tears. She was thus carried off in a state of consternation to the cottage over the rough road, where the wheels went with a din and lurch over the stones, and dug deep into the sand, eliciting a succession of little shrieks from her oppressed bosom. "I shall be shaken all to bits," she said, grasping the arm of the old gentleman to steady herself. Mr. Tatham was not displeased to be the champion of a lady of title. He assured her in dulcet tones that his springs were very good and his horses very sure—"though it is not a very nice road."

"Oh, it is a dreadful road!" said Lady Mariamne.

But in due time they did arrive at the cottage, where her ladyship could not wait for the gathering of the company, but demanded at once something to eat. "I can't really go another moment without food. I must have something or I shall die. Phil, come here this instant and get me something. They have brought me off at the risk of my life, and there's nobody to attend to me. Don't stand spooning there," cried Lady Mariamne, "but do what I tell you. Do you think I should ever have put myself into this position but for you?"

"You would never have been asked here if they had consulted me. I knew what a nuisance you'd be. Here, get this lady something to eat, old man," said the bridegroom, tapping Mr. Tatham on the back, who did, indeed, look rather like a waiter from that point of view.

"I shall have to help myself," said the lady in despair. And she sat down at the elaborate table in the bride's place and began to hack at the chicken. The gentlemen coming in at the moment roared again with laughter over the Jew's impatience; but it was not regarded with the same admiration by the rest of the guests.

These little incidents, perhaps, helped to wile away the weary hours until it was time for the bridal pair to depart. Mrs. Dennistoun was so angry that it kept up a little fire, so to speak, in her heart when the light of her house was extinguished. Lady Mariamne, standing in the porch with a bag full of rice to throw, kept up the spirit of the mistress of the house, which otherwise might, perhaps, have failed her altogether at that inconceivable moment; for though she had been looking forward to it for months it was inconceivable when it came, as death is inconceivable. Elinor going away!—not on a visit, or to be back in a week, or a month, or a year—going away for ever! ending, as might be said, when she put her foot on the step of the carriage. Her mother stood by and looked on with that cruel conviction that overtakes all at the last. Up to this moment had it not seemed as if the course of affairs was unreal, as if something must happen to prevent it? Perhaps the world will end to-night, as the lover says in the "Last Ride." But now here was the end: nothing had happened, the world was swinging on in space in its old careless way, and Elinor was going—going away for ever and ever. Oh, to come back, perhaps—there was nothing against that—but never the same Elinor. The mother stood looking, with her hand over her eyes to shield them from the sun. Those eyes were quite dry, and she stood firm and upright by the carriage door. She was not "breaking down" or "giving way," as everybody feared. She was "bearing up," as everybody was relieved to see. And in a moment it was all over, and there was nothing before her eyes—no carriage, no Elinor. She was so dazed that she stood still, looking with that strange kind of smile for a full minute after there was nothing to smile at, only the vacant air and the prospect of the combe, coming in in a sickly haze which existed only in her eyes.

But, by good luck, there was Lady Mariamne behind, and the fire of indignation giving a red flicker upon the desolate hearth.

"I caught Phil on the nose," said that lady, in great triumph; "spoilt his beauty for him for to-day. But let's hope she won't mind. She thinks him beautiful, the little goose. Oh, my Puggy-wuggy, did that cruel Algy pull your little, dear tail, you darling? Come to oos own mammy, now those silly wedding people are away."

"Your little dog, I presume, is of a very rare sort," said Mr. Tatham, to be civil. He had proposed the bride and bridegroom's health in a most appropriate speech, and he felt that he had deserved well of his kind, which made him more amiable even than usual. "Your ladyship's little dog," he added, after a moment, as she did not take any notice, "I presume, is of a rare kind?"

Lady Mariamne gave him a look, or rather a stare. "Is Puggy

of a rare sort?" she said over her shoulder, to one of the attendant tribe.

"Don't be such a duffer, Jew! You know as well as any one what breed he's of," Harry Compton said.

"Oh, I forgot," said the fine lady. She was standing full in front of the entrance, keeping Mrs. Dennistoun in the full sun outside. "I hope there's a train very soon," she said. "Did you look, Algy, as I told you? If it hadn't been that Phil would have killed me I should have gone now. It would have been such fun to have spied upon the turtle doves!"

The men thought it would have been rare fun with obedient delight, but that Phil would have cut up rough, and made a scene. At this Lady Mariamne held up her finger, and made a portentous face.

"Oh, you naughty, naughty boy," she cried, "telling tales out of school."

"Perhaps, my dear lady," said Mr. Tatham, quietly, "you would let Mrs. Dennistoun pass."

"Oh!" said Lady Mariamne, and stared at him again for half a minute; then she turned and stared at the tall lady in grey satin. "Anybody can pass," she said: "I'm not so very big."

"That is quite true—quite true. There is plenty of room," said the little gentleman, holding out his hand to his cousin.

"My dear John," said Mrs. Dennistoun, "I am sure you will be kind enough to lend your carriage again to Lady Mariamne, who is in a hurry to get away. There is another train, which stops at Downforth station, in half an hour, and there will just be time to get there, if you will order it at once. I told your man to be in readiness: and it would be a thousand pities to lose this train, for there is not another for an hour."

"By Jove, Jew! there's a slap in the face for you," said, in an audible whisper, one of the train, who had been standing in front of all the friends, blocking out the view. As for Lady Mariamne, she stared more straight than ever into Mrs. Dennistoun's eyes, but for the moment did not seem to find anything to say. She was left in the hall with her band while the mistress of the house went into the drawing-room, followed by all the country ladies, who had not lost a word, and who were already whispering to each other over that terrible betrayal about the temper of Phil.

"Cut up rough! Oh! poor little Elinor, poor little Elinor!" the ladies said to each other under their breath.

"I am not at all surprised. It is not any news to me. You could see it in his eyes," said Miss Mary Dale. And then they all were silent to listen to the renewed laughter that came bursting from the hall. Mrs. Hudson questioned her husband afterwards as to what it was that made everybody laugh, but the Rector had not much to say. "I really could not tell you, my dear," he said. "I don't remember anything that was said—but it seemed funny somehow, and as they all laughed one had to laugh too."

The great lady came in, however, dragged by her brother to say good-by. "It has all gone off very well, I am sure, and Nell looked very nice, and did you great credit," she said, putting out her hand. "And it's very kind of you to take so much trouble to get us off by the first train."

"Oh, it is no trouble," Mrs. Dennistoun said.

"Shouldn't you like to say good-by to Puggy-muggy?" said Lady Mariamne, touching the little black nose upon her arm. "He enjoyed that *pâté* so much. He really never has *foie gras* at home: but he doesn't at all mind if you would like to give him a little kiss just here."

"Good-by, Lady Mariamne," said Mrs. Dennistoun, with one of the curtseys of the old school. But there was another gust of laughter as Lady Mariamne was placed in the carriage, and a shrill little trumpet gave forth the satisfaction of the departing guest at having "got a rise out of the old girl." The gentlemen heaped themselves into Mr. Tatham's carriage, and swept off along with her, all but civil Harry, who waited to make their apologies, and to put up along with his own Dick Bolsover's "things." And thus the bridegroom's party, the new associates of Elinor, the great family into which the Honourable Mrs. Phil Compton had been so lucky as to marry, to the great excitement of all the country round, departed and was seen no more. Harry, who was civil, walked home with the Hudsons when all was over, and said the best he could for the Jew and her friends. "You see, she has been regularly spoiled: and then when a girl's so dreadful shy, as often as not it sounds like impudence." "Dear me, I should never have thought Lady Mariamne was shy," the gentle Rector said. "That's just how it is," said Harry. He went over again in the darkening to take his leave of Mrs. Dennistoun. He found her sitting out in the garden before the open door, looking down the misty walk. The light had gone out of the skies, but the usual cheerful lights had not yet appeared in the house, where the hum of a great occasion still reigned. The Tathams were at the Rectory, and Mrs. Dennistoun was alone. Harry Compton had a good heart, and though he could not conceive the possibility of a woman not being glad to have married her daughter, the loneliness and darkness touched him a little in contrast with the gayety of the previous night. "You must think us a dreadful noisy lot," he said, "and as if my sister had no sense. But it's only the Jew's way. She's made like that—and at bottom she's not at all a bad sort."

"Are you going away?" was all the answer that Mrs. Dennistoun made.

"Oh, yes, and we shall be a good riddance," said Harry; "but please don't think any worse of us than you can help——Phil—well, he's got a great deal of good in him—he has indeed, and she'll bring it all out."

It was very good of Harry Compton. He had a little choking in his throat as he walked back. "Blest if I ever thought of it in that light before," he said to himself.

But I doubt if what he said, however well meant, brought much comfort to Mrs. Dennistoun's heart.

CHAPTER XVII.

Thus Elinor Dennistoun disappeared from Windyhill and was no more seen. There are many ways in which a marriage is almost like a death, especially when the marriage is that of an only child. The young go away, the old remain. There is all the dreary routine of the solitary life unbrightened by that companionship which is all the world to the one who is left behind. So little—only the happy going away into brighter scenes of one whose happiness was the whole thought of that dreary survivor at the chimney corner—and yet so much. And if that survivor is a woman she has to smile and tell her neighbours of the bride's happiness, and how great the comfort to herself that her Elinor's life is assured, and her own ending is now of no particular importance to her daughter; if it is a man, he is allowed to lament, which is a curious paradox, but one of the many current in this world. Mrs. Dennistoun had to put a very brave face upon it all the more because of the known unsatisfactoriness of Elinor's husband: and she had to go on with her life, and sit down at her solitary meals, and invent lonely occupations for herself, and read and read, till her brains were often dazed by the multiplicity of the words, which lost their meaning as she turned over page by page. To sit alone in the house, without a sound audible, except perhaps the movement of the servants going up-stairs or down to minister to the wants, about which she felt she cared nothing whether they were ministered to or not, of their solitary mistress, where a little while ago there used to be the rhythm of the one quick step, the sound of the one gay voice which made the world a warm inhabited place to Mrs. Dennistoun—this was more dismal than words could say. To be sure, there were some extraordinary and delightful differences; there were the almost daily letters, which afforded the lonely mother all the pleasure that life could give; and there was always the prospect, or at least possibility and hope, of seeing her child again. Those two particulars, it need scarcely be said, make a difference which is practically infinite: but yet for Mrs. Dennistoun, sitting alone all the day and night, walking alone, reading alone, with little to do that was of the slightest consequence, not even the reading—for what did it matter to her dreary, lonely consciousness whether she kept afloat of general literature or improved her mind or not? this separation by marriage was dreadfully like the dreary separation by death, and in one respect it was almost worse; for death, if it reaches our very hearts, takes away at least the gnawing pangs of anxiety. He or she who is gone that way is well; never more can trouble touch them, their feet cannot err nor their hearts ache; while who can tell what troubles and miseries may be befalling, out there in the unknown, the child who has embarked upon the troubled sea of mortal life?

And it may be imagined with what anxious eyes those letters, which made all the difference, were read; how the gradually changing tone in them was noted as it came in, slowly but also surely. Sometimes they got to be very hurried, and then Mrs. Dennistoun saw as in a glass the impatient husband waiting, wondering what she could constantly find to say to her mother; sometimes they were long and detailed, and that meant, as would appear perhaps by a phrase slurred over in the postscript, that Phil had gone away somewhere. There was never a complaint in them, never a word that could be twisted into a complaint: but the anxious mother read between the lines innumerable things, not half of them true. There is perhaps never a half true of what anxiety may imagine: but then the half that is true!

John Tatham was very faithful to her during that winter. As soon as he came back from Switzerland, at the end of the long vacation, he went down to see her, feeling the difference in the house beyond anything he had imagined, feeling as if he were stepping into some darkened outer chamber of the grave: but with a cheerful face and eager but confident interest in "the news from Elinor." "Of course she is enjoying herself immensely," he said, and Mrs. Dennistoun was able to reply with a smile that was a little wistful, that yes, Elinor was enjoying herself immensely. "She seems very happy, and everything is new to her and bright," she said. They were both very glad that Elinor was happy, and they were very cheerful themselves. Mrs. Dennistoun truly cheered by his visit and by the necessity for looking after everything that John might be comfortable, and the pleasure of seeing his face opposite to her at table. "You can't think what it is to see you there; sitting down to dinner is the most horrible farce when one is alone." "Poor aunt!" John Tatham said: and nobody would believe how many Saturdays and Sundays he gave up to her during the long winter. Somehow he himself did not care to go anywhere else. In Elinor's time he had gone about freely enough, liking a little variety in his Saturday to Mondays, though always happiest when he went to Windyhill: but now somehow the other houses seemed to pall upon him. He liked best to go down to that melancholy house which his presence made more or less bright, where there was an endless talk of Elinor, where she was, what she was doing, and what was to be her next move, and, at last, when she was coming to town. Mrs. Dennistoun did not say, as she did at first, "when she is coming home." That possibility seemed to slip away somehow, and no one suggested it. When she was coming to town, that was what they said between themselves. She had spent the spring on the Riviera, a great part of it at Monte Carlo, and her letters were full of the beauty of the place; but she said less and less about people, and more and more about the sea and the mountains, and the glorious road which gave at every turn a new and beautiful vision of the hills and the sea. It was a little like a guide-book, they sometimes felt, but neither said it; but at last it became certain that in the month of May she was coming to town.

More than that, oh, more than that! One evening in May,

when it was fine but a little chilly, when Mrs. Dennistoun was walking wistfully in her garden, looking at the moon shining in the west, and wondering if her child had arrived in England, and whether she was coming to a house of her own, or a lodging, or to be a visitor in some one else's house, details which Elinor had not given—her ear was suddenly caught by the distant rumbling of wheels, heavy wheels, the fly from the station certainly. Mrs. Dennistoun had no expectation of what it could be, no sort of hope: and yet a woman has always a sort of hope when her child lives and everything is possible. The fly seemed to stop, not coming up the little cottage drive; but by and by, when she had almost given up hoping, there came a rush of flying feet, and a cry of joy, and Elinor was in her mother's arms. Elinor! yes, it was herself, no vision, no shadow such as had many a time come into Mrs. Dennistoun's dreams, but herself in flesh and blood, the dear familiar figure, the face which, between the twilight and those ridiculous tears which come when one is too happy, could scarcely be seen at all. "Elinor, Elinor! it is you, my darling!" "Yes, mother, it is me, really me. I could not write, because I did not know till the last minute whether I could get away."

It may be imagined what a coming home that was. Mrs. Dennistoun, when she saw her daughter even by the light of the lamp, was greatly comforted. Elinor was looking well; she was changed in that indescribable way in which marriage changes (though not always) the happiest woman. And her appearance was changed; she was no longer the country young lady very well dressed and looking as well as any one could in her carefully made clothes. She was now a fashionable young woman, about whose dresses there was no question, who wore everything as those do who are at the fountain-head, no matter what it was she wore. Mrs. Dennistoun's eyes caught this difference at once, which is also indescribable to the uninitiated, and a sensation of pride came into her mind. Elinor was improved, too, in so many ways. Her mother had never thought of calling her anything more, even in her inmost thoughts, than very pretty, very sweet;

179

but it seemed to Mrs. Dennistoun now as if people might use a stronger word, and call Elinor beautiful. Her face had gained a great deal of expression, though it was always an expressive face; her eyes looked deeper; her manner had a wonderful youthful dignity. Altogether, it was another Elinor, yet, God be praised, the same.

It was but for one night, but that was a great deal, a night subtracted from the blank, a night that seemed to come out of the old times—those old times that had not been known to be so very happy till they were over and gone. Elinor had naturally a great deal to tell her mother, but in the glory of seeing her, of hearing her voice, of knowing that it was actually she who was speaking, Mrs. Dennistoun did not observe, what she remembered afterwards, that again it was much more of places than of people that Elinor talked, and that though she named Phil when there was any occasion for doing so, she did not babble about him as brides do, as if he were altogether the sun, and everything revolved round him. It is not a good sign, perhaps, when the husband comes down to his "proper place" as the representative of the other half of the world too soon. Elinor looked round upon her old home with a mingled smile and sigh. Undoubtedly it had grown smaller, perhaps even shabbier, since she went away: but she did not say so to her mother. She cried out how pretty it was, how delightful to come back to it! and that was true too. How often it happens in this life that there are two things quite opposed to each other, and yet both of them true.

"John will be delighted to hear that you have come, Elinor," her mother said.

"John, dear old John! I hope he is well and happy, and all that; and he comes often to see you, mother? How sweet of him! You must give him ever so much love from his poor Nelly. I always keep that name sacred to him."

"But why should I give him messages as if you were not sure to meet? of course you will meet—often."

"Do you think so?" said Elinor. She opened her eyes a little in surprise, and then shook her head. "I am afraid not, mamma. We are in two different worlds."

"I assure you," said Mrs. Dennistoun, "John is a very rising man. He is invited everywhere."

"That I don't doubt at all."

"And why then shouldn't you meet?"

"I don't know. I don't fancy we shall go to the same places. John has a profession; he has something to do. Now you know we have nothing to do."

She laughed and laid a little emphasis on the *we*, by way of taking off the weight of the words.

"I always thought it was a great pity, Elinor."

"It may be a pity or not," said Elinor, "but it is, and it cannot be helped. We have got to make up our minds to it. I would rather Phil did nothing than mixed himself up with companies. Thank heaven, at present he is free of anything of that kind."

"I hope he is free of that one at least, that he was going to invest all your money in, Elinor. I hope you found another investment that was quite steady and safe."

"Oh, I suppose so," said Elinor, with some of her old petulance: "don't let us spoil the little time I have by talking about money, mamma!"

And then it was that Mrs. Dennistoun noticed that what Elinor did talk of, hurrying away from this subject, were things of not the least importance—the olive woods on the Riviera, the wealth of flowers, the strange little old towns upon the hills. Surely even the money, which was her own and for her comfort, would be a more interesting subject to discuss. Perhaps Elinor herself perceived this, for she began immediately to ask questions about the Hudsons and Hills, and all the people of the parish, with much eagerness of questioning, but a flagging interest in the replies, as her mother soon saw. "And Mary Dale, is she still there?" she asked. Mrs. Dennistoun entered into a little history of how Mary Dale had gone away to nurse a distant cousin who had been ill, and finally had died and left a very comfortable little fortune to her kind attendant. Elinor listened with little nods and appropriate exclamations, but before the evening was out asked again, "And Mary Dale?" then hastily corrected herself with an "Oh, I remember! you told me." But it was perhaps safer not to question her how much she remembered of what she had been told.

Thus there were notes of disquiet in even that delightful evening, such a contrast as it was to all the evenings since she had left home. Even when John came, what a poor substitute for Elinor! The ingratitude of those whose heart is set on one object made Mrs. Dennistoun thus make light of what had been her great consolation. He was very kind, very good, and oh, how glad she had been to see him through that heavy winter—but he was not Elinor! It was enough for Elinor to step across her mother's threshold to make Mrs. Dennistoun feel that there was no substitute for her—none: and that John was of no more consequence than the Rector or any habitual caller. But, at the same time, in all the melody of the home-coming, in the sweetness of Elinor's voice, and look, and kiss, in the perfection of seeing her there again in her own place, and listening to her dear step running up and down the no longer silent house, there were notes of disquiet which could not be mistaken. She was not unhappy, the mother thought; her eyes could not be so bright, nor her colour so fair unless she was happy. Trouble does not embellish, and Elinor was embellished. But yet—there were notes of disquiet in the air.

Next day Mrs. Dennistoun drove her child to the railway in order not to lose a moment of so short a visit, and naturally, though she had received that unexpected visit with rapture, feeling that a whole night of Elinor was worth a month, a year of anybody else, yet now that Elinor was going she found it very short. "You'll come again soon, my darling?" she said, as she stood at the window of the carriage ready to say good-bye.

"Whenever I can, mother dear, of that you may be sure; whenever I can get away."

"I don't wish to draw you from your husband. Don't get away—come with Philip from Saturday to Monday. Give him my love, and tell him so. He shall not be bored; but Sunday is a day without engagements."

"Oh, not now, mamma. There are just as many things to do on Sundays as on any other day."

There were a great many words on Mrs. Dennistoun's lips, but she did not say them; all she did say was, "Well, then, Elinor—when you can get away."

"Oh, you need not doubt me, mamma." And the train, which sometimes lingers so long, which some people that very day were swearing at as so slow, "Like all country trains," they said—that inevitable heartless thing got into motion, and Mrs. Dennistoun watched it till it disappeared; and—what was that that came over Elinor's face as she sank back into the corner of her carriage, not knowing her mother's anxious look followed her still—what was it? Oh, dreadful, dreadful life! oh, fruitless love and longing!—was it relief? The mother tried to get that look out of her mind as she drove silently and slowly home, creeping up hill after hill. There was no need to hurry. All that she was going to was an empty and silent house, where nobody awaited her. What was that look on Elinor's face? Relief! to have it over, to get away again, away from her old home and her fond mother, away to her new life. Mrs. Dennistoun was not a jealous mother nor unreasonable. She said to herself—Well! it was no doubt a trial to the child to come back—to come alone. All the time, perhaps, she was afraid of being too closely questioned, of having to confess that *he* did not want to come, perhaps grudged her coming. She might be afraid that her mother would divine something—some hidden opposition, some dislike, perhaps, on his part. Poor Elinor! and when everything had passed over so well, when it was ended, and nothing had been between them but love and mutual understanding, what wonder if there came over her dear face a look of relief! This was how this good woman, who had seen a great many things in her passage through life, explained her child's look: and though she was sad was not angry, as many less tolerant and less far-seeing might have been in her place.

John, that good John, to whom she had been so ungrateful, came down next Saturday, and to him she confided her great news, but not all of it. "She came down—alone?" he said.

"Well," said Mrs. Dennistoun, bravely; "she knew very well it was her I wanted to see, and not Philip. They say a great deal about mothers-in-law, but why shouldn't we in our turn have our fling at sons-in-law, John? It was not him I wanted to see: it was my own child: and Elinor understood that, and ran off by herself. Bless her for the thought."

"I understand that," said John. He had given the mother more than one look as she spoke, and divined her better than she supposed. "Oh, yes, I can understand that. The thing I don't understand is why he let her; why he wasn't too proud to bring her back to you, that you might see she had taken no harm. If it had been I——"

"Ah, but it was not you," said Mrs. Dennistoun; "you forget that. It never could have been you."

He looked quickly at her again, and it was on his lips to ask, "Why could it never have been I?" but he did not; for he knew that if it had ever been him, it could not have been for years. He was too prudent, and Elinor, even if she had escaped Phil Compton, would have met some one else. He had no right to say, or even think, what, in the circumstances, he would have done. He did not make any answer, but she understood him as he understood her.

And later in the evening she asked his advice as to what she should do. "I am not fond of asking advice," she said, "and I don't think there is another in the world I would ask it from but you. What should I do? It would cost me nothing to run up to town for a part of the season at least. I might get a little house, and be near her, where she could come to me when she pleased. Should I do it, or would it be wise not to do it? I don't want to spy upon her or to force her to tell me more than she wishes. John, my dear, I will tell you what I would tell no one else. I caught a glimpse of her dear face when the train was just going out of sight, and she was sinking back in her corner with a look of relief——"

"Of relief!" he cried.

"John, don't form any false impression! it was no want of love: but I think she was thankful to have seen me, and to have satisfied me, and that I had asked no questions that she could not answer—in a way."

John clenched his fist, but he dared not make any gesture of disgust, or suggest again, "If it had been I."

"Well, now," she said, "remember I am not angry—fancy being angry with Elinor!—and all I mean is for her benefit. Should I go? it might be a relief to her to run into me whenever she pleased; or should I not go? lest she might think I was bent on finding out more than she chose to tell?"

"Wouldn't it be right that you should find out?"

"That is just the point upon which I am doubtful. She is not unhappy, for she is—she is prettier than ever she was, John. A girl does not get like that—her eyes brighter, her colour clearer, looking—well, beautiful!" cried the mother, her eyes filling with bright tears, "if she is unhappy. But there may be things that are not quite smooth, that she might think it would make me unhappy to know, yet that if let alone might come all right. Tell me, John, what should I do?"

And they sat debating thus till far on in the night.

CHAPTER XVIII.

Mrs. Dennistoun did not go up to town. There are some women who would have done so, seeing the other side of the subject—at all hazards; and perhaps they would have been right—who can tell? She did not—denying herself, keeping herself by main force in her solitude, not to interfere with the life of her child, which was drawn on lines so different from any of hers—and perhaps she was wrong. Who knows, except by the event, which is the best or the worst way in any of our human movements, which are so short-sighted? And twice during the season Elinor found means to come to the cottage for a night as she had done at first. These were occasions of great happiness, it need not be said—but of many thoughts and wonderings too. She had always an excuse for Phil. He had meant until the last moment to come with her—some one had turned up, quite unexpectedly, who had prevented him. It was a fatality; especially when she came down in July did she insist upon this. He had been invited quite suddenly to a political dinner to meet one of the Ministers from whom he had hopes of an appointment. "For we find that we can't go on enjoying ourselves for ever," she said gayly, "and Phil has made up his mind he must get something to do."

"It is always the best way," said Mrs. Dennistoun.

"I am not so very sure, mamma, when you have never been used to it. Of course, some people would be wretched without work. Fancy John with nothing to do! How he would torment his wife—if he had one. But Phil never does that. He is very easy to live with. He is always after something, and leaves me as free as if he had a day's work in an office."

This slipped out, with a smile: but evidently after it was said

Elinor regretted she had said it, and thought that more might be drawn from the admission than she intended. She added quietly, "Of course a settled occupation would interfere with many things. We could not go out together continually as we do now."

Was there any way of reconciling these two statements? Mrs. Dennistoun tried and tried in vain to make them fit into each other: and yet no doubt there was some way.

"And perhaps another season, mother, if Phil was in a public office—it seems so strange to think of Phil having an office—you might come up, don't you think, to town for a time? Would it be a dreadful bore to you to leave the country just when it is at its best? I'm afraid it would be a dreadful bore: but we could run about together in the mornings when he was busy, and go to see the pictures and things. How pleasant it would be!"

"It would be delightful for me, Elinor. I shouldn't mind giving up the country, if it wouldn't interfere with your engagements, my dear."

"Oh, my engagements! Much I should care for them if Phil was occupied. I like, of course, to be with him."

"Of course," said Mrs. Dennistoun.

"And it is good for him, too, I think." This was another of the little admissions that Elinor regretted the moment they were made. "I mean it's a pity, isn't it, when a man likes to have his wife with him that she shouldn't always be there, ready to go?"

"A great pity," said Mrs. Dennistoun, and then she changed the subject. "I thought it required all sorts of examinations and things for a man to get into a public office now."

"So it does for the ordinary grades, which would be far, far too much routine for Phil. But they say a minister always has things in his power. There are still posts——"

"Sinecures, Elinor?"

"I did not mean exactly sinecures," she said, with an embarrassed laugh, "though I think those must have been fine things; but posts where it is not merely routine, where a man may have a chance of acting for himself and distinguishing himself, perhaps. And to be in the service of the country is always better, safer, than that dreadful city. Don't you think so?"

"I have never thought the city dreadful, Elinor. I have had many friends connected with the city."

"Ah, but not in those horrid companies, mamma. Do you know that company which we just escaped, which Phil saved my money out of, when it was all but invested—I believe that has ruined people right and left. He got out of it, fortunately, just before the smash; that is, of course, he never had very much to do with it, he was only on the Board."

"And where is your money now?"

"Oh, I can answer that question this time," said Elinor, gayly. "He had just time to get it into another company which pays—beautifully! The Jew is in it, too, and the whole lot of them. Oh! I beg your pardon, mamma. I tried hard to call her by her proper name, but when one never hears any other, one can't help getting into it!"

"I hope," said Mrs. Dennistoun, "that Philip was not much mixed up with this company if other people have been ruined, and he has escaped?"

"How could that be?" said Elinor, with a sort of tremulous dignity. "You don't suppose for a moment that he——. But of course you don't," she added with a heightened colour and a momentary cloud over her eyes, "of course you don't. There was a dreadful manager who destroyed the books and then fled, so that there never could be a right winding up of the affairs."

"I hope Philip will take great care never to have to do with anything of the kind again."

"Oh, no, he has promised me he will not. I will not have it. He has a kind of ornamental directorship on this new company, just for the sake of his name: but he has promised me he will have nothing more to do with it for my peace of mind."

"I wonder that they should care in the city for so small a matter as a peer's younger son."

"Oh, do you think it a small matter, mamma? I don't mean

that I care, but people give a good deal of weight to it, you know."

"I meant only in the city, Elinor."

"Oh!" Elinor said. She was half offended with her mother's indifference. She had found that to be the Hon. Mrs. Compton was something, or so at least she supposed: and she began timidly to give her mother a list of her engagements, which were indeed many in number, and there were some dazzling names among a great many with which Mrs. Dennistoun was unacquainted. But how could she know who were the fashionable people nowadays, a woman living so completely out of the world?

John Tatham, for his part, went through his engagements that year with a constant expectation of seeing Elinor, which preoccupied him more than a rising young barrister going everywhere ought to have been preoccupied. He thought he went everywhere, and so did his family at home, especially his sister, Mary Tatham, who was his father's nurse and attendant, and never had any chance of sharing these delights. She made all the more, as was natural, of John's privileges and social success from the fact of her own seclusion, and was in the habit of saying that she believed there was scarcely a party in London to which John was not invited—three or four in a night. But it would seem with all this that there were many parties to which he was not invited, for the Phil Comptons (how strange and on the whole disgusting to think that this now meant Elinor!) also went everywhere, and yet they very seldom met. It was true that John could not expect to meet them at dinner at a Judge's or in the legal society in high places which was his especial sphere, and nothing could be more foolish than the tremor of expectation with which this very steady-going man would set out to every house in which the fashionable world met with the professional, always thinking that perhaps——But it was rarely, very rarely, that this perhaps came to pass. When it did it was amid the crowd of some prodigious reception to which people "looked in" for half an hour, and where on one occasion he found Elinor alone, with that curious dignity about her, a little tragical, which comes of neglect. He agreed with her mother, that he had never imagined Elinor's youthful prettiness could have come to anything so near beauty. There was a strained, wide open look in her eyes, which was half done by looking out for some one, and half by defying any one to think that she felt herself alone, or was pursuing that search with any anxiety. She stood exceedingly erect, silent, observing everything, yet endeavouring to appear as if she did not observe, altogether a singular and very striking figure among the fashionable crowd, in which it seemed everybody was chattering, smiling, gay or making believe to be gay, except herself. When she saw John a sudden gleam of pleasure, followed by a cloud of embarrassment, came over her face: but poor Elinor could not help being glad to see some one she knew, some one who more or less belonged to her; although it appeared she had the best of reasons for being alone. "I was to meet Phil here," she said, "but somehow I must have missed him." "Let us walk about a little, and we'll be sure to find him," said John. She was so glad to take his arm, almost to cling to him, to find herself with a friend. "I don't know many people here," she confided to John, leaning on his arm, with the familiar sisterly dependence of old, "and I am so stupid about coming out by myself. It is because I have never been used to it. There has always been mamma, and then Phil; but I suppose he has been detained somewhere to-night. I think I never felt so lost before, among all these strange people. He knows everybody, of course."

"But you have a lot of friends, Elinor."

"Oh, yes," she said, brightly enough; "in our own set: but this is what Phil calls more serious than our set. I should not wonder in the least if he had shirked it at the last, knowing I would be sure to come."

"That is just the reason why I should have thought he would not shirk it," said John.

"Ah, that's because you're not married," said Elinor, but with a laugh in which there was no bitterness. "Don't you know one good of a wife is to do the man's social duties for him, to appear at the dull places and save his credit? Oh, I don't object at all; it is quite a legitimate division of labour. I shall get into it in time: but I am so stupid about coming into a room alone, and instead of looking about to see what people I really do know, I just stiffen into a sort of shell. I should never have known you if you had not come up to me, John."

"You see I was looking out for you, and you were not looking out for me, that makes all the difference."

"You were looking out for us!"

"Ever since the season began I have been looking out for you, everywhere," said John, with a rather fierce emphasis on the pronoun, which, however, as everybody knows, is plural, and means two as much as one, though it was the reverse of this that John Tatham meant to show.

"Ah!" said Elinor. "But then I am afraid our set is different, John. There will always be some places—like this, for instance—where I hope we shall meet; but our set perhaps is a little frivolous, and your set a little—serious, don't you see? You are professional and political, and all that; and Phil is—well, I don't know exactly what Phil is—more fashionable and frivolous, as I said. A race-going, ball-going, always in motion set."

"Most people," said John, "go more or less to races and balls."

"More or less, that makes the whole difference. We go to them all. Now you see the distinction, John. You go to Ascot perhaps on the cup day; we go all the days and all the other days, at the other places."

"How knowing you have become!"

"Haven't I?" she said, with a smile that was half a sigh.

"But I shouldn't have thought that would have suited you, Elinor."

"Oh, yes, it does," she said, and then she eyed him with something of the defiance that had been in her look when she was standing alone. She did not avoid his look as a less brave woman might have done. "I like the fun of it," she said.

And then there was a pause, for he did not know what to reply.

"We have been through all the rooms," she said at last, "and we have not seen a ghost of Phil. He cannot be coming now. What o'clock is it? Oh, just the time he will be due at—— I'm sure he can't come now. Do you think you could get my carriage for me? It's only a brougham that we hire," she said, with a smile, "but the man is such a nice, kind man. If he had been an old family coachman he couldn't take more care of me."

"That looks as if he had to take care of you often, Elinor."

"Well," she said, looking him full in the face again, "you don't suppose my husband goes out with me in the morning shopping? I hope he has something better to do."

"Shouldn't you like to have your mother with you for the shopping, etc.?"

"Ah, dearly!" then with a little quick change of manner, "another time—not this season, but next, if I can persuade her to come; for next year I hope we shall be more settled, perhaps in a house of our own, if Phil gets the appointment he is after."

"Oh, he is after an appointment?"

"Yes, John; Phil is not so lucky as to have a profession like you."

This was a new way of looking at the matter, and John Tatham found nothing to say. It seemed to him, who had worked very hard for it, a little droll to describe his possession of a profession as luck. But he made no remark. He took Elinor down-stairs and found her brougham for her, and the kind old coachman on the box, who was well used to taking care of her, though only hired from the livery stables for the season—John thought the old man looked suspiciously at him, and would have stopped him from accompanying her, had he designed any such proceeding. Poor little Nelly, to be watched over by the paternal fly-man on the box! she who might have had—— but he stopped himself there, though his heart felt as heavy as a stone to see her go away thus, alone from the smart party where she had been doing duty for her husband. John could not take upon himself to finish his sentence—she who might have had love and care of a very different kind. No, he had never offered her that love and care.

Had Phil Compton never come in her way it is possible that John Tatham might never have offered it to her—not, at least, for a long time. He could never have had any right to be a dog in the manger, neither would he venture to pretend now that it was her own fault if she had chosen the wrong man; was it his fault then, who had never put a better man within her choice? but John, who was no coxcomb, blushed in the dark to himself as this question flitted through his mind. He had no reason to suppose that Elinor would have been willing to change the brotherly tie between them into any other. Thank heaven for that brotherly tie! He would always be able to befriend her, to stand by her, to help her as much as any one could help a woman who was married, and thus outside of all ordinary succour. And as for that blackguard, that *dis*-Honourable Phil—— But here John, who was a man of just mind, paused again. For a man to let his wife go to a party by herself was not after all so dreadful a thing. Many men did so, and the women did not complain; to be sure they were generally older, more accustomed to manage for themselves than Elinor: but still, a man need not be a blackguard because he did that. So John stopped his own ready judgment, but still I am afraid in his heart pronounced Phil Compton's sentence all the same. He did not say a word about this encounter to Mrs. Dennistoun; at least, he did tell her that he had met Elinor at the So-and-So's, which, as it was one of the best houses in London, was pleasing to a mother to hear.

"And how was she looking?" Mrs. Dennistoun cried.

"She was looking—beautiful——" said John. "I don't flatter, and I never thought her so in the old times—but it is the only word I can use——"

"Didn't I tell you so?" said the mother, pleased. "She is quite embellished and improved—therefore she must be happy."

"It is certainly the very best evidence——"

"Isn't it? But it so often happens otherwise, even in happy marriages. A girl feels strange, awkward, out of it, in her new life. Elinor must have entirely accustomed herself, adapted herself to it, and to them, or she would not look so well. That is the greatest comfort I can have."

And John kept his own counsel about Elinor's majestic solitude and the watchful old coachman in the hired brougham. Her husband might still be full of love and tenderness all the same. It was a great effort of the natural integrity of his character to pronounce like this; but he did it in the interests of justice, and for Elinor's sake and her mother's said nothing of the circumstances at all.

It may be supposed that when Elinor paid the last of her sudden visits at the cottage it was a heavy moment both for mother and daughter. It was the time when fashionable people finish the season by going to Goodwood—and to Goodwood Elinor was going with a party, Lady Mariamne and a number of the "set." She told her mother, to amuse her, of the new dresses she had got for this important occasion. "Phil says one may go in sackcloth and ashes the remainder of the year, but we must be fine for Goodwood," she said. "I wanted him to believe that I had too many clothes already, but he was inexorable. It is not often, is it, that one's husband is more anxious than one's self about one's dress?"

"He wants you to do him credit, Elinor."

"Well, mamma, there is no harm in that. But more than that— he wants me to look nice, for myself. He thinks me still a little shy—though I never was shy, was I?—and he thinks nothing gives you courage like feeling yourself well dressed—but he takes the greatest interest in everything I wear."

"And where do you go after Goodwood, Elinor?"

"Oh, mamma, on such a round of visits!—here and there and everywhere. I don't know," and the tears sprang into Elinor's eyes, "when I may see you again."

"You are not coming back to London," said the mother, with the heart sinking in her breast.

"Not now—they all say London is insupportable—it is one of the things that everybody says, and I believe that Phil will not set foot in it again for many months. Perhaps I might get a moment, when he is shooting, or something, to run back to you; but it is a long way from Scotland—and he must be there, you know, for the 12th. He would think the world was coming to an end if he did not get a shot at the grouse on that day."

"But I thought he was looking for an appointment, Elinor?"

A cloud passed over Elinor's face. "The season is over," she said, "and all the opportunities are exhausted—and we don't speak of that any more."

She gave her mother a very close hug at the railway, and sat with her head partly out of the window watching her as she stood on the platform, until the train turned round the corner. No relief on her dear face now, but an anxious strain in her eyes to see her mother as long as possible. Mrs. Dennistoun, as she walked again slowly up the hills that the pony might not suffer, said to herself, with a chill at her heart, that she would rather have seen her child sinking back in the corner, pleased that it was over, as on the first day.

CHAPTER XIX.

The next winter was more dreary still and solitary than the first at Windyhill. The first had been, though it looked so long and dreary as it passed, full of hope of the coming summer, which must, it seemed, bring Elinor back. But now Mrs. Dennistoun knew exactly what Elinor's coming back meant, and the prospect was less cheering. Three days in the whole long season—three little escapades, giving so very little hope of more sustained intercourse to come. Mrs. Dennistoun, going over all the circumstances—she had so little else to do but to go over them in her long solitary evenings—came to the conclusion that whatever might happen, she herself would go to town when summer came again. She amused herself with thinking how she would find a little house—quite a small house, as there are so many—in a good situation, where even the most fashionable need not be ashamed to come, and where there would be room enough for Elinor and her husband if they chose to establish themselves there. Mrs. Dennistoun was of opinion, already expressed, that if mothers-in-law are obnoxious to men, sons-in-law are very frequently so to women, which is a point of view not popularly perceived. And Philip Compton was not sympathetic to her in any point of view. But still she made up her mind to endure him, and even his family, for the sake of Elinor. She planned it all out—it gave a little occupation to the vacant time—how they should have their separate rooms and even meals if that turned out most convenient; how she would interfere with none of their ways: only to have her Elinor under her roof, to have her when the husband was occupied—in the evenings, if there were any evenings that she spent alone; in the mornings, when perhaps

Phil got up late, or had engagements of his own; for the moment's freedom when her child should be free. She made up her mind that she would ask no questions, would never interfere with any of their habits, or oppose or put herself between them—only just to have a little of Elinor every day.

"For it will not be the same thing this year," she said to John, apologetically. "They have quite settled down into each other's ways. Philip must see I have no intention of interfering. For the most obdurate opponent of mothers-in-law could not think—could he, John?—that I had any desire to put myself between them, or make myself troublesome now."

"There is no telling," said John, "what such asses might think."

"But Philip is not an ass; and don't you think I have behaved very well, and may give myself this indulgence the second year?"

"I certainly think you will be quite right to come to town: but I should not have them to live with you, if I were you."

"Shouldn't you? It might be a risk: but then I shouldn't do it unless there was room enough to leave them quite free. The thing I am afraid of is that they wouldn't accept."

"Oh, Phil Compton will accept," said John, hurriedly.

"Why are you so sure? I think often you know more about him than you ever say."

"I don't know much about him, but I know that a man of uncertain income and not very delicate feelings is generally glad enough to have the expenses of the season taken off him: and even get all the more pleasure out of it when he has his living free."

"That's not a very elevated view to take of the transaction, John."

"My dear aunt, I did not think you expected anything very elevated from the Comptons. They are not the sort of family from which one expects——"

"And yet it is the family that my Elinor belongs to: she is a Compton."

"I did not think of that," said John, a little disconcerted. Then

197

he added, "There is no very elevated standard in such matters. Want of money has no law: and of course there are better things involved, for he might be very glad that Elinor should have her mother to go out with her, to stand by when—a man might have other engagements."

Mrs. Dennistoun looked at him closely and shook her head. She was not very much reassured by this view of the case. "At all events I shall try it," she said.

Quite early in the year, when she was expecting no such pleasure, she was rewarded for her patience by another flying visit from her child, who this time telegraphed to say she was coming, so that her mother could go and meet her at the station, and thus lose no moment of her visit. Elinor, however, was not in good spirits on this occasion, nor was she in good looks. She told her mother hurriedly that Phil had come up upon business; that he was very much engaged with the new company, getting far more into it than satisfied her. "I am terrified that another catastrophe may come, and that he might share the blame if things were to go wrong"—which was by no means a good preface for the mission with which it afterwards appeared Elinor herself was charged.

"Phil told me to say to you, mamma, that if you were not satisfied with any of your investments, he could help you to a good six or seven per cent.——"

She said this with her head turned away, gazing out of the window, contemplating the wintry aspect of the combe with a countenance as cloudy and as little cheerful as itself.

There was an outcry on Mrs. Dennistoun's lips, but fortunately her sympathy with her child was so strong that she felt Elinor's sentiments almost more forcibly than her own, and she managed to answer in a quiet, untroubled voice.

"Philip is very kind, my dear: but you know my investments are all settled for me and I have no will of my own. I get less interest, but then I have less responsibility. Don't you know I belong to the time in which women were not supposed to be good for anything, and consequently I am in the hands of my trustees."

"I think he foresaw that, mother," said Elinor, still with her head averted and her eyes far away; "but he thought you might represent to the trustees that not only would it give you more money, but it would be better in the end for me. Oh, how I hate to have to say this to you, mamma!"

How steadily Mrs. Dennistoun kept her countenance, though her daughter now flung herself upon her shoulder with uncontrollable tears!

"My darling, it is quite natural you should say it. You must tell Philip that I fear I am powerless. I will try, but I don't think anything will come of it. I have been glad to be free of responsibility, and I have never attempted to interfere."

"Mother, I am so thankful. I oughtn't to go against him, ought I? But I would not have you take his advice. It is so dreadful not to appear——"

"My dear, you must try to think that he understands better than you do: men generally do: you are only a girl, and they are trained more or less to business."

"Not Phil! not Phil!"

"Well, he must have some capacity for it, some understanding, or they would not want him on those boards; and you cannot have, Elinor, for you know nothing about it. To hear you speak of per cents. makes me laugh." It was a somewhat forlorn kind of laugh, yet the mother executed it finely: and by and by the subject dropped, and Elinor was turned to talk of other things—other things of which there was a great deal to say, and over which they cried and laughed together as nature bade.

In the same evening, the precious evening of which she did not like to waste a moment, Mrs. Dennistoun unfolded her plan for the season. "I feel that I know exactly the kind of house I want; it will probably be in some quiet insignificant place, a Chapel Street, or a Queen Street, or a Park Street somewhere, but in a good situation. You shall have the first floor all to yourself to receive your visitors, and if you think that Philip would prefer a separate table——"

"Oh, mamma, mamma!" cried Elinor, clinging to her, kissing passionately her mother's cheek, which was still as soft as a child's.

"It is not anything you have told me now that has put this into my head, my darling. I had made it all up in my own mind. Then, you know, when your husband is engaged with those business affairs—in the city—or with his own friends—you would have your mother to fall back upon, Elinor. I should have just the *moments perdus*, don't you see, when you were doing nothing else, when you were wanted for nothing else. I promise you, my darling, I should never be *de trop*, and would never interfere."

"Oh, mamma, mamma!" Elinor cried again as if words failed her; and so they did, for she said scarcely anything more, and evaded any answer. It went to her mother's heart, yet she made her usual excuses for it. Poor child, once so ready to decide, accepting or rejecting with the certainty that no opposition would be made to her will, but now afraid to commit herself, to say anything that her husband would not approve! Well! Mrs. Dennistoun said to herself, many a young wife is like that, and yet is happy enough. It depends so much on the man. Many a man adores his wife and is very good to her, and yet cannot bear that she should seem to settle anything without consulting his whim. And Philip Compton had never been what might be called an easy-going man. It was right of Elinor to give no answer till she knew what he would like. The dreadful thing was that she expressed no pleasure in her mother's proposal, scarcely looked as if she herself would like it, which was a thing which did give an unquestionable wound.

"Mamma," she said, as they were driving to the station, not in the pony carriage this time, but in the fly, for the weather was bad, "don't be vexed that I don't say more about your wonderful, your more than kind offer."

"Kind is scarcely a word to use, Elinor, between you and me."

"I know, I know, mamma—and I as good as refuse it, saying nothing. Oh, if I could tell you without telling you! I am so frightened—how can I say it?—that you should see things you would not approve!"

"My dear, I am of one generation and you are of another. I am an old woman, and your husband is a young man. But what does that matter? We can agree to differ. I will never thrust myself into his private affairs, and he——"

"Oh, mother, mother darling, it is not that," Elinor said. And she went away without any decision. But in a few days there came to Mrs. Dennistoun a letter from Philip himself, most nobly expressed, saying that Elinor had told him of her mother's kind offer, and that he hastened to accept it with the utmost gratitude and devotion. He had just been wondering, he wrote, how he was to muster all things necessary for Elinor, with the business engagements which were growing upon himself. Nobody could understand better than Nell's good mother how necessary it was that he should neglect no means of securing their position, and he had found that often he would have to leave his darling by herself: but this magnificent, this magnanimous offer on her part would make everything right. Need he say how gratefully he accepted it? Nell and he being on the spot would immediately begin looking out for the house, and when they had a list of three or four to look at he hoped she would come up to their rooms and select what she liked best. This response took away Mrs. Dennistoun's breath, for, to tell the truth, she had her own notions as to the house she wanted and as to the time to be spent in town, and would certainly have preferred to manage everything herself. But in this she had to yield, with thankfulness that in the main point she was to have her way.

Did she have her way? It is very much to be doubted whether in such a situation of affairs it would have been possible. The house that was decided upon was not one which she would have chosen for herself, neither would she have taken it from Easter to July. She had meant a less expensive place and a shorter season; but after all, what did that matter for once if it pleased Elinor? The worst of it was that she could not at all satisfy herself that it pleased Elinor. It pleased Philip, there was no doubt, but then it had not been intended except in a very secondary way to please him. And when the racket of the season began Mrs. Dennistoun had a good deal to bear. Philip, though he was supposed to be a man of business and employed in the city, got up about noon, which was dreadful to all her orderly country habits; the whole afternoon through there was a perpetual tumult of visitors, who, when by chance she encountered them in the hall or on the stairs, looked at her superciliously as if she were the landlady. The man who opened the door, and brushed Philip Compton's clothes, and was in his service, looked superciliously at her too, and declined to have anything to say to "the visitors for down-stairs." A noise of laughter and loud talk was (distinctly) in her ears from noon till late at night. When Philip came home, always much later than his wife, he was in the habit of bringing men with him, whose voices rang through the house after everybody was in bed. To be sure, there were compensations. She had Elinor often for an hour or two in the morning before her husband was up. She had her in the evenings when they were not going out, but these were few. As for Philip, he never dined at home. When he had no engagements he dined at his club, leaving Elinor with her mother. He gave Mrs. Dennistoun very little of his company, and when they did meet there was in his manner too a sort of reflection of the superciliousness of the "smart" visitors and the "smart" servant. She was to him, too, in some degree the landlady, the old lady down-stairs. Elinor, as was natural, redoubled her demonstrations of affection, her excuses and sweet words to make up for this neglect: but all the time there was in her mother's mind that dreadful doubt which assails us when we have committed ourselves to one act or another, "Was it wise? Would it not have been better to have denied herself and stayed away?" So far as self-denial went, it was more exercised in Curzon Street than it would have been at the Cottage. For she had to see many things that displeased her and to say no word; to guess at the tears, carefully washed away from Elinor's eyes, and to ask no questions, and to see what she could not but feel was the violent career downward, the rush that must lead to a catastrophe, but make no sign. There was one evening when Elinor, not looking well or feeling well, had stayed at home, Philip having a whole long list of engagements in hand; men's engagements, his wife explained, a stockbroking dinner, an adjournment to somebody's chambers, a prolonged sitting, which meant play, and a great deal of wine, and other attendant circumstances into which she did not enter. Elinor had no engagement for that night, and was free to be petted and fêted by her mother. She was put at her ease in a soft and rich dressing-gown, and the prettiest little dinner served, and the room filled with flowers, and everything done that used to be done when she was recovering from some little mock illness, some child's malady, just enough to show how dear above everything was the child to the mother, and with what tender ingenuity the mother could invent new delights for the child. These delights, alas! did not transport Elinor now as they once had done, and yet the repose was sweet, and the comfort of this nearest and dearest friend to lean upon something more than words could say.

On this evening, however, in the quiet of those still hours, poor Elinor's heart was opened, or rather her mouth, which on most occasions was closed so firmly. She said suddenly, in the midst of something quite different, "Oh, I wish Phil was not so much engaged with those dreadful city men."

"My dear!" said Mrs. Dennistoun, who was thinking of far other things; and then she said, "there surely cannot be much to fear in that respect. He is never in the city—he is never up, my dear, when the city men are doing their work."

"Ah," said Elinor, "I don't think that matters; he is in with them all the same."

"Well, Elinor, there is no reason that there should be any harm in it. I would much rather he had some real business in hand than be merely a butterfly of fashion. You must not entertain that horror of city men."

"The kind he knows are different from the kind you know, mamma."

"I suppose everything is different from what it was in my time: but it need not be any worse for that——"

"Oh, mother! you are obstinate in thinking well of everything; but sometimes I am so frightened, I feel as if I must do something dreadful myself—to precipitate the ruin which nothing I can do will stop——"

"Elinor, Elinor, this is far too strong language——"

"Mamma, he wants me to speak to you again. He wants you to give your money——"

"But I have told you already I cannot give it, Elinor."

"Heaven be praised for that! But he will speak to you himself, he will perhaps try to—bully you, mamma."

"Elinor!"

"It is horrible, what I say; yes, it is horrible, but I want to warn you. He says things——"

"Nothing that he can say will make me forget that he is your husband, Elinor."

"Ah, but don't think too much of that, mamma. Think that he doesn't know what he is doing—poor Phil, oh, poor Phil! He is hurried on by these people; and then it will break up, and the poor people will be ruined, and they will upbraid him, and yet he will not be a whit the better. He does not get any of the profit. I can see it all as clear—— And there are so many other things."

Mrs. Dennistoun's heart sank in her breast, for she too knew what were the other things. "We must have patience," she said; "he is in his hey-day, full of—high spirits, and thinking everything he touches must go right. He will steady down in time."

"Oh, I am not complaining," cried Elinor, hurriedly dashing her tears away; "if you were not a dreadfully good mamma, if you would grumble sometimes and find fault, that I might defend him! It is the sight of you there, seeing everything and not saying a word that is too much for me."

"Then I will grumble, Elinor. I will even say something to him for our own credit. He should not come in so late—at least when he comes in he should come in to rest and not bring men with him to make a noise. You see I can find fault as much as heart could desire. I am dreadfully selfish. I don't mind when he goes out now and then without you, for then I have you; but he should not bring noisy men with him to disturb the house in the middle of the night. I think I will speak to him——"

"No," said Elinor, with a clutch upon her mother's arm; "no, don't do that. He does not like to be found fault with. Unless in the case—if you were giving him that money, mother."

"Which I cannot do: and Elinor, my darling, which I would not do if I could. It is all you will have to rely upon, you and——"

"It would have been the only chance," said Elinor. "I don't say it would have been much of a chance. But he might have listened, if—— Oh, no, dear mother, no. I would not in my sober senses wish that you should give him a penny. It would do no good, but only harm. And yet if you had done it, you might have said—— and he might have listened to you for once——"

CHAPTER XX.

A few days after this Philip Compton came in, in the afternoon, to the little room down-stairs which Mrs. Dennistoun had made into a sitting-room for herself. Elinor had gone out with her sister-in-law, and her mother was alone. It was a very rare thing indeed for Mrs. Dennistoun's guest—who, indeed, was to all intents and purposes the master of the house, and had probably quite forgotten by this time that he was not in reality so—to pay a visit "down-stairs." "Down-stairs" had a distinct meaning in the Compton vocabulary. It was spoken of with significance, and with a laugh, as something half hostile, half ridiculous. It meant a sort of absurd criticism and inspection, as of some old crone sitting vigilant, spying upon everything—a mother-in-law. Phil's cronies thought it was the most absurd weakness on his part to let such an intruder get footing in his house. "You will never get rid of her," they said. And Phil, though he was generally quite civil to his wife's mother (being actually and at his heart more a gentleman than he had the least idea he was), did not certainly in any way seek her society. He scarcely ever dined at home, as has been said; when he had not an engagement—and he had a great many engagements—he found that he was obliged to dine at his club on the evenings when he might have been free; and as this was the only meal which was supposed to be common, it may be perceived that Phil had little means of meeting his mother-in-law; and that he should come to see her of his own free will was unprecedented. Phil Compton had not improved since his marriage. His nocturnal enjoyments, the noisy parties up-stairs in the middle of the night, had not helped to dissipate the effect of the anxieties of the city, which his wife so deplored. Mrs.

Dennistoun that very day, when she came down-stairs in the fresh summer morning to her early breakfast, had seen through an open door the room up-stairs which was appropriated to Phil, with a lamp still burning in the daylight, cards lying strewn about the floor, and all in that direful disorder which a room so occupied overnight shows in the clear eye of the day. The aspect of the room had given her a shock almost more startling than any moral certainty, as was natural to a woman used to all the decorums and delicacies of a well-ordered life. There is no sin in going late to bed, or even letting a lamp burn into the day; but the impression that such a sight makes even upon the careless is always greater than any mere apprehension by the mind of the midnight sitting, the eager game, the chances of loss and ruin. She had not been able to get that sight out of her eyes. Though on ordinary occasions she never entered Phil's rooms, on this she had stolen in to put out the lamp, with the sensation in her mind of destroying some evidence against him, which someone less interested than she might have used to his disadvantage. And she had sent up the housemaid to "do" the room, with an admonition. "I cannot have Mr. Compton's rooms neglected," she said. "The gentlemen is always so late," the housemaid said in self-defence. "I hears them let themselves out sometimes after we're all up down-stairs." "I don't want to hear anything about the gentlemen. Do your work at the proper time; that is all that is asked of you." Phil's servant appeared at the moment pulling on his coat, with the air of a man who has been up half the night— which, indeed, was the case, for "the gentlemen" when they came in had various wants that had to be supplied. "What's up now?" he said to the housemaid, within hearing of her mistress, casting an insolent look at the old lady, who belonged to "down-stairs." "She've been prying and spying about like they all do——" Mrs. Dennistoun had retreated within the shelter of her room to escape the end of this sentence, which still she heard, with the usual quickness of our faculties in such cases. She swallowed her simple breakfast with what appetite she might, and her stout spirit for the moment broke down before this insult which was ridiculous, she said to herself, from a saucy servant-man. What did it matter to her what Johnson did or said? But it was like the lamp burning in the sunshine: it gave a moral shock more sharp than many a thing of much more importance would have been capable of doing, and she had not been able to get over it all day.

It may be supposed, therefore, that it was an unfortunate moment for Phil Compton's visit. Mrs. Dennistoun had scarcely seen them that day, and she was sitting by herself, somewhat sick at heart, wondering if anything would break the routine into which their life was falling; or if this was what Elinor must address herself to as its usual tenor. It would be better in the country, she said to herself. It was only in the bustle of the season, when everybody of his kind was congregated in town, that it would be like this. In their rounds of visits, or when the whole day was occupied with sport, such nocturnal sittings would be impossible—and she comforted herself by thinking that they would not be consistent with any serious business in the city such as Elinor feared. The one danger must push away the other. He could not gamble at night in that way, and gamble in the other among the stockbrokers. They were both ruinous, no doubt, but they could not both be carried on at the same time— or so, at least, this innocent woman thought. There was enough to be anxious and alarmed about without taking two impossible dangers into her mind together.

And just then Phil knocked at her door. He came in smiling and gracious, and with that look of high breeding and *savoir faire* which had conciliated her before and which she felt the influence of now, although she was aware how many drawbacks there were, and knew that the respect which her son-in-law showed was far from genuine. "I never see you to have a chat," he said; "I thought I would take the opportunity to-day, when Elinor was out. I want you to tell me how you think she is."

"I think she is wonderfully well," said Mrs. Dennistoun.

"*Wonderfully* well—you mean considering—that there is too

much racket in her life?"

"Partly, I mean that—but, indeed, I meant it without condition; she is wonderfully well. I am surprised, often——"

"It is rather a racket of a life," said Phil.

"Too much, indeed—it is too much—for a woman who is beginning her serious life—but if you think that, it is a great thing gained, for you can put a stop to it, or moderate—'the pace' don't you call it?" she said, with a smile.

"Well, yes. I suppose we could moderate the pace—but that would mean a great deal for me. You see, when a man's launched it isn't always so easy to stop. Nell, of course, if you thought she wanted it—might go to the country with you."

Mrs. Dennistoun's heart gave a leap. "Might go to the country with you!" It seemed a glimpse of Paradise that burst upon her. But then she shook her head. "You know Elinor would not leave you, Philip."

"Well! she has a ridiculous partiality," he said, with a laugh, "though, of course, I'd make her—if it was really for her advantage," he added, after a moment; "you don't think I'd let that stand in her way."

"In the meantime," said Mrs. Dennistoun, with hesitation, "without proceeding to any such stringent measures—if you could manage to be a little less late at night."

"Oh, you listen for my coming in at night?"

His face took a sombre look, as if a cloud had come over it.

"I do not listen—for happily for me I have been asleep for hours. I generally jump up thinking the house is on fire at the sound of voices, which make listening quite unnecessary, Philip."

"Ah, yes, the fellows are rather noisy," he said, carelessly, "but Nell sleeps like a top, and pays no attention—which is the best thing she can do."

"I would not be too sure she slept like a top."

"It's true; women are all hypocrites alike. You never know when you have them," Phil said.

And then there was a pause; for she feared to say anything

more lest she should go too far; and he for once in his life was embarrassed, and did not know how to begin what he had to say.

"Well," he said, quickly, getting up, "I must be going. I have business in the city. And now that I find you're satisfied about Nell's health—— By the way, you never show in our rooms; though Nell spends every minute she has to spare here."

"I am a little old perhaps for your friends, Philip, and the room is not too large."

"Well, no," he said, "they are wretched little rooms. Good-by, then; I'm glad you think Nell is all right."

Was this all he meant to say? There was, however, an uncertainty about his step, and by the time he had opened the door he came to a pause, half closed it again, and said, "Oh, by the bye!"

"What is it?" said Mrs. Dennistoun.

He closed the door again and came back half a step. "I almost forgot, I meant to tell you: if you have any money to invest, I could help you to—— The best thing I've heard of for many a day!"

"You are very kind, Philip; but you know everything I have is in the hands of trustees."

"Oh, bother trustees. The only thing they do is to keep your dividends down to the lowest amount possible and cut short your income. Come, you're quite old enough to judge for yourself. You might give them a jog. At your time of life they ought to take a hint from you."

"I have never done it, Philip, and they would pay no attention to me."

"Oh, nonsense, mamma. Why, except you, who has a right to be consulted except Nell? and if I, her husband, am your adviser——"

"I know they would do nothing but mock at me."

"Rubbish! I'd like to see who would mock at you. Just you send them to me, that is all."

"Philip, will you not believe me when I say that it is impossible?

I have never interfered. They would ask what made me think of such a thing now."

"And you could tell them a jolly good opportunity, as safe as the bank, and paying six or seven per cent.—none of your fabulous risky ten or twelve businesses, but a solid steady——How could it be to my interest to mislead you? It would be Nell who would be the loser. I should be simply cutting off my own head."

"That is true, no doubt——"

"And," he said, scarcely waiting for her reply, "Nell is really the person who should be consulted: for if there was loss eventually it would come upon her—and so upon me. I mean taking into consideration all the chances of the future: for it is perfectly safe for your time, you may be quite sure of that."

No one, though he might be ninety, likes to have his time limited, and his heir's prospects dwelt upon as the only things of any importance, and Mrs. Dennistoun was a very long way from ninety. She would have sacrificed everything she had to make her child happy, but she did not like, all the same, to be set down as unimportant so far as her own property was concerned.

"I am afraid," she said, with a slight quaver in her voice, "that my trustees would not take Elinor's wishes into consideration in the first place, nor yours either, Philip. They think of me, and I suppose that is really their duty. If I had anything of my own—
—"

"Do you mean to say," he said, bluntly, "that with a good income and living in the country in a hole, in the most obscure way, you have saved nothing all these years?"

"If I had," said Mrs. Dennistoun, roused by his persistent attack, "I should be very sorry to fling it away."

"Oh, that is what you think?" he said. "Now we're at the bottom of it. You think that to put it in my hands would be to throw it away! I thought there must be something at the bottom of all this pretty ignorance of business and so forth. Good gracious! that may be well enough for a girl; but when a grandmother pretends not to know, not to interfere, etc., that's too much. So this is what you meant all the time! To put it into my hands would be throwing it away!"

"I did not mean to say so, Philip—I spoke hastily, but I must remind you that I am not accustomed to this tone——"

"Oh, no, not at all accustomed to it, you all say that—that's Nell's dodge—never was used to anything of the kind, never had a rough word said to her, and so forth and so forth."

"Philip—I hope you don't say rough words to my Elinor."

"Oh!" he said, "I have got you there, have I. *Your* Elinor—no more yours than she is—Johnson's. She is my Nell, and what's more, she'll cling to me, whatever rough words I may say, or however you may coax or wheedle. Do you ever think when you refuse to make a sacrifice of one scrap of your hoards for her, that if I were not a husband in a hundred I might take it out of her and make her pay?"

"For what?" said Mrs. Dennistoun, standing up and confronting him, her face pale, her head very erect—"for what would you make her pay?"

He stood staring at her for a moment and then he broke out into a laugh. "We needn't face each other as if we were going to have a stand-up fight," he said. "And it wouldn't be fair, mamma, we're not equally matched, the knowing ones would all lay their money on you. So you won't take my advice about investing your spare cash? Well, if you won't you won't, and there's an end of it: only stand up fair and don't bother me with nonsense about trustees."

"It is no nonsense," she said.

His eyes flashed, but he controlled himself and turned away, waving his hand. "I'll not beat Nell for it when I come home to-night," he said.

Once more Phil dined at his club that evening and Elinor with her mother. She was in an eager and excited state, looking anxiously in Mrs. Dennistoun's eyes, but it was not till late in the evening that she made any remark. At last, just before they parted for the night, she threw herself upon her mother with a little cry—"Oh, mamma, I know you are right, I know you are quite right. But if you could have done it, it would have given you an influence! I don't blame you—not for a moment—but it might have given you an opening to speak. It might have—given you a little hold on him."

"My darling, my darling!" said Mrs. Dennistoun.

"No," said Elinor, "there's nothing to pity me about, nothing at all—Phil is always kind and good to me—but you would have had a standing ground. It might have given you a right to speak—about those dreadful, dreadful city complications, mamma."

Mrs. Dennistoun went to bed that night a troubled woman, and lay awake watching and expecting when the usual midnight tumult should arise. But that evening there was none. No sound but the key in the latch, the shutting of a door or two, and all quiet. Compunctions filled the mother's heart. What was the wrong if, perhaps, she could satisfy Elinor, perhaps get at the heart of Phil, who had a heart, though it was getting strangled in all those intricacies of gambling and wretched business. She turned over and over in her mind all that she had, and all that she had any power over. And she remembered a small sum she had in a mortgage, which was after all in her own power. No doubt it would be to throw the money away, which would be so much gone from the future provision of Elinor—but if by that means she could acquire an influence as Elinor said—be allowed to speak—to protest or perhaps even insist upon a change of course? Thinking over such a question for a whole sleepless night, and feeling beneath all that at least, at worst, this sacrifice would give pleasure to Elinor, which was really the one and sole motive, the only thing that could give her any warrant for such a proceeding—is not a process which is likely to strengthen the mind. In the morning, as soon as she knew he was up, which was not till late enough, she sent to ask if Phil would give her five minutes before he went out. He appeared after a while, extremely correct and *point device*, grave but polite. "I must ask you to excuse me," he said, "if I am hurried, for to-day is one of my Board days."

"It was only to say, Philip—you spoke to me yesterday of money—to be invested."

"Yes?" he said politely, without moving a muscle.

"I have been thinking it all over, and I remember that there is a thousand pounds or two which John Tatham placed for me in a mortgage, and which is in my own power."

"Ah!" he said, "a thousand pounds or two," with a shrug of his shoulders; "it is scarcely worth while, is it, changing an investment for so small a matter as a thousand pounds?"

"If you think so, Philip—it is all I can think of that is in my own power."

"It is really not worth the trouble," he said, "and I am in a hurry." He made a step towards the door and then turned round again. "Well," he said, "just to show there is no ill-feeling, I'll find you something, perhaps, to put your tuppenceha'penny in to-day."

And then there was John Tatham to face after that!

CHAPTER XXI.

It cost Mrs. Dennistoun a struggle to yield to her daughter and her daughter's husband, and with her eyes open and no delusion on the subject to throw away her two thousand pounds. Two thousand pounds is a big thing to throw away. There are many people much richer than Mrs. Dennistoun who would have thought it a wicked thing to do, and some who would have quarrelled with both daughter and son-in-law rather than do so foolish a thing. For it was not merely making a present, so to speak, of the money, it was throwing it away. To have given it to Elinor would have been nothing, it would have been a pleasure; but in Phil's investment Mrs. Dennistoun had no confidence. It was throwing her money after Elinor's money into that hungry sea which swallows up everything and gives nothing again.

But if that had been difficult for her, it may be imagined with what feelings she contemplated her necessary meeting with John Tatham. She knew everything he would say—more, she knew what he would look: his astonishment, his indignation, the amazement with which he would regard it. John was far from being incapable of a sacrifice. Mrs. Dennistoun, indeed, did him more than justice in that respect, for she believed that he had himself been on the eve of asking Elinor to marry him when she was snatched up by, oh, so much less satisfactory a man! which the reader knows is not quite the case, though perhaps it required quite as much self-denial on John's part to stand by Elinor and maintain her cause under her altered circumstances as if it had been the case. But notwithstanding this, she knew that John would be angry with what she had done or promised to do, and would put every possible impediment in her way: and when she sent for him, in order that she might carry out her promise, it was with a heart as sick with fright and as much disturbed by the idea of a scolding as ever child's was.

John had been very little to the house at Curzon Street. He had dined two or three times with Mrs. Dennistoun alone, and once or twice Elinor had been of the party; but the Comptons had never any guests at that house, and the fact already mentioned that Philip Compton never dined at home made it a difficult matter for Mrs. Dennistoun to ask any but her oldest friends to the curious little divided house, which was neither hers nor theirs. Thus Cousin John had met, but no more, Elinor's husband, and neither of the gentlemen had shown the least desire to cultivate the acquaintance. John had not expressed his sentiments on the subject to any one, but Phil, as was natural, had been more demonstrative. "I don't think much of your relations, Nell," he said, "if that's a specimen: a prig if ever there was one—and that old sheep that was at the wedding, the father of him, I suppose——"

"As they are my relations, Phil, you might speak of them a little more respectfully."

"Oh, respectfully! Bless us all! I have no respect for my own, and why I should have for yours, my little dear, I confess I can't see. Oh, by the way, this is Cousin John, who I used to think by your blushing and all that——"

"Phil, I think you are trying to make me angry. Cousin John is the best man in the world; but I never blushed—how ridiculous! I might as well have blushed to speak of my brother."

"I put no confidence in brothers, unless they're real ones," said Phil; "but I'm glad I've seen him, Nell. I doubt after all that you're such a fool, when you see us together—eh?" He laughed that laugh of conscious superiority which, when it is not perfectly well-founded, sounds so fatuous to the hearer. Elinor did not look at him. She turned her head away and made no reply.

John, on his part, as has been said, made no remark. If he had possessed a wife at home to whom he could have confided his sentiments, as Phil Compton had, it is possible that he might have said something not unsimilar. But then had he had a wife at home he would have been more indifferent to Phil, and might not have cared to criticise him at all.

Mrs. Dennistoun received him when he came in obedience to her call, as a child might do who had the power of receiving its future corrector. She abased herself before him, servilely choosing his favourite subjects, talking of what she thought would please him, of former times at the Cottage, of Elinor, and her great affection for Cousin John, and so forth. I imagine that he had a suspicion of the cause of all this sweetness. He looked at her suspiciously, though he allowed himself to be drawn into reminiscences, and to feel a half pleasure, half pain in the affectionate things that Elinor had said. At length, after some time had passed, he asked, in a pause of the conversation, "Was this all you wanted with me, aunt, to talk of old times?"

"Wasn't it a good enough pretext for the pleasure of seeing you, John?"

He laughed a little and shook his head.

"An excellent pretext where none was wanted. It is very kind of you to think it a pleasure: but you had something also to say?"

"It seems there is no deceiving you, John," she said, and with many hesitations and much difficulty, told him her story. She saw him begin to flame. She saw his eyes light up, and Mrs. Dennistoun shook in her chair. She was not a woman apt to be afraid, but she was frightened now.

Nevertheless, when she had finished her story, John at first spoke no word: and when he did find a tongue it was only to say,

"You want to get back the money you have on that mortgage. My dear aunt, why did not you tell me so at once?"

"But I have just told you, John."

"Well, so be it. You know it will take a little time; there are some formalities that must be gone through. You cannot make a demand on people in that way to pay you cash at once."

"Oh, I thought it was so easy to get money—on such very good security and paying such a good adequate rate of interest."

"It is easy," he said, "perfectly easy; but it wants a little time: and people will naturally wonder, if it is really good security and good interest, why you should be in such a hurry to get out of it."

"But surely, to say private reasons—family reasons, that will be enough."

"Oh, there is no occasion for giving any reason at all. You wish to do it; that is reason enough."

"Yes," said Mrs. Dennistoun, with diffidence, yet also a little self-assertion, "I think it is enough."

"Of course, of course." But his eyes were flaming, and Mrs. Dennistoun would not allow herself to believe that she had got off. "And may I ask—not that I have any right to ask, for of course you have better advisers—what do you mean to put the money in, when you have got it back?"

"Oh, John," said Mrs. Dennistoun, "you are implacable, though you pretend different. You know what I want with the money, and you disapprove of it, and so do I. I am going to throw it away. I know that just as well as you do, and I am ashamed of myself: but I am going to do it all the same."

"You are going to give it to Elinor? I don't think there is anything to disapprove of in that. It is the most natural thing in the world."

"If I could be sure that Elinor would get any good by it," she said.

And then his face suddenly blazed up, so that the former flame in his eyes was nothing. He sat for a moment staring at her, and then he said, "Yes, if—but I suppose you take the risk." There were a great many things on his lips to say, but he said none of them, except hurriedly, "You have a motive, I suppose——"

"I have a motive—as futile probably as my act—if I could by that means, or any other, acquire an influence——"

John was very seldom, if ever, rude—it was not in his way—but at this moment he was so bitterly exasperated that he forgot his manners altogether. He burst out into a loud laugh, and then he jumped up to his feet and said, "Forgive me. I really have a dozen engagements. I can't stay. I'll see to having this business done for you as soon as possible. You would rather old Lynch had no hand in it? I'll get it done for you at once."

She followed him out to the door as if they had been in the country, and that the flowery cottage door, with the great world of down and sky outside, instead of Curzon Street: longing to say something that would still, at the last moment, gain her John's approval, or his understanding at least. But she could think of nothing to say. He had promised to manage it all for her: he had not reproached her; and yet not content with that she wanted to extort a favourable word from him before he should go. But she could not find a word to say. He it was only who spoke. He asked when she was going to return home, with his hand upon the street door.

"I don't know. I have not made any plans. The house is taken till July."

"And you have enjoyed it?" he said. "It has answered?"

What a cruel, cruel question to put to her! She going so unsuspectingly with him to the very door! Philip Compton's servant, always about when he was not wanted, spying about to see whom it was that "down-stairs" was letting out, came strolling into sight. Anyhow, whether that was the reason or not, she made him no reply. He caught her look—a look that said more than words—and turned round quickly and held out his hand. "I did not mean to be cruel," he said.

"Oh, no, no, no—you did not mean it—you were not cruel. The reverse—you are always so kind. Yes, it has answered—I am more glad than I can tell you—that I came."

He it was now that looked at her anxiously, while she smiled that well-worn smile which is kept for people in trouble. She went in afterwards and sat silent for some time, covering her face with her hands; in which attitude Elinor found her after her afternoon visitors had gone away.

"What is it, mother? What is it, dear mother? Something has

happened to vex you."

"Nothing, nothing, Elinor. John Tatham has been here. He is going to do that little piece of business for me."

"And he—has been bullying you too? poor mamma!"

"On the contrary, he did not say a word. He considered it—quite natural."

Elinor gave her mother a kiss. She had nothing to say. Neither of them had a word to say to the other. The thought that passed through both their minds was: "After all it is only two thousand pounds"—and then, *après*? was Elinor's thought. And then, never more, never more! was what passed through Mrs. Dennistoun's mind.

Phil Compton smiled upon her that day she handed him over the money. "It is a great pity you took the trouble," he said. "It is a pity to change an investment for such a bagatelle as two thousand pounds. Still, if you insist upon it, mamma. I suppose Nell's been bragging of the big interest, but you never will feel it on a scrap like this. If you would let me double your income for you now."

"You know, Philip, I cannot. The trustees would never consent."

"Bother trustees. They are the ruin of women," he said, and as he left the room he turned back to ask her how long she was going to stay in town.

"How long do you stay?"

"Oh, till Goodwood always," said Phil. "Nell's looking forward to it, and there's generally some good things just at the end when the heavy people have gone away; but I thought you might not care to stay so long."

"I came not for town, but for Elinor, Philip."

"Exactly so. But don't you think Elinor has shown herself quite able to take care of herself—not to say that she has me? It's a thousand pities to keep you from the country which you prefer, especially as, after all, Nell can be so little with you."

"It would be much better for her at present, Philip, to come with me, and rest at home, while you go to Goodwood. For the sake of the future you ought to persuade her to do it."

"I daresay. Try yourself to persuade her to leave me. She won't, you know. But why should you bore yourself to death staying on here? You don't like it, and nobody——"

"Wants me, you mean, Philip."

"I never said anything so dashed straightforward. I am not a chap of that kind. But what I say is, it's a shame to keep you hanging on, disturbed in your rest and all that sort of thing. That noisy beggar, Dismar, that came in with us last night must have woke you up with his idiotic bellowing."

"It doesn't matter for me; but Elinor, Philip. It does matter for your wife. If her rest is broken it will react upon her in every way. I wish you would consent to forego those visitors in the middle of the night."

He looked at her with a sort of satirical indifference. "Sorry I can't oblige you," he said. "When a girl's friends fork out handsomely a man has some reason for paying a little attention. But when there's nothing, or next to nothing, on her side, why of course he must pick up a little where he can, as much for her sake as his own."

"Pick up a little!" said Mrs. Dennistoun.

"I wish you wouldn't repeat what I say like that. It makes a fellow nervous. Yes, of course, a man that knows what he's about does pick up a little. About your movements, however. I advise you to take my advice and go back to your snug little house. It would kill me in a week, but I know it suits you. Why hang on for Nell? She's as well as can be, and there's a few things that it would be good for us to do."

"Which you cannot do while I am here? Is that what you mean, Philip?"

"I never saw any good in being what the French call brutal," he said, "I hate making a woman cry, or that sort of thing. But you're a woman of sense, and I'm sure you must see that a young couple like Nell and me, who have our way to make in the world——"

"You know it was for her sake entirely that I came here."

"Yes, oh, yes. To do coddling and that sort of thing—which

221

she doesn't require a bit; but if I must be brutal you know there's things of much consequence we could do if——"

"If what, Philip?"

"Well," he said, turning on his heel, "if we had the house to ourselves."

This was the influence Mrs. Dennistoun hoped to acquire by the sacrifice of her two thousand pounds! When he was gone, instead of covering her face as she had done when John left her, Mrs. Dennistoun stared into the vacant air for a minute and then she burst into a laugh. It was not a mirthful laugh, it may be supposed, or harmonious, and it startled her as she heard it pealing into the silence. Whether it was loud enough to wake Elinor up-stairs, or whether she was already close by and heard it, I cannot tell, but she came in with a little tap at the door and a smile, a somewhat anxious and forced smile, it is true, upon her face.

"What is the joke?" she said. "I heard you laugh, and I thought I might come in and share the fun. Somehow, we don't have so much fun as we used to have. What is it, mamma?"

"It is only a witticism of Philip's, who has been in to see me," said Mrs. Dennistoun. "I won't repeat it, for probably I should lose the point of it—you know I always did spoil a joke in repeating it. I have been speaking to him," she said, after a little pause, during which both her laugh and Elinor's smile evaporated in the most curious way, leaving both of them very grave—"of going away, Elinor."

"Of going away!" Elinor suddenly assumed a startled look; but there is a difference between doing that and being really startled, which her mother, alas! was quite enlightened enough to see; and surely once more there was that mingled relief and relaxation in the lines of her face which Mrs. Dennistoun had seen before.

"Yes, my darling," she said, "it is June, and everything at the Cottage will be in full beauty. And, perhaps, it would do you more good to come down there for a day or two when there is nothing doing than to have me here, which, after all, has not been of very much use to you."

"Oh, don't say that, mamma. Use!—it has been of comfort unspeakable. But," Elinor added, hurriedly, "I see the force of all you say. To remain in London at this time of the year must be a far greater sacrifice than I have any right to ask of you, mamma."

Oh, the furtive, hurried, unreal words! which were such pain and horror to say with the consciousness of the true sentiment lying underneath; which made Elinor's heart sink, yet were brought forth with a sort of hateful fervour, to imitate truth.

Mrs. Dennistoun saw it all. There are times when the understanding of such a woman is almost equal to those "larger other eyes" with which it is our fond hope those who have left us for a better country see, if they are permitted to see, our petty doings, knowing, better than we know ourselves, what excuses, what explanations, they are capable of. "As for the sacrifice," she said, "we will say nothing of that, Elinor. It is a vain thing to say that if my life would do you any pleasure—for you don't want to take my life, and probably the best thing I can do for you is to go on as long as I can. But in the meantime there's no question at all of sacrifice—and if you can come down now and then for a day, and sleep in the fresh air——"

"I will, I will, mamma," said Elinor, hiding her face on her mother's shoulder; and they would have been something more than women if they had not cried together as they held each other in that embrace—in which there was so much more than met either eye or ear.

CHAPTER XXII.

It was about the 10th of June when Mrs. Dennistoun left London. She had been in town for about five weeks, which looked like as many months, and it was with a mingled sense of relief, and of that feeling which is like death in the heart, the sense of nothing further to be done, of the end of opportunity, the conclusion of all power to help, which sometimes comes over an anxious mind, without in any respect diminishing the anxiety, giving it indeed a depth and pang beyond any other feeling that is known to the heart of man. What could she do more for her child? Nothing. It was her only policy to remain away, not to see, certainly not to remark anything that was happening, to wait if perhaps the moment might come when she would be of use, and to hope that perhaps that moment might never need to come, that by some wonderful turn of affairs all might yet go well. She went back to Windyhill with the promise of a visit "soon," Philip himself had said—in the pleasure of getting the house, which was her house, which she had paid for and provisioned, to himself for his own uses. Mrs. Dennistoun could not help hearing through her maid something of the festivities which were in prospect after she was gone, the dinners and gay receptions at which she would have been *de trop*. She did not wish to hear of them, but these are things that will make themselves known, and Mrs. Dennistoun had to face the fact that Elinor was more or less consenting to the certainty of her mother being *de trop*, which gave her a momentary pang. But after all, what did it matter? It was not her fault, poor child. I have known a loving daughter in whose mind there was a sentiment almost of relief amid her deep grief when her tender mother died. Could such a thing be possible? It was;

224

because after then, however miserable she might be, there was no conflict over her, no rending of the strained heart both ways. A woman who has known life learns to understand and forgive a great many things; and Mrs. Dennistoun forgave her Elinor, her only child, for whose happiness she had lived, in that she was almost glad when her mother went away.

Such things, however, do not make a lonely little house in the country more cheerful, or tend to make it easier to content one's self with the Rector's family, and the good old, simple-minded, retired people, with their little complaints, yet general peacefulness, and incompetence to understand what tragedy was. They thought on the whole their neighbour at the Cottage ought to be very thankful that she had got her daughter well, or, if not very well, at least fashionably, married, with good connections and all that, which are always of use in the long run. It was better than marrying a poor curate, which was almost the only chance a girl had on Windyhill.

It was a little hard upon Mrs. Dennistoun, however, that she lost not only Elinor, but John, who had been so good about coming down when she was all alone at first. Of course, during the season, a young rising man, with engagements growing upon him every day, was very unlikely to have his Saturdays to Mondays free. So many people live out of town nowadays, or, at least, have a little house somewhere to which they go from Saturday to Monday, taking their friends with them. This was no doubt the reason why John never came; and yet the poor lady suspected another reason, and though she no longer laughed as she had done on that occasion when the Honourable Phil gave her her dismissal, a smile would come over her face sometimes when she reflected that with her two thousand pounds she had purchased the hostility of both Philip and John.

John Tatham was indeed exceedingly angry with her for the weakness with which she had yielded to Phil Compton's arguments, though indeed he knew nothing of Phil Compton's arguments, nor whether they had been exercised at all on the woman who was first of all Elinor's mother and ready to sacrifice everything to her comfort. When he found that this foolish step on her part had been followed by her retirement from London, he was greatly mystified and quite unable to understand. He met Elinor some time after at one of those assemblies to which "everybody" goes. It was, I think, the soirée at the Royal Academy—where amid the persistent crowd in the great room there was a whirling crowd, twisting in and out among the others, bound for heaven knows how many other places, and pausing here and there on tiptoe to greet an acquaintance, at the tail of which, carried along by its impetus, was Elinor. She was not looking either well or happy, but she was responding more or less to the impulse of her set, exchanging greetings and banal words with dozens of people, and sometimes turning a wistful and weary gaze towards the pictures on the walls, as if she would gladly escape from the mob of her companions to them, or anywhere. It was no impulse of taste or artistic feeling, however, it is to be feared, but solely the weariness of her mind. John watched her for some time before he approached her. Phil was not of the party, which was nothing extraordinary, for little serious as that assembly is, it was still of much too serious a kind for Phil; but Lady Mariamne was there, and other ladies with whom Elinor was in the habit of pursuing that gregarious hunt after pleasure which carries the train of votaries along at so breakneck a pace, and with so little time to enjoy the pleasure they are pursuing. When he saw indications that the stream was setting backwards to the entrance, again to separate and take its various ways to other entertainments, he broke into the throng and called Elinor's attention to himself. For a moment she smiled with genuine pleasure at the sight of him, but then changed her aspect almost imperceptibly. "Oh, John!" she said with that smile: but immediately looked towards Lady Mariamne, as if undecided what to do.

"You need not look—as if I would try to detain you, Elinor."

"Do you think I am afraid of your detaining me? I thought I should be sure to meet you to-night, and was on the outlook.

How is it that we never see you now?"

He refused the natural retort that she had never asked to see him, and only said, with a smile, "I hear my aunt is gone."

"Do you mean to say that you only came for her? That is an unkind speech. Yes, she has gone. It was cruel to keep her in town for the best part of the year."

"But she intended to stay till July, Elinor."

"Did she? I think you are mistaken, John. She intended to watch over me—dear mamma, she thinks too much of me—but when she saw that I was quite well——"

"You don't look to me so extraordinarily well."

"Don't I? I must be a fraud then. Nobody could be stronger. I'm going to a multitude of places to-night. Wherever my Hebrew leader goes I go," said Elinor, with a laugh. "I have given myself up for to-night, and she is never satisfied with less than a dozen."

"Ten minutes to each."

"Oh, half an hour at least: and with having our carriage found for us at every place, and the risk of getting into a *queue*, and all the delays of coming and going, it cannot be much less than three-quarters of an hour. This is the third. I think three more will weary even the Jew."

"You are with Lady Mariamne then, Elinor?"

"Yes—oh, you need not make that face. She is as good as the rest, and pretends to nothing, at least. I have no carriage, you know, and Phil took fright at my dear old fly. He thought a hired brougham was not good when I was alone."

"That was quite true. Nevertheless, I should like above all things to keep you here a little longer to look at some of the pictures, and take you home in a hansom after."

She laughed. "Oh, so should I—fancy, I have not seen the pictures, not at all. We came in a mob to the private view; and then one day I was coming with mamma, but was stopped by something, and now—— Always people, people—nothing else. 'Did you see So-and-so? There's some one bowing to you, Nell. Be sure you speak a word to the Thises or the Thats'—while I don't care for one of them. But I fear the hansom would not do, John."

"It would have done very well in the old days. Your mother would not have been displeased."

"The old days are gone and will never return," she said, half sad, half smiling, shaking her head. "So far as I can see, nothing ever returns. You have your day, and if you do not make the best of that——"

She stopped, shaking her head again with a laugh, and there were various ways in which that speech might be interpreted. John for one knew a sense of it which he believed had never entered Elinor's head. He too might have had his day and let it slip. "So you are making the most of yours," he said. "I hear that you are very gay."

Elinor coloured high under his look. "I don't know who can have told you that. We have had a few little dinners since mamma left us, chiefly Phil's business friends. I would not have them while she was with us—that is to say, to be honest," cried Elinor, "while we were with her: which of course was the real state of the case. I myself don't like those people, John, but they would have been insupportable to mamma. It was for her sake——"

"I understand," he said.

"Oh, but you must not say 'I understand' with that air of knowing a great deal more than there is to understand," she said, with heat. "Mamma said it would do me much more good to go—home for a night now and then and sleep in the fresh air than for her to stay; and though I think she is a little insane on the subject of my health, still it was certainly better than that she should stay here, making herself wretched, her rest broken, and all that. You know we keep such late hours."

"I should not have thought she would have minded that."

"But what would you have thought of me if I did not mind it for her? There, John, do you see they are all going? Ah, the pictures! I wish I could have stayed with you and gone round the rooms. But it must not be to-night. Come and see me!" she said, turning round to him with a smile, and holding out her hand.

"I would gladly, Elinor—but should not I find myself in the way of your fine friends like——"

He had not the heart to finish the sentence when he met her eyes brimming full of tears.

"Not my fine friends, but my coarse friends," she said; "not friends at all, our worst enemies, I am sure."

"Nell!" cried Lady Mariamne, in her shrill voice.

"You will come and see me, John?"

"Yes," he said, "and in the meantime I will take you downstairs, let your companions think as they please."

It proved when he did so that John had to escort both ladies to the carriage, which it was not very easy to find, no other cavalier being at hand for the moment; and that Lady Mariamne invited him to accompany them to their next stage. "You know the Durfords, of course. You are going there? What luck for us, Nell! Jump in, Mr. Tatham, we will take you on."

"Unfortunately Lady Durford has not taken the trouble to invite me," said John.

"What does that matter? Jump in, all the same, she'll be delighted to see you, and as for not asking you, when you are with me and Nell——"

But John turned a deaf ear to this siren's song.

He went to Curzon Street a little while after to call, as he had been invited to do, and went late to avoid the bustle of the tea-table, and the usual rabble of that no longer intimate but wildly gregarious house. And he was not without his reward. Perhaps a habit he had lately formed of passing by Curzon Street in the late afternoon, when he was on his way to his club, after work was over, had something to do with his choice of this hour. He found Elinor, as he had hoped, alone. She was sitting so close to the window that her white dress mingled with the white curtains, so that he did not at first perceive her, and so much abstracted in her own thoughts that she did not pay any attention to the servant's hurried murmur of his name at the door. When she felt rather than saw that there was some one in the room, Elinor jumped up with a shock of alarm that seemed unnecessary in her own drawing-room; then seeing who it was, was so much and so suddenly moved that she shed a few tears in some sudden revulsion of feeling as she said, "Oh, it is you, John!"

"Yes," he said, "but I am very sorry to see you so nervous."

"Oh, it's nothing. I was always nervous"—which indeed was the purest invention, for Elinor Dennistoun had not known what nerves meant. "I mean I was always startled by any sudden entrance—in this way," she cried, and very gravely asked him to be seated, with a curious assumption of dignity. Her demeanour altogether was incomprehensible to John.

"I hope," he said, "you were not displeased with me, Elinor, for going off the other night. I should have been too happy, you know, to go with you anywhere; but Lady Mariamne is more than I can stand."

"I was very glad you did not come," she said with a sigh; then smiling faintly, "But you were ungrateful, for Mariamne formed a most favourable opinion of you. She said, 'Why didn't you tell me, Nell, you had a cousin so presentable as that?'"

"I am deeply obliged, Elinor; but it seems that what was a compliment to me personally involved something the reverse for your other relations."

"It is one of their jokes," said Elinor, with a voice that faltered a little, "to represent my relations as—not in a complimentary way. I am supposed not to mind, and it's all a joke, or so they tell me; but it is not a joke I like," she said, with a flash from her eyes.

"All families have jokes of that description," said John; "but tell me, Nelly, are you really going down to the cottage, to your mother?"

Her eyes thanked him with a gleam of pleasure for the old familiar name, and then the light went out of them. "I don't know," she said, abruptly. "Phil was to come; if he will not, I think I will not either. But I will say nothing till I make sure."

"Of course your first duty is to him," said John; "but a day now or a day then interferes with nothing, and the country would be good for you, Elinor. Doesn't your husband see it? You are not looking like yourself."

"Not like myself? I might easily look better than myself. I wish I could. I am not so bigoted about myself."

"Your friends are, however," he said: "no one who cares for you wants to change you, even for another Elinor. Come, you are nervous altogether to-night, not like yourself, as I told you. You always so courageous and bright! This depressed state is not one of your moods. London is too much for you, my little Nelly."

"Your little Nellie has gone away somewhere John. I doubt if she'll ever come back. Yes, London is rather too much for me, I think. It's such a racket, as Phil says. But then he's used to it, you know. He was brought up to it, whereas I—I think I hate a racket, John—and they all like it so. They prefer never having a moment to themselves. I daresay one would end by being just the same. It keeps you from thinking, that is one very good thing."

"You used not to think so, Elinor."

"No," she said, "not at the Cottage among the flowers, where nothing ever happened from one year's end to another. I should die of it now in a week—at least if not I, those who belong to me. So on the whole perhaps London is the safest—unless Phil will go."

"I can only hope you will be able to persuade him," said John, rising to go away, "for whatever you may think, you are a country bird, and you want the fresh air."

"Are you going, John? Well, perhaps it is better. Good-by. Don't trouble your mind about me whether I go or stay."

"Do you mean I am not to come again, Elinor?"

"Oh, why should I mean that?" she said. "You are so hard upon me in your thoughts;" but she did not say that he was wrong, and John went out from the door saying to himself that he would not go again. He saw through the open door of the dining-room that the table was prepared sumptuously for a dinner-party. It was shining with silver and crystal, the silver Mrs. Dennistoun's old service, which she had brought up with her from Windyhill, and which as a matter of convenience she had left behind with her daughter. Would it ever, he wondered, see Windyhill again?

He went on to his club, and there some one began to amuse him with an account of Lady Durford's ball, to which Lady Mariamne had wished to take him. "Are not those Comptons relations of yours, Tatham?" he said.

"Connections," said John, "by marriage."

"I'm very glad that's all. They are a queer lot. Phil Compton you know—the dis-Honourable Phil, as he used to be called—but I hear he's turned over a new leaf——"

"What of him?" said John.

"Oh, nothing much: only that he was flirting desperately all the evening with a Mrs. Harris, an American widow. I believe he came with her—and his own wife there—much younger, much prettier, a beautiful young creature—looking on with astonishment. You could see her eyes growing bigger and bigger. If it had not been kind of amusing to a looker-on, it would be the most pitiful sight in the world."

"I advise you not to let yourself be amused by such trifles," said John Tatham, with a look of fire and flame.

CHAPTER XXIII.

As a matter of fact, Elinor did not go to the Cottage for the fresh air or anything else. She made one hurried run in the afternoon to bid her mother good-by, alone, which was not a visit, but the mere pretence of a visit, hurried and breathless, in which there was no time to talk of anything. She gave Mrs. Dennistoun an account of the usual lists of visits that her husband and she were to make in the autumn, which the mother, with the usual instinct of mothers, thought too much. "You will wear yourself to death, Elinor."

"Oh, no," she said, "it is not that sort of thing that wears one to death. I shall—enjoy it, I suppose, as other people do——"

"I don't know about enjoyment, Elinor, but I am sure it would be much better for you to come and stay here quietly with me."

"Oh, don't talk to me of any paradises, mamma. We are in the working-day world, and we must make out our life as we can."

"But you might let Philip go by himself and come and stay quietly here for a little, for the sake of your health, Elinor."

"Not for the world, not for the world," she cried. "I cannot leave Phil." and then with a laugh that was full of a nervous thrill, "You are always thinking of my health, mamma, when my health is perfect: better, far better, than almost anybody's. The most of them have headaches and that sort of thing, and they stay in bed for a day or two constantly, but I never need anything of the kind."

"My darling, it would not be leaving Philip to take, say, a single week's rest."

"While he went off without me I should not know where," she said, sullenly; then gave her mother a guilty look and laughed

233

again. "No, no, mamma; he would not like it. A man does not like his wife to be an incapable, to have to leave him and be nursed up by her mother. Besides, it is to the country we are going, you know, to Scotland, the finest air; better even, if that were possible, than Windyhill."

This was all that was said, and there was indeed time for little more; for as the visit was unexpected the Hudsons, by bad luck, appeared to take tea with Mrs. Dennistoun by way of cheering her in her loneliness, and were of course enchanted to see Elinor, and to hear, as Mrs. Hudson said, of all her doings in the great world. "We always look out for your name at all the parties. It gives one quite an interest in fashionable life," said the Rector's wife, nodding her head, "and Alice was eager to hear what the last month's novelties were in the fashions, and if Elinor had any nice new patterns, especially for under-things. But what should you want with new under-things, with such a trousseau as you had?" she added, regretfully. Elinor in fact was quite taken from her mother for that hour. Was it not, perhaps, better so? Her mother herself was half inclined to think that it was, though with an ache in her heart, and there could be no doubt that Elinor herself was thankful that it so happened. When there are many questions on one side that must be asked, and very little answer possible on the other, is it a good thing when the foolish outside world breaks in with its *banal* interest and prevents this dangerous interchange?

So short time did Elinor stay that she had kept the fly waiting which brought her from the station: and she took leave of her mother with a sort of determination, not allowing it even to be suggested that she should accompany her. "I like to bid you good-by here," she said, "at our own door, where you have always come all my life to see me off, even when I was only going to tea at the Rectory. Good-by, good-by, mother dear." She drove off waving her hand, and Mrs. Dennistoun sat out in the garden a long time till she saw the fly go round the turn of the road, the white line which came suddenly in sight from among the trees and as suddenly disappeared again round the side of the hill. Elinor waved her handkerchief from the window and her mother answered—and then she was gone like a dream, and the loneliness closed down more overwhelming than ever before.

Elinor was at Goodwood, her name in all the society papers, and even a description of one of her dresses, which delighted and made proud the whole population of Windyhill. The paper which contained it, and which, I believe, belonged originally to Miss Dale, passed from hand to hand through almost the entire community; the servants getting it at last, and handing it round among the humbler friends, who read it, half a dozen women together round a cottage door, wiping their hands upon their aprons before they would touch the paper, with many an exclamation and admiring outcry. And then her name appeared among the lists of smart people who were going to the North—now here, now there—in company with many other fine names. It gave the Windyhill people a great deal of amusement, and if Mrs. Dennistoun did not quite share this feeling it was a thing for which her friends blamed her gently. "For only think what a fine thing for Elinor to go everywhere among the best people, and see life like that!" "My dear friend," said the Rector, "you know we cannot hope to keep our children always with us. They must go out into the world while we old birds stay at home; and we must not—we really must not—grudge them their good times, as the Americans say." It was more wonderful than words could tell to Mrs. Dennistoun that it should be imagined she was grudging Elinor her "good time!"

The autumn went on, with those occasional public means of following her footsteps which, indeed, made even John Tatham—who was not in an ordinary way addicted to the *Morning Post*, being after his fashion a Liberal in politics and far from aristocratical in his sentiments generally—study that paper, and also other papers less worthy: and with, of course, many letters from Elinor, which gave more trustworthy accounts of her proceedings. These letters, however, were far less long, far less detailed, than they had once been; often written in a hurry, and short, containing notes of where she was going, and of a continual change of address, rather than of anything that could be called information about herself. John, I think, went only once to the Cottage during the interval which followed. He went abroad as usual in the Long Vacation, and then he had this on his mind—that he had half-surreptitiously obtained a new light upon the position of Elinor, which he had every desire to keep from her mother; for Mrs. Dennistoun, though she felt that her child was not happy, attributed that to any reason rather than a failure in her husband's love. Elinor's hot rejection of the very idea of leaving Phil, her dislike of any suggestion to that effect, even for a week, even for a day, seemed to her mother a proof that her husband, at all events, remained as dear to her as ever; and John would rather have cut his tongue out than betray any chance rumour he heard—and he heard many—to this effect. He was of opinion, indeed, that in London, and especially at a London club, not only is everything known that is to be known, but much is known that has never existed, and never will exist if not blown into being by those whose office it is to invent the grief to come; therefore he thought it wisest to keep away, lest by any chance something might drop from him which would awaken a new crowd of disquietudes in Mrs. Dennistoun's heart. Another incident, even more disquieting than gossip, had indeed occurred to John. It had happened to him to meet Lady Mariamne at a great *omnium gatherum* of a country house, where all sorts of people were invited, and where that lady claimed his acquaintance as one of the least alarming of the grave "set." She not only claimed his acquaintance, but set up a sort of friendship on the ground of his relationship to Elinor, and in an unoccupied moment after dinner one day poured a great many confidences into his ear.

"Isn't it such a pity," she said, "that Phil and she do not get on? Oh, they did at first, like a house on fire! And if she had only minded her ways they might still have been as thick—— But these little country girls, however they may disguise it at first, they all turn like that. The horridest little puritan! Phil does no more than a hundred men—than almost all men do: amuse himself with anything that throws itself in his way, don't you know. And sometimes, perhaps, he does go rather far. I think myself he sometimes goes a little too far—for good taste you know, and that sort of thing."

It was more amazing to hear Lady Mariamne talk of good taste than anything that had ever come in John Tatham's way before, but he was too horribly, desperately interested to see the fun.

"She will go following him about wherever he goes. She oughtn't to do that, don't you know. She should let him take his swing, and the chances are it will bring him back all right. I've told her so a dozen times, but she pays no attention to me. You're a great pal of hers. Why don't you give her a hint? Phil's not the sort of man to be kept in order like that. She ought to give him his head."

"I'm afraid," said John, "it's not a matter in which I can interfere."

"Well, some of her friends should, anyhow, and teach her a little sense. You're a cautious man, I see," said Lady Mariamne. "You think it's too delicate to advise a woman who thinks herself an injured wife. I didn't say to console her, mind you," she said with a shriek of a laugh.

It may be supposed that after this John was still more unwilling to go to the Cottage, to run the risk of betraying himself. He did write to Elinor, telling her that he had heard of her from her sister-in-law; but when he tried to take Lady Mariamne's advice and "give her a hint," John felt his lips sealed. How could he breathe a word even of such a suspicion to Elinor? How could he let her know that he thought such a thing possible?— or presume to advise her, to take her condition for granted? It was impossible. He ended by some aimless wish that he might meet her at the Cottage for Christmas; "you and Mr. Compton," he said—whom he did not wish to meet, the last person in the world: and of whom there was no question that he should go to the Cottage at Christmas or any other time. But what could John do or say? To suggest to her that he thought her an injured wife was beyond his power.

It was somewhere about Christmas—just before—in that dread moment for the lonely and those who are in sorrow and distress, when all the rest of the world is preparing for that family festival, or pretending to prepare, that John Tatham was told one morning in his chambers that a lady wanted to see him. He was occupied, as it happened, with a client for whom he had stayed in town longer than he had intended to stay, and he paid little more attention than to direct his clerk to ask the lady what her business was, or if she could wait. The client was long-winded, and lingered, but John's mind was not free enough nor his imagination lively enough to rouse much curiosity in him in respect to the lady who was waiting. It was only when she was ushered in by his clerk, as the other went away, and putting up her veil showed the pale and anxious countenance of Mrs. Dennistoun, that the shock as of sudden calamity reached him. "Aunt!" he cried, springing from his chair.

"Yes, John—I couldn't come anywhere but here—you will feel for me more than any one."

"Elinor?" he said.

Her lips were dry, she spoke with a little difficulty, but she nodded her head and held out to him a telegram which was in her hand. It was dated from a remote part of Scotland, far in the north. "Ill—come instantly," was all it said.

"And I cannot get away till night," cried Mrs. Dennistoun, with a burst of subdued sobbing. "I can't start till night."

"Is this all? What was your last news?"

"Nothing, but that they had gone there—to somebody's shooting-box, which was lent them, I believe—at the end of the world. I wrote to beg her to come to me. She is—near a moment—of great anxiety. Oh, John, support me: let me not break down."

"You will not," he said; "you are wanted; you must keep all

your wits about you. What were they doing there at this time of the year?"

"They have been visiting about—they were invited to Dunorban for Christmas, but she persuaded Philip, so she said, to take this little house. I think he was to join the party while she—I cannot tell you what was the arrangement. She has written very vaguely for some time. She ought to have been with me—I told her so—but she has always said she could not leave Philip."

Could not leave Philip! The mother, fortunately, had no idea why this determination was. "I went so far as to write to Philip," she said, "to ask him if she might not come to me, or, at least begging him to bring her to town, or somewhere where she could have proper attention. He answered me very briefly that he wished her to go, but she would not: as he had told me before I left town—that was all. It seemed to fret him—he must have known that it was not a fit place for her, in a stranger's house, and so far away. And to think I cannot even get away till late to-night!"

John had to comfort her as well as he could, to make her eat something, to see that she had all the comforts possible for her night journey. "You were always like her brother," the poor lady said, finding at last relief in tears. And then he went with her to the train, and found her a comfortable carriage, and placed her in it with all the solaces his mind could think of. A sleeping-carriage on the Scotch lines is not such a ghastly pretence of comfort as those on the Continent. The solaces John brought her—the quantities of newspapers, the picture papers and others, rugs and shawls innumerable—all that he possessed in the shape of wraps, besides those which she had with her. What more could a man do? If she had been young he would have bought her sugar-plums. All that they meant were the dumb anxieties of his own breast, and the vague longing to do something, anything that would be a help to her on her desolate way.

"You will send me a word, aunt, as soon as you get there?"

"Oh, at once, John."

"You will tell me how she is—say as much as you can—no three words, like that. I shall not leave town till I hear."

"Oh, John, why should this keep you from your family? I could telegraph there as easily as here."

He made a gesture almost of anger. "Do you think I am likely to put myself out of the way—not to be ready if you should want me?"

How should she want him?—a mother summoned to her daughter at such a moment—but she did not say so to trouble him more: for John had got to that maddening point of anxiety when nothing but doing something, or at least keeping ready to do something, flattering yourself that there must be something to do, affords any balm to the soul.

He saw her away by that night train, crowded with people going home—people noisy with gayety, escaping from their daily cares to the family meeting, the father's house, all the associations of pleasure and warmth and consolation—cold, but happy, in their third-class compartments—not wrapped up in every conceivable solace as she was, yet no one, perhaps, so heavy-hearted. He watched for the last glimpse of her face just as the train plunged into the darkness, and saw her smile and wave her hand to him; then he, too, plunged into the darkness like the train. He walked and walked through the solitary streets not knowing where he was going, unable to rest. Had he ever been, as people say, in love with Elinor? He could not tell—he had never betrayed it by word or look if he had. He had never taken any step to draw her near him, to persuade her to be his and not another's; on the contrary, he had avoided everything that could lead to that. Neither could he say, "She was as my sister," which his relationship might have warranted him in doing. It was neither the one nor the other— she was not his love nor his sister—she was simply Elinor; and perhaps she was dying; perhaps the news he would receive next day would be the worst that the heart can hear. He walked and walked through those dreary, semi-respectable streets of London, the quiet, the sordid, the dismal, mile after mile, and street after street, till half the night was over and he was tired out, and might have a hope of rest.

But for three whole days—days which he could not reckon, which seemed of the length of years—during which he remained closeted in his chambers, the whole world having, as it seemed, melted away around him, leaving him alone, he did not have a word. He did not go home, feeling that he must be on the spot, whatever happened. Finally, when he was almost mad, on the morning of the third day, he received the following telegram: "Saved—as by a miracle; doing well. Child—a boy."

"Child—a boy!" Good heavens! what did he want with that? it seemed an insult to him to tell him. What did he care for the child, if it was a boy or not?—the wretched, undesirable brat of such parentage, born to perpetuate a name which was dishonoured. Altogether the telegram, as so many telegrams, but lighted fresh fires of anxiety in his mind. "Saved—as by a miracle!" Then he had been right in the dreadful fancies that had gone through his mind. He had passed by Death in the dark; and was it now sure that the miracle would last, that the danger would have passed away?

CHAPTER XXIV.

───────────

It was not till nearly three weeks after this that John received another brief dispatch. "At home: come and see us." He had indeed got a short letter or two in the interval, saying almost nothing—a brief report of Elinor's health, and of the baby, against whom he had taken an unreasoning disgust and repugnance. "Little beast!" he said to himself, passing over that part of the bulletin: for the letters were scarcely more than bulletins, without a word about the circumstances which surrounded her. A shooting lodge in Ross-shire in the middle of the winter! What a place for a delicate woman! John was well enough aware that many elements of comfort were possible even in such a place; but he shut his eyes, as was natural, to anything that went against his own point of view.

And now this telegram from Windyhill—"At home: come and see us"—*us*. Was it a mistake of the telegraph people?—of course they must make mistakes. They had no doubt taken the *me* in Mrs. Dennistoun's angular writing for *us*—or was it possible——John had no peace in his mind until he had so managed matters that he could go and see. There was no very pressing business in the middle of January, when people had hardly yet recovered the idleness of Christmas. He started one windy afternoon, when everything was grey, and arrived at Hurrymere station in the dim twilight, still ruddy with tints of sunset. He was in a very contradictory frame of mind, so that though his heart jumped to see Mrs. Dennistoun awaiting him on the platform, there mingled in his satisfaction in seeing her and hearing what she had to tell so much sooner, a perverse conviction of cold and discomfort in the long drive up in the pony carriage which he felt sure was before him. He was mistaken, however, on this point, for the first thing she said was, "I have secured the fly, John. Old Pearson will take your luggage. I have so much to tell you." There was an air of excitement in her face, but not that air of subdued and silent depression which comes with solitude. She was evidently full of the report she had to make; but yet the first thing she did when she was ensconced in the fly with John beside her was to cover her face with her hands, and subside into her corner in a silent passion of tears.

"For mercy's sake tell me what is the matter. What has happened? Is Elinor ill?"

He had almost asked is Elinor dead?

She uncovered her face, which had suddenly lighted up with a strange gleam of joy underneath the tears. "John, Elinor is here," she said.

"Here?"

"At home—safe. I have brought her back—and the child."

"Confound the child!" John said in his excitement. "Brought her back! What do you mean?"

"Oh, John, it is a long story. I have a hundred things to tell you, and to ask your advice upon; but the main thing is that she is here. I have brought her away from him. She will go back no more."

"She has left her husband?" he said, with a momentary flicker of exultation in his dismay. But the dismay, to do him justice, was the strongest. He looked at his companion almost sternly. "Things," he said, "must have been very serious to justify that."

"They were more than serious—they had become impossible," Mrs. Dennistoun said.

And she told him her story, which was a long one. She had arrived to find Elinor alone in the little solitary lodge in the midst of the wilds, not without attention indeed or comfort, but alone, her husband absent. She had been very ill, and he had been at the neighbouring castle, where a great party was assembled, and where, the mother discovered at last, there was—the woman

243

who had made Elinor's life a burden to her. "I don't know with what truth. I don't know whether there is what people call any harm in it. It is possible he is only amusing himself. I can't tell. But it has made Elinor miserable this whole autumn through, that and a multitude of other things. She would not let me send for him when I got there. It had gone so far as that. She said that the whole business disgusted him, that he had lost all interest in her, that to hear it was over might be a relief to him, but nothing more. Her heart has turned altogether against him, John, in every way. There have been a hundred things. You think I am almost wickedly glad to have her home. And so I am. I cannot deny it. To have her here even in her trouble makes all the difference to me. But I am not so careless as you think. I can look beyond to other things. I shrink as much as you do from such a collapse of her life. I don't want her to give up her duty, and now that there is the additional bond of the child——"

"Oh, for heaven's sake," said John, "leave the child out of it! I want to hear nothing of the child!"

"That is one chief point, however, that we want your advice about, John. A man, I suppose, does not understand it; but her baby is everything to Elinor: and I suppose—unless he can really be proved as guilty as she thinks—he could take the child away."

John smiled to himself a little bitterly: this was why he was sent for in such a hurry, not for the sake of his society, or from any affection for him, but that he might tell them what steps to take to secure them in possession of the child. He said nothing for some time, nor did Mrs. Dennistoun, whose disappointment in the coldness of his response was considerable, and who waited in vain for him to speak. At length she said, almost tremblingly, "I am afraid you disapprove very much of the whole business, John."

"I hope it has not been done rashly," he said. "The husband's mere absence, though heartless as—as I should have expected of the fellow—would yet not be reason enough to satisfy any—court."

"Any court! You don't think she means to bring him before any court? She wants only to be left alone. We ask nothing from him, not a penny, not any money—surely, surely no revenge—only not to be molested. There shall not be a word said on our side, if he will but let her alone."

John shook his head. "It all depends upon the view the man takes of it," he said.

Now this was very cold comfort to Mrs. Dennistoun, who had by this time become very secure in her position, feeling herself entirely justified in all that she had done. "The man," she said, "the man is not the sufferer: and surely the woman has some claim to be heard."

"Every claim," said John. "That is not what I was thinking of. It is this: if the man has a leg to stand upon, he will show fight. If he hasn't—why that will make the whole difference, and probably Elinor's position will be quite safe. But you yourself say——"

"John, don't throw back upon me what I myself said. I said that perhaps things were not so bad as she believed. In my experience I have found that folly, and playing with everything that is right is more common than absolute wrong—and men like Philip Compton are made up of levity and disregard of everything that is serious."

"In that case," said John, "if you are right, he will not let her go."

"Oh, John! oh, John! don't make me wish that he may be a worse man than I think. He could not force her to go back to him, feeling as she does."

"Nobody can force a woman to do that; but he could perhaps make her position untenable; he would, perhaps, take away the child."

"John," said Mrs. Dennistoun, in alarm, "if you tell her that, she will fly off with him to the end of the world. She will die before she will part with the child."

"I suppose that's how women are made," said John, not yet cured of his personal offence.

245

"Yes," she said, "that's how women are made."

"I beg your pardon," he said, coming to himself; "but you know, aunt, a man may be pardoned for not understanding that supreme fascination of the baby who cares no more for one than another, poor little animal, so long as it gets its food and is warm enough. We must await and see what the man will do."

"Is that the best?—is there nothing we can do to defend ourselves in the meantime—to make any sort of barricade against him?"

"We must wait and see what he is going to do," said John; and they went over and over the question, again and again, as they climbed the hills. It grew quite dark as they drove along, and when they came out upon the open part of the road, from which the Cottage was visible, they both looked out across the combe to the lights in the windows with an involuntary movement. The Cottage was transformed; instead of the one lonely lighted window which had indicated to John in former visits where Mrs. Dennistoun sat alone, there was now a twinkle from various points, a glow of firelight, a sensation of warmth, and company. Mrs. Dennistoun looked out upon it and her face shone. It was not a happy thing that Elinor should have made shipwreck of her life, should have left her husband and sought refuge in her mother's house. But how could it be otherwise than happy that Elinor was there—Elinor and the other little creature who was something more than Elinor, herself and yet another? As for John, he looked at it too, with an interest which stopped all arguments on the cause of it. She was there—wrong, perhaps, impatient; too quick to fly as she had been too quick to go—but still Elinor all the same, whether she was right or wrong.

The cab arrived soberly at the door, where Pearson with the pony carriage, coming by the shorter way with the luggage, had just arrived also. Mrs. Dennistoun said, hurriedly, "You will find Elinor in the drawing-room, John," and herself went hastily through the house and up the stairs. She was going to the baby! John guessed this with a smile of astonishment and half contempt. How strange it was! There could not be a more sad position than that in which, in their rashness, these two women had placed themselves; and yet the mother, a woman of experience, who ought to have known better, got out of the carriage like a girl, without waiting to be helped or attended to, and went up-stairs like the wind, forgetting everything else for that child—that child, the inheritor of Phil Compton's name and very likely of his qualities—fated from his birth (most likely) to bring trouble to everybody connected with him! And yet Elinor was of less interest to her mother. What strange caprices of nature! what extraordinary freaks of womankind!

The Cottage down-stairs was warm and bright with firelight and lamplight, and in the great chair by the fire was reclining, lying back with her book laid on her lap and her face full of eager attention to the sounds outside, a pale young woman, surrounded by cushions and warm wraps and everything an invalid could require, who raised to him eyes more large and shining than he had ever seen before, suffused with a dew of pain and pleasure and eager welcome. Elinor, was it Elinor? He had never seen her in any way like an invalid before—never knew her to be ill, or weak, or unable to walk out to the door and meet him or anyone she cared for. The sight of her ailing, weak, with those large glistening eyes, enlarged by feebleness, went to his very heart. Fortunately he did not in any way connect this enfeebled state with the phenomenon up-stairs, which was best for all parties. He hurried up to her, taking her thin hands into his own.

"Elinor! my poor little Nelly—can this be you!"

The water that was in her eyes rolled over in two great tears; a brief convulsion went over her face. "Yes, John," she said, almost in a whisper. "Strange as it may seem, this is all that is left of me."

He sat down beside her and for a moment neither of them spoke. Pity, tenderness, wrath, surged up together in John's breast; pity, tender compassion, most strong of all. Poor little thing; this was how she had come back to her home; her heart broken, her wings broken, as it were; all her soaring and swiftness and energy gone.

He could scarcely look upon her for the pity that overflowed his heart. But underneath lay wrath, not only against the man who had brought her to such a pass, but against herself too.

"John," she said, after a while, "do you remember saying to me that I was not one to bear, to put up with things, to take the consequences if I tried a dangerous experiment and failed?"

"Did I ever say anything so silly and so cruel?"

"Oh, no, no; it was neither silly nor unkind, but quite, quite true. I have thought of it so often. I used to think of it to stir up my pride, to remind myself that I ought to try to be better than my nature, not to allow you to be a true prophet. But it was so, and I couldn't change it. You can see you were right, John, for I have not been like a strong woman, able to endure; I have only been able to run away."

"My poor little Nelly!"

"Don't pity me," she said, the tears running over again. "I am too well off; I am too well taken care of. A prodigal should not be made so much of as I am."

"Don't call yourself a prodigal, Nelly! Perhaps things may not be as bad as they appear. At least, it is but the first fall—the greatest athlete gets many before he can stand against the world."

"I'll never be an athlete, John. Besides, I'm a woman, you know, and a fall of any kind is fatal to a woman, especially anything of this kind. No, I know very well it's all over; I shall never hold up my head again. But that's not the question—the question is, to be safe and as free as can be. Mamma takes me in, you know, just as if nothing had happened. She is quite willing to take the burden of me on her shoulders—and of baby. She has told you that there are two of me, now, John—my baby, as well as myself."

John could only nod an assent; he could not speak.

"It's a wonderful thing to come out of a wreck with a treasure in one's arms; everything going to pieces behind one; the rafters coming down, the walls falling in and yet one's treasure in one's arms. Oh, I had not the heart or the strength to come out of the tumbling house. My mother did it all, dragged me out, wrapped me up in love and kindness, carried me away. I don't want you to think I was good for anything. I should just have lain there and died. One thing, I did not mind dying at all—I had quite made up my mind. That would not have been so disgraceful as running away."

"There is nothing that is disgraceful," said John, "for heaven's sake don't say so, Nelly. It is unfortunate—beyond words—but that is all. Nobody can think that you are in any way disgraced. And if you are allowed just to stay quietly here in your natural home, I suppose you desire nothing more."

"What should I desire more, John? You don't suppose I should like to go and live in the world again, and go into society and all that? I have had about enough of society. Oh, I want nothing but to be quiet and unmolested, and bring up my baby. They could not take my baby from me, John?"

"I do not think so," he said, with a grave face.

"You do not—think so? Then you are not *sure*? My mother says dreadful things, but I cannot believe them. They would never take an infant from its mother to give it to—to give it to—a man—who could do nothing, nothing for it. What could a man do with a young child? a man always on the move, who has no settled home, who has no idea what an infant wants? John, I know law is inhuman, but surely, surely not so inhuman as that."

"My dear Nelly," he said, "the law, you know, which, as you say, is often inhuman, recognizes the child as belonging to the father. He is responsible for it. For instance, they never could come upon you for its maintenance or education, or anything of that kind, until it had been proved that the father——"

"May I ask," said Elinor, with uplifted head, "of what or of whom you are talking when you say *it*?"

It was all John could do not to burst into a peal of aggrieved and indignant laughter. He who had been brought from town, from his own comforts such as they were, to be consulted about this brat, this child which belonged to the dis-Honourable Phil; and Elinor, *Elinor*, of all people in the world, threw up her

249

head and confronted him with disdain because he called the brat it, and not him or her, whichever it was. John recollected well enough that sentence at which he had been so indignant in the telegram—"child, a boy "—but he affected to himself not to know what it was for the indulgence of a little contumely: and the reward he had got was contumely upon his own head. But when he looked at Elinor's pale face, the eyes so much larger than they ought to be, with tears welling out unawares, dried up for a moment by indignation or quick hasty temper, the temper which made her sweeter words all the more sweet he had always thought—then rising again unawares under the heavy lids, the lips so ready to quiver, the pathetic lines about the mouth: when he looked at all these John's heart smote him. He would have called the child anything, if there had been a sex superior to him the baby should have it. And what was there that man could do that he would not do for the deliverance of the mother and the child?

CHAPTER XXV.

It cannot be said that this evening at the Cottage was an agreeable one. To think that Elinor should be there, and yet that there should be so little pleasure in the fact that the old party, which had once been so happy together, should be together again, was bewildering. And yet there was one member of it who was happy with a shamefaced unacknowledged joy. To think that that which made her child miserable should make her happy was a dreadful thought to Mrs. Dennistoun, and yet how could she help it? Elinor was there, and the baby was there, the new unthought-of creature which had brought with it a new anxiety, a rush of new thoughts and wishes. Already everything else in the mind of Elinor's mother began to yield to the desire to retain these two—the new mother and the child. But she did not avow this desire. She was mostly silent, taking little part in the discussion, which was indeed a very curious discussion, since Elinor, debating the question how she was to abandon her husband and defend herself against him, never mentioned his name.

She did not come in to dinner, which Mrs. Dennistoun and John Tatham ate solemnly alone, saying but little, trying to talk upon indifferent topics, with that very wretched result which is usual when people at one of the great crises of life have to make conversation for each other while servants are about and the restraints of common life are around them. Whether it is the terrible flood of grief which has to be barred and kept within bounds so that the functions of life may not altogether be swept away, or the sharper but warmer pang of anxiety, that which cuts like a serpent's tooth, yet is not altogether beyond the reach of hope, what poor pretences these are at interest in ordinary subjects; what miserable gropings after something that can furnish a thread of conversation just enough to keep the intercourse of life going! These two were not more successful than others in this dismal pursuit. Mrs. Dennistoun found a moment when the meal was over before she left John, poor pretence! to his wine. "Remember that she will not mention his name; nothing must be said about him," she said. "How can we discuss him and what he is likely to do without speaking of him?" said John, with a little scorn. "I don't know," replied the poor lady. "But you will find that she will not have his name mentioned. You must try and humour her. Poor Elinor! For I know that you are sorry for her, John."

Sorry for her! He sat over his glass of mild claret in the little dining-room that had once been so bright; even now it was the cosiest little room, the curtains all drawn, shutting out the cold wind, which in January searches out every crevice, the firelight blazing fitfully, bringing out all the pretty warm decorations, the gleam of silver on the side-board, the pictures on the wall, the mirror over the mantelpiece. There was nothing wanted under that roof to make it the very home of domestic warmth and comfort. And yet—sorry for Elinor! That was not the word. His heart was sore for her, torn away from all her moorings, drifting back a wreck to the little youthful home, where all had been so tranquil and so sweet. John had nothing in him of that petty sentiment which derives satisfaction from a calamity it has foreseen, nor had he even an old lover's thrill of almost pleasure in the downfall of the clay idol that has been preferred to his gold. His pain for Elinor, the constriction in his heart at thought of her position, were unmixed with any baser feeling. Sorry for her! He would have given all he possessed to restore her happiness—not in his way, but in the way she had chosen, even, last abnegation of all, to make the man worthy of her who had never been worthy. Even his own indignation and wrath against that man were subservient in John's honest breast to the desire of somehow finding that it might be possible to whitewash him, nay to reform him, to make him as near as possible something which she could tolerate for life. I doubt if a woman, notwithstanding the much more ready power of sacrifice which women possess, could have so fully desired this renewal and amendment as John did. It was scarcely too much to say that he hated Phil Compton: yet he would have given the half of his substance at this moment to make Phil Compton a good man; nay, even to make him a passable man—to rehabilitate him in his wife's eyes.

John stayed a long time over "his wine," the mild glass of claret (or perhaps it was Burgundy) which was all that was offered him—partly to think the matter over, but also partly perhaps because he heard certain faint gurglings, and the passage of certain steps, active and full of energy, past the door of the room within which he sat, going now to the drawing-room, now up-stairs, from which he divined that the new inmate of the house was at present in possession of the drawing-room, and of all attention there. He smiled at himself for his hostility to the child, which, of course, was entirely innocent of all blame. Here the man was inferior to the woman in comprehension and sympathy; for he not only could not understand how they could possibly obtain solace in their trouble from this unconscious little creature, but he was angry and scornful of them for doing so. Phil Compton's brat, no doubt the germ of a thousand troubles to come, but besides that a nothing, a being without love or thought, or even consciousness, a mere little animal feeding and sleeping—and yet the idol and object of all the thoughts of two intelligent women, capable of so much better things! This irritated John and disgusted him in the midst of all his anxious thoughts, and his profound compassion and deliberations how best to help: and it was not till the passage of certain feeble sounds outside his door, which proceeded audibly up-stairs, little bleatings in which, if they had come from a lamb, or even a puppy, John would have been interested, assured him that the small enemy had disappeared—that he finally rose and proceeded to "join the ladies," as if he had been holding a little private debauch all by himself.

There was a little fragrance and air of the visitor still in the room, a little disturbance of the usual arrangements, a surreptitious, quite unjustifiable look as of pleasure in Elinor's eyes, which were less expanded, and if as liquid as ever, more softly bright than before. Something white actually lay on the sofa, a small garment which Mrs. Dennistoun whisked away. They were conscious of John's critical eye upon them, and received him with a warmth of conciliatory welcome which betrayed that consciousness. Mrs. Dennistoun drew a chair for him to the other side of the fire. She took her own place in the middle at the table with a large piece of white knitting, to which she gave her whole attention, and thus the deliberation began.

"Elinor wants to know, John, what you think we ought to do— to make quite sure—that there will be no risk, about the baby."

"I must know more of the details of the question before I can give any advice," said John.

"John," said Elinor, raising herself in her chair, "here are all the details that are necessary. I have come away. I have come home, finding that life was impossible there. That is the whole matter. It may be, probably it is, my own fault. It is simply that life became impossible. You know you said that I was not one to endure, to put up with things. I scoffed at you then, for I did not expect to have anything to put up with; but you were quite right, and life had become impossible—that is all there is any need to say."

"To me, yes," said John, "but not enough, Elinor, if it ever has to come within the reach of the law."

"But why should it come within the reach of the law? You, John, you are a lawyer; you know the rights of everything. I thought you might have arranged it all. Couldn't you try to make a kind of a bargain? What bargain? Oh, am I a lawyer, do I know? But you, John, who have it all at your fingers' ends, who know what can be done and what can't be done, and the rights that one has and that another has! Dear John! if you were to try, don't you think that you could settle it all, simply as between people who don't want any exposure, any struggle, but only to be quiet and to be let alone?"

"Elinor, I don't know what I could do with so little information as I have. To know that you found your life impossible is enough for me. But you know most people are right in their own eyes. If we have some one opposed to us who thinks, for instance, that the fault was yours?"

"Well," she cried, eagerly, "I am willing to accept that: say that the fault was mine! You could confirm it, that it was likely to be mine. You could tell them what an impatient person I was, and that you said I was not one to try an experiment, for I never, never could put up with anything. John, you could be a witness as well as an advocate. You could prove that you always expected—and that I am quite, quite willing to allow that it was I——"

"Elinor, if I could only make you understand what I mean! I am told that I am not to mention any names?"

"No, no names, no names! What is the good? We both know very well what we mean."

"But I don't know very well what you mean. Don't you see that if it is your fault—if the other party is innocent—there can be no reason in the world why he should consent to renounce his rights. It is not a mere matter of feeling. There is right in it one way or another—either on your side or else on the other side; and if it is on the other side, why should a man give up what belongs to him, why should he renounce what is—most dear to him?"

"Oh, John, John, John!" she made this appeal and outcry, clasping her hands together with a mixture of supplication and impatience. Then turning to her mother—"Oh, tell him," she cried, "tell him!"—always clasping those impatient yet beseeching hands.

"You see, John," said Mrs. Dennistoun, "Elinor knows that the right is on her side: but she will consent to say nothing about it to any one—to give herself out as the offender rather—that is to say, as an ill-disciplined person that cannot put up with anything, as you seem to have said."

John laughed with vexation, yet a kind of amusement. "I never said it nor thought it: still if it pleases her to think so—— The wiser thing if this separation is final——"

"If it is final!" Elinor cried. She raised herself up again in her chair, and contemplated the unfortunate John with a sort of tragic superiority. "Do you think that of me," she said, "that I would take such a step as this and that it should not be final? Is dying final? Could one do such a thing as this and change?"

"Such things have been done," said John. "Elinor, forgive me. I must say it—it is all your life that is in the balance, and another life. There is this infant to be struggled over, perhaps rent in two by those who should have united to take care of him—and it's a boy, I hear. There's his name and his after-life to think of—a child without a father, perhaps the heir of a family to which he will not belong. Elinor—tell her, aunt, you understand: is it my wish to hand her back to—to—— No, I'll speak no names. But you know I disliked it always, opposed it always. It is not out of any favour to—to the other side. But she ought to take all these things into account. Her own position, and the position in the future of the child——"

Elinor had crushed her fan with her hands, and Mrs. Dennistoun let the knitting with which she had gone on in spite of all fall at last in her lap. There was a little pause. John Tatham's voice itself had began to falter, or rather swelled in sound as when a stream swells in flood.

"I do not go into the question about women and what they ought to put up with," said John, resuming. "There's many things that law can do nothing for—and nature in many ways makes it harder for women, I acknowledge. We cannot change that. Think what her position will be—neither a wife nor with the freedom of a widow; and the boy, bearing the name of one he must almost be taught to think badly of—for one of them must be in the wrong——"

"He shall never, never hear that name; he shall know nothing, he shall be free of every bond; his mind shall never be cramped or twisted or troubled by any—man—if I live."

This Elinor said, lifting her pale face from her hands with eyes that flashed and shone with a blaze of excitement and weakness.

"There already," said John, "is a tremendous condition—if you live! Who can make sure that they will live? We must all die—some sooner, some later—and you wearing yourself out with excitement, that never were strong; you exposing your heart, the weakest organ——"

"John," said Mrs. Dennistoun, grasping him by the arm, "you are talking nonsense, you don't know what you are saying. My darling! she was never weak nor had a feeble heart, nor—anything! She will live to bring up *his* children, her baby's children, upon her knees."

"And what would it matter?" said Elinor—looking at him with clear eyes, from which the tears had disappeared in the shock of this unlooked-for suggestion—"suppose I have no more strength than that, suppose I were to die? you shall be his guardian, John, bring him up a good man; and his Heavenly Father will take care of him. I am not afraid."

A man had better not deal with such subjects between two women. What with Mrs. Dennistoun's indignant protest and Elinor's lofty submission, John was at his wits' end. "I did not mean to carry things to such a bitter end as that," he said. "You want to force me into a corner and make me say things I never meant. The question is serious enough without that."

There was again a little pause, and then Elinor, with one of those changes which are so perplexing to sober-minded people, suddenly turned to him, holding out both her hands.

"John—we'll leave that in God's hands whatever is to happen to me. But in the meantime, while I am living—and perhaps my life depends upon being quiet and having a little peace and rest. It is not that I care very much for my life," said Elinor, with that clear, open-eyed look, like the sky after rain—"I am shipwrecked, John, as you say—but my mother does, and it's of—some—consequence—to baby; and if it depends upon whether I am left alone, you are too good a friend to leave me in the lurch. And you said—one night—whatever happened I was to send for you."

John sprang up from his seat, dropping the hands which he had taken into his own. She was like Queen Katherine, "about to weep," and her breast strained with the sobbing effort to keep it down.

"For God's sake," he cried, "don't play upon our hearts like this! I will do anything—everything—whatever you choose to tell me. Aunt, don't let her cry, don't let her go on like that. Why, good heavens!" he cried, bursting himself into a kind of big sob, "won't it be bad for that little brat of a baby or something if she keeps going on in this way?"

Thus John Tatham surrendered at discretion. What could he do more? A man cannot be played upon like an instrument without giving out sounds of which he will, perhaps, be ashamed. And this woman appealing to him—this girl—looking like the little Elinor he remembered, younger and softer in her weakness and trouble than she had been in her beauty and pride—was the creature after all, though she would never know it, whom he loved best in the world. He had wanted to save her, in the one worldly way of saving her, from open shipwreck, for her own sake, against every prejudice and prepossession of his mind. But if she would not have that, why it was his business to save her as she wished, to do for her whatever she wanted; to act as her agent, her champion, whatever she pleased.

He was sent away presently, and accepted his dismissal with thankfulness, to smoke his cigar. This is one amusing thing in a feminine household. A man is supposed to want all manner of little indulgences and not to be able to do without them. He is carefully left alone over "his wine"—the aforesaid glass of claret; and ways and means are provided for him to smoke his cigar, whether he wishes it or not. He had often laughed at these regulations of his careful relatives, but he was rather glad of them to-night. "I am going to get Elinor to bed," said Mrs. Dennistoun. "It has, perhaps, been a little too much for her: but when you have finished your cigar, John, if you will come back to the drawing-room for a few minutes you will find me here."

John did not smoke any cigar. It is all very well to be soothed and consoled by tobacco in your own room, at your own ease: but when you are put into a lady's dining-room, where everything is nice, and where the curtains will probably smell of smoke next morning: and when your mind is exercised beyond even the power of the body to keep still, that is not a time to enjoy such calm and composing delights. But he walked about the room in which he was shut up like a wild beast in his cage, sometimes with long strides from wall to wall, sometimes going round, with that abstract trick of his, staring at the pictures, as if he did not know every picture in the place by heart. He forgot that he was to go back to the drawing-room again after Elinor had been taken to bed, and it was only after having waited for him a long time that Mrs. Dennistoun came, almost timidly, knocking at her own dining-room door, afraid to disturb her visitor in the evening rites which she believed in so devoutly. She did go in, however, and they stood together over the fire for a few minutes, he staring down upon the glow at his feet, she contemplating fitfully, unconsciously, her own pale face and his in the dim mirror on the mantelpiece. They talked in low tones about Elinor and her health, and her determination which nothing would change.

"Of course I will do it," said John; "anything—whatever she may require of me—there are no two words about that. There is only one thing: I will not compromise her by taking any initiative. Let us wait and see what they are going to do——"

"But, John, might it not be better to disarm him by making overtures? anything, I would do anything if he would but let her remain unmolested—and the baby."

"Do you mean money?" he said.

Mrs. Dennistoun gave him an abashed look, deprecatory and wistful, but did not make any reply.

"Phil Compton is a cad, and a brute, and a scamp of the first water," said John, glad of some way to get rid of his excitement;

"but I do not think that even he would sell his wife and his child for money. I wouldn't do him so much discredit as that."

"Oh, I beg your pardon, John," Mrs. Dennistoun said.

CHAPTER XXVI.

John left the Cottage next morning with the full conduct of the affairs of the family placed in his hands. The ladies were both a little doubtful if his plan was the best—they were still frightened for what might happen, and kept up a watch, as John perceived, fearing every step that approached, trembling at every shadow. They remembered many stories, such as rush to the minds of persons in trouble, of similar cases, of the machinations of the bad father whose only object was to overcome and break down his wife, and who stole his child away to let it languish and die. There are some circumstances in which people forget all the shades of character, and take it for granted that a man who can go wrong in one matter will act like a very demon in all. This was doubly strong in Mrs. Dennistoun, a woman full of toleration and experience; but the issues were so momentous to her, and the possible results so terrible, that she lost her accustomed good sense. It was more natural, perhaps, that Elinor, who was weak in health and still full of the arbitrariness of youth, should entertain this fear—without considering that Phil was the very last man in the world to burden himself with an infant of the most helpless age—which seemed to John an almost quite unreasonable one. Almost—for, of course, he too was compelled to allow, when driven into a corner, that there was nothing that an exasperated man might not do. Elinor had come down early to see her cousin before he left the house, bringing with her in her arms the little bundle of muslin and flannel upon the safety of which her very life seemed to depend. John looked at it, and at the small pink face and unconscious flickering hands that formed the small centre to all those wrappings, with a curious mixture of pity and repugnance. It was like any other blind new-born kitten or puppy, he thought, but not so amusing—no, it was not blind, to be sure. At one moment, without any warning, it suddenly opened a pair of eyes, which by a lively exercise of fancy might be supposed like Elinor's, and seemed to look him in the face, which startled him very much, with a curious notification of the fact that the thing was not a kitten or a puppy. But then a little quiver came over the small countenance, and the attendant said it was "the wind." Perhaps the opening of the eyes was the wind too, or some other automatic effect. He would not hold out his finger to be clasped tight by the little flickering fist, as Elinor would have had him. He would none of those follies; he turned away from it not to allow himself to be moved by the effect, quite a meretricious one, of the baby in the young mother's arms. That was all poetry, sentiment, the trick of the painter, who had found the combination beautiful. Such ideas belonged, indeed, to the conventional-sacred, and he had never felt any profane resistance of mind against the San Sisto picture or any of its kind. But Phil Compton's brat was a very different thing. What did it matter what became of it? If it were not for Elinor's perverse feeling on the subject, and that perfectly imbecile prostration of her mother, a sensible woman who ought to have known better, before the little creature, he would himself have been rather grateful to Phil Compton for taking it away. But when he saw the look of terror upon Elinor's face when an unexpected step came to the door, when he saw her turn and fly, wrapping the child in her arms, on her very heart as it seemed, bending over it, covering it so that it disappeared altogether in her embrace, John's heart was a little touched. It was only a hawking tramp with pins and needles, who came by mistake to the hall door, but her panic and anguish of alarm were a spectacle which he could not get out of his eyes.

"You see, she never feels safe for a moment. It will be hard to persuade her that that man, though I've seen him about the roads for years, is not an emissary—or a spy—to find out if she is here."

"I am sure it is quite an unnecessary panic," said John. "In the first place, Phil Compton's the last man to burden himself with a child; in the second, he's not a brute nor a monster."

"You called him a brute last night, John."

"I did not mean in that way. I don't mean to stand by any rash word that may be forced from me in a moment of irritation. Aunt, get her to give over that. She'll torture herself to death for nothing. He'll not try to take the child away—not just now, at all events, not while it is a mere—— Bring her to her senses on that point. You surely can do that?"

"If I was quite sure of being in my own," Mrs. Dennistoun said, with a forlorn smile. "I am as much frightened as she is, John. And, remember, if there is anything to be done—anything——"

"There is nothing but a little common sense wanted," said John. But as he drove away from the door, and saw the hawker with the needles still about, the ladies had so infected him that it was all he could do to restrain an inclination to take the vagrant by the collar and throw him down the combe.

"Who's that fellow hanging about?" he said to Pearson, who was driving him; "and what does he want here?"

"Bless you, sir! that's Joe," Pearson said. "He's after no harm. He's honest enough as long as there ain't nothing much in his way; and he's waiting for the pieces as cook gives him once a week when he comes his rounds. There's no harm in poor Joe."

"I suppose not, since you say so," said John; "but you know the ladies are rather nervous, Pearson. You must keep a look-out that no suspicious-looking person hangs about the house."

"Bless us! Mr. John," said Pearson, "what are they nervous about?—the baby? But nobody wants to steal a baby, bless your soul!"

"I quite agree with you," said John, much relieved (though he considered Pearson an old fool, in a general way) to have his own opinion confirmed. "But, all the same, I wish you would be doubly particular not to admit anybody you don't know; and if any man should appear to bother them send for me on the moment. Do you hear?"

"What do you call any man, sir?" said Pearson, smartly. He had ideas of his own, though he might be a fool.

"I mean what I say," said John, more sharply still. "Any one that molests or alarms them. Send me off a telegram at once—'You're wanted!' That will be quite enough. But don't go with it to the office yourself; send somebody—there's always your boy about the place—and keep about like a dragon yourself."

"I'll do my best, sir," said Pearson, "though I don't know what a dragon is, except it's the one in the Bible; and that's not a thing anybody would want about the place."

It was a comfort to John, after all his troubles, to be able to laugh, which he did with a heartiness which surprised Pearson, who was quite unaware that he had made any joke.

These fears, however, which were imposed upon him by the contagion of the terrors of the others, soon passed from John's mind. He was convinced that Phil Compton would take no such step; and that, however much he might wish his wife to return, the possession of the baby was not a thing which he would struggle over. It cannot be denied, however, that he was anxious, and eagerly inspected his letters in the morning, and looked out for telegrams during the day. Fortunately, however, no evil tidings came. Mrs. Dennistoun reported unbroken peace in the Cottage and increasing strength on the part of Elinor; and, in a parenthesis with a sort of apology, of the baby. Nobody had come near them to trouble them. Elinor had received no letters. The tie between her and her husband seemed to be cut as with a knife. "We cannot of course," she said, "expect this tranquillity to last."

And it came to be a very curious thought with John, as week after week passed, whether it was to last—whether Phil Compton, who had never been supposed wanting in courage, intended to let his wife and child drop off from him as if they had never been. This seemed a thing impossible to conceive: but John said to himself with much internal contempt that he knew nothing of the workings of the mind of such a man, and that it might for aught he knew be a common incident in life with the Phil

Comptons thus to shake off their belongings when they got tired of them. The fool! the booby! to get tired of Elinor! That rumour which flies about the world so strangely and communicates information about everybody to the vacant ear, to be retailed to those whom it may concern, provided him, as the days went by, with many particulars which he had not been able to obtain from Elinor. Phil, it appeared, had gone to Glenorban—the great house to which he had been invited—alone, with an excuse for his wife, whose state of health was not appropriate to a large party, and had stayed there spending Christmas with a brilliant houseful of guests, among whom was the American lady who had captivated him. Phil had paid one visit to the lodge to see Elinor, by her mother's summons, at the crisis of her illness, but had not hesitated to go away again when informed that the crisis was over. Mrs. Dennistoun never told what had passed between them on that occasion, but the gossips of the club were credibly informed that she had bullied and stormed at Phil, after the fashion of mothers-in-law, till she had driven him away. Upon which he had returned to his party and flirted with Mrs. Harris more than ever. John discovered also that the party having dispersed some time ago, Phil had gone abroad. Whether in ignorance of his wife's flight or not he could not discover; but it was almost impossible to believe that he would have gone to Monte Carlo without finding out something about Elinor—how and where she was. But whether this was the cause of his utter silence, or whether it was the habit of men of his class to treat such tremendous incidents in domestic life with levity, John Tatham could not make out. He was congratulating himself, however, upon keeping perfectly quiet, and leaving the conduct of the matter to the other party, when the silence was disturbed in what seemed to him the most curious way.

One afternoon when he returned from the court he was aware, when he entered the outer office in which his clerk abode, of what he described afterwards as a smell fit to knock you down. It would have been described more appropriately in a French novel as the special perfume, subtle and exquisite, by which a beautiful woman may be recognised wherever she goes. It was, indeed, neither more nor less than the particular scent used by Lady Mariamne, who came forward with a sweep and rustle of her draperies, and the most ingratiating of her smiles.

"It appears to be fated that I am to wait for you," she said. "How do you do, Mr. Tatham? Take me out of this horrible dirty place. I am quite sure you have some nice rooms in there." She pointed as she spoke to the inner door, and moved towards it with the air of a person who knew where she was going, and was fully purposed to be admitted. John said afterwards, that to think of this woman's abominable scent being left in his room in which he lived (though he also received his clients in it) was almost more than he could bear. But, in the meantime, he could do nothing but open the door to her, and offer her his most comfortable chair.

She seated herself with all those little tricks of movement which are also part of the stock-in-trade of the pretty woman. Lady Mariamne's prettiness was not of a kind which had the slightest effect upon John, but still it was a kind which received credit in society, being the product of a great deal of pains and care and exquisite arrangement and combination. She threw her fur cloak back a little, arranged the strings of her bonnet under her chin, which threw up the daintiness and rosiness of a complexion about which there were many questions among her closest friends. She shook up, with what had often been commented upon as the prettiest gesture, the bracelets from her wrists. She arranged the veil, which just came over the tip of her delicate nose, she put out her foot as if searching for a footstool—which John made haste to supply, though he remained unaffected otherwise by all these pretty preliminaries.

"Sit down, Mr. Tatham," then said Lady Mariamne. "It makes me wretchedly uncomfortable, as if you were some dreadful man waiting to be paid or something, to see you standing there."

Though John's first impulse was that of wrath to be thus

requested to sit down in his own chambers, the position was amusing as well as disagreeable, and he laughed and drew a chair towards his writing-table, which was as crowded and untidy as the writing-table of a busy man usually is, and placed himself in an attitude of attention, though without asking any question.

"Well," said Lady Mariamne, slowly drawing off her glove; "you know, of course, why I have come, Mr. Tatham—to talk over with you, as a man who knows the world, this deplorable business. You see it has come about exactly as I said. I knew what would happen: and though I am not one of those people who always insist upon being proved right, you remember what I said——"

"I remember that you said something—to which, perhaps, had I thought I should have been called upon to give evidence as to its correctness—I should have paid more attention, Lady Mariamne."

"How rude you are!" she said, with her whole interest concentrated upon the slow removal of her glove. Then she smoothed a little, softly, the pretty hand which was thus uncovered, and said, "How red one's hands get in this weather," and then laughed. "You don't mean to tell me, Mr. Tatham," she said, suddenly raising her eyes to his, "that, considering what a very particular person we were discussing, you can't remember what I said?"

John was obliged to confess that he remembered more or less the gist of her discourse, and Lady Mariamne nodded her head many times in acceptance of his confession.

"Well," she said, "you see what it has come to. An open scandal, a separation, and everything broken up. For one thing, I knew if she did not give him his head a little that's what would happen. I don't believe he cares a brass farthing for that other woman. She makes fun of everybody, and that amused him. And it amused him to put Nell in a state—that as much as anything. Why couldn't she see that and learn to *prendre son parti* like other people? She was free to say, 'You go your way and I'll go mine.'

the most of us do that sooner or later: but to make a vulgar open rupture, and go off—like this."

"I fail to see the vulgarity in it," said John.

"Oh, of course; everything she does is perfect to you. But just think, if it had been your own case—followed about and bullied by a jealous woman, in a state of health that of itself disgusts a man——"

"Lady Mariamne, you must pardon me if I refuse to listen to anything more of this kind," said John, starting to his feet.

"Oh, I warn you, you'll be compelled to listen to a great deal more if you're her agent as I hear! Phil will find means of compelling you to hear if you don't like to take your information from me."

"I should like to know how Mr. Phil Compton will succeed in compelling me—to anything I don't choose to do."

"You think, perhaps, because there's no duelling in this country he can't do anything. But there is, all the same. He would shame you into it—he could say you were—sheltering yourself——"

"I am not a man to fight duels," said John, very angry, but smiling, "in any circumstances, even were such a thing not utterly ridiculous; but even a fighting man might feel that to put himself on a level with the dis-Hon——"

He stopped himself as he said it. How mean it was—to a woman!—descending to their own methods. But Lady Mariamne was too quick for him.

"Oh," she said; "so you've heard of that, a nickname that no gentleman——" then she too paused and looked at him, with a momentary flush. He was going to apologize abjectly, when with a slight laugh she turned the subject aside.

"Pretty fools we are, both of us, to talk such nonsense. I didn't come here carrying Phil on my shoulders, to spring at your throat if you expressed your opinion. Look here—tell me, don't let us go beating about the bush, Mr. Tatham—I suppose you have seen Nell?"

"I know my cousin's mind, at least," he said.

"Well, then, just tell me as between friends—there's no need we should quarrel because they have done so. Tell me this, is she going to get up a divorce case——"

"A divorce——!"

"Because," said Lady Mariamne, "she'll find it precious difficult to prove anything. I know she will. She may prove the flirting and so forth—but what's that? You can tell her from me, it wants somebody far better up to things than she is to prove anything. I warn her as a friend she'll not get much good by that move."

"I am not aware," said John, "whether Mrs. Compton has made up her mind about the further steps——"

"Then just you advise her not," cried Lady Mariamne. "It doesn't matter to me: I shall be none the worse whatever she does: but if you are her true friend you will advise her not. She might tell what she thinks, but that's no proof. Mr. Tatham, I know you have great influence with Nell."

"Not in a matter like this," said John, with great gravity. "Of course she alone can be the judge."

"What nonsense you talk, you men! Of course she is not the least the judge, and of course she will be guided by you."

"You may be sure she shall have the best advice that I can give," John said with a bow.

"You want me to go, I see," said Lady Mariamne; "you are dreadfully rude, standing up all the time to show me I had better go." Hereupon she recommenced her little *manège*, drawing on her glove, letting her bracelets drop again, fastening the fur round her throat. "Well, Mr. Tatham," she said, "I hope you mean to have the civility to see after my carriage. I can't go roaming about hailing it as if it were a hansom cab—in this queer place."

CHAPTER XXVII.

John went down to Windyhill that evening. His appearance alarmed the little household more than words could say. As he was admitted at once by the servants, delighted to see him, he walked in suddenly into the midst of a truly domestic scene. The baby lay on Elinor's knee in the midst of a mass of white wrappings, kicking out a pair of pink little legs in the front of the fire. Elinor herself was seated on a very low chair, and illuminated by the cheerful blaze, which threw a glare upon her countenance, and called out unthought-of lights in her hair, there was no appearance in her looks of anxiety or trouble. She was altogether given up to the baby and the joy of its new life. The little kicking limbs, the pleasure of the little creature in the warmth, the curling of its rosy little toes in the agreeable sensation of the heat, were more to Elinor and to her mother, who was kneeling beside her on the hearth-rug, than the most refined and lofty pleasures in the world. The most lofty of us have to come down to those primitive sources of bliss, if we are happy enough to have them placed in our way. The greatest poet by her side, the music of the spheres sounding in her ear, would not have made Elinor forget her troubles like the stretching out towards the fire of those little pink toes.

When the door opened, and the voice and step of a man—dreaded sounds—were audible, a thrill of terror ran over this little group. Mrs. Dennistoun sprang to her feet and placed herself between the intruder and the young mother, while Elinor gathered up, covering him all over, so that he disappeared altogether, her child in her arms.

"It is John," said Mrs. Dennistoun. "God be thanked, it is only

John."

But Elinor, quite overcome by the shock, burst suddenly into tears, to which the baby responded by a vigorous cry, not at all relishing the sudden huddling up among its shawls to which it had been subjected. It may be supposed what an effect this cloudy side of the happiness, which he had not been able to deny to himself made a very pretty scene, had upon John. He said, not without a little offence, "I am sure I beg your pardon humbly. I'll go away."

Elinor turned round her head, smiling through her tears. "It was only that you gave me a fright," she said. "I am quite right again; don't, oh, don't go away! unless you object to the sight of baby, and to hear him cry; but he'll not cry now, any more than his silly mother. Mamma, make John sit down and tell us—Oh, I am sure he has something to tell us—Perhaps I took comfort too soon; but the very sight of John is a protection and a strength," she said, holding out her hand to him. This sudden change of front reduced John, who had been perhaps disposed for a moment to stand on his dignity, to utter subjection. He neither said nor even thought a word against the baby, who was presently unfolded again, and turned once more the toes of comfort towards the fire. He did not approach too near, feeling that he had no particular share in the scene, and indeed cut an almost absurd figure in the midst of that group, but sat behind, contemplating it from a little distance against the fire. The evening had grown dark by this time, but the two women, absorbed by their worship, had wanted no light. It had happened to John by an extreme piece of luck to catch the express train almost as soon as Lady Mariamne had left him, and to reach the station at Hurrymere before the February day was done.

"You have something to tell us, John—good news or bad?" Mrs. Dennistoun said.

"Good; or I should not have come like this unannounced," he said. "The post is quick enough for bad. I think you may be quite at your ease about the child—no claim will be made on the child.

Elinor, I think, will not be disturbed if—she means to take no steps on her side."

"What steps?" said Mrs. Dennistoun. Elinor turned her head to look at him anxiously over the back of her chair.

"I have had a visit this afternoon," he said.

"From—" Elinor drew a long hurried breath. She said no name, but it was evident that one was on her lips—a name she never meant to pronounce more, but to which her whole being thrilled still even when it was unspoken. She looked at him full of eagerness to hear yet with a hand uplifted, as if to forbid any utterance.

"From Lady Mariamne."

How her countenance fell! She turned round again, and bent over her baby. It was a pang of acute disappointment, he could not but see, that went through her, though she would not have allowed him to say that name. Strange inconsistency! it ran over John too with a sense of keen indignation, as if he had taken from her an electric touch.

"——Whose object in coming to me was to ascertain whether you intended to bring a suit for—divorce."

A cry rang through the room. Elinor turned upon him for a moment a face blazing with hot and painful colour. The lamp had been brought in, and he saw the fierce blush and look of horror. Then she turned round and buried it in her hands.

"Divorce!" said Mrs. Dennistoun. "Elinor——! To drag her private affairs before the world. Oh, John, John, that could not be. You would not wish that to be."

"I!" he cried with a laugh of tuneless mirth. "Is it likely that I would wish to drag Elinor before the world?"

Elinor did not say anything, but withdrew one hand from her burning cheek and put it into his. These women treated John as if he were a man of wood. What he might be feeling, or if he were feeling anything, did not enter their minds.

"It was like her," said Elinor after a time in a low hurried voice, "to think of that. She is the only one who would think of it. As if

I had ever thought or dreamed——"

"It is possible, however," he said, "that it might be reasonable enough. I don't speak to Elinor," who had let go his hand hastily, "but to you, aunt. If it is altogether final, as she says, to be released would perhaps be better, from a bond that was no bond."

"John, John, would you have her add shame to pain?"

"The shame would not be to her, aunt."

"The shame is to every one concerned—to every one! My Elinor's name, her dear name, dragged through all that mud! She a party, perhaps, to revelations—Oh, never, never! We would bear anything rather."

"This of course," said John, "is perhaps a still more bitter punishment for the other side."

She looked round at him again. Looking up with a look of pale horror, her eyelids in agonised curves over her eyes, her mouth quivering. "What did you say, John?"

"I said it might be a more bitter punishment still for—the other side."

Elinor lifted up her baby to her breast, raising herself with a new dignity, with her head high. "I meant no punishment," she said, "I want none. I have left—what killed me—behind me; many things, not one only. I have brought my boy away that he may never—never— But if it would be better that—another should be free—"

"I will never give my consent to it, Elinor."

"Nor I with my own mind; but if it is vindictive—if it is revenge, mother! I am not alone to think of myself. If it were better for —— that he should be free; speak to John about it and tell me. I cannot, cannot discuss it. I will leave it all to John and you. It will kill me! but what does that matter?—it is not revenge that I seek."

She turned with the baby pressed to her breast and walked away, her every movement showing the strain and excitement of her soul.

"Why did you do this, John, without at least consulting me?

273

You have thrown a new trouble into her mind. She will never, never do this thing—nor would I permit it. There are some things in which I must take a part. I could not forbid her marriage; God grant that I had had the strength to do it—but this I will forbid, to expose her to the whole world, when everything we have done has been with the idea of concealing what had happened. Never, never. I will never consent to it, John."

"I had no intention of proposing such a step; but the other side—as we are bound to call him—are frightened about it. And when I saw her look up, so young still, so sweet, with all her life before her, and thought how she must spend it—alone; with no expanding, no development, in this cottage or somewhere else, a life shipwrecked, a being so capable, so full of possibilities—lost."

"I have spent my life in this cottage," said Mrs. Dennistoun. "My husband died when I was thirty—my life was over, and still I was young; but I had Elinor. There were some who pitied me too, but their pity was uncalled for. Elinor will live like her mother, she has her boy."

"But it is different; you cannot but see the difference."

"Yes, I see it—it is different; but not so different that my Elinor's name should be placarded about the streets and put in all the newspapers. Oh, never, never, John. If the man suffers, it is his fault. She will suffer, and it is not her fault; but I will not, to release him, drag my child before the world."

Mrs. Dennistoun was so much excited that she began to pace about the room, she who was usually so sober and self restrained. She had borne much, but this she was unable even to contemplate with calm. For once in her life she had arrived at something which she would not bear. John felt his own position very strange sitting looking on as a spectator, while this woman, usually so self-controlled, showed her impatience of circumstances and fate. It was ruefully comic that this should be, so to speak, his doing, though he was the last in the world to desire any exposure of Elinor, or to have any sympathy with those who sought justice for themselves or revenge on others at such a cost.

"I was rash perhaps to speak as I did," he said; "I had no intention of doing it when I came. It was a mere impulse, seeing Elinor: but you must know that I agree with you perfectly. I see that Elinor's lot is fixed anyhow. I believe that no decree of a court would make any difference to her, and she would not change the name that is the child's name. All that I recognise. And one thing more, that neither you nor Elinor has recognised. They—he is afraid of any proceedings—I suppose I may mention him to you. It's rather absurd, don't you think, speaking of a fellow of that sort, or rather, not speaking of him at all, as if his name was sacred? He is afraid of proceedings—whatever may be the cause."

"John, can't you understand that she cannot bear to speak of him, a man she so fought for, against us all? And now her eyes are opened, she is undeceived, she knows him all through and through, more, far more, than we do. She opened her mind to me once, and only once. It was not *that* alone; oh, no, no. There are things that rankle more than that, something he did before they were married, and made her help him to conceal. Something dishon—I can't say the word, John."

"Oh," said John, grimly, "you need not mind me."

"Well, the woman—I blush to have to speak to you even of such a thing—the woman, John, was not the worst. She almost might, I think, have forgiven that. It was one thing after another, and that, that first business the worst of all. She found it out somehow, and he had made her take a part—I can't tell what. She would never open her lips on the subject again. Only that once it all burst forth. Oh, divorce! What would that do to her, besides the shame? You understand some things, John," said Mrs. Dennistoun, with a smile, "though you are a man. She would never do anything to give herself a name different from her child's."

"Yes," said John, with a laugh, "I think I understand a thing or two, though, as you say, my dear aunt, I am only a man. However, it is just as well I am that imperfect creature, to take care of you. It understands the tactics of the wicked better than you do. And now you must persuade Elinor and persuade yourself of what I came here on purpose to tell you—not to disturb you, as I have been so unfortunate as to do. You are perfectly safe from him. I will not let the enemy know your sentiments, or how decided you are on the subject. I will perhaps, if you will let me, crack the whip a little over their heads, and keep them in a pleasing uncertainty. But as long as he is afraid that she will take proceedings against him, he will take none, you may be sure, against her. So you may throw aside all your precautions and be happy over your treasure in your own way."

"Thank God for what you say, John; you take a weight off my heart. But happy—how can you speak of being happy after such a catastrophe?"

"I thought I came in upon a very happy little scene. It might be only pretence, but it looked uncommonly like the real thing."

"You mean the baby, John, the dear infant that knows no harm. He does take off our thoughts a little, and enable us to bear——"

"Oh, aunt, don't be a hypocrite; that was never a fault of yours. Confess that with all your misery about Elinor you are happy to have her here and her child—notwithstanding everything—happy as you have not been for many a day."

She sat down by him and gave him her hand. "John, to be a man you have wonderful insight, and it's I who am a very, very imperfect creature. You don't think worse of me to be glad to have her, even though it is purchased by such misery and trouble? God knows," cried the poor lady, drying her eyes, "that I would give her up to-morrow, and with joy, and consent never to see her again, if that would be for her happiness. John! I've not thrust myself upon them, have I, nor done anything against him, nor said a word? But now that she is here, and the baby, and all to myself—which I never hoped—would I not be an ungrateful woman if I did not thank God for it, John?"

"You are an excellent special pleader, aunt," he said, with a laugh, "as most women whom I have known are: and I agree with you in everything. You behaved to them, while it was *them*, angelically: you effaced yourself, and I fully believe you never said a word against him. Also, I believe that if circumstances changed, if anything happened to make her see that she could go back to him——"

Mrs. Dennistoun started in spite of herself, and pressed her hands together, with a half sob of dismay.

"I don't think it likely, but if it were so, you would sacrifice yourself again—I haven't a doubt of it. Why, then, set up this piece of humbug to me who know you so well, and pretend that you are not very happy for the moment? You are, and you have a good right to be: and I say enjoy it, my dear aunt; take all the good of it, you will have no trouble from him."

"You think so, you really think so, John?"

"I have no doubt of it: and you must persuade Elinor. Don't think I am making light of the situation: you'll have plenty to trouble you no doubt, when that little shaver grows up——"

"John!"

"Well, he is a little shaver (whatever that may mean I'm sure I don't know), if he were a little prince. When he grows up you will have your business laid out for you, and I don't envy you the clearing up——"

"John don't speak as if a time would come when you would not stand by us. I mean stand by Elinor."

"Your first phrase was much the best. I will stand by you both as a matter of course."

"You must consider I shall be an old woman then; and who knows if I may live to see the poor little darling grow up?"

"The poor little darling may never grow up, and none of us may live to see it. One prediction is as good as another: but I think better things of you, aunt, than that you would go and die and desert Elinor, unless 'so be as you couldn't help it,' as Pearson says. But, however, in the meantime, dying of anybody is not in the question, and I hope both you and she will take as much pleasure out of the baby and be as happy as circumstances will allow. And I'll tell Pearson that there is no need for him to act the dragon—either the Bible one, whom he did not think you would like to have about the house, or any other—for the danger is over. Trust me at least for that."

"I trust you for everything, John; but," added Mrs. Dennistoun, "I wouldn't say anything to Pearson. If you've told him to be a dragon, let him be a dragon still. I am sure you are right, and I will tell Elinor so, and comfort her heart; but we may as well keep a good look out, and our eyes about us, all the same."

"They are sure I am right, but think it better to go on as if I were wrong," John said to himself as he went to dress for dinner. And while he went through this ceremony, he had a great many thoughts—half-impatient, half-tender—of the wonderful ways of women which are so amazing to men in general, as the ways of men are amazing to women, and will be so, no doubt, as long as the world goes on. The strange mixture of the wise and the foolish, the altogether heroic, and the involuntarily fictitious, struck his keen perception with a humourous understanding, and amusement, and sympathy. That Mrs. Dennistoun should pose a little as a sufferer while she was unmitigatedly happy in the possession of Elinor and the child, and be abashed when she was forced to confess how ecstatic was the fearful joy which she snatched in the midst of danger, was strange enough. But that Elinor, at this dreadful crisis of her life, when every bond was rent asunder, and all that is ordinarily called happiness wrecked for ever, should be moved to the kind of rapture he had seen in her face by the reaching out and curling in of those little pink toes in the warm light of the fire, was inconceivable—a thing that was not in any philosophy. She had made shipwreck of her life. She had torn the man whom she loved out of her heart, and fled from his neglect and treachery—a fugitive to her mother's house. And yet as she sat before the fire with this little infant cooing in the warmth—like a puppy or a little pig, or any other little animal you can suggest—this was the thought of the irreverent man—there was a look of almost more than common happiness, of blessedness, in her face. Who can fathom these things? They were at least beyond the knowledge, though not the sympathy, of this very rising member of the bar.

CHAPTER XXVIII.

Thus there came a sort of settling down and composure of affairs. Phil Compton and all belonging to him disappeared from the scene, and Elinor returned to all the habits of her old life— all the habits, with one extraordinary and incalculable addition which changed all these habits. The baby—so inconsiderable a little creature, not able to show a feeling, or express a thought, or make even a tremulous step from one pair of loving arms to another—an altogether helpless little bundle, but nevertheless one who had already altered the existence of the cottage and its inhabitants, and made life a totally different thing for them. Can I tell how this was done? No doubt for the wisest objects, to guard the sacred seed of the race as mere duty could never guard it, rendering it the one thing most precious in the world to those to whom it is confided—at least to most of them. When that love fails, then is the deepest abyss of misery reached. I do not say that Elinor was happy in this dreadful breaking up of her life, or that her heart did not go back, with those relentings which are the worst part of every disruption, to the man who had broken her heart and unsettled her nature. The remembrance of him in his better moments would flash upon her, and bear every resentment away. Dreadful thoughts of how she might herself have done otherwise, have rendered their mutual life better, would come over her; and next moment recollections still more terrible of what he had done and said, the scorn she had borne, the insults, the neglect, and worse of all the complicity he had forced upon her, by which he had made her guilty when she knew and feared nothing—when these thoughts overcame her, as they did twenty times in a day, for it is the worst of such troubles that they will not be settled by one struggle, but come back and back, beginning over again at the same point, after we have wrestled through them, and have thought that we had come to a close— when these thoughts, I say, overcame her, she would rush to the room in which the baby held his throne, and press him to the heart which was beating so hotly, till it grew calm. And in the midst of all to sit down by the fire with the little atom of humanity in her lap, and see it spread and stretch its rosy limbs, would suffice to bring again to her face that beatitude which had filled John Tatham with wonder unspeakable. She took the baby and laid him on her heart to take the pain away: and so after a minute or two there was no more question of pain, but of happiness, and delicious play, and the raptures of motherhood. How strange were these things! She could not understand it herself, and fortunately did not try, but accepted that solace provided by God. As for Mrs. Dennistoun, she made no longer any pretences to herself, but allowed herself, as John had advised, to take her blessedness frankly without hypocrisy. When Elinor's dear face was veiled by misery her mother was sympathetically miserable, but at all other moments her heart sang for joy. She had her child again, and she had her child's child, an endless occupation, amusement, and delight. All this might come to an end—who can tell when?—but for the moment her house was no more lonely, the requirements of her being were satisfied. She had her Elinor—what more was to be said? And yet there was more to be said, for in addition there was the boy.

This was very well so far as the interior of the house and of their living was concerned, but very soon other difficulties arose. It had been Mrs. Dennistoun's desire, when she returned home, to communicate some modified version of what had happened to the neighbours around. She had thought it would not only be wise, but easier for themselves, that their position should be understood in the little parish society which, if it did not know authoritatively, would certainly inquire and investigate and divine, with the result of perhaps believing more than the truth, perhaps setting up an entirely fictitious explanation which it would be impossible to set aside, and very hard to bear. It is the worst of knowing a number of people intimately, and being known by them from the time your children were in their cradles, that every domestic incident requires some sort of explanation to this close little circle of spectators. But Elinor, who had not the experience of her mother in such matters, nor the knowledge of life, made a strenuous opposition to this. She would not have anything said. It was better, she thought, to leave it to their imagination, if they chose to interfere with their neighbours' concerns and imagine anything. "But why should they occupy themselves about us? And they have no imaginations," she said, with a contempt of her neighbours which is natural to young people, though very unjustifiable. "But, my darling," Mrs. Dennistoun would say, "the position is so strange. There are not many young women who—And there must be some way of accounting for it. Let us just tell them——"

"For heaven's sake, mamma, tell them nothing! I have come to pay you a long visit after my neglect of you for these two years, which, of course, they know well enough. What more do they want to know? It is a very good reason: and while baby is so young of course it is far better for him to be in a settled home, where he can be properly attended to, than moving about. Isn't that enough?"

"Well, Elinor; at least you will let me say as much as that——"

"Oh, they can surely make it out for themselves. What is the use of always talking a matter over, to lead to a little more, and a little more, till the appetite for gossip is satisfied? Surely, in our circumstances, least said is soonest mended," Elinor said, with that air of superior understanding which almost always resides in persons of the younger generation. Mrs. Dennistoun said no more to her, but she did take advantage of the explanation thus suggested. She informed the anxious circle at the Rectory that Elinor had come to her on a long visit, "partly for me, and partly for the baby," she said, with one of those smiles which are either the height of duplicity or the most pathetic evidence of self-control, according as you choose to regard them. "She thinks she has neglected her mother, though I am sure I have never blamed her; and she thinks—of which there can be no doubt—that to carry an infant of that age moving about from place to place is the worst thing in the world; and that I am very thankful she should think so, I need not say."

"It is very nice for you, dear Mrs. Dennistoun," Mrs. Hudson said.

"And a good thing for Elinor," said Alice, "for she is looking very poorly. I have always heard that fashionable life took a great deal out of you if you are not quite brought up to it. I am sure I couldn't stand it," the young lady said with fervour, who had never had that painful delight in her power.

"That is all very well," said the Rector, rubbing his hands, "but what does Mr. Compton say to it? I don't want to say a word against your arrangements, my dear lady, but you know there must be some one on the husband's side. Now, I am on the husband's side, and I am sorry for the poor young man. I hope he is going to join his wife. I hope, excuse me for saying it, that Elinor—though we are all so delighted to see her—will not forsake him, for too long."

And then Mrs. Dennistoun felt herself compelled to embroider a little upon her theme.

"He has to be a great deal abroad during this year," she said; "he has a great many things to do. Elinor does not know when he will be—home. That is one reason——"

"To be sure, to be sure," the Rector said, rubbing his hands still more, and coming to her aid just as she was breaking down. "Something diplomatic, of course. Well, we must not inquire into the secrets of the State. But what an ease to his mind, my dear lady, to think that his wife and child will be safe with you while he's away!"

Mary Dale not being present could not of course say anything. She was a person who was always dreadfully well informed. It was a comfort unspeakable that at this moment she was away!

This explanation made the spring pass quietly enough, but not without many questions that brought the blood to Elinor's face. When she was asked by some one, for the first time, "When do you expect Mr. Compton, Elinor?" the sudden wild flush of colour which flooded her countenance startled the questioner as much as the question did herself. "Oh, I beg your pardon!" said the injudicious but perfectly innocent seeker for information. I fear that Elinor fell upon her mother after this, and demanded to know what she had said. But as Mrs. Dennistoun was innocent of anything but having said that Philip was abroad, there was no satisfaction to be got out of that. Some time after, one of the Miss Hills congratulated Elinor, having seen in the papers that Mr. Compton was returning to town for the season. "I suppose, dear Elinor, we shan't have you with us much longer," this lady said. And then it became known at the Cottage that Mary Dale was returning to the Rectory. This was the last aggravation, and Elinor, who had now recovered her strength and energy, and temper along with it, received the news with an outburst of impatience which frightened her mother. "You may as well go through the parish and ring the bell, and tell everybody everything," she said. "Mary Dale will have heard all, and a great deal more than all; she will come with her budget, and pour it out far and wide; she will report scenes that never took place: and quarrels, and all that—that woman insinuated to John—and she will be surrounded with people who will shake their heads, and sink their voices when we come in and say, 'Poor Elinor!' I cannot bear it, I cannot bear it," she cried.

"My darling! that was bound to come sooner or later. We must set our faces like a rock, and look as if we were unaware of anything——"

"I cannot look as if I were unaware. I cannot meet all their cruel eyes. I can see, now, the smile on Mary Dale's face, that will say, 'I told you so.' I shall hear her say it even when I am in my room, with the combe between. I know exactly how she will say

284

it—'If Elinor had listened to me——'"

"Elinor," said poor Mrs. Dennistoun, "I cannot contradict you, dear. It will be so—but none of them are cruel, not even Mary Dale. They will make their remarks—who could help it? we should ourselves if it were some one else's case: but they will not be cruel—don't think so—they will be full of sympathy——"

"Which is a great deal worse," Elinor said, in her unreason; "the one might be borne, but the other I will not endure. Sympathy, yes! They will all be sorry for me—they will say they knew how it would be. Oh, I know I have not profited as I ought by what has happened to me. I am unsubdued. I am as impatient and as proud as ever. It is quite true, but it cannot be mended. It is more than I can bear."

"My darling," said her mother, again. "We all say that in our trouble, and yet we know that we have got to bear it all the same. It is intolerable—one says that a thousand times—and yet it has to be put up with. All the time that we have been flattering ourselves that nobody took any notice it has been a delusion, Elinor. How could it be otherwise? We must set our faces——"

"Not I, mamma!" she said. "Not I! I must go away——"

"Go away? Elinor!"

"Among strangers; where nobody has heard of me before—where nobody can make any remark. To live like this, among a crowd of people who think they ought to know everything that one is doing—who are nothing to you, and yet whom you stand in awe of and must explain everything to!—it is this that is intolerable. I cannot, cannot bear it. Mother, I will take my baby, and I will go away——"

"Where?" said Mrs. Dennistoun, with all the colour fading out of her face. What panic had taken her I cannot tell. She grew pale to her lips, and the words were almost inaudible which she breathed forth. I think she thought for a moment that Elinor's heart had turned, that she was going back to her husband to find refuge with him from the strife of tongues which she could not encounter alone. All the blood went back upon the mother's

285

heart—yet she set herself to suppress all emotion, and if this should be so, not to oppose it—for was it not the thing of all others to be desired—the thing which everybody would approve, the reuniting of those whom God had put together? Though it might be death to her, not a word of opposition would she say.

"Where? how can I tell where—anywhere, anywhere out of the world," cried Elinor, in the boiling tide of her impatience and wretchedness, "where nobody ever heard of us before, where there will be no one to ask, no one to require a reason, where we should be free to move when we please and do as we please. Let me go, mother. It seemed too dear, too peaceful to come home, but now home itself has become intolerable. I will take my baby and I will go—to the farthest point the railway can take me to—with no servant to betray me, not even an address. Mother, let me go away and be lost; let me be as if I had never been."

"And me—am I to remain to bear the brunt behind?"

"And you—mamma! Oh, I am the most unworthy creature. I don't deserve to have you, I that am always giving you pain. Why should I unroot you from your place where you have lived so long—from your flowers, and your landscape, and your pretty rooms that were always a comfort to think of in that horrible time when I was away? I always liked to think of you here, happy and quiet, in the place you had chosen."

"Flowers and landscapes are pretty things," said Mrs. Dennistoun, whose colour had begun to come again a little, "but they don't make up for one's children. We must not do anything rashly, Elinor; but if what you mean is really that you will go away to a strange place among strangers——"

"What else could I mean?" Elinor said, and then she in her turn grew pale. "If you thought I could mean that I would go—back——"

"Oh, my darling, my darling! God knows if we are right or wrong—I not to advise you so, or you not to take my advice. Elinor, it is my duty, and I will say it though it were to break my heart. There only could you avoid this strife of tongues. John spoke the truth. He said, as the boy grew up we should have—many troubles. I have known women endure everything that their children might grow up in a natural situation, in their proper sphere. Think of this—I am saying it against my own interest, against my own heart. But think of it, Elinor. Whatever you might have to bear, you would be in your natural place."

Elinor received this agitated address standing up, holding her head high, her nostrils expanded, her lips apart. "Have you quite done, mother?" she said.

Mrs. Dennistoun made an appealing movement with her hands, and sank, without any power to add a word, into a chair.

"I am glad you said it against your heart. Now you must feel that your conscience is clear. Mother, if I had to wander the world from place to place, without even a spot of ground on which to rest my foot, I would never, never do what you say. What! take my child to grow up in that tainted air; give him up to be taught such things as they teach! Never, never, never! His natural place, did you say? I would rather the slums of London were his natural place. He would have some chance there! If I could bear it for myself, yet I could not for him—for him most of all. I will take him up in my arms. Thank God, I am strong now and can carry him—and go away—among strangers, I don't care where—where there can be no questions and no remarks."

"But not without me, Elinor!"

"Oh, mother, mother! What a child I am to you, to rend your heart as I have done, and now to tear you out of your house and home!"

"My home is where my children are," Mrs. Dennistoun said: and then she made a little pause. "But we must think it over, Elinor. Such a step as this must not be taken rashly. We will ask John to come down and advise us. My dear——"

"No, mother, not John or any one. I will go first if you like and find a place, and you will join me after. That woman" (it was poor Mary Dale, who was indeed full of information, but meant no harm) "is coming directly. I will not wait here to see her, or their faces after she has told them all the lies she will have heard. I am not going to take advice from any one. Let me alone, mother. I must, I must go away."

"But not by yourself, Elinor," Mrs. Dennistoun said.

This was how it happened that John Tatham, who had meant to go down to the Cottage the very next Saturday to see how things were going, was driven into a kind of stupefaction one morning in May by a letter which reached him from the North, a letter conveying news so unexpected and sudden, so unlike anything that had seemed possible, that he laid it down, when it was half read, with a gasp of astonishment, unable to believe his eyes.

CHAPTER XXIX.

It was Mrs. Dennistoun whose letter brought John Tatham such dismay. It was dated Lakeside, Waterdale, Penrith—an address with which he had no associations whatever, and which he gazed at blankly for a moment before he attempted to read the letter, not knowing how to connect it with the well-known writing which was as familiar as the common day.

"You will wonder to see this address," she wrote. "You will wonder still more, dear John, when I tell you we have come here for good. I have left the Cottage in an agent's hands with the hope of letting it. Windyhill is such a healthy place that I hope somebody will soon be found to take it. You know Elinor would not let me make any explanation. And the constant questions and allusions to *his* movements which people had seen in the papers, and so forth, had got on her nerves, poor child. You can understand how easily this might come about. At last she got that she could not bear it longer. Mary Dale, who always lives half the year with her sister at the Rectory, was coming back. You know it was she who brought the first tale about him, and she knows, I think, all the gossip that ever was got up about any one. Poor Elinor—though I don't believe Mary had any bad meaning; and it would, alas! have been for all our good had we listened to what she said—Elinor cannot bear her; and when she heard she was coming, she declared she would take her baby and go away. I tried to bring her to reason, but I could not. Naturally it was she who convinced me—you know the process, John. Indeed, in many things I can see it is the best thing we could do. I am not supremely attached to Windyhill. The Cottage had got to be

289

very homelike after living in it so long, but home is where those are whom one loves. And to live among one set of people for so many years, if it has great advantages, has at the same time very great disadvantages too. You can't keep anything to yourself. You must explain every step you take, and everything that happens to you. This is a lovely country, a little cold as yet, and a little damp perhaps, being so near the lake—but the mountains are beautiful, and the air delicious. Elinor is out all the day long, and baby grows like a flower. You must come and see us as soon as ever you can. That is one dreadful drawback, that we shall not have you running up and down from Saturday to Monday: and I am afraid you will be vexed with us that we did not take your advice first—you, who have always been our adviser. But Elinor would not hear a word of any advice. I think she was afraid you would disapprove: and it would have been worse to fly in your face if you had disapproved than to come away without consulting you: and you know how impetuous she is. At all events the die is cast. Write kindly to her; don't say anything to vex her. You can let yourself out, if you are very angry, upon me.

"One thing more. She desires that if you write you should address her as *Mrs. Compton* only, no Honourable. That might attract attention, and what we desire is to escape notice altogether, which I am sure is a thing you will thoroughly understand, now that we have transplanted ourselves so completely. Dear John, form the most favourable idea you can of this sudden step, and come and see us as soon as it is possible.

"Yours affectly.,
"M. D."

To say that John was thunderstruck by this letter is to describe his sensations mildly, for he was for a time bitterly angry, wounded, disappointed, disturbed to the bottom of his soul; but perhaps if truth were told it could scarcely be said that he disapproved. He thought it over, which he naturally did all that day, to the great detriment of his work, first with a sort of rage against Elinor and her impetuosity, which presently shaded down into understanding of her feelings, and ended in a sense that he might have known it from the first, and that really no other conclusion was possible. He came gradually to acquiesce in the step the ladies had taken. To have to explain everything to the Hudsons, and Hills, and Mary Dales, to open up your most sacred heart in order that they might be able to form a theory sufficient for their outside purposes of your motives and methods, or, what was perhaps worse still—to know that they were on the watch, guessing what you did not tell them, putting things together, explaining this and that in their own way—would have been intolerable. "That is the good of having attached friends," John exclaimed to himself, very unjustly: for it is human nature that is to blame, if there is any blame attaching to an exercise of ingenuity so inevitable. As a matter of fact, when Miss Dale brought the true or something like the true account to Windyhill, the warmth of the sympathy for Elinor, the wrath of the whole community with her unworthy husband, was almost impassioned. Had she been there it would not have been possible for those good people altogether to conceal from her how sorry and how indignant they were; even perhaps there might have been some who could not have kept out of their eyes, who must have betrayed in some word or shake of the head the "I told you so" which is so dear to human nature. But how was it possible that they could remain uninterested, unaffected by the trouble in the midst of them, or even appear to be so? John, like Elinor, threw a fiery dart of impatience at the country neighbours, not allowing that everywhere in the greatest town, in the most cosmopolitan community, this would have been the same.

"The chattering gossips!" he said, as if a club would not have been a great deal worse, as if indeed his own club, vaguely conscious of a connection by marriage between him and the dis-Honourable Phil, had not discussed it all, behind his back, long ago.

But on the whole John was forced not to disapprove. To say

that he went the length of approving would be too much, and to deny that he launched forth a tremendous letter upon Mrs. Dennistoun, who always bore the brunt, is more than my conscience would permit. He did do this, throwing out, as the French say, fire and flame, but a few days after followed it up by a much milder letter (need I say this was addressed to Elinor?), allowing that he understood their motives, and that perhaps, from their own point of view, they were not so very much to blame. "You will find it very damp, very cold, very different from Windyhill," he said, with a sort of savage satisfaction. But as it happened to be unusually good weather among the lakes when his letter came, this dart did not do much harm. And that John felt the revolution in his habits consequent upon this move very much, it would be futile to deny. To have nowhere to go to freely when he pleased from Saturday to Monday (he had at least a score of places, but none like the Cottage) made a wonderful difference in his life. But perhaps when he came to think of it soberly, as he did so often in the brilliant Saturday afternoons of early summer, when the sunshine on the trees made his heart a little sick with the idea that he had, as he said to himself, nowhere to go to, he was not sure that the difference was not on the whole to his advantage. A man perhaps should not have it in his power to enjoy, in the most fraternal intimacy, the society of another man's wife whenever he pleased, even if to her he was, as he knew, of as little importance (notwithstanding that she was, as she would have said, so fond of John) as the postman, say, or any other secondary (yet sufficiently interesting) figure in the country neighbourhood. John knew in his heart of hearts that this was not a good thing nor a wholesome thing for him. He was not a man, as has been said, who would ever have hurried events, or insisted upon appropriating a woman, even when he loved her, and securing her as his very own. He would always have been able to put that off, to subordinate it to the necessity of getting on in the world, and securing his position: and he was by no means sure when he questioned his own heart (which was a thing he did seldom, knowing, like a wise man, that that shifty subject often made queer revelations, and was not at all an easy object to cross-examine), that the intercourse which he had again dropped into with Elinor was not on the whole as much as he required. There was no doubt that it kept him alive from one period to another; kept his heart moderately light and his mind wonderfully contented—as nothing else had ever done. He looked forward to his fortnightly or monthly visit to the Cottage (sometimes one, and sometimes the other; he never indulged himself so far as to go every week), and it gave him happiness enough to tide over all the dull moments between: and if anything came in his way and detained him even from his usual to a later train, he was ridiculously, absurdly angry. What right had he to feel so in respect to another man's wife? What right had he to watch the child—the child whom he disliked so much to begin with—developing its baby faculties with an interest he was half ashamed of, but which went on increasing? Another man's wife and another man's child. He saw now that it was not a wholesome thing for him, and he could never have given it up had they remained. It had become too much a part of his living; should he not be glad therefore that they had taken it into their own hands, and gone away? When it suddenly occurred to John, however, that this perhaps had some share in the ladies' hasty decision, that Mrs. Dennistoun perhaps (all that was objectionable was attributed to this poor lady) had been so abominably clear-sighted, so odiously presuming as to have suspected this, his sudden blaze of anger was *foudroyant*. Perhaps she had settled upon it for his sake, to take temptation out of his way. John could scarcely contain himself when this view of the case flashed upon him, although he was quite aware for himself that though it was a bitter wrench, yet it was perhaps good for him that Elinor should go away.

It was probably this wave of fierce and, as we are aware, quite unreasonable anger rushing over him that produced the change which everybody saw in John's life about this time. It was about

293

the beginning of the season when people's enjoyments begin to multiply, and for the first time in his life John plunged into society like a very novice. He went everywhere. By this time he had made a great start in life, had been brought into note in one or two important cases, and was, as everybody knew, a young man very well thought of, and likely to do great things at the bar; so that he was free of many houses, and had so many invitations for his Sundays that he could well afford to be indifferent to the loss of such a humble house as the Cottage at Windyhill. Perhaps he wanted to persuade himself that this was the case, and that there really was nothing to regret. And it is certain that he did visit a great deal during that season at one house where there were two or three agreeable daughters; the house, indeed, of Sir John Gaythorne, who was Solicitor-General at that time, and a man who had always looked upon John Tatham with a favourable eye. The Gaythornes had a house near Dorking, where they often went from Saturday to Monday with a few choice *convives*, and "picknicked," as they themselves said, but it was a picknicking of a highly comfortable sort. John went down with them the very Saturday after he received that letter—the Saturday on which he had intended to go to Windyhill. And the party was very gay. To compare it for a moment with the humdrum family at the Cottage would have been absurd. The Gaythornes prided themselves on always having pleasant people with them, and they had several remarkably pleasant people that day, among whom John himself was welcomed by most persons; and the family themselves were lively and agreeable to a high degree. A distinguished father, a very nice mother, and three charming girls, up to everything and who knew everybody; who had read or skimmed all the new books of any importance, and had seen all the new pictures; who could talk of serious things as well as they could talk nonsense, and who were good girls to boot, looking after the poor, and visiting at hospitals, in the intervals of their gaieties, as was then the highest fashion in town. I do not for a moment mean to imply that the Miss Gaythornes did their good work because it was the fashion: but the fact that it is the fashion has liberated many girls, and allowed them to carry out their natural wishes in that way, who otherwise would have been restrained and hampered by parents and friends, who would have upbraided them with making themselves remarkable, if in a former generation they had attempted to go to Whitechapel or St. Thomas's with any active intentions. And Elinor had never done anything of this kind, any more than she had pursued music almost as a profession, which was what Helena Gaythorne had done; or learned to draw, like Maud (who once had a little thing in the Royal Academy); or studied the Classics, like Gertrude. John thought of her little tunes as he listened to Miss Gaythorne's performance, and almost laughed out at the comparison. He was very fond of music, and Miss Gaythorne's playing was something which the most cultivated audience might have been glad to listen to. He was ashamed to confess to himself that he liked the "tunes" best. No, he would not confess it even to himself; but when he stood behind the performer listening, it occurred to him that he was capable of walking all the miles of hill and hollow which divided the one place from the other, only for the inane satisfaction of seeing that baby spread on Elinor's lap, or hearing her play to him one of her "tunes."

He went with the Gaythornes to their country-place twice in the month of June, and dined at the house several times, and was invited on other occasions, becoming, in short, one of the *habitués* when there was anything going on in the house—till people began to ask, which was it? It was thought generally that Helena was the attraction, for John was known to be a musical man, always to be found where specially good music was going. Some friends of the family had even gone so far as to say among themselves what a good thing it was that dear Helena's lot was likely to be cast with one who would appreciate her gift. "It generally happens in these cases that a girl marries somebody who does not know one note from another," they said to each other. When, all at once, John flagged in his visits; went no more to Dorking; and finally ceased to be more assiduous or more remarked than the other young men who were on terms of partial intimacy at the Gaythorne house. He had, indeed, tried very hard to make himself fall in love with one of Sir John's girls. It would have been an excellent connection, and the man might think himself fortunate who secured any one of the three for his wife. Proceeding from his certainty on these points, and also a general liking for their company, John had gone into it with a settled purpose, determined to fall in love if he could: but he found that the thing was not to be done. It was a pity; but it could not be helped. He was in a condition now when it would no longer be rash to marry, and he knew now that there was the makings of a domestic man in him. He never could have believed that he would take an interest in the sprawling of the baby upon its mother's knee, and he allowed to himself that it might be sweet to have that scene taking place in a house of his own. Ah! but the baby would have to be Elinor's. It must be Elinor who should sit on that low chair with the firelight on her face. And that was impossible. Helena Gaythorne was an exceedingly nice girl, and he wished her every success in life (which she attained some time after by marrying Lord Ballinasloe, the eldest son of the Earl of Athenree, a marriage which everybody approved), but he could not persuade himself to be in love with her, though with the best will in the world.

During this time he did not correspond much with his relations in the country. He had, indeed, some letters to answer from his father, in which the interrogatories were very difficult: "Where has Mary Dennistoun gone? What's become of Elinor and her baby? Has that fashionable fellow of a husband deserted her? What's the meaning of the move altogether?" And, "Mind you keep yourself out of it," his father wrote. John had great trouble in wording his replies so as to convey as little information as possible. "I believe Aunt Mary has got a house somewhere in the North, probably to suit Elinor, who would be able to be more with her if she were in that neighbourhood." (It must be confessed that he thought this really clever as a way of getting over the question.) "As for Compton, I know very little about him. He was never a man much in my way." Mr. Tatham's household saw nothing remarkable in these replies; upon which, however, they built an explanation, such as it was, of the other circumstances. They concluded that it must be in order to be near Elinor that Mrs. Dennistoun had gone to the North, and that it was a very good thing that Elinor's husband was not a man who was in John's way. "A scamp, if I ever saw one!" Mr. Tatham said. "But what's that Jack says about Gaythorne? Mary, I remember Gaythorne years ago; a capital friend for a young man. I'm glad your brother's making such nice friends for himself; far better than mooning about that wretched little cottage with Mary Dennistoun and her girl."

CHAPTER XXX.

It happened thus that it was not till the second autumn after the settlement of the ladies in Waterdale, when all the questions had died out, and there was no more talk of them, except on occasions when a sudden recollection cropped up among their friends at Windyhill, that John Tatham paid them his first visit. He had been very conscientious in his proposed bestowal of himself. Perhaps it is scarcely quite complimentary to a woman when she is made choice of by a man who is consciously to himself "on the outlook," thinking that he ought to marry, and investigating all the suitable persons about with an eye to finding one who will answer his requirements. This sensible way of approaching the subject of matrimony does not somehow commend itself to our insular notions. It is the right way in every country except our own, but it has a cold-blooded look to the Anglo-Saxon; and a girl is not flattered (though perhaps she ought to be) by being the subject of this sensible choice. "As if I were a housekeeper or a cook!" she is apt to say, and is far better pleased to be fallen in love with in the most rash and irresponsible way than to be thus selected from the crowd: though that, everybody must allow, after due comparison and inspection, is by far the greater compliment. John having arrived at the conclusion that it would be better for him in many ways to marry, and specially in the way of Elinor, fortifying him for ever from all possible complications, and making it possible for him to regard her evermore with the placid feelings of a brother, which was, he expected, to be the consequence—worked at the matter really with great pertinacity and consistency. He kept his eyes open upon the whole generation of girls whom he met with in society.

When he went abroad during the long vacation (instead of going to Lakeside, as he was invited to do), he directed his steps rather to the fashionable resorts, where families disport themselves at the foot of the mountains, than to the Alpine heights where he had generally found a more robust amusement. And wherever he went he bent his attention on the fairer portion of the creation, the girls who fill all the hotels with the flutter of their fresh toilettes and the babble of their pleasant voices. It was very mean and poor of him, seeing he was a mountaineer himself—but still it must be recorded that the only young ladies he systematically neglected were those in very short petticoats, with very sunburnt faces and nails in their boots, who ought to have been most congenial to him as sharing his own tastes. It is said, I don't know with what truth, that at Ouch, or Interlachen, or some other of the most mundane and banal resorts of the tourists, he came upon one girl who he thought might make him a suitable wife: and that, though with much moderation and prudence, he more or less followed her party for some time, meeting them over and over again, with expressions of astonishment, round the most well-known corners, and persisting for a considerable time in this quest. But whether he ever came the length of proposing at all, or whether the young lady was engaged beforehand, or if she thought the prospect of making a suitable wife not good enough, I cannot say, and I doubt whether any one knows—except, of course, the parties immediately concerned. It is very clear, at all events, that it came to nothing. John did not altogether give it up, I fancy, for he went a great deal into society still, especially in that *avant saison*, which people who live in London declare to be the most enjoyable, and when it is supposed you can enjoy the best of company at your ease without the hurry and rush of the summer crowd. He would have been very glad, thankful, indeed, if he could have fallen in love. How absurd to think that any silly boy can do it, to whom it is probably nothing but a disadvantage and the silliest of pastimes, and that he, a reasonable man with a good income, and arrived at a time of life when it is becoming and rational to marry, could not do it, let him try as he would! There was something ludicrous in it, when you came to think, as well as something very depressing. Mothers who wanted a good position for their daughters divined him, and many of them were exceedingly civil to John, this man in search of a wife; and many of the young ladies themselves divined him, and with the half indignation, half mockery, appropriate to the situation, were some of them not unaverse to profit by it, and accordingly turned to him their worst side in the self-consciousness produced by that knowledge. And thus the second year turned round towards the wane, and John was farther from success than ever.

He said to himself then that it was clear he was not a marrying man. He liked the society of ladies well enough, but not in that way. He was not made for falling in love. He might very well, he was aware, have dispensed with the tradition, and found an excellent wife, who would not at all have insisted upon it from her side. But he had his prejudices, and could not do this. Love he insisted upon, and love would not come. Accordingly, when the second season was over he gave up both the quest and the idea, and resolved to think of marrying no more, which was a sensible relief to him. For indeed he was exceedingly comfortable as he was; his chambers were excellent, and he did not think that any street or square in Belgravia would have reconciled him to giving up the Temple. He had excellent servants, a man and his wife, who took the greatest care of him. He had settled into a life which was arranged as he liked, with much freedom, and yet an agreeable routine which John was too wise to despise. He relinquished the idea of marrying then and there. To be sure there is never any prophesying what may happen. A little laughing gipsy of a girl may banish such a resolution out of a man's mind in the twinkling of an eye, at any moment. But short of such accidents as that, and he smiled at the idea of anything of the kind, he quite made up his mind on this point with a great sensation of relief.

It is curious how determined the mind of the English public

at least is on this subject—that the man or woman who does not marry (especially the woman, by-the-bye) has an unhappy life, and that a story which does not end in a wedding is no story at all, or at least ends badly, as people say. It happened to myself on one occasion to put together in a book the story of some friends of mine, in which this was the case. They were young, they were hopeful, they had all life before them, but they did not marry. And when the last chapter came to the consciousness of the publisher he struck, with the courage of a true Briton, not ashamed of his principles, and refused to pay. He said it was no story at all— so beautiful is marriage in the eyes of our countrymen. I hope, however, that nobody will think any harm of John Tatham because he concluded, after considerable and patient trial, that he was not a marrying man. There is no harm in that. A great number of those Catholic priests whom it was the habit in my youth to commiserate deeply, as if they were vowed to the worst martyrdom, live very happy lives in their celibacy and prefer it, as John Tatham did. It will be apparent to the reader that he really preferred it to Elinor, while Elinor was in his power. And though afterwards it gave a comfort and grace to his life to think that it was his faithful but subdued love for Elinor which made him a bachelor all his days, I am by no means certain that this was true. Perhaps he never would have made up his mind had she remained always within his reach. Certain it is that he was relieved when he found that to give up the idea of marriage was the best thing for him. He adopted the conclusion with pleasure. His next brother had already married, though he was younger than John; but then he was a clergyman, which is a profession naturally tending to that sort of thing. There was, however, no kind of necessity laid upon him to provide for the continuance of the race. And he was a happy man.

By what sequence of ideas it was that he considered himself justified, having come to this conclusion, in immediately paying his long-promised visit to Lakeside, is a question which I need not enter into, and indeed do not feel entirely able to cope with. It suited him, perhaps, as he had been so long a time in Switzerland last year: and he had an invitation to the far north for the grouse, which he thought it would be pleasant to accept. Going to Scotland or coming from it, Waterdale of course lies full in the way. He took it last on his way home, which was more convenient, and arrived there in the latter part of September, when the hills were golden with the yellow bracken. The Cumberland hills are a little cold, in my opinion, without the heather, which clothes with such a flush of life and brightness our hills in the north. The greenness is chilly in the frequent rain; one feels how sodden and slippery it is—a moisture which does not belong to the heather: but when the brackens have all turned, and the slopes reflect themselves in the tranquil water like hills of gold, then the landscape reaches its perfect point. Lakeside was a white house standing out on a small projection at the head of the lake, commanding the group of hills above and part of the winding body of water below, in which all these golden reflections lay. A little steamer passed across the reflected glory, and came to a stop not a hundred yards from the gate of the house. It was a scene as unlike as could be conceived to the Cottage at Windyhill: the trees were all glorious in colour; yellow birches like trees made of light, oaks all red and fiery, chestnuts and elms and beeches in a hundred hues. The house was white, with a sort of broad verandah round, supported on pillars, furnishing a sheltered walk below and a broad balcony above, which gave it a character of more importance than perhaps its real size warranted. When John approached there ran out to meet him into the wide gravel drive before the door a little figure upon two sturdy legs, calling out, in inarticulate shoutings, something that sounded a little like his own name. It was, "'tle John! 'tle John!" made into a sort of song by the baby, nearly two years old, and "very forward," as everybody assured the stranger, for his age. Uncle John! his place was thus determined at once by that little potentate and master of the house. Behind the child came Elinor, no longer pale and languid as he had seen her last, but matured into vigorous beauty, bright-eyed, a little sober, as might have become maturer years than hers. Perhaps there was something in the style of her dress that favoured the idea, not of age indeed, but of matronly years, and beyond those which Elinor counted. She was dressed in black, of the simplest description, not of distinctive character like a widow's, yet something like what an ideal widow beyond fashion or conventionalities of woe might wear. It seemed to give John the key-note of the character she had assumed in this new sphere.

Mrs. Dennistoun, who had not changed in the least, stood in the open door. They gave him a welcome such as John had not had, he said to himself, since he had seen them before. They were unfeignedly glad to see him, not wounded (which, to think of afterwards, wounded him a little) that he had not come sooner, but delighted that he was here now. Even when he went home it was not usual to John to be met at the door in this way by all his belongings. His sister might come running down the stairs when she heard the dog-cart draw up, but that was all. And Mary's eagerness to see him was generally tempered by the advice she had to give, to say that or not to say this, because of papa. But in the present case it was the sight of himself which was delightful to all, and, above all, though the child could have no reason for it, to the little shouting excited boy. "'Tle John! 'tle John!" What was Uncle John to him? yet his little voice filled the room with shouts of joy.

"What does he know about me, the little beggar, that he makes such a noise in my honour?" said John, touched in spite of himself. "But I suppose anything is good enough for a cry at that age."

"Come," said Elinor, "you are not to be contemptuous of my boy any longer. You called him *it* when he was a baby."

"And what is he now?" said John, whose heart was affected by strange emotions, he, the man who had just decided (with relief) that he was not a marrying man. There came over him a curious wave of sensation which he had no right to. If he had had a right to it, if he had been coming home to those who belonged to him, not distantly in the way of cousinship, but by a dearer right, what sensations his would have been! But sitting at the corner of the fire (which is very necessary in Waterdale in the end of September) a little in the shadow, his face was not very clearly perceptible: though indeed had it been so the ladies would have thought nothing but that John's kind heart was touched, as was so natural, by this sight.

"What is he now? Your nephew! Tell Uncle John what you are now," said Elinor, lifting her child on her lap; at which the child between the kisses which were his encouragement and reward produced, in a large infant voice, very treble, yet simulating hers, the statement, "Mamma's bhoy."

"Now, Elinor," said Mrs. Dennistoun, "he has played his part beautifully; he has done everything you taught him. He has told you who he is and who Uncle John is. Let him go to his nursery now."

"Come up-stairs, Pippo. Mother will carry her boy," said Elinor. "They don't want us any more, these old people. Say good-night to Uncle John, and come to bed."

"Dood-night, 'tle John," said the child; which, however, was not enough, for he tilted himself out of his mother's arms and put his rosy face and open mouth, sweet but damp, upon John's face. This kiss was one of the child's accomplishments. He himself was aware that he had been good, and behaved himself in every way as a child should do, as he was carried off crowing and jabbering in his mother's arms. He had formed a sort of little human bridge between them when he made that dive from Elinor's arms upon John's face. Ah, heaven! if it had been the other way, if the child and the mother had both been his!

"He has grown up very sweet. You may think we are foolish, John; but you can't imagine what a delight that child is. Hasn't he grown up sweet?"

"If you call that grown up!"

"Oh, yes, I know he is only a baby still; but so forward for his age, such a little man, taking care of his mother before he is two years old!"

"What did I hear her call him?" John asked, and it seemed to Mrs. Dennistoun that there was something severe in the sound of his voice.

"He had to be Philip. It is a pretty name, though we may have reason to mourn the day—and belongs to his family. We must not forget that he belongs to a known family, however he may have suffered by it."

"Then you intend the child to know about his family? I am glad to hear it," said John, though his voice perhaps was not so sweet as his words.

"Oh, John, that is quite another thing! to know about his family—at two! He has his mother—and me to take care of them both, and what does he want more?"

"But he will not always be two," said John, the first moment almost of his arrival, before he had seen the house, or said a word about the lake, or anything. She was so disappointed and cast down that she made him no reply.

"I am a wretched croaker," he said, after a moment, "I know. I ought after all this time to try to make myself more agreeable; but you must pardon me if this was the first thing that came into my mind. Elinor is looking a great deal better than when I saw her last."

"Isn't she! another creature. I don't say that I am satisfied, John. Who would be satisfied in such a position of affairs? but while the child is so very young nothing matters very much. And she is quite happy. I do think she is quite happy. And so well— this country suits them both perfectly. Though there is a good deal of rain, they are both out every day. And little Pippo thrives, as you see, like a flower."

"That is a very fantastic name to give the child."

"How critical you are, John! perhaps it is, but what does it matter at his age? any name does for a baby. Why, you yourself, as grave as you are now——"

"Don't, aunt," said John. "It is a grave matter enough as it appears to me."

"Not for the present; not for the present, John."

"Perhaps not for the present: if you prefer to put off all the difficulties till they grow up and crush you. Have there been any overtures, all this time, from—the other side?"

"Dear John, don't overwhelm me all in a moment, in the first pleasure of seeing you, both with the troubles that are behind and the troubles that are in front of us," the poor lady said.

CHAPTER XXXI.

The weather was fine, which was by no means always a certainty at Waterdale, and Elinor had become a great pedestrian, and was ready to accompany John in his walks, which were long and varied. It was rather a curious test to which to subject himself after the long time he had been away, and the other tests through which he had gone. Never had he been so entirely the companion of Elinor, never before had they spent so many hours together without other society. At Windyhill, indeed, their interviews had been quite unrestrained, but then Elinor had many friends and interests in the parish and outside of it, visits to pay and duties to perform. Now she had her child, which occupied her mornings and evenings, but left her free for hours of rambling among the hills, for long walks, from which she came back blooming with the fresh air and breezes which had blown her about, ruffling her hair, and stirring up her spirits and thoughts. Sometimes when there has been heavy and premature suffering there occurs thus in the young another spring-time, an almost childhood of natural, it may be said superficial pleasure—the power of being amused, and of enjoying every simple satisfaction without any *arrière pensée* like a child. She had recovered her strength and vigour in the mountain air—and in that freedom of being unknown, with no look ever directed to her which reminded her of the past, no question which brought back her troubles, had blossomed out into that fine youthful maturity of twenty-six, which has already an advantage over the earlier girlhood, the perfection of the woman grown. Elinor had thought of many things and understood many things, which she had still regarded with the high assumptions of ignorance three or four years ago.

And poor John, who had tried so hard to find himself a mate that suited him, who had studied so many girls more beautiful, more accomplished than Elinor, in the hope of goading himself, so to speak, into love, and had not succeeded—and who had felt so strongly that another man's wife must not occupy so much of his thoughts, nor another man's child give him an unwilling pleasure which was almost fatherly—poor John felt himself placed in a position more trying than any he had known before, more difficult to steer his way through. He had never had so much of her company, and she did not conceal the pleasure it was to her to have some one to walk with, to talk with, who understood what she said and what she did not say, and was in that unpurchasable sympathy with herself which is not to be got by beauty, or by will, or even by love itself, but comes by nature. Elinor felt this with simple pleasure. Without any complicating suspicion, she said, "What a brother John is! I always felt him so, but now more than ever." "You have been, so to speak, brought up together," said Mrs. Dennistoun, whose mind was by no means so easy on the subject. "That is the reason, I suppose," said Elinor, with happy looks.

But poor John said nothing of this kind. What he felt was that he might have spared himself the trouble of all those researches of his; that to roam about looking for a young lady whom he might—not devour, but learn to love, was pains as unnecessary as ever man took. He still hugged himself, however, over the thought that in no circumstances would he have been a marrying man; that if Elinor had been free he would have found plenty of reasons why they should remain on their present terms and go no farther. As it was clear that they must remain on their present terms, and could go no farther, it was certainly better that he should cherish that thought.

And curiously enough, though they heard so little from the outside world, they had heard just so much as this, that John's assiduities to the Miss Gaythornes (which the reader may remember was the first of all his attempts, and quite antiquated in his recollection) had occasioned remarks, and he had not been many evenings at Lakeside before he was questioned on the subject. Had it been true, or had he changed his mind or had the lady——? It vexed him that there was not the least little opposition or despite in their tones, such as a man's female friends often show towards the objects of his admiration, not from any feeling on their own part, except that most natural one, which is surprised and almost hurt to find that, "having known me, he could decline"—a feeling which, in its original expression, was not a woman's sentiment, but a man's, and therefore is, I suppose, common to both sides. But the ladies at Lakeside did not even betray this feeling. They desired to know if there had been anything in it—with smiles, it is true; but Mrs. Dennistoun at the same time expressed her regret warmly.

"We were in great hopes something would come of it, John. Elinor has met the Gaythornes, and thought them very nice; and if there is a thing in the world that would give me pleasure, it would be to see you with a nice wife, John."

"I am sure I am much obliged to you, aunt; but there really was nothing in it. That is, I was seized with various impulses on the subject, and rather agreed with you: but I never mentioned the matter to any of the Miss Gaythornes. They are charming girls, and I don't suppose would have looked at me. At the same time, I did not feel it possible to imagine myself in love with any of them. That's quite a long time since," he added with a laugh.

"Then there have been others since then? Let us put him in the confessional, mother," cried Elinor with a laugh. "He ought not to have any secrets of that description from you and me."

"Oh, yes, there have been others since," said John. "To tell the truth, I have walked round a great many nice girls asking myself whether I shouldn't find it very delightful to have one of them belonging to me. I wasn't worthy the least attractive of them all, I quite knew; but still I am about the same as other men. However, as I've said, I never mentioned the matter to any of them."

"Never?" cried Mrs. Dennistoun, feeling a hesitation in his

tone.

He laughed a little, shamefaced: "Well, if you like, I will say hardly ever," he said. "There was one that might, perhaps, have taken pity upon me—but fortunately an old lover of hers, who was much more enterprising, turned up before anything decisive had been said."

"Fortunately, John?"

"Well, yes, I thought so. You see I am not a marrying man. I tried to screw myself up to the point, but it was altogether, I am afraid, as a matter of principle. I thought it would be a good thing, perhaps, to have a wife."

"That was a very cold-blooded idea. No wonder you—it never came to anything. That is not the way to go about it," said Elinor with the ringing laugh of a child.

And yet her way of going about it had been far from a success. How curious that she did not remember that!

"Yes," he said, "I am quite aware that I did not go about it in the right way, but then that was the only way in which it presented itself to me; and when I had made up my mind at last that it was a failure, I confess it was with a certain sense of relief. I suppose I was born to live and die an old bachelor."

"Do not be so sure of that," said Elinor. "Some day or other, in the most unlooked-for moment, the fairy princess will bound upon the scene, and the old bachelor will be lost."

"We'll wait quite contentedly for that day—which I don't believe in," he said.

Mrs. Dennistoun did not take any part in the later portion of this discussion; her smile was feeble at the places where Elinor laughed. She said seriously after this fireside conference, when he got up to prepare for dinner, putting her hand tenderly on his shoulder, "I wish you had found some one you could have loved, John."

"So did I—for a time," he said, lightly. "But you see, it was not to be."

She shook her head, standing against the firelight in the dark room, so that he could not see her face. "I wish," she said, "I wish—that I saw you with a nice wife, John."

"You might wish—to see me on the woolsack, aunt."

"Well—and it might come to pass. I shall see you high up—if I live long enough; but I wish I was as sure of the other, John."

"Well," he said with a laugh, "I did my best; but there is no use in struggling against fate."

No, indeed! how very, very little use there was. He had kept away from them for nearly two years; while he had done his best in the meantime to get a permanent tenant for his heart which should prevent any wandering tendencies. But he had not succeeded; and now if ever a man could be put in circumstances of danger it was he. If he did not appear in time for their walk Elinor would call him. "Aren't you coming, John?" And she overflowed in talk to him of everything—excepting always of that one dark passage in her life of which she never breathed a word. She asked him about his work, and about his prospects, insisting upon having everything explained to her—even politics, to which he had a tendency, not without ideas of their use in reaching the higher ranks of his profession. Elinor entered into all with zest and almost enthusiasm. She wrapped him up in her sympathy and interest. There was nothing he did that she did not wish to know about, did not desire to have a part in. A sister in this respect is, as everybody knows, often more full of enthusiasm than a wife, and Elinor, who was vacant of all concerns of her own (except the baby) was delighted to take up these subjects of excitement, and follow John through them, hastening after him on every line of indication or suggestion which he gave—nay, often with her lively intelligence hastening before him, making incursions into undiscovered countries of which he had not yet perceived the importance. They walked over all the country, into woods which were a little damp, and up hill-sides where the scramble was often difficult enough, and along the side of the lake—or, for a variety, went rowing across to the other side, or far down the gleaming water, out of sight, round the wooded corner which, with all its autumnal colours, blazed like a brilliant sentinel into the air above and the water below. Mrs. Dennistoun watched them, sometimes with a little trouble on her face. She would not say a word to throw suspicions or doubts between them. She would not awaken in Elinor's mind the thought that any such possibilities as arise between two young people free of all bonds could be imagined as affecting her and any man such as her cousin John. Poor John! if he must be the victim, the victim he must be. Elinor could not be disturbed that he might go free. And indeed, what good would it have done to disturb Elinor? It would but have brought consciousness, embarrassment, and a sense of danger where no such sense was. She was trebly protected, and without a thought of anything but the calm yet close relations that had existed so long. He—— but he could take care of himself, Mrs. Dennistoun reflected in despair; he must take care of himself. He was a man and must understand what his own risks and perils were.

"And do you think this plan is a success?" John asked her one day as they were rowing homeward up the lake. The time of his visit was drawing to a close; indeed it had drawn to a close several times, and been lengthened very unadvisedly, yet very irresistibly as he felt.

Her face grew graver than usual, as with a sudden recollection of that shadow upon her life which Elinor so often seemed to have forgotten. "As much of a success," she said, "as anything of the kind is likely to be."

"It suits you better than Windyhill?"

"Only in being more out of the world. It is partially out of the world for a great part of the year; but I suppose no place is so wholly. It seems impossible to keep from making acquaintances."

"Of course," he said, "I have noticed. You know people here already."

"How can we keep from knowing people? Mamma says it is the same thing everywhere. If we lived up in that little house which they say is the highest in England—at the head of the pass—we should meet people I suppose even there."

"Most likely," he replied; "but the same difficulties can hardly arise."

"You mean we shall not know people so well as at—at home, and will not be compelled to give an account of ourselves whatever we do? Heaven knows! There is a vicarage here, and there is a squire's house: and there are two or three people besides who already begin to inquire if we are related to So-and-So, if we are the Scotch Dennistouns, or the Irish Comptons, or I don't know what; and whether we are going to Penrith or any other capital city for the winter." Elinor ended with a laugh.

"So soon?" John said.

"So soon—very much sooner, the first year: with mamma so friendly as she is and with me so silly, unable to keep myself from smiling at anybody who smiles at me!"

"Poor Elinor!"

"Oh, you may laugh; but it is a real disadvantage. I am sure there was not very much smile in me when we came; and yet, notwithstanding, the first pleasant look is enough for me, I cannot but respond; and I shall always be so, I suppose," she said, with a sigh.

"I hope so, Elinor. It would be an evil day for all of us if you did not respond."

"For how many, John? For my mother and—ah, you are so good, more like my brother than my cousin—for you, perhaps, a little; but what is it to anybody else in the world whether I smile or sigh? It does not matter, however," she said, flinging back her head; "there it is, and I can't help it. If you smile at me I must smile back again—and so we make friends; and already I get a great deal of advice about little Pippo. If we live here till he grows up, the same thing will happen as at the Cottage. We will require to account to everybody for what we do with him—for the school he goes to, and all he does; to explain why he has one kind of training or another; and, in short, all that I ran away from: the world wherever one goes seems to be so much the same."

"The world is very much the same everywhere; and you cannot get out of it were you to take refuge in a cave on the hill. The best thing is generally to let it know all that can be known, and so save the multitude of guesses it always makes."

Elinor looked at him for a moment with her lips pressed tightly together, and a light in her eyes; then she looked away across the water to the golden hills, and said nothing; but there was a great deal in that look of eager contradiction, yet forced agreement, of determination above all, with which right and wrong had nothing to do.

"Elinor," he said, "do you mean that child to grow up here between your mother and you—in ignorance of all that there is in the world besides you two?"

"That child!" she cried. "John, I think you dislike my boy; for, of course, it is Pippo you mean."

"I wish you would not call him by that absurd name."

"You are hard to please," she said, with an angry laugh. "I think it is a very sweet little name."

"The child will not always be a baby," said John.

"Oh, no: I suppose if we all live long enough he will some time be a—possibly disagreeable man, and punish us well for all the care we have spent upon him," Elinor said.

"I don't want to make you angry, Elinor——"

"No, I don't suppose you do. You have been very nice to me, John. You have neither scolded me nor given me good advice. I never expected you would have been so forbearing. But I have always felt you must mean to give me a good knock at the end."

"You do me great injustice," he said, much wounded. "You know that I think only of what is best for you—and the child."

They were approaching the shore, and Mrs. Dennistoun's white cap was visible in the waning light, looking out for them from the door. Elinor said hastily, "And the child? I don't think that you care much for the child."

"There you are mistaken, Elinor. I did not perhaps at first: but I acknowledge that a little thing like that does somehow creep into one's heart."

Her face, which had been gloomy, brightened up as if a sunbeam had suddenly burst upon it. "Oh, bless you, John— Uncle John; how good and how kind, and what a dear friend and brother you are! And I such a wretch, ready to quarrel with those I love best! But, John, let me keep quiet, let me keep still, don't make me rake up the past. He is such a baby, such a baby! There cannot be any question of telling him anything for years and years!"

"I thought you were lost," said Mrs. Dennistoun, calling to them. "I began to think of all kinds of things that might have happened—of the steamboat running into you, or the boat going on a rock, or——"

"You need not have had any fear when I was with John," Elinor said, with a smile that made him warm at once, like the sun. He knew very well, however, that it was only because he had made that little pleasant speech about her boy.

CHAPTER XXXII.

There passed after this a number of years of which I can make no record. The ladies remained at Lakeside, seldom moving. When they took a holiday now and then, it was more for the sake of the little community which, just as in Windyhill, had gathered round them, and which inquired, concerned, "Are you not going to take a little change? Don't you think, dear Mrs. Dennistoun, your daughter would be the better for a change? Do you really think that a little sea air and variety wouldn't be good for the boy?" Forced by these kind speeches they did go away now and then to unknown seaside places in the north when little Philip was still a child, and to quiet places abroad when he grew a boy, and it was thought a good thing for him to learn languages, and to be taught that there were other countries in the world besides England. They were absent for one whole winter in France and another in Germany with this motive, that Philip should learn these languages, which he did *tant bien que mal* with much assistance from his mother, who taught herself everything that she thought the boy should know, and shared his lessons in order to push him gently forward. And on the whole, he did very well in this particular of language, showing much aptitude, though not perhaps much application. I would not assert that the ladies, with an opinion very common among women, and also among youth in general, did not rather glory in the thought that he could do almost anything he liked (which was their opinion, and in some degree while he was very young, the opinion of his masters), with the appearance of doing nothing at all. But on the whole, his education was the most difficult matter in which they had yet been engaged. How was he to be educated? His birth and condition pointed to one of the great public schools, and Mrs. Dennistoun, who had made many economics in that retirement, was quite able to give the child what they both called the best education. But how could they send him to Eton or Harrow? A boy who knew nothing about his parentage or his family, a boy bearing a well-known name, who would be subject to endless questions where he came from, who he belonged to? a hundred things which neither in Waterdale nor in their travels had ever been asked of him. What the Waterdale people thought on the subject, or how much they knew, I should not like to inquire. There are ways of finding out everything, and people who possess family secrets are often extraordinarily deceived in respect to what is known and what is not known of those secrets. My own opinion is that there is scarcely such a thing as a secret in the world. If any moment of great revolution comes in your life you generally find that your neighbours are not much surprised. They have known it, or they have suspected it, all along, and it is well if they have not suspected more than the truth. So it is quite possible that these excellent people knew all about Elinor: but Elinor did not think so, which was the great thing.

However, there cannot be any question that Philip's education was a very great difficulty. John Tatham, who paid them a visit soberly from time to time, but did not now come as of old, never indeed came as on that first occasion when he had been so happy and so undeceived. To be sure, as Philip grew up it was of course impossible for any one to be like that. From the time Pippo was five or six he went everywhere with his mother, her sole companion in general, and when there was a visitor always making a third in the party, a third who was really the first, for he appealed to his mother on every occasion, directed her attention to everything. He only learned with the greatest difficulty that it was possible she should find it necessary to give her attention in a greater degree to any one else. When she said, "You know, Pippo, I must talk to Uncle John," Pippo opened his great eyes, "Not than to me, mamma?"

"Yes, dearest, more than to you for the moment: for he has come a long way to see us, and he will soon have to go away again." When this was first explained to him, Pippo inquired particularly when his Uncle John was going away, and was delighted to hear that it was to be very soon. However, as he grew older the boy began to take great pleasure in Uncle John, and hung upon his arm when they went out for their walks, and instead of endeavouring to monopolise his mother, turned the tables upon her by monopolising this the only man who belonged to him, and to whom he turned with the instinct of budding manhood. John too was very willing to be thus appropriated, and it came to pass that now and then Elinor was left out, or left herself out of the calculation, urging that the walk they were planning was too far for her, or too steep for her, or too something, so that the boy might have the enjoyment of the man's society all to himself. This changed the position in many ways, and I am not sure that at first it did not cost Elinor a little thus to stand aside and put herself out of that first place which had always been by all of them accorded to her. But if this was so, it was soon lost in the consideration of how good it was for Pippo to have a man like John to talk to and to influence him in every way. A man like John! That was the thing; not a common man, not one who might teach him the baseness, or the frivolity, or the falsehood of the world, but a good man, who was also a distinguished man, a man of the world in the best sense, knowing life in the best sense, and able to modify the boy's conception of what he was to find in the world, as women could never do.

"For after all that can be said, we are not good for much on those points, mother," Mrs. Compton would say.

"I don't know, Elinor; I doubt whether I would exchange my own ideas for John's," the elder lady replied.

"Ah, perhaps, mother; but for Pippo his experience and his knowledge will do so much. A boy should not be brought up entirely with women any more than a girl should be with men."

"I have often thought, my dear," said Mrs. Dennistoun, "if in

318

God's providence it had been a girl instead of a boy——"

"Oh!" said the younger mother, with a flush, "how can you speak—how could you think of any possible child but Pippo? I would not give him for a score of girls."

"And if he had been a girl you would not have changed him for scores of boys," said Mrs. Dennistoun, who added after a while, with a curious sense of competition, and a determination to allow no inferiority, "You forget, Elinor, that my only child is a girl." The elder lady (whom they began to call the old lady) showed a great deal of spirit in defence of her own.

But Philip was approaching fourteen, and the great question had to be decided now or never; where was he to be sent to school? It was difficult now to send him to bed to get him out of the way, he who was used to be the person of first importance in the house—in order that the others might settle what was to be his fate. And accordingly the two ladies came down-stairs again after the family had separated in the usual way, in order to have their consultation with their adviser. There was now a room in the house furnished as a library in order that Philip might have a place in which to carry on his studies, and where "the gentlemen" might have their talks by themselves, when there was any one in the house. And here they found John when they stole in one after the other, soft-footed, that the boy might suspect no complot. They had their scheme, it need not be doubted, and John had his. He pronounced at once for one of the great public schools, while the ladies on their part had heard of one in the north, an old foundation as old as Eton, where there was at the moment a head master who was quite exceptional, and where boys were winning honours in all directions. There Pippo would be quite safe. He was not likely to meet with anybody who would put awkward questions, and yet he would receive an education as good as any one's. "Probably better," said Elinor: "for Mr. Sage will have few pupils like him, and therefore will give him the more attention."

"That means," said John, "that the boy will not be among his equals, which is of all things I know the worst for a boy."

319

"We are not aristocrats, as you are, John. They will be more than his equal in one way, because many of them will be bigger and stronger than he, and that is what counts most among boys. Besides, we have no pretensions."

"My dear Elinor," said John Tatham (who was by this time an exceedingly successful lawyer, member for his native borough, and within sight of a Solicitor-Generalship), "your modesty is a little out of character, don't you think? There can be no two opinions about what the boy is: an aristocrat—if you choose to use that word, every inch of him—a little gentleman, down to his fingers' ends."

"Oh, thank you, John," cried Pippo's inconsistent mother; "that is the thing of all others that we hoped you would say."

"And yet you are going to send him among the farmers' sons. Fine fellows, I grant you, but not of his kind. Have you heard," he said, more gravely, "that Reginald Compton died last year?"

"We saw it in the papers," said Mrs. Dennistoun. Elinor said nothing, but turned her head away.

"And neither of the others are married, or likely to marry; one of them is very much broken down——"

"Oh, John, John, for God's sake don't say anything more!"

"I must, Elinor. There is but one good life, and that in a dangerous climate, and with all the risks of possible fighting, between the boy and——"

"Don't, don't, John!"

"And he does not know who he is. He is ignorant of everything, even the fact, the great fact, which you have no right to keep from him——"

"John," she cried, starting to her feet, "the boy is mine: I have a right to deal with him as I think best. I will not hear a word you have to say."

"It is vain to say anything," said Mrs. Dennistoun; "she will not hear a word."

"That is all very well, so far as she is concerned," said John, "but I have a part of my own to play. You give me the name of adviser and so forth—a man cannot be your adviser if his mouth is closed before he speaks. I have a right to speak, being summoned for that purpose. I tell you, Elinor, that you have no right to conceal from the boy who he is, and that his father is alive."

She gave a cry as if he had struck her, and shrank away behind her mother, hiding her face in her hands.

"I am, more or less, of your opinion, John. I have told her the same. While he was a baby it mattered nothing, now that he is a rational creature with an opinion of his own, like any one of us——"

"Mother," cried Elinor, "you are unkind. Oh, you are unkind! What did it matter so long as he was a baby? But now he is just at the age when he would be—if you don't wish to drive me out of my senses altogether, don't say a word more to me of this kind."

"Elinor," said John, "I have said nothing on the subject for many years, though I have thought much: and you must for once hear reason. The boy belongs—to his father as much as to you. I have said it! I cannot take it back. He belongs to the family of which he may one day be the head. You cannot throw away his birthright. And think, if you let him grow up like this, not knowing that he has a family or a—unaware whom he belongs to."

"Have you done, John?" asked Elinor, who had made two or three efforts to interrupt, and had been beating her foot impatiently upon the ground.

"If you ask me in that tone, I suppose I must say yes: though I have a great deal more that I should like to say."

"Then hear me speak," cried Elinor. "Of us three at least, I am the only one to whom he belongs. I only have power to decide for him. And I say, No, no: whatever argument there may be, whatever plea you may bring forward, No and no, and after that No! What! at fourteen, just the age when anything that was said to him would tell the most; when he would learn a lesson the quickest, learn what I would die to keep him from! When he would take everything for gospel that was said to him, when the very charm of—of that unknown name——"

She stopped for a moment to take breath, half choked by her own words.

"And you ought to remember no one has ever laid claim to him. Why should I tell him of one that never even inquired—— No, John, no, no, no! A baby he might have been told, and it would have done him no harm. Perhaps you were right, you and mother, and I was wrong. He might have known it from the first, and thought very little of it, and he may know when he is a man, and his character is formed and he knows what things mean— but a boy of fourteen! Imagine the glamour there would be about the very name; how he would feel we must all have been unjust and the—the other injured. You know from yourself, John, how he clings to you—you who are only a cousin; he knows that, yet he insists upon Uncle John, the one man who belongs to him, and looks up to you, and thinks nothing of any of us in comparison. I like it! I like it!" cried Elinor, dashing the tears from her eyes. "I am not jealous: but fancy what it would be with the—other, the real, the—— I cannot, cannot, say the word; yes, the father. If it is so with you, what would it be with him?"

John listened with his head bent down, leaning on his hand: every word went to his heart. Yes, he was nothing but a cousin, it was true. The boy did not belong to him, was nothing to him. If the father stepped in, the real father, the man of whom Philip had never heard, in all the glory of his natural rights and the novelty and wonder of his existence, how different would that be from any feeling that could be raised by a cousin, an uncle, with whom the boy had played all his life! No doubt it was true: and Phil Compton would probably charm the inexperienced boy with his handsome, disreputable grace, and the unknown ways of the man of the world. And yet, he thought to himself, there is a perspicacity about children which is not always present in a man. Philip had no precocious instincts to be tempted by his father's habits; he had the true sight of a boy trained amid everything that was noble and pure. Would it indeed be more dangerous now, when the boy was a boy, with all those safeguards of nature, than when he was a man? John kept his mind to this question with the firmness of a trained intelligence, not letting himself go off into other matters, or pausing to feel the sting that was in Elinor's words, the reminder that though he had been so much, he was still nothing to the family to whom he had consecrated so much of his life, so much now of his thoughts.

"I do not think I agree with you, Elinor," he said at last. "I think it would have been better had he always known that his father lived, and who he was, and what family he belonged to; that is not to say that you were to thrust him into his father's arms. And I think now that, though we cannot redeem the past, it should be done as soon as possible, and that he should know before he goes to school. I think the effect will be less now than if the discovery bursts upon him when he is a young man, when he finds, perhaps, as may well be, that his position and all his prospects are changed in a moment, when he may be called upon without any preparation to assume a name and a rank of which he knows nothing."

"Not a name. He has always borne his true name."

"His true name may be changed at any moment, Elinor. He may become Lord Lomond, and the heir——"

"My dear," said Mrs. Dennistoun, growing red, "that is a chance we have never taken into account."

"What has that to do with it?" she said. "Is his happiness and his honour to be put in comparison with a chance, a possibility that may never come true? John, for the sake of everything that is good, let him wait till he is a man and knows good from evil."

"It is that I am thinking of, Elinor; a boy of fourteen often knows good from evil much better than a youth of twenty-one, which is, I suppose, what you call a man. My opinion is that it would be better and safer now."

"No!" she said. "And no! I will never consent to it. If you go and poison my boy's mind I will never forgive you, John."

"I have no right to do anything," he said; "it is of course you

323

who must decide, Elinor: I advise only; and I might as well give that up," he added, "don't you think? for you are not to be guided by me."

And she was of course supreme in everything that concerned her son. John, when he could do no more, knew how to be silent, and Mrs. Dennistoun, if not so wise in this respect, was yet more easily silenced than John. And Philip Compton went to the old grammar-school among the dales, where was the young and energetic head-master, who, as Elinor anticipated, found this one pupil like a pearl among the pebbles of the shore, and spared no pains to polish him and perfect him in every way known to the ambitious schoolmaster of modern times.

CHAPTER XXXIII.

It is needless to say that the years which developed Elinor's child into a youth on the verge of manhood, had not passed by the others of the family without full evidence of its progress. John Tatham was no longer within the elastic boundaries of that conventional youth which is allowed to stretch so far when a man remains unmarried. He might have been characterized as *encore jeune*, according to the fine distinction of our neighbours in France, had he desired it. But he did not desire it. He had never altogether neglected society, having a wholesome liking for the company of his fellow creatures, but neither had he ever plunged into it as those do who must keep their places in the crowd or die. John had pursued the middle path, which is the most difficult. He had cultivated friends, not a mob of acquaintances, although as people say he "knew everybody," as a man who had attained his position and won his success could scarcely fail to do. He had succeeded indeed, not in the fabulous way that some men do, but in a way which most men in his profession looked upon as in the highest degree satisfactory. He had a silk gown like any dowager. He had been leading counsel in many cases which were now of note. He was among, not the two or three perhaps, but the twenty or thirty, who were at the head of his profession. If he had not gone further it was perhaps more from lack of ambition than from want of power. He had been for years in Parliament, but preferred his independence to the chance of office. It is impossible to tell how John's character and wishes might have been modified had he married and had children round him like other men. Had the tall boy in the north, the young hero of Lakeside, been his, what a difference would that have made in

his views of life! But Philip was not his, nor Philip's mother—
probably, as he always said to himself, from his own fault. This,
as the reader is aware, had always been fully recognised by John
himself. Perhaps in the old days, in those days when everything
was possible, he had not even recognised that there was but one
woman in the world whom he could ever wish to marry. Probably
it was only her appropriation by another that revealed this fact to
him. There are men like this to be found everywhere; not so hotly
constituted as to seize for themselves what is most necessary for
their personal happiness—possessed by so many other subjects
that this seems a thing to be thought of by-and-by—which by-
and-by is generally too late.

But John Tatham was neither a disappointed nor an unhappy
man. He might have attained a higher development and more
brilliant and full life, but that was all; and how few men are there
of whom this could not be said! He had become Mr. Tatham of
Tatham's Cross, as well as Q.C. and M.P., a county gentleman of
modest but effective standing, a lawyer of high reputation, quite
eligible either for the bench or for political elevation, had he cared
for either, a member of Parliament with a distinct standing, and
therefore importance of his own. There was probably throughout
England no society in which he could have found himself where
his position and importance would have been unknown. He was
a man approaching fifty, who had not yet lost any of the power of
enjoyment or begun to feel the inroads of decay, at the very height
of life, and unconscious that the ground would shortly begin
to slope downwards under his feet; indeed, it showed no such
indication as yet, and probably would not do so for years. The
broad plateau of middle age lasts often till sixty, or even beyond.
There was no reason to doubt that for John Tatham it would last
as long as for any man. His health was perfect, and his habits
those of a man whose self had never demanded indulgences of
the vulgar kind. He had given up with some regret, but years
before, his chambers in the Temple: that is, he retained them as
chambers, but lived in them no longer. He had a house in one

of the streets about Belgrave Square, one of those little bits of awkward, three-cornered streets where there are some of the pleasantest houses of a moderate kind in London; furnished from top to bottom, the stairs, the comfortable quaint landings, the bits of corridor and passage, nothing naked or neglected about it—no cold corner; but nothing fantastic; not very much ornament, a few good pictures, a great deal of highly-polished, old-fashioned dark mahogany, with a general flavour of Sherraton and Chippendale: and abundance of books everywhere. John was able to permit himself various little indulgences on which wives are said to look with jealous eyes. He had a fancy for rare editions (in which I sympathise) and also for bindings, which seems to me a weakness—however, it was one which he indulged in moderation. He possessed in his drawing-room (which was not very much used) a beautiful old-fashioned harpsichord, and also he had belonging to him a fiddle of value untold. I ought, of course, to say violin, or rather to distinguish the instrument by its family name; I have no doubt it was a Stradivarius. But there is an affectionate humour in the fiddle which does not consist with fine titles. He had always been fond of music, but even the Stradivarius did not beguile him, in the days of which I speak, to play, nor perhaps was his performance worthy of it, though his taste was said to be excellent. It will be perceived by all this that John Tatham's life had many pleasures.

And I am not myself sorry for him because he was not married, as many people will be. Perhaps it is a little doleful coming home, when there is never anybody looking out for you, expecting you. But then he had never been accustomed to look for that, and the effect might have been irksome rather than pleasant. His household went on velvet under the care of a respectable couple who had "done for" Mr. Tatham for years. He would not have submitted to extortion or waste, but everything was ample in the house; the cook by no means stinted in respect to butter or any of those condiments which are as necessary to good cooking as air is to life. Mr. Tatham would not have understood a lack of anything, or that what was served to him should not have been the best, supplied and served in the best way. Failure on such points would have so much surprised him that he would scarcely have known what steps to take. But Jervis, his butler, knew what was best as well as Mr. Tatham did, and was quite as little disposed to put up with any shortcoming. I say I am not sorry for him that he was not married—up to this time. But, as a matter of fact, the time does come when one becomes sorry for the well-to-do, highly respectable, refined, and agreeable man who has everything that heart can desire, except the best things in life—love, and the companionship of those who are his very own. When old age looms in sight everything is changed. But Mr. Tatham, as has been said, was not quite fifty, and old age seemed as far off as if it could never be.

He was a man who was very good to a number of people, and spent almost as much money in being kind as if he had possessed extravagant children of his own. His sister Mary, for instance, had married a clergyman not very well off, and the natural result had followed. How they could have existed without Uncle John, much less how they could have stumbled into public schools, scholarships, and all the rest of it, would be difficult to tell, especially now in these days when a girl's schooling ought, we are told, to cost as much as a boy's. This latter is a grievance which must be apparent to the meanest capacity. Unless the girl binds herself by the most stringent vows *not* to marry a poor curate or other penniless man the moment that you have completed her expensive education, I do not think she should in any case be permitted to go to Girton. It is all very well when the parents are rich or the girls have a sufficiency of their own. But to spend all that on a process which, instead of fructifying in other schools and colleges, or producing in life a highly accomplished woman, is to be lost at once and swallowed up in another nursery, is the most unprofitable of benefactions. This is what Mary Tatham's eldest girl had just done, almost before her bills at Newnham had been paid. A wedding present had, so to speak, been demanded from Uncle John at the end of the bayonet to show his satisfaction in the event which had taken all meaning out of his exertions for little Mary. He had given it indeed—in the shape not of a biscuit-box, which is what she would have deserved, but of a cheque—but he was not pleased. Neither was he pleased, as has been seen, by the proceedings of Elinor, who had slighted all his advice yet clung to himself in a way some women have. I do not know whether men expect you to be quite as much their friend as ever after they have rejected your counsel and taken their own (exactly opposite) way: but women do, and indeed I think expect you to be rather grateful that they have not taken amiss the advice which they have rejected and despised. This was Elinor's case. She hoped that John was ashamed of advising her to make her boy acquainted with his family and the fact of his father's existence, and that he duly appreciated the fact that she did not resent that advice; and then she expected from him the same attention to herself and her son as if the boy had been guided in his and not in her way. Thus it will be seen his friends and relations expected a very great deal from John.

He had gone to his chambers one afternoon after he left the law courts, and was there very busily engaged in getting up his notes for to-morrow's work, when he received a visit which awakened at once echoes of the past and alarms for the future in John's mind. It was very early in the year, the end of January, and the House was not sitting, so that his public duties were less overwhelming than usual. His room was the same in which we have already seen on various occasions, and which Elinor in her youth, before anything had happened to make life serious for her, had been in the habit of calling the Star Chamber, for no reason in the world except that law and penalties or judgments upon herself in her unripe conviction, and suggestions of what ought to be done, came from that place to which Mrs. Dennistoun had made resort in her perplexities almost from the very beginning of John's reign there. Mr. Tatham had been detained beyond his usual time by the importance of the case for which he was preparing, and a clerk, very impatient to get free, yet obliged to simulate content, had lighted the lamp and replenished the fire. It had always been a comfortable room. The lamp by which John worked had a green shade which concentrated the light upon a table covered with that litter of papers in which there seemed so little order, yet which Mr. Tatham knew to the last scrap as if they had been the tidiest in the world. The long glazed book-case which filled up one side of the room gave a dark reflection of the light and of the leaping brightness of the fire. The curtains were drawn over the windows. If the clerk fumed in the outer rooms, here all was studious life and quiet. No spectator could have been otherwise than impressed by the air of absolute self-concentration with which the eminent lawyer gave himself up to his work. He was like his lamp, giving all the light in him to the special subject, indifferent to everything outside.

"What is it, Simmons?" he said abruptly, without looking up.

"A lady, sir, who says she has urgent business and must see you."

"A lady—who *must* see me." John Tatham smiled at the very ineffectual *must*, which meant coercion and distraction to him. "I don't see how she is going to accomplish that."

"I told her so," said the clerk.

"Well, you must tell her so again." He had scarcely lifted his head from his work, so that it was unnecessary to return to it when the door closed, and Mr. Tatham went on steadily as before.

It is easy to concentrate the light of the lamp when it is duly shaded and no wind to blow it about, and it is easy to concentrate a man's attention in the absolute quiet when nothing interrupts him; but when there suddenly rises up a wind of talk in the room which is separated from him only by a door, a tempest of chattering words and laughter, shrill and bursting forth in something like shrieks, making the student start, that is altogether a different business. The lady outside, who evidently had multiplied herself—unless it was conceivable that the serious Simmons had made himself her accomplice—had taken the cleverest way of showing that she was not to be beat by any passive resistance of busy man, though not even an audible conversation with Simmons would have startled or disturbed his master, to whom it would have been apparent that his faithful vassal was thus defending his own stronghold and innermost retirement. But this was quite independent of Simmons, a discussion in two voices, one high-pitched and shrill, the other softer, but both absolutely unrestrained by any consciousness of being in a place where the chatter of strange voices is forbidden, and stillness and quiet a condition of being. The sound of the talk rang through Mr. Tatham's head as if all the city bells were ringing. One of the unseen ladies had a very shrill laugh, to which she gave vent freely. John fidgeted in his chair, raised up his eyes above the level of his spectacles (he wore spectacles, alas! by this time habitually when he worked) as if lifting a voiceless appeal to those powers who interest themselves in law cases to preserve him from disturbance, then made a manly effort to disregard the sounds that filled the air, returning with a shake of his head to his reading. But at the end of a long day, and in the dulness of the afternoon, perhaps a man is less capable than at other moments to fight against interruption of this kind and finally he threw down his papers and touched his bell. Simmons came in full of pale indignation, which made itself felt even beyond the circle illuminated by the lamp.

"What can I do?" he said. "They've planted themselves by the fire, and there they mean to stay. 'Oh, very well, we'll wait,' they said, quite calm. And I make no doubt they will, having nothing else to do, till all is blue."

Mr. Simmons had a gift of expression of which all his friends were flatteringly sensible, and he was very friendly and condescending to John, of whom he had taken care for many years.

"What is to be done?" said Mr. Tatham. "Can't you do anything to get them away?"

Simmons shook his head. "There's two of them," he said, "and they entertain each other, and they think it's fun to jabber like that in a lawyer's office. The young one says, 'What a queer place!' and the other, she holds forth about other times when she's been here."

"Oh, she's been here other times—— Do you know her, Simmons?"

"Not from Adam, Mr. Tatham—or, I should say, from Eve, as she's a lady. But a real lady I should say, though she don't behave herself as such—one of the impudent ones. They are never impudent like that," said Mr. Simmons, with profound observation, "unless they are real high or—real low."

"Hum!" said John, hesitating. And then he added, "There is a young one, you say?"

But I do not myself think, though the light-minded may imagine it to be so, that it was because there was a young one that John gave in. It was because he could do nothing else, the noise and chatter of the voices being entirely destructive of that undisturbed state of the atmosphere in which work can be done. It was not merely the sounds but the vibration they made in the air, breaking all its harmony and concentration. He tried a little longer, but was unsuccessful, and finally in despair he said to Simmons, "You had better show them in, and let me get done with them," in an angry tone.

"Oh, he will see us after all," said the high-pitched voice. "So good of Mr. Tatham; but of course I should have waited all the same. Dolly, take Toto; I can't possibly get up while I have him on my knee. You can tell Mr. Tatham I did not send in my name to disturb him, which makes it all the more charitable of him to receive me; but, dear me, of course I can tell him that himself as he consents to see us. Dolly, don't strangle my poor darling! I never saw a girl that didn't know how to take up a dear dog before."

"He's only a snappish little demon, and you spoil him so," said the other voice. This was attended by the sound of movement as if the party were getting under weigh.

332

"My poor darling pet, it is only her jealousy: is that the way? Yes, to be sure it is the next room. Now, Dolly, remember this is where all the poor people are ruined and done for. Leave hope behind all ye who enter here." A little shriek of laughter ended this speech. And John, looking up, taking off his spectacles, and raising a little the shade of the lamp, saw in the doorway Lady Mariamne, altered as was inevitable by the strain and stress of nearly twenty years.

CHAPTER XXXIV.

I do not mean to assert that John Tatham had not seen Lady Mariamne during these twenty years, or that her changed appearance burst upon him with anything like a shock. In society, when you are once a member of that little world within a world, everybody sees everybody else from time to time. He had not recognised her voice, for he was not in the smallest degree thinking of Lady Mariamne or of any member of her family, notwithstanding that they now and then did make a very marked appearance in his mind in respect of the important question of that connection which Elinor in her foolishness tried to ignore. And John was not at all shocked by the progress of that twenty years, as reflected in the appearance of this lady, who was about his own standing, a woman very near fifty, but who had fought strenuously against every sign of her age, as some women foolishly do. The result was in Lady Mariamne's case, as in many others, that the number of her years looked more like a hundred and fifty than their natural limit. A woman of her class has but two alternatives as she gets old. She must get stout, in which case, though she becomes unwieldy, she preserves something of her bloom; or she may grow thin, and become a spectre upon which art has to do so much that nature, flouted and tortured, becomes vindictive, and withdraws every modifying quality. Lady Mariamne had, I fear, false hair, false teeth, false complexion, everything that invention could do in a poor little human countenance intended for no such manipulation. The consequence was that every natural advantage (and there are some which age confers, as well as many that age takes away) was lost. The skin was parchment, the eyes were like eyes of fishes, the teeth—too white and too perfect—looked like the horrible things in the dentists' windows, which was precisely what they were. On such a woman, the very height of the fashion, to which she so often attaches herself with desperation, has an antiquated air. Everything "swears," as the French say, with everything else. The softness, the whiteness, the ease, the self-abnegation of advancing age are all so many ornaments if people but knew. But Lady Mariamne had none of these. She wore a warm cloak in her carriage, it is true, but that had dropped from her shoulders, leaving her in all the bound-up rigidity in which youth is trim and slim and elastic, as becomes it. It is true that many a woman of fifty is, as John Tatham was, serenely dwelling on that tableland which shows but little difference between thirty-five, the crown of life, and fifty-five; but Lady Mariamne was not one of these. She had gone "too fast," she would herself have allowed; "the pace" had been too much for such survivals. She was of the awful order of superannuated beauties of which Mr. Rider Haggard would in vain persuade us "She" was not one. I am myself convinced that "She's" thousands of years were all written on her fictitious complexion, and that other people saw them clearly if not her unfortunate lover. And Lady Mariamne had come to be of the order of "She." By dint of wiping out the traces of her fifty years, she had made herself look as if she might have been a thousand, and in this guise she appeared to the robust, ruddy, well-preserved man of her own age, as she stood, with a fantastic little giggle, calling his attention, on the threshold of his door.

Behind Lady Mariamne was a very different figure—that of the serious and independent girl without any illusions, who is in so many cases the child of such a mother, and who is in revolt so complete from all that mother's traditions, so highly set on the crown of every opposite principle, that nature vindicates itself by the possibility that she may at any moment topple over and become again what her mother was. He would have been a bold man, however, who in the present stage would have prophesied any such fate for Dolly Prestwich, who between working at

Whitechapel, attending on a ward in St. Thomas's, drawing three days a week in the Slade School, and other labours of equally varied descriptions, had her time very fully taken up, and only on special occasions had time to accompany her mother. She had been beguiled on this occasion by the family history which was concerned, and which, *fin de siècle* as Dolly was, excited her curiosity almost as much as if she had been born in the "forties." Dolly was never unkind, sometimes indeed was quite the reverse, to her mother. When Mr. Tatham, with a man's brutal unconsciousness of what is desirable, placed a chair for Lady Mariamne in front of the fire, Dolly twisted it round with a dexterous movement so as to shield the countenance which was not adapted for any such illumination. For herself, Dolly cared nothing, whether it was the noonday sun or the blaze of a furnace that shone upon her; she defied them both to make her wink. As for complexion, she scorned that old-fashioned vanity. She had not very much, it is true. Having been scorched red and brown in Alpine expeditions in the autumn, she was now of a somewhat dry whitish-greyish hue, the result of much loss of cuticle and constant encounter with London fogs and smoke. She carried Toto—who was a shrinking, chilly Italian greyhound—in a coat, carelessly under one arm, and sat down beside her mother, studying the papers on John's table with exceedingly curious eyes. She would have liked to go over all his notes about his case, and form her own opinion on it—which she would have done, we may be sure, much more rapidly, and with more decision, than Mr. Tatham could do.

"So here I am again, you will say," said Lady Mariamne. She had taken off her gloves, and was smoothing her hands, from the points of the fingers downwards, not, I believe, with any intention of demonstrating their whiteness, but solely because she had once done so, and the habit remained. She wore several fine rings, and her hands were still pretty, and—unlike the rest of her—younger than her age. They made a little show with their sparkling diamonds, just catching the edge of the light from

336

John's shaded lamp. Her face by Dolly's help was in the shadow of the green shade. "You will say so, Mr. Tatham, I know: here she is again—without thinking how self-denying I have been, never to come, never to ask a single question, for all these years."

"The loss is mine, Lady Mariamne," said John, gravely.

"It's very pretty of you to say that, isn't it, Dolly? One's old flirts don't always show up so well." And here the lady gave a laugh, such as had once been supposed to be one of Lady Mariamne's charms, but which was rather like a giggle now—an antiquated giggle, which is much less satisfactory than the genuine article. "How I used to worry you about poor Phil, and that little spitfire of a Nell—and what a mess they have made of it! I suppose you know what changes have happened in the family, Mr. Tatham, since those days?"

"I heard indeed, with regret, Lady Mariamne, that you had lost a brother——"

"A brother! two!" she cried. "Isn't it extraordinary—poor Hal, that was the picture of health? How little one knows! He just went, don't you know, without any one ever thinking he would go. Regg in India was different—you expect that sort of thing when a man is in India. But poor Hal! I told you Mr. Tatham wouldn't have heard of it, Dolly, not being in our own set, don't you know."

"It was in all the papers," said Miss Dolly.

"Ah, well, you didn't notice it, I suppose: or perhaps you were away. I always say it is of no use being married or dying or anything else in September—your friends never hear of it. You will wonder that I am not in black, but black was always very unbecoming to me, and dark grey is just as good, and doesn't make one quite so ghastly. But the funny thing is that now Phil— who looked as if he never could be in the running, don't you know—is heir presumptive. Isn't it extraordinary? Two gone, and Phil, that lived much faster than either of them, and at one time kept up an awful pace, has seen them both out. And St. Serf has never married. He won't now, though I have been at him on the subject for years. He says, not if he knows it, in the horrid way men have. And I don't wonder much, for he has had some nasty experiences, poor fellow. There was Lady—— Oh, I almost forgot you were there, Dolly."

"You needn't mind me," said Dolly, gravely; "I've heard just as bad."

"Well," said Lady Mariamne, with a giggle, "did you ever know anything like those girls? They are not afraid of anything. Now, when I was a girl—don't you remember what an innocent dear I was, Mr. Tatham?—like a lamb; never suspecting that there was any naughtiness in the world——"

John endeavoured to put on a smile, in feeble sympathy with the uproariousness of Lady Mariamne's laugh—but her daughter took no such trouble. She sat as grave as a young judge, never moving a muscle. The dog, however, held in her arms, and not at all comfortable, then making prodigious efforts to struggle on to its mistress's more commodious lap, burst out into a responsive bark, as shrill and not much unlike.

"Darling Toto," said Lady Mariamne, "come!—it always knows what it's mummy means. Did you ever see such a darling little head, Mr. Tatham?—and the faithful pet always laughs when I laugh. What was I talking of?—St. Serf and his ladies. Well, it is not much wonder, you know, is it? for he has always been a sort of an invalid, and he will never marry now—and poor Hal being gone there's only Phil. Phil's been going a pace, Mr. Tatham; but he has had a bad illness, too, and the other boys going has sobered him a bit; and I do believe, *now*, that he'll probably mend. And there he is, you know, tied to a—— Oh, of course, *she* is as right as a—as right as a—trivet, whatever that may be. Those sort of heartless people always are: and then there's the child. Is it living, Mr. Tatham?—that's what I want to know."

"Philip is alive and well, Lady Mariamne, if that is what you want to know."

"Philip!—she called him after Phil, after all! Well, that is something wonderful. I expected to hear he was John, or

338

Jonathan, or something. Now, where is he?" said Lady Mariamne, with the most insinuating air.

John burst into a short laugh. "I don't suppose you expect me to tell you," he said.

"Why not?—you can't hide a boy that is heir to a peerage, Mr. Tatham!—it is impossible. Nell has done the best she could in that way. They know nothing about her in that awful place she was married from—of course you remember it—a dreadful place, enough to make one commit suicide, don't you know. The Cottage, or whatever they call it, is let, and nobody knows anything about them. I took the trouble to go there, I assure you, on my own hook, to see if I could find out something. Toto nearly died of it, didn't you, darling? Not a drop of cream to be had for him, the poor angel; only a little nasty skim milk. But Mr. Tatham has the barbarity to smile," she went on, with a shrill outcry. "Fancy, Toto—the cruelty to smile!"

"No cream for the angel, and no information for his mistress," said John.

"You horrid, cruel, cold-blooded man!—and you sit there at your ease, and will do nothing for us——"

"Should you like me," said John, "to send out for cream for your dog, Lady Mariamne?"

"Cream in the Temple?" said the lady. "What sort of a compound would it be, Dolly? All plaster of Paris, or stuff of that sort. Perhaps you have tea sometimes in these parts——"

"Very seldom," said John; "but it might be obtainable if you would like it." He put forward his hand, but not with much alacrity, to the bell.

"Mother never takes any tea," said Miss Dolly, hastily; "she only crumbles down cake into it for that little brute."

"It is you who are a little brute, you unnatural child. Toto likes his tea very much—he is dying for it. But you must have patience, my pet, for probably it would be very bad, and the cream all stucco, or something. Mr. Tatham, do tell us what has become of Nell? Now, have you hidden her somewhere in London, St. John's

Wood, and that sort of thing, don't you know? or where is she? Is the old woman living? and how has that boy been brought up? At a dame's school, or something of that sort, I suppose."

"Mother," said Dolly, "you ought to know there are now no dame's schools. There's Board Schools, which is what you mean, I suppose; and it would be very good for him if he had been there. They would teach him a great deal more than was ever taught to Uncle Phil."

"Teach him!" said Lady Mariamne, with another shriek. "Did I ask anything about teaching? Heaven forbid! Mr. Tatham knows what I mean, Dolly. Has he been at any decent place—or has he been where it will never be heard of? Eton and Harrow one knows, and the dame's schools one knows, but horrible Board Schools, or things, where they might say young Lord Lomond was brought up—oh, goodness gracious! One has to bear a great many things, but I could not bear that."

"It does not matter much, does it, so long as he does not come within the range of his nearest relations?" This was from John, who was almost at the end of his patience. He began to put his papers back in a portfolio, with the intention of carrying them home with him, for his hour's work had been spoilt as well as his temper. "I am afraid," he added, "that I cannot give you any information, Lady Mariamne."

"Oh, such nonsense, Mr. Tatham!—as if the heir to a peerage could be hid."

It was not often that Lady Mariamne produced an unanswerable effect, but against this last sentence of hers John had absolutely nothing to say. He stared at her for a moment, and then he returned to his papers, shovelling them into the portfolio with vehemence. Fortunately, she did not herself see how potent was her argument. She went on diluting it till it lost all its power.

"There is the 'Peerage,' if it was nothing else—they must have the right particulars for that. Why, Dolly is at full length in it, her age and all, poor child; and Toto, too, for anything I know. Is du in the 'Peerage,' dear Toto, darling? And yet Toto can't succeed, nor Dolly either. And this year Phil will be in as heir presumptive and his marriage and all—and then a blank line. It's ridiculous, it's horrible, it's a thing that can't, can't be! Only think of all the troops of people, nice people, the best people, that read the 'Peerage,' Mr. Tatham!—and that know Phil is married, and that there is a child, and yet will see nothing but that blank line. Nell was always a little fool, and never could see things in a common-sense way. But a man ought to know better—and a lawyer, with chambers in the Temple! Why, people come and consult you on such matters—I might be coming to ask you to send out detectives, and that sort of thing. How do you dare to hide away that boy?"

Lady Mariamne stamped her foot at John, but this proceeding very much incommoded Toto, who, disturbed in his position on her knee, got upon his feet and began to bark furiously, first at his mistress and then, following her impulse, at the gentleman opposite to her, backing against the lady's shoulder and setting up his little nose furiously with vibrations of rage against John, while stumbling upon the uncertain footing of the lap, volcanically shaken by the movement. The result of this onslaught was to send Lady Mariamne into shrieks of laughter, in the midst of which she half smothered Toto with mingled endearments and attempts at restraint, until Dolly, coming to the rescue, seized him summarily and snatched him away.

"The darling!" cried Lady Mariamne, "he sees it, and you can't see it, a great big lawyer though you are. Dolly, don't throttle my angel child. Stands up for his family, don't he, the dear? Mr. Tatham, how can you be so bigoted and stubborn, when our dear little Toto—— But you always were the most obstinate man. Do you remember once, when I wanted to take you to Lady Dogberry's dance—wasn't it Lady Dogberry's?—well, it was Lady Somebody's—and you said you were not asked, and I said, what did it matter: but to make you go, and Nell was with me—we might as well have tried to make St. Paul's go——"

"My dear Lady Mariamne," said John.

She held up a finger at him with the engaging playfulness of old. "How can I be your dear Lady Mariamne, Mr. Tatham, when you won't do a thing I ask you? What, Dolly? Yes, we must go, of course, or I shall not have my nap before dinner. I always have a nap before dinner, for the sake of my complexion, don't you know—my beauty nap, they call it. Now, Mr. Tatham, come to me to-morrow, and you shall give Toto his cream, to show you bear no malice, and tell me all about the boy. Don't be an obstinate pig, Mr. Tatham. Now, I shall look for you—without fail. Shan't we look for him, Dolly?—and Toto will give you a paw and forgive you—and you must tell me all about the boy."

CHAPTER XXXV.

To tell her all about the boy!

John Tatham shovelled his papers into his portfolio, and shut it up with a snap of embarrassment, a sort of confession of weakness. He pushed back his chair with the same sharpness, almost making a noise upon the old Turkey carpet, and he touched his bell so that it sounded with a shrill electric ping, almost like a pistol-shot. Simmons understood all these signs, and he was very sympathetic when he came in to take Mr. Tatham's last orders and help him on with his coat.

"Spoilt your evening's work," said Simmons, compassionately. "I knew they would. Ladies never should enter a gentleman's chambers if I could help it. They've got nothing to do in the Temple."

"You forget some men in the Temple are married, Simmons."

"What does that matter?" said the clerk; "let 'em see their wives at home, sir. What I will maintain is that ladies have no business here."

This was a little ungrateful, it must be said, for Simmons probably got off three-quarters of an hour earlier than he would have done had Mr. Tatham remained undisturbed. As it was, John had some ten minutes to wait before his habitual hansom drew up at the door.

It was not the first time by many times that Mr. Tatham had considered the question which he now took with him into his hansom, and which occupied him more or less all the way to Halkin Street. Lady Mariamne, however, had put it very neatly and very conclusively when she said that you can't hide the heir to a peerage—more concisely at least than John had himself put it in his many thoughts on the subject—for, to tell the truth, John had never considered the boy in this aspect. That he should ever be the heir to a peerage had seemed one of those possibilities which so outrage nature, and are so very like fiction, that the sober mind rejects them with almost a fling of impatience. And yet how often they come true! He had never heard—a fact of which he felt partly ashamed, for it was an event of too much importance to be ignored by any one connected with Elinor—of Hal Compton's death. John was not acquainted with Hal Compton any more than he was with other men who come and go in society, occasionally seen, but open to no particular remark. A son of Lord St. Serf—the best of the lot—a Compton with very little against him: these were things which he had heard said and had taken little notice of. Hal was healthier, less objectionable, a better life than Phil's, and yet Hal was gone, who ought by all rights to have succeeded his invalid brother. It was true that the invalid brother, who had seen the end of two vigorous men, might also see out Phil. But that would make little difference in the position, unless indeed by modifying Elinor's feelings and removing her reluctance to make her boy known. John shook his head as he went on with his thoughts, and decided within himself that this was the very reason why Phil Compton should survive and become Lord St. Serf, and make the imbroglio worse, if worse were possible. It had not required this to make it a hideous imbroglio, the most foolish and wanton that ever a woman made. He wondered at himself when he thought of it how he had ever consented to it, ever permitted such a state of affairs; and yet what could he have done? He had no right to interfere even in the way of advice, which he had given until everybody was sick of him and his counsels. He could not have betrayed his cousin. To tell her that she was conducting her affairs very foolishly, laying up untold troubles for herself, was what he had done freely, going to the very edge of a breach. And he had no right to do any more. He could not force her to adopt his method, neither could he betray her when she took her own way. Nevertheless, there can be no doubt that John felt himself almost an accomplice, involved in this unwise folly, with a sort of responsibility for it, and almost guilt. It did not indeed change young Philip's moral position in any way, or make the discovery that he had a father living more likely to shock and bewilder him that this discovery should come mingled with many extraneous wonders. And yet these facts did alter the circumstances. "You cannot hide the heir to a peerage." Lady Mariamne was far, very far, from being a philosopher or a person of genius, and yet this which she had said was in reality quite unanswerable. Phil Compton might have been ignored for ever by his wife and child had he remained only the *dis*-Honourable Phil, a younger son and a nobody. But Phil Compton as Lord St. Serf could not be ignored. Elinor had been wise enough never to change her name, that is to say, she had been too proud to do so, though nobody knew of the existence of that prefix which was so inappropriate to her husband's character. But now Mrs. Compton would no longer be her name; and Philip, the boy at the big northern grammar-school, would be Lord Lomond. An unlooked-for summons like this has sometimes the power of turning the heads of the heirs so suddenly ennobled, but it did anything but convey elation to John's mind in the prospect of its effect upon his relations. Would she see reason *now*? Would she be brought to allow that something must be done, or would she remain obdurate to the end of the chapter? A great impatience with Elinor filled John's mind. She was, as the reader knows, the only woman to John Tatham; but what does that matter? He did not approve of her any more on that account. He was even more conscious of the faults of which she was guilty. He was aware of her obstinacy, her determined adherence to her own way as no other man in the world was. Would she acknowledge now at last that she was wrong, and give in? I am obliged to confess that the giving in of Elinor was the last spectacle in heaven or earth which John Tatham could conceive.

He went over these circumstances as he drove through all of London that is to some people worth calling London, on that dark January night, passing from the light of the busy streets into the comparative darkness of those in which people live, without in the least remarking where he was going, except in his thoughts. He had not the least intention of accepting the invitation of Lady Mariamne, nor did his mind dwell upon her or the change that age had wrought in her. But yet the Compton family had gained an interest in John's eyes which it did not possess even at the time when Elinor's marriage first brought its name into his thoughts. Philip—young Philip—the boy, as John called him in his own mind, in fond identification—was as near John's own child as anything ever could be in this world. He had many nephews and nieces belonging to him by a more authentic title, but none of these was in the least like Philip, whom none of all the kindred knew but himself, and who, so far as he was aware, had but one kinsman in the world, who was Uncle John. He had followed the development of the boy's mind always with a reference to those facts of which Philip knew nothing, which would be so wonderful to him when the revelation came. To John that little world at Lakeside—where the ladies had made an artificial existence for themselves, which was at the same time so natural, so sweet, so full of all the humanities and charities—was something like what we might suppose this erring world to be to some archangel great enough to see how everything is, not great enough to give the impulse that would put it right. If the great celestial intelligences are allowed to know and mark out perverse human ways, how much impatience with us must mingle with their tenderness and pity! John Tatham had little perhaps that was heavenly about him, but he loved Elinor and her son, and was absolutely free of selfishness in respect to them. Never, he was aware, could either woman or child be more to him than they were now. Nay, they were everything to him, but on their own account, not his; he desired their welfare absolutely, and not his own through them. Elinor was capable at any moment of turning upon him, of saying, if not in words, yet in undeniable inference, what is it to you? and the boy, though he gladly referred to Uncle John when Uncle John was in the way, took him with perfect composure as a being apart from his life. They were everything to him, but he was nothing to them. His whole heart was set upon their peace, upon their comfort and well-being, but as much apart from himself as if he had not been.

Mr. Tatham was dining out that night, which was a good thing for him to distract his thoughts from this problem, which he could only torment himself about and could not solve; and there was an evening party at the same house—one of those quieter, less-frequented parties which are, people in London tell you, so much more agreeable than in the crowd of the season. It was a curious kind of coincidence that at this little assembly, which might have been thought not at all in her way, he met Lady Mariamne, accompanied by her daughter, again. It was not in her way, being a judge's house, where frivolity, though it had a certain place, was not the first element. But then when there are few things to choose from, people must not be too particular, and those who cannot have society absolutely of their own choosing, are bound, as in other cases of necessity, to take what they can get. And then Dolly liked to hear people talking of things which she did not understand. When Lady Mariamne saw that John Tatham was there she gave a little shriek of satisfaction, and rushed at him as if they had been the dearest friends in the world. "So delighted to see you *again*," she cried, giving everybody around the idea of the most intimate relationship. "It was the most wonderful good fortune that I got my Toto home in safety, poor darling; for you know, Mr. Tatham, you would not give him any tea, and Dolly, who is quite unnatural, pitched him into the carriage and simply sat upon him—sat upon him, Mr. Tatham! before I could interfere. Oh, you do not know half the trials a woman has to go through! And now please take me to have some coffee or something, and let us finish the conversation we were having when Dolly made me go away."

John could not refuse his arm, nor his services in respect to the coffee, but he was mute on the subject on which his companion was bent. He tried to divert her attention by some questions on the subject of Dolly instead.

"Dolly! oh, yes, she's a girl of the period, don't you know—not what a girl of the period used to be in *our* day, Mr. Tatham, when those nasty newspaper people wrote us down. Look at her talking to those two men, and laying down the law. Now, we never laid down the law; we knew best about things in our sphere—dress, and the drawing-room, and what people were doing in society. But Dolly would tell you how to manage your next great case, Mr. Tatham, or she could give one of those doctor-men a wrinkle about cutting off a leg. Gracious, I should have fainted only to hear of such a thing! Tell me, are those doctor-men supposed to be in society?" Lady Mariamne cried, putting up her thin shoulder (which was far too like a specimen of anatomy) in the direction of a famous physician who was blandly smiling upon the instruction which Miss Dolly assuredly intended to convey.

"As much as lawyer-men are in society," replied John.

"Oh, Mr. Tatham, such nonsense! Lawyers have always been in society. What are the Attorney General and Lord Chancellor and so forth? They are all lawyers; but I never heard of a doctor that was in the Cabinet, which makes all the difference. Here is a quiet corner, where nobody can disturb us. Sit down; it will be for all the world like sitting out a dance together: and tell me about Nell and her boy."

"And what if I have nothing to tell?" said John, who did not feel at all like sitting out a dance; but, on the contrary, was much more upright and perpendicular than even a queen's counsel of fifty has any need to be.

"Oh, sit down, *please!* I never could bear a man standing over me, as if he had swallowed a poker. Why did she go off and leave Phil? Where did she go to? I told you I went off on my own hook to that horrid place where they lived, and knocked up the old clergyman and the woman who wanted me to put on a shawl over one of the prettiest gowns I ever had. Fancy, the Vandal! But they knew nothing at all of her there. Where is Nell, Mr. Tatham?

You don't pretend not to know. And the boy? Why he must be about eighteen—and if St. Serf were to die—— Mr. Tatham, you know it is quite, quite intolerable, and not to be borne! I don't know what steps Phil has taken. He has been awfully good—he has never said a word. To hear him you would think she was far too nice to be mixed up with a set of people like us. But now, you know, he must be got hold of—he must, he must! Why, he'd be Lomond if St. Serf were to die! and everybody would be crying out, 'Where's the heir?' After Phil there's the Bagley Comptons, and they would set up for being heirs presumptive, unless you can produce that boy."

"But the boy is not mine that I should produce him," said John.

"Oh, Mr. Tatham! when Nell is your relation, and always, always was advised by you. You may tell that to the Marines, or anybody that will believe it. You need not think you can take me in."

"I hope not to take in anybody. If being advised by me means persistently declining to do what I suggest and recommend——"

"Oh, then, you are of the same opinion as I am!" said Lady Mariamne. "Bravo! now we shall manage something. If you had been like that years ago when I used to go to you, don't you remember, to beg you to smooth things down—but you would never see it, till the smash came."

"I wish," said John, not without a little bitterness, "that I could persuade you how little influence I have. There are some women, I suppose, who take advice when it is given to them; but the women whom I have ever had anything to do with, I am sorry to say——"

"I'll promise," cried Lady Mariamne, putting her hands and rings together in an attitude of supplication, "to do what you tell me faithfully, if you'll advise me where I'll find the boy. Oh, let Nell alone, if you want to keep her to yourself—I sha'n't spoil sport, Mr. Tatham, I promise you," she cried, with her shrill laugh; "only tell me where I'll find the boy. What is it you want, Dolly, coming after me like a policeman? Don't you see I am busy? We are sitting out the dance, Mr. Tatham and I."

Dolly did not join in her mother's laugh nor unbend in the least. "As there is no dancing," she said, "and everybody is going, I thought you would prefer to go too."

"But we shall see you to-morrow, Mr. Tatham? Now, I cannot take any refusal. You must come, if it were only for Toto's sake; and Dolly will go out, I hope, on one of her great works and will not come to disturb us, just when I have persuaded you to speak—for you were just going to open your mouth. Now you know you were! Five o'clock to-morrow, Mr. Tatham, whatever happens. Now remember! and you are to tell me everything." She held up her finger to him, half threatening, half coaxing, and then, with a peal of laughter, yielded to Dolly, and was taken away.

"I did not know, Tatham," said the Judge who was his host, "that you were on terms of such friendship with Lady Mariamne."

"Nor did I," said John Tatham, with a yawn.

"Queer thing this is about that old business, in which her brother was mixed up—haven't you heard? one of those companies that came to smash somewhere about twenty years ago. The manager absconded, and there was something queer about the books. Well, the fellow, the manager, has been caught at last, and there will be a trial. It's in your way—you will be offered a brief, no doubt, with refreshers every day, you lucky fellow. I have just as much trouble and no refreshers. What a fool a man is, Tatham, ever to change the Bar for the Bench! Don't you do it, my dear fellow—take a man's advice who knows."

"At least I shall wait till I am asked," said John.

"Oh, you will be asked sooner or later—but don't do it—take example by those who have gone before you," said the great functionary, shaking his learned head.

And the Judge's wife had also a word to say. "Mr. Tatham," she said, as he took his leave, "I know now what I have to do when I want to secure Lady Mariamne—I shall ask you."

"Do you often want to secure Lady Mariamne?" said John.

"Oh, it is all very well to look as if you didn't care! She is, perhaps, a little *passée*, but still a great many people think her charming. Isn't there a family connection?" Lady Wigsby said, with a curiosity which she tried not to make too apparent, for she was acquainted with the ways of the profession, and knew that was the last thing likely to procure her the information she sought.

"It cannot be called a connection. There was a marriage—which turned out badly."

"Oh, I beg your pardon, Mr. Tatham, if the question was indiscreet! I hear Lord St. Serf is worse again, and not likely to last long; and there is some strange story about a lost heir."

"Good-night, Lady Wigsby," John replied.

And he added, "Confound Lord St. Serf," under his breath, as he went down-stairs.

But it was not Lord St. Serf, poor man, who had done him no harm, whom John wished to be confounded because at last, after many threatenings, he was about to be so ill-advised as to die. It was some one very different. It was the woman who for much more than twenty years had been the chief object of John Tatham's thoughts.

CHAPTER XXXVI.

Things relapsed into quietness for some time after that combination which seemed to be directed against John's peace of mind. If I said that it is not unusual for the current of events to run very quietly before a great crisis, I should not be saying anything original, since the torrent's calmness ere it dash below has been remarked before now. But it certainly was so in this instance. John, I need scarcely say, did not present himself at Lady Mariamne's on the afternoon at five when he was expected. He wrote a very civil note to say that he was unable to come, and still less able to give the information her ladyship required; and, to tell the truth, in his alarm lest Lady Mariamne should repeat her invasion, Mr. Tatham was guilty of concerting with his clerk, the excellent Simmons, various means of eluding such a danger. And he exercised the greatest circumspection in regard to his own invitations, and went nowhere where there was the least danger of meeting her. In this way for a few months he had kept himself safe.

It may be imagined, then, how great was his annoyance when Simmons came in again, very diffident, coughing behind his hand, and taking shelter in the shaded part of the room, with the hesitating statement that a lady—who would take no denial, who looked as if she knew the chambers as well as he did, and could hardly be kept from walking straight in—was waiting to see Mr. Tatham. John sprang to his feet with words which were not benedictions. "I thought," he said, "you ass, that you knew exactly what to say."

"But, sir," said Simmons, "it is not the same lady—it is not at all the same lady. It is a lady who——"

But here the question was summarily settled, for the door was pushed open though Simmons still held it with his hand, and a voice, which was more like the voice of Elinor Dennistoun at eighteen than that of Mrs. Compton, said quickly, "I know, John, that your door can't be shut for me."

"Elinor!" he said, getting up from his chair.

"I know," she repeated, "that there must be some mistake— that your door could not be shut for me."

"No, of course not," he said. "It is all right, Simmons; but who could have thought of seeing you here? It was a contingency I never anticipated. When did you come? where are you staying? Is Philip with you?" He overwhelmed her with questions, perhaps by way of stopping her mouth lest she should put questions still more difficult to answer to himself.

"Let me take breath a little," she said. "I scarcely have taken breath since the—thing happened which has brought me here; but I feel a little confidence now with the strong backing I have in you, John."

"My dear Elinor," he said, "I am afraid you must not look for any strong backing in me."

"Why?" she cried. "Have you judged it all beforehand? And do you know—are you quite, quite sure, John, that I cannot avoid it in any way, that I am obliged at all costs to appear? I would rather fly the country, I would rather leave Lakeside altogether and settle abroad. There is nothing in the world that I would not rather do."

"Elinor," said John, with some sternness, "you cannot believe that I would oppose you in any possible thing. Your pleasure has been a law to me. I may have differed with you, but I have never made any difference."

"John! you do not mean to say," she cried, turning pale, "that you are going to abandon me now?"

"Of course, that is merely a figure of speech," he said. "How could I abandon you? But it is quite true what that woman says, and I entirely agree with her and not with you in this respect, that the heir to a peerage cannot be hid——"

"The heir to a peerage!" she faltered, looking at him astonished. Gradually a sort of slowly growing light seemed to diffuse itself over her face. "The heir to a peerage, John! I don't know what you mean."

"Is this not your reason for coming to town?"

"There is nothing—that I know of—about the heir to a peerage. Who is this heir to a peerage? I don't know what you mean, but you frighten me. Is that a reason why I should be dragged out of my seclusion and made to appear in his defence? Oh, no—surely no; if he is *that*, they will let him off. They will not press it. I shall not be wanted. John, the more reason that you should stand by me——"

"We are at cross-purposes, Elinor. What has brought you to London? Let me know on your side and then I shall understand what I have got to do."

"*That* has brought me to London." She handed him a piece of paper which John knew very well the appearance of. He understood it better than she did, and he was not afraid of it, which she was, but he opened it all the same with a great deal of surprise. It was a subpœna charging Elinor Compton to appear and bear testimony—in the case of the *Queen* versus *Brown*.

"The *Queen* versus *Brown!* What have you got to do with such a case? You, Elinor, of all people in the world! Oh!" he said suddenly as a light, but a dim one, began to break upon him. It was the case of which his friend the judge had spoken, and in which he had been offered a retainer, as a matter of fact, shortly after that talk. He had been obliged to refuse, his time being already fully taken up, and he had not looked into the case. But now it began slowly to dawn upon him that the trial was that of the once absconded manager of a certain joint-stock company, and that this was precisely the company in which Elinor's money had been all but invested by her husband. It might be upon that subject that she had to appear.

"Well," he said, "I can imagine a possible reason why you

should be called, and yet not a good one; for it was not of course you who were acting, but your—husband for you. It is he that should appear, and not you."

"Oh, John," she cried. "Oh, John!" wringing her hands. She had followed his looks eagerly, noticing the light that seemed to dawn over his face with a strange anxiety and keen interest. But John, it was evident, had not got the clue which she expected, and her face changed into impatience, disappointment, exasperation. "You have not heard anything about it," she said; "you don't know."

"It was brought to me," he said, "but I could not take it up—no, I don't know—except that it's curious from the lapse of time— twenty years or thereabouts: that's all I know."

"The question is," she said, "about a date. There were some books destroyed, and it is not known who did it. Suspicion fell upon one—who might have been guilty: but that on that day—he arrived at the house of the girl—whom he was going to marry: and consequently could not have been there——"

"Elinor!"

"Yes," she said, "that is what I am wanted for, John, an excellent reason after all these years. I must appear to—clear my husband: and that is how Pippo will find out that I have a husband and he a father. Oh, John, John! support me with your approval, and help me, oh, help me to go away."

"Good gracious!" was all that John could say.

"I should have gone first and asked you after," she cried, "for you are a lawyer, and I suppose you will think you must not advise any one to fly in the face of the law. And I don't even know whether it will be of any use to fly. Will they have it in the papers all the same? Will they put it in that his wife refused to appear on his behalf, that she had gone away to avoid the summons? Will it be all there for Pippo to guess and wonder at the name and come to me with questions, mother, who is this? and mother, what is that? John, can't you answer me, you that I came to to guide me, to tell me what I must do; have you nothing, nothing to say?"

"I am too much bewildered to know what I am doing, Elinor. This is all sprung upon me like a mine: and there was plenty before."

"There was nothing before," she cried, indignantly, "it was all plain sailing before. He knew nothing of family troubles—how should he, poor child, being so young? That was simple enough. And I think I see a way still, John. I will take him off at Easter for a trip abroad, and when we have started to go to Switzerland or somewhere, I will change my mind, and make him think of Greece or somewhere far, far away—the East where there will be no newspapers. Tell me when the trial will come on, and how long you think it will last, and I will keep him away till it is all over. John! you have nothing surely to say against that? Think from how much it will save the boy."

"It is impossible, Elinor, that the boy can be saved. I never knew of this complication, but there are other circumstances, of which I have lately heard."

"What can any other circumstances have to do with it, John, even if he must hear? I know, I know, you have always been determined upon that. Is that the way you would have him hear, not only that he has a father, but that his father was involved in—in transactions like that before ever he was born?"

"Elinor, let us understand each other," said Mr. Tatham. "You mean that you have it in your power to exonerate your husband, and he has had you subpœnaed, knowing this?"

She looked at him with a look which he could not fathom. Was it reluctance to save Phil Compton that was in Elinor's eyes? Was she ready to leave her husband to destruction when she could prevent it, in order to save her boy from the knowledge of his existence? John Tatham was horrified by the look she fixed upon him, though he could not read it. He thought he could read it, and read it that way, in the way of hate and deliberate preference of her own will to all law and justice. There could be no such tremendous testimony to the power of that long continued, absolutely-faithful, visionary love which John Tatham bore to

Elinor than that this discovery which he thought he had made did not destroy it. He was greatly shocked, but it made no difference in his feelings. Perhaps there was more of the brotherly character in them than he thought. For a moment they looked at each other, and he thought he made this discovery—while she met his eyes with that look which she did not know was inscrutable, which she feared was full of self-betrayal. "I believe," she said, bending her head, "that that is what he thinks."

"If it had been me," said John Tatham, moved out of his habitual calm, "I would rather be proved guilty of anything than owe my safety to such an expedient as that. Drag in a woman who hates me to prove my alibi as if she loved me! By Jove, Elinor! you women have the gift of drawing out everything that's worst in men."

"It seems to make you hate me, John, which I don't think I have deserved."

"Oh, no, I don't hate you. It's a consequence, I suppose, of use and wont. It makes little difference to me——"

She gave him another look which he did not understand—a wistful look, appealing to something, he did not know what—to his ridiculous partiality, he thought, and that stubborn domestic affection to which it was of so little importance what she did, as long as she was Elinor; and then she said with a woman's soft, endless pertinacity, "Then you think I may go?"

He sprang from his seat with that impatient despair which is equally characteristic of the man. "Go!" he said, "when you are called upon by law to vindicate a man's character, and that man your husband! I ought not to be surprised at anything with my experience, but, Elinor, you take away my breath."

She only smiled, giving him once more that look of appeal.

"How can you think of it?" he said. "The subpœna is enough to keep any reasonable being, besides the other motive. You must not budge. I should feel my own character involved, as well as yours, if after consulting me on the subject you were guilty of an evasion after all."

"It would not be your fault, John."

"Elinor! you are mad—it must not be done," he cried. "Don't defy me, I am capable of informing upon you, and having you stopped—by force—if you do not give this idea up."

"By force!" she said, with her nostril dilating. "I shall go, of course, if I am threatened."

"Then Philip must not go. Do you know what has happened in the family to which he belongs, and must belong, whether you like it or not? Do you know—that the boy may be Lord Lomond before the week is out? that his uncle is dying, and that your husband is the heir?"

She turned round upon him slowly, fixing her eyes upon his, with simple astonishment and no more in her look. Her mind, so absorbed in other thoughts, hardly took in what he could mean.

"Have you not heard this, Elinor?"

"But there is Hal," she said, "Hal—the other brother—who comes first."

"Hal is dead, and the one in India is dead, and Lord St. Serf is dying. The boy is the heir. You must not, you cannot, take him away. It is impossible, Elinor, it is against all nature and justice. You have had him for all these years; his father has a right to his heir."

"Oh, John!" she cried, in a bitter note of reproach, "oh, John, John!"

"Well," he cried, "is not what I tell you the truth? Would Philip give it up if it were offered to him? He is almost a man—let him judge for himself."

"Oh, John, John! when you know that the object of my life has been to keep him from knowing—to shut that chapter of my life altogether; to bring him up apart from all evil influences, from all instructions——"

"And from his birthright, Elinor?"

She stopped, giving him another sudden look, the natural language of a woman brought to bay. She drew a long breath in impatience and desperation, not knowing what to reply; for what could she reply? His birthright! to be Lord Lomond, Lord St. Serf, the head of the house. What was that? Far, far better Philip Dennistoun, of Lakeside, the heir of his mother and his grandmother, two stainless women, with enough for everything that was honest and of good report, enough to permit him to be an unworldly scholar, a lover of art, a traveller, any play-profession that he chose if he did not incline to graver work. Ah! but she had not been so wise as that, she had not brought him up as Philip Dennistoun. He was Philip Compton, she had not been bold enough to change his name. She stood at bay, surrounded as it were by her enemies, and confronted John Tatham, who had been her constant companion and defender, as if all that was hostile to her, all that was against her peace was embodied in him.

"I must go a little further, Elinor," said John, "though God knows that to add to your pain is the last thing in the world I wish. You have been left unmolested for a very long time, and we have all thought your retreat was unknown. I confess it has surprised me, for my experience has always been that everything is known. But you have been subpœnaed for this trial, therefore, my dear girl, we must give up that idea. Everybody, that is virtually everybody, all that are of any consequence, know where you are and all you are about now."

She sank into a chair, still keeping her eyes upon him, as if it were possible that he might take some advantage of her if she withdrew them; then, still not knowing what to reply, seized at the last words because they were the last, and had little to do with the main issue. "All about me?" she said faintly, as if there had been something else besides the place of her refuge to conceal.

"You know what I mean, Elinor. The moment that your home is known all is known. That Philip lives and is well, a promising boy; that you have brought him up to do honour to any title or any position."

He could not help saying this, and partly in the testimony to her, partly for love of the boy, John Tatham's voice faltered a little and the water came into his eyes.

"Ah, John! you say that!" she cried, as if it had been an admission forced from him against his will.

"What could I say otherwise? Elinor, because I don't approve of all your proceedings, because I don't think you have been wise in one respect, is that to say that I do not understand and know *you?* I am not such a fool or a formalist as you give me credit for being. You have made him all that the fondest and proudest could desire. You have done far better for him, I do not doubt for a moment, than—— But, my dear cousin, my dear girl, my poor Nellie——"

"Yes, John?"

He paused a moment, and then he said, "Right is right, and justice is justice at the end of all."

CHAPTER XXXVII.

When Elinor received the official document which had so extraordinary an effect upon her life, and overturned in a moment all the fabric of domestic quiet and security which she had been building up for years, it was outside the tranquil walls of the house at Lakeside, in the garden which lay between it and the high-road, opening upon that not very much-frequented road by a pair of somewhat imposing gates, which gave the little establishment an air of more pretension than it really possessed. Some fine trees shrouded the little avenue, and Elinor was standing under one of them, stooping over a little nest of primroses at its roots, from which the yellow buds were peeping forth, when she heard behind her the sound of a vehicle at the gates, and the quick leap to the ground of someone who opened them. Then there was a pause; the carriage, whatever it was, did not come farther, and presently she herself, a little curious, turned round to see a man approaching her, whom she did not know. A dog-cart driven by another, whose face she recognized, waited in the road while the stranger came forward. "You are Mrs. Compton, ma'am?" he said. A swift thrill of alarm, she could scarcely tell why, ran over Elinor from head to foot. She had been settled for nearly eighteen years at Lakeside. What could happen to frighten her now? but it tingled to her very fingers' ends. And then he said something to her which she scarcely understood, but which sent that tingle to her very heart and brain, and gave her the suspicious looking blue paper which he held in his hand. It all passed in a moment of time to her dazed yet excited consciousness. The early primrose which she had gathered had not had time to droop in her grasp, though she crushed the stalk unconsciously in her fingers, before the gates were closed again, the sound of the departing wheels growing faint on the road, and she herself standing like one paralyzed with that thing in her hand. A subpœna!—what was a subpœna? She knew as little, perhaps less, than the children in the parish school, who began to troop along the road in their resounding clogs at their dinner hour. The sound of this awoke her a little to a frightened sense that she had better put this document out of sight, at least until she could manage to understand it. And then she sped swiftly away past the pretty white house lying in the sunshine, with all its doors and windows open, to the little wood behind, where it would be possible to think and find out at her leisure what this was. It was a small wood and a public path ran through it; but where the public was so limited as at Lakeside this scarcely impaired the privacy of the inhabitants, at least in the morning, when everybody in the parish was at work. Elinor hurried past the house that her mother might not see her, and climbed the woody hillock to a spot which was peculiarly her own, and where a seat had been placed for her special use. It was a little mount of vision from which she could look out, up and down, at the long winding line of the lake cleaving the green slopes, and away to the rugged and solemn peaks among which lay, in his mountain fastnesses, Helvellyn, with his hoary brethren crowding round him. Elinor had watched the changes of many a north-country day, full of endless vicissitudes, of flying clouds and gleams of sunshine, from that seat, and had hoped and tried to believe that nothing, save these vicissitudes of nature, would ever again disturb her. Had she really believed that? Her heart thumping against her breast, and the pulses of her brain beating loud in her ears, answered "No." She had never believed it—she had known, notwithstanding all her obstinacy, and indignant opposition to all who warned her, that some day or other her home must be broken up, and the storm burst upon her. But even such a conviction, desperately fought against and resisted, is a very different matter from the awful sense of certainty that it has come, *now*——

The trees were thick enough to conceal her from any passer-by on the path, the young half-unfolded foliage of the birches fluttered over her head, while a solid fir or two stood, grim guardians, yet catching pathetic airs from every passing wind to soothe her. But Elinor neither heard nor saw lake, mountain, nor sunshine, nor spring breezes, but only the bit of paper in her hand, and the uncomprehended words she had heard when it was given to her. It was not long, however, before she perceived and knew exactly what it meant. It was a subpœna in the case of "The Queen *versus* Brown," to attend and give evidence on a certain day in May, in London. It was for a few minutes a mystery to her as great as it was alarming, notwithstanding the swift and certain mental conviction she had that it concerned infallibly the one secret and mystery of her life. But as she sat there pondering, those strange strays of recollection that come to the mind, of things unnoted, yet unconsciously stored by memory, drew gradually about her, piecing out the threads of conviction. She remembered to have heard her mother read, among the many scraps which Mrs. Dennistoun loved to read out when the newspaper arrived, something about a man who had absconded, whose name was Brown, who had brought ruin on many, and had at length, after a number of years, ventured back to England and had been caught. It was one of the weaknesses of Mrs. Dennistoun's advancing years to like these bits of news, though there might be little interest in them to so quiet a household; and her daughter was wont to listen with a very vague attention, noting but a word now and then, answering vaguely the lively remarks her mother would make on the subjects. In this case even she had paid no attention; and yet, the moment that strong keynote had been struck, which vibrated through her whole being, this echo suddenly woke up and resounded as if it had been thundered in her ears—"Brown!" She began to remember bit by bit—and yet what had she to do with Brown? He had not defrauded her; she had never seen him; she knew nothing about his delinquencies. Then there came another note faintly out of the distance of the years: her husband's image, I need not say, had come suddenly into her sight with the first burst of this new event. His voice seemed to be in the air saying half-forgotten things. What had he to do with this man? Oh, she knew very well there was something—something! which she would have given her life not to recollect; which she knew in another moment would flash completely upon her as she tried not to remember it. And then suddenly her working mind caught another string which was not that; which was a relief to that for the moment. Brown!—who was it that had talked of Brown?—and the books that were destroyed—and the——and the—— day that Phil Compton arrived at Windyhill?

Elinor rose up from her seat with a gasp. She put her arm round the rough stem of the fir-tree to support herself, but it shook with her though there was no wind, only the softest of morning airs. She saw before her a scene very different from this—the flowery garden at the cottage with the copse and the sandy road beyond, and the man whom Phil had expected, whom he had been so anxious to see—and his fingers catching hers, keeping her by him, and the questions to which she had replied. Twenty years! What a long time it is! time enough for a boy to grow into almost a man who had not been born or thought of—and yet what a moment, what a nothing! Her mind flashed from that scene in the garden to the little hall in the cottage, the maid stooping down fastening the bolt of the door, the calendar hanging on the wall with the big 6 showing so visible, so obtrusive, forcing itself as it were on the notice of all. "Only ten days, Nell!" And the maid's glance upwards of shy sympathy, and the blank of Mrs. Dennistoun's face, and his look. Oh, that look of his! which was true and yet so false; which meant so much besides, and yet surely, surely meant love too!

The young fir-tree creaked and swayed in Elinor's grip. She unloosed it as if the slim thing had cried under the pressure, and sat down again. She had nothing to grasp at, nothing. Oh, her life had not been without support! Her mother—how extraordinary had been her good fortune to have her mother to fall back upon when she was shipwrecked in her life—to have a home, a shelter, a perpetual protector and champion, who, whether she approved or disapproved, would forsake her never. And then the boy, God bless him! who might quiver like the little fir if she flung herself upon him, but who, she knew, would stand as true. Oh, God forbid, God forbid that he should ever know! Oh, God help her, God help her! how was she to keep it from his knowledge? Elinor flung herself down upon the mossy knoll in her despair as this came pouring into her mind a flood of horrible light, of unimaginable bitterness. He must not know, he must not know; and yet how was it to be kept from his knowledge? It was a public thing; it could not be hid. It would be in all the papers, his father's name: and the boy did not know he had a father living. And his mother's evidence on behalf of her husband; and the boy thought she had no husband.

This was what had been said to her again and again and again. Sometime the boy must know—and she had pushed it from her angrily, indignantly asking why should he know? though in the bottom of her own heart she too was aware that it was the delusion of a fool, and that the time must come—— But how could she ever have thought that it would come like this, that the boy would discover his father through the summons of his mother to a public court to defend her husband from a criminal accusation? Oh, life that pardons nothing! Oh, severe, unchanging heaven!—that this should be the way!

And then there came into Elinor's mind wild thoughts of flight. She was not a woman whose nature it was to endure. When things became intolerable to her she fled from them, as the reader knows; escaped, shutting her ears to all advice and her heart to all thoughts except that life had become intolerable, and that she could bear it no longer. It is not easy to hold the balance even in such matters. Had Elinor fulfilled what would appear to many her first duty, and stood by Phil through neglect, ill-treatment, and misery, as she had vowed, for better, for worse, she would by this time have been not only a wretched but a deteriorated woman, and her son most probably would have been injured both in his moral and intellectual being. What she had done was not the abstract duty of her marriage vow, but it had been better— had it not been better for them both? In such a question who is to be the judge? And now again there came surging up into Elinor's veins the impulse of flight. To take the boy and fly. She could take him where he wished most to go, to the scenes of that literature and history of which his schoolboy head was full, to the happiest ideal wandering, his mother and he, two companions almost better than lovers. How his eyes would brighten at the thought! among the summer seas, the golden islands, the ideal countries—away from all the trouble and cares, all the burdens of the past, all the fears of the future! Why should she be held by that villainous paper and obey that dreadful summons? Why allow all her precautions, all the fabric of her life to fall in a moment? Why pour upon the boy the horror of that revelation, when everything she had done and planned all his life had been to keep it from him? In the sudden energy of that new possibility of escape Elinor rose up again from the prostration of despair. She saw once more the line of shining water at her feet full of heavenly splendour, the mountain tops sunning themselves in the morning light, the peace and the beauty that was over all. And there was nothing needed but a long journey, which would be delightful, full of pleasure and refreshment, to secure her peace to her, and to save her boy.

When she had calmed herself with this new project, which, the moment it took form in her mind seemed of itself, without reference to the cause, the most delightful project in the world and full of pleasure—Elinor smoothed back her hair, put her garden hat, which had got a little out of order, straight, and took her way again towards the house. Her heart had already escaped from the shock and horror and was beating softly, exhausted yet refreshed, in her bosom. She felt almost like a child who had sobbed all its troubles out, or like a convalescent recovering from a brief but violent illness, and pathetically happy in the cessation of pain. She went along quietly, slowly, by the woodland path among the trees full of the sweetness of the morning which seemed to have come back to her. Should she say anything about it to her mother, or only by degrees announce to her the plan she had begun to form for Pippo's pleasure, the long delightful ramble which would come between his school-time and the university? She had almost decided that she would do this when she went into the house; but she had not been half an hour with her mother when her intention became untenable, for the good reason that she had already told Mrs. Dennistoun of the new incident. They were not in the habit of keeping secrets from each other, and in that case there is nothing in the world so difficult. It requires training to keep one's affairs to one's self in the constant presence of those who are our nearest and dearest. Some people may be capable of this effort of self-control, but Elinor was not. She had showed that alarming paper to her mother with a partial return of her own terror at the sight of it before she knew. And I need not say that for a short time Mrs. Dennistoun was overwhelmed by that natural horror too.

"But," she said, "what do you know, what can you tell about this Mr. Brown, Elinor? You never saw him in your life."

"I think I know what it means," said Elinor, with a sudden dark glow of colour, which faded instantly, leaving her quite pale. She added hurriedly, "There were some books destroyed. I cannot tell you the rights of the story. It is too dreadful altogether, but—another was exculpated by the date of the day he arrived at Windyhill. This must be the reason I am called."

"The date he arrived—before your marriage, Elinor? But then they might call me, and you need not appear."

"Not for the world, mother!" cried Elinor. The colour rose again and faded. "Besides, you do not remember."

"Oh, I could make it out," said Mrs. Dennistoun. "It was when he came from Scotland, and went off in the evening next day. I don't at this moment remember what the day was, but I could make it out. It was about a fortnight before, it was——"

"Do you remember, mother, the little calendar in the hall, and what it marked, and what he said?"

"I remember, of course, perfectly well the little calendar in the hall. You gave it me at Christmas, and it was always out of order, and never kept right. But I could make it out without that."

"You must not think of it for a moment," cried Elinor, with a shudder. There had been so many things to think of that it had scarcely occurred to her what it was to which she had to bear witness. She told her mother hurriedly the story of that incident, and then she added, without stopping to take breath, "But I will not appear. I cannot appear. We must keep it out of the papers, at every cost. Mother, do not think it dreadful of me. I will run away with Pippo; far away, if you will not be anxious. This is just his chance between school and college. I will take him to Greece."

"To Greece, Elinor?" Mrs. Dennistoun cried, with almost a shriek.

"Mother, dear, it is not so very far away."

"I am not thinking how far away it is, Elinor. And leave his father's reputation to suffer? Leave him perhaps to be ruined—by a false charge?"

"Oh, mother," cried Elinor, starting to her feet. She was quite unprepared for such remonstrance.

"My dear, I have not opposed you; though there have been many things I have scarcely approved of. But, Elinor, this must not be. Run away from the law? Allow another to suffer when you can clear him? Elinor, Elinor, this must not be—unless I can go and be his witness in your place. I might do that," said Mrs. Dennistoun, seriously. She paused a moment, and then she said, "But I think you are wrong about the sixth. He stayed only one night, and the night he went away was the night that Alick Hudson—who was going up for his examination. I can make it out exactly, if you will give me a little time to think it over. My poor child! that you should have this to disturb your peace. But I will go, Elinor. I can clear him as well as you."

Elinor stood up before her, pallid as a ghost. "For God's sake, mother, not another word," she said, with a dreadful solemnity. "The burden is mine, and I must bear it. Let us not say a word more."

CHAPTER XXXVIII.

I will not confuse the reader with a description of all Elinor's thoughts during the slow progress of that afternoon and evening, which were as the slow passing of a year to her impatient spirit. She took the usual afternoon walk with her mother soberly, as became Mrs. Dennistoun's increasing years, and then she made a pretext of some errands in the village to occupy her until dark, or rather to leave her free to twist the thread of her own thoughts as she went along the silent country road. Her thoughts varied in the afternoon from those which had seized upon her with such vulture's claws in the morning; but they were not less overwhelming in that respect. Her mother's suggestion that *she* and not Elinor should be the witness of that date, and then her ponderings as to that date, her slow certainty that she could make it out, or puzzle it out, as Elinor in her impatience said, which was the last of all things to be desired—had stung the daughter into a new and miserable realization of what it was that was demanded of her, which nobody could do but she. What was it that would be demanded of her? To stand up in the face of God and man and swear to tell the truth, and tell—a lie: or else let the man who had been her husband, the love of her youth, the father of her boy, sink into an abyss of shame. She thought rapidly, knowing nothing, that surely there could be no punishment for him, even if it were proved, at the long interval of twenty years. But, shame—there would be shame. Nothing could save him from that. Shame which would descend more or less to his son. And then Elinor reflected, with hot moisture coming out upon her forehead against the cold breeze of the spring night, on what would be asked of her. Oh, no doubt, it would be cleverly done! She would be asked if she remembered his visit, and why she remembered it. She would be led on carefully to tell the story of the calendar in the hall, and of how it was but ten days before her marriage—the last hurried, unexpected visit of the lover before he came as a bridegroom to take her away. It would be all true, every word, and yet it would be a lie. And standing up there in that public place, she would be made to repeat it, as she had done in the flowery garden, in the sunshine, twenty years ago—then dazed and bewildered, not knowing what she did, and with something of the blind confidence of youth and love in saying what she was told to say; but now with clearer insight, with a horrible certainty of the falsehood of that true story, and the object with which it was required of her. Happily for herself, Elinor did not think of the ordeal of cross-examination through which witnesses have to pass. She would not, I think, have feared that if the instinct of combativeness had been roused in her: her quick wit and ready spirit would not have failed in defending herself, and in maintaining the accuracy of the fact to which she had to bear witness. It was herself, and not an opposing counsel, that was alarming to Elinor. But I have promised that the reader should not be compelled to go through all the trouble and torment of her thoughts.

Dinner, with the respect which is necessary for the servant who waits, whether that may be a solemn butler with his myrmidons, or a little maid—always makes a pause in household communications; but when the ladies were established afterwards by the pleasant fireside which had been their centre of life for so many years, and with the cheerful lamp on the table between them which had lighted so many cheerful talks, readings, discussions, and consultations, the new subject of anxiety and interest immediately came forth again. It was Mrs. Dennistoun who spoke first. She had grown older, as we all do; she wore spectacles as she worked, and often a white shawl on her shoulders, and was—as sometimes her daughter felt, with shame of herself to remark it—a little slower in speech, a little more pertinacious and insistent, not perhaps perceiving with such quick sympathy the changes and fluctuations of other minds, and whether it was advisable or not to follow a subject to the bitter end. She said, looking up from her knitting, with a little rhetorical movement of her hand which Elinor feared, and which showed that she felt herself on assured and certain ground:

"My dear, I have been thinking. I have made it out day by day. God knows there were plenty of landmarks in it to keep any one from forgetting. I can now make out certainly the day—of which we were speaking; and if you will give me your attention for a minute or two, Elinor, you will see that whatever the calendar said—which I never noticed, for it was as often wrong as right—you are making a mis——"

"Oh, for Heaven's sake, mother," cried Elinor, "don't let us talk of that any more!"

"I have no desire to talk of it, my dear child; but for what you said I should never—— But of course we must take some action about this thing—this paper you have got. And it seems to me that the best thing would be to write to John, and see whether he could not manage to get it transferred from you to me. I can't see what difficulty there could be about that."

"I would not have it for the world, mother! And what good would it do? The great thing in it, the dreadful thing, would be unchanged. Whether you appear or me, Pippo would be made to know, all the same, what it has been our joint object to conceal from him all his life."

Mrs. Dennistoun did not say anything, but she would not have been mortal if she had not, very slightly, but yet very visibly to keen eyes, shaken her head.

"I know what you mean," said Elinor, vehemently, "that it has been I, and not we, whose object has been to conceal it from him. Oh, yes, I know you are right; but at least you consented to it, you have helped in it, it is your doing as well as mine."

"Elinor, Elinor!" cried her mother, who, having always protested, was not prepared for this accusation.

"Is there any advantage to be got," said Elinor, like an injured and indignant champion of the right, "in opening up the whole question over again now?"

What could poor Mrs. Dennistoun do? She was confounded, as she often had been before, by those swift and sudden tactics. She gave a glance up at her daughter over her spectacles, but she said nothing. Argument, she knew by long experience, was difficult to keep up with such an opponent.

"But John is an idea," said Elinor. "I don't know why I should not have thought of him. He may suggest something that could be done."

"I thought of him, of course, at once," said Mrs. Dennistoun, not able to refrain from that small piece of self-assertion. "It is not a time that it would be easy for him to leave town; but at least you could write and lay your difficulties before him, and suggest——"

"Oh, you may be sure, mother," cried Elinor, "I know what I have to say."

"I never doubted it, my dear," said Mrs. Dennistoun, gently.

And then there was a little pause. They sat and worked, the elder lady stumbling a little over her knitting, her thoughts being so much engaged; the younger one plying a flying needle, the passion and impetus of her thoughts lending only additional swiftness and vigour to everything she did. And for ten minutes or more there was nothing to be heard in the room but the little drop of ashes from the fire, the sudden burst of a little gas-flame from the coals, the rustle of Elinor's arm as it moved. The cat sat with her tail curled round her before the fire, the image of dignified repose, winking at the flames. The two human inhabitants, save for the movements of their hands, might have been in wax, they were so still. Suddenly, however, the quietness was broken by an energetic movement. Elinor threw her work down on the table and rose from her chair. She went to the window and drew the curtain aside, and looked out upon the night. She shut it carefully again, and going to the writing-table, struck a match and lighted the candles there, and sat down and began, or appeared to begin, to write. Then she rose quickly again and returned to the table at which Mrs. Dennistoun was still seated, knitting on, but watching every movement of her restless companion. "Mother," she said, "I can't write, I have far too much to say. I will run up to town to-morrow myself and see John."

"To town, Elinor, by yourself? My dear, you forget it is not an hour's journey, as it was to Windyhill."

"I know that very well, mother. But even the journey will be an advantage. The movement will do me good, and I can tell John much better than I could write. Who could write about a complicated business like this? He will understand me when he sees me at half a word; whereas in writing one can never explain. Don't oppose me, please, mother! I feel that to do something, to get myself in motion, is the only thing for me now."

"I will not oppose you, Elinor. I have done so, perhaps, too little, my dear; but we will not speak of that. No doubt, as you say, you will understand each other better if you tell him the circumstances face to face. But, oh, my dear child, do nothing rash! Be guided by John; he is a prudent adviser. The only thing is that he, no more than I, has ever been able to resist you, Elinor, if you had set your heart upon any course. Oh, my dear, don't go to John with a foregone conclusion. Hear first what he has to say!"

Elinor came behind her mother with one of those quick returns of affectionate impulse which were natural to her, and put her arms suddenly round Mrs. Dennistoun. "You have always been far too good to me, mamma," she said, kissing her tenderly, "both John and you."

And next morning she carried out her swiftly conceived intention and went to town, as the reader is aware. A long railway journey is sometimes soothing to one distracted with agitation and trouble. The quiet and the noise, which serves as a kind of accompaniment, half silencing, half promoting too active thought; the forced abstraction and silence, and semi-imprisonment of mind and body, which are equally restless, but which in that enclosure are bound to self-restraint, exercise, in spite of all struggles of the subject, a subduing effect. And it was a strange thing that in the seclusion of the railway compartment in which she travelled alone there came for the first time to Elinor a softening thought, the sudden sensation of a feeling, of which she had not been sensible for years, towards the man whose name she bore. It occurred to her quite suddenly, she could not tell how, as if some one invisible had thrown that reflection into her mind (and I confess that I am of opinion they do: those who are around us, who are unseen, darting into our souls thoughts which do not originate with us, thoughts not always of good, blasphemies as well as blessings)—it occurred to her, I say, coming into her mind like an arrow, that after all she had not been so well hidden as she thought all these years, seeing that she had been found at once without difficulty, it appeared, when she was wanted. Did this mean that he had known where she was all the time—known, but never made any attempt to disturb her quiet? The thought startled her very much, revealing to her a momentary glimpse of something that looked like magnanimity, like consideration and generous self-restraint. Could these things be? He could have hurt her very much had he pleased, even during the time she had remained at Windyhill, when certainly he knew where she was: and he had not done so. He might have taken her child from her: at least he might have made her life miserable with fears of losing her child: and he had not done so. If indeed it was true that he had known where she was all the time and had never done anything to disturb her, what did that mean? This thought gave Elinor perhaps the first sense of self-reproach and guilt that she had ever known towards this man, who was her husband, yet whom she had not seen for more than eighteen years.

And then there was another thing. After that interval he was not afraid to put himself into her hands—to trust to her loyalty for his salvation. He knew that she could betray him—and he knew equally well that she would not do so, notwithstanding

the eighteen years of estrangement and mutual wrong that lay
between. It did not matter that the loyalty he felt sure of would
be a false loyalty, an upholding of what was not true. He would
think little of that, as likely as not he had forgotten all about
that. He would know that her testimony would clear him, and
he would not think of anything else; and even did he think of
it the fact of a woman making a little mis-statement like that
would never have affected Philip. But the strange thing was that
he had no fear she would revenge herself by standing up against
him—no doubt of her response to his appeal; he was as ready
to put his fate in her hands as if she had been the most devoted
of wives—his constant companion and champion. This had the
most curious effect upon her mind, almost greater than the other.
She had shown no faith in him, but he had faith in her. Reckless
and guilty as he was, he had not doubted her. He had put it in her
power to convict him not only of the worst accusation that was
brought against him, but of a monstrous trick to prove his *alibi*,
and a cruel wrong to her compelling her to uphold that as true.
She was able to expose him, if she chose, as no one else could do;
but he had not been afraid of that. This second thought, which
burst upon Elinor without any volition of her own, had the most
curious effect upon her. She abstained carefully, anxiously, from
allowing herself to be drawn into making any conclusion from
these darts of unintended thoughts. But they moved her in spite
of herself. They made her think of him, which she had for a long
time abstained from doing. She had shut her heart for years from
any recollection of her husband, trying to ignore his existence
in thought as well as in fact. And she had succeeded for a long
time in doing this. But now in a moment all her precautions were
thrown to the winds. He came into her memory with a sudden
rush for which she was no way responsible, breaking all the
barriers she had put up against him: that he should have known
where she was all this time, and never disturbed her, respected
her solitude all these years—that when the moment of need
came he should, without a word to conciliate her, without an

explanation or an apology, have put his fate into her hands——
To the reader who understands I need not say more of the effect
upon the mind of Elinor, hasty, generous, impatient as she was of
these two strange facts. There are many in the world who would
have given quite a different explanation—who would have made
out of the fact that he had not disturbed her only the explanation
that Phil Compton was tired of his wife and glad to get rid of
her at any price: and who would have seen in his appeal to her
now only audacity combined with the conviction that she would
not compromise herself by saying anything more than she could
help about him. I need not say which of these interpretations
would have been the true one. But the first will understand and
not the other what it was that for the first time for eighteen years
awakened a struggle and controversy which she could not ignore,
and vainly endeavoured to overcome, in Elinor's heart.

CHAPTER XXXIX.

Elinor had not been three days gone, indeed her mother had but just received a hurried note announcing her arrival in London, when as she sat alone in the house which had become so silent, Mrs. Dennistoun suddenly became aware of a rising of sound of the most jubilant, almost riotous description. It began by the barking of Yarrow, the old colley, who was fond of lying at the gate watching in a philosophic way of his own the mild traffic of the country road, the children trooping by to school, who hung about him in clusters, with lavish offerings of crust and scraps of biscuit, and all the leisurely country *flâneurs* whom the good dog despised, not thinking that he himself did nothing but *flâner* at his own door in the sun. A bark from Yarrow was no small thing in the stillness of the spring afternoon, and little Urisk, the terrier, who lay wrapt in dreams at Mrs. Dennistoun's feet, heard where he lay entranced in the folds of sleep and cocked up an eager ear and uttered a subdued interrogation under his breath. The next thing was no bark, but a shriek of joy from Yarrow, such as could mean nothing in the world but "Philip!" or Pippo, which was what no doubt the dogs called him between following their mistress. Urisk heard and understood. He made but one spring from the footstool on which he lay and flung himself against the door. Mrs. Dennistoun sat for a moment and listened, much disturbed. When some troublous incident occurs in the deep quiet of domestic life how often is it followed by another, and her heart turned a little sick. She was not comforted even by the fact that Urisk was waggling not his tail only, but his whole little form in convulsions of joy, barking, crying aloud for the door to open, to let him forth. By this time all the friendly dogs about had taken up the sound out of sympathy with Yarrow's yells of delight—and into this came the clang of the gate, the sound of wheels, an outcry in a human voice, that of Barbara, the maid—and then a young shout that rang through the air—"Where's my mother, Barbara, where's granny?" Philip, it may be imagined, did not wait for any answer, but came in headlong. Yarrow leaping after him, Urisk springing into the air to meet him—himself in too great a hurry to heed either, flinging himself upon the astonished lady who rose to meet him, with a sudden kiss, and a "Where's my mother, granny?" of eager greeting.

"Pippo! Good gracious, boy, what's brought you home now?"

"Nothing but good news," he said, "so good I thought I must come. I've got it, granny: where *is* my mother——"

"You've got it?" she said, so full of other thoughts that she could not recollect what it was he meant. Pippo thought, as Elinor sometimes thought, that his granny was getting slow of understanding—not so bright as she used to be in her mind.

"Oh, granny, you've been dozing: the scholarship! I've got it—I thought you would know the moment you heard me at the door——"

"My dear boy," she said, putting her arms about him, while the tall boy stood for the homage done to him—the kiss of congratulation. "You have got the scholarship! notwithstanding Howard and Musgrave and the hard fight there was to be——"

Pippo nodded, with a bright face of pleasure. "But," he said—"I can't say I'm sorry I've got it, granny—but I wish there had been another for Musgrave: for he worked harder than I did, and he wanted so to win. But so did I, for that matter. And where is my mother all this time?"

"How delighted she will be: and what a comfort to her just now when she is upset and troubled! My dear, it'll be a dreadful disappointment to you: your mother is in London. She had to hurry off the day before yesterday—on business."

"In London!" cried Pippo. His countenance fell: he was so much disappointed that for a moment, big boy as he was, he looked ready to cry. He had come in bursting with his news, expecting a reception almost as tumultuous as that given him by the dogs outside. And he found only his grandmother, who forgot what it was he was "in for"—and no mother at all!

"It is a disappointment, Pippo—and it will be such a disappointment to her not to hear it from your own lips: but you must telegraph at once, and that will be next best. She has some worrying business—things that she hates to look after—and this will give her a little heart."

"What a bore!" said Pippo, with his crest down and the light gone out of him. He gave himself up to the dogs who had been jumping about him, biding their time. "Yarrow knew," he said, laughing, to get the water out of his eyes. "He gave me a cheer whenever he saw me, dear old fellow—and little Risky too——"

"And only granny forgot," said Mrs. Dennistoun; "that was very hard upon you, Pippo; my thoughts were all with your mother. And I couldn't think how you could get back at this time——"

"Well," said the boy, "my work's over, you know. There's nothing for a fellow to do after he's got the scholarship. I needn't go back at all—unless you and my mother wish it. I've—in a sort of a way, done everything that I can do. Don't laugh at me, granny!"

"Laugh at you, my boy! It is likely I should laugh at you. Don't you know I am as proud of you as your mother herself can be? I am glad and proud," said Mrs. Dennistoun, "for I am glad for her as well as for you. Now, Pippo, you want something to eat."

The boy looked up with a laugh. "Yes, granny," he said, "you always divine that sort of thing. I do."

Mrs. Dennistoun did not occupy her mind with any thought of that little unintentional and grateful jibe—that she always divined that sort of thing. Among the other great patiences of her life she had learnt to know that the mother and son, loving and tender as they were, had put her back unconsciously into the proper place of the old woman—always consulted, always thought of, never left out; but divining chiefly *that sort of thing*, the actual needs, the more apparent thoughts of those about her.

She knew it, but she did not dwell upon it—sometimes it made her smile, but it scarcely hurt her, and never made her bitter, she comprehended it all so well. Meanwhile Pippo, left alone, devoted himself to the dogs for a minute or two, making them almost too happy. Then, at the very climax of riotous enjoyment, cast them off with a sudden, "Down, Yarrow!" which took all the curl in a moment out of the noble tail with which Yarrow was sweeping all the unconsidered trifles off Mrs. Dennistoun's work-table. The young autocrat walked to the window as he shook off his adoring vassal, and stared out for a little with his hands deeply dug into his pockets. And then a new idea came into Pippo's head; the most brilliant new idea, which restored at once the light to his eyes and elevation to his crest. He said nothing of this, however, till he had done justice to the excellent luncheon, while his grandmother, seated beside him in the dining-room with her knitting, looked on with pride and pleasure and saw him eat. This was a thing, they were all of accord, which she always thoroughly understood.

"You will run out now and telegraph to your mother. She is in the old rooms in Ebury Street, Pippo."

"Yes, granny; don't you think now a fellow of my age, having done pretty well and all that, might be trusted to—make a little expedition out of his own head?"

"My dear! you have always been trusted, Pippo, you know. I can't remember when your mother or I either have shown any want of trust——"

"Oh, it's not that," said Pippo, confused. "I know I've had lots, lots—far more than most fellows—of my own way. It was not that exactly. I meant without consulting any one, just to do a thing out of my own head."

"I have no doubt it will be quite a right thing, Pippo; but I should know better if you were to tell me."

"That would scarcely be doing it out of my own head, would it, granny? But I can't keep a thing to myself; now Musgrave can, you know; that's the great difference. I suppose it is having nobody but my mother and you, who always spoil me, that has

381

made me that I can't keep a secret."

"It is something about making it up to Musgrave for not winning the scholarship?"

Philip grew red all over with a burning blush of shame. "What a beast I am!" he said. "You will scarcely believe me, but I had forgotten that—though I do wish I could. I do wish there was any way—— No, granny, it was all about myself."

"Well, my dear?" she said, in her benignant, all-indulgent grandmother's voice.

"It is no use going beating about the bush," he said. "Granny, I'm not going to telegraph to mamma. I'll run up to London by the night mail."

"Pippo!"

"Well, it isn't so extraordinary; naturally I should like to tell her better than to write. It didn't quite come off, my telling it to you, did it? but my mother will be excited about it—and then it will be a surprise seeing me at all—and then if she is worried by business it will be a good thing to have me to stand by her. And— why there are a hundred reasons, granny, as you must see. And then I should like it above all."

"My dear," said Mrs. Dennistoun, trembling a little. She had time during this long speech to collect herself, to get over the first shock, but her nerves still vibrated. "In ordinary circumstances, I should think it an excellent plan. And you have worked well for it, and won your holiday; and your mother always enjoys wandering about town with you. Still, Pippo——"

"Now what can there be against it?" the boy said, with the same spark of fire coming into his blue eyes which had often been seen in Elinor's hazel ones. He was like the Comptons, a refined image of his father, with the blue eyes and very dark hair which had once made Phil Compton irresistible. Pippo had the habit, I am sorry to say, of being a little impatient with his grandmother. Her objections seemed old-world and obsolete at the first glance.

"The chief thing against it is that I don't think your mother— would wish it, Pippo."

"Mamma—think me a bore, perhaps!" the lad cried, with a laugh of almost scornful amusement at this ridiculous idea.

"She would never, of course, think you a bore in any circumstances—but she will be very much confined—she could not take you with her to—lawyers' offices. She will scarcely have any time to herself."

"What is this mysterious business, granny?"

"Indeed, Pippo, I can scarcely tell you. It is something connected with old times—that she wishes to have settled and done with. I did not inquire very closely; neither, I think, should you. You know your poor mother has had troubles in her life——"

"Has she?" said Pippo, with wide open eyes. "I have never seen any. I think, perhaps, don't you know, granny, ladies—make mountains of molehills—or so at least people say——"

"Do they?" said Mrs. Dennistoun, with a laugh. "So you have begun to learn that sort of thing already, Pippo, even here at the end of the world!"

Pippo was a little mortified by her laugh, and a little ashamed of what he had said. It is very tempting at eighteen to put on a man's superiority, yet he was conscious that it was perhaps a little ungenerous, he who owed all that he was and had to these two ladies; but naturally he was the more angry because of this.

"I suppose," he said, "that what is in every book that ever was written is likely to be true! But that has nothing to do with the question. I won't do anything against you if you forbid me absolutely, granny; but short of that I will go——"

Mrs. Dennistoun looked at the boy with all the heat in him of his first burst of independence. It is only wise to compute the forces opposed to one before one launches a command which one may not have force to ensure obedience to. He said that he would not disobey her "absolutely" with his lips; but his eyes expressed a less dutiful sentiment. She had no mind to be beaten in such a struggle. Elinor had complained of her mother in her youth that she was too reasonable, too unwilling to command, too reluctant to assume the responsibility of an act; and it was not to be supposed that she had mended of this, in all the experience she had had of her impatient daughter, and under the influence of so many additional years. She looked at Philip, and concluded that he would at least find some way of eluding her authority if she exercised it, and it did not consist with her dignity to be either "absolutely" or partially disobeyed.

"You forget," she said, "that I have never taken such authority upon me since you were a child. I will not forbid you to do what you have set your heart upon. I can only say, Philip, that I don't think your mother would wish you to go——"

"If that's all, granny," said the boy, "I think I can take my mother into my own hands. But why do you call me Philip? You never call me that but when you are angry."

"Was I ever angry?" she said, with a smile; "but if we are to consider you a man, looking down upon women, and taking your movements upon your own responsibility, my dear, it would be ridiculous that you should be little Pippo any more."

"Not little Pippo," he said, with a boyish, complacent laugh, rising up to his full height. A young man nearly six feet high, with a scholarship in his pocket, how is he to be expected to take the law from his old grandmother as to what he is to do?

And young Philip did go to town triumphantly by the night mail. He had never done such a thing before, and his sense of manly independence, of daring, almost of adventure, was more delightful than words could say. There was not even any one, except the man who had driven him into Penrith, to see him away, he who was generally accompanied to the last minute by precautions, and admonitions, and farewells. To feel himself dart away into the night with nobody to look back to on the platform, no gaze, half smiling, half tearful, to follow him, was of itself an emancipation to Pippo. He was a good boy and no rebel against the double maternal bond which had lain so lightly yet so closely upon him all his life. It was only for a year or two that he had suspected that this was unusual, or even imagined that for a growing man the sway of two ladies, and even their devotion, might make others smile. Perhaps he had been a little more particular in his notions, in his manners, in his fastidious dislike to dirt and careless habits, than was common in the somewhat rough north country school which had so risen in scholastic note under the last head master, but which was very far from the refinements of Eton. And lately it had begun to dawn upon him that a mother and a grandmother to watch over him and care for him in everything might be perhaps a little absurd for a young man of his advanced age. Thus his escapade, which was against the will of his elder guardian, and without the knowledge of his mother—which was entirely his own act, and on his own responsibility, went to Philip's head, and gave him a sort of intoxication of pleasure. That his mother should be displeased, really displeased, should not want him—incredible thought! never entered into his mind save as an accountable delusion of granny's. His mother not want him! All the arguments in the world would never have got that into young Pippo's head.

Mrs. Dennistoun waking up in the middle of the night to think of the boy rushing on through the dark on his adventurous way, recollected only then with much confusion and pain that she ought to have telegraphed to Elinor, who might be so engaged as to make it very embarrassing for her in her strange circumstances to see Pippo—that the boy was coming. In her agitation she had forgotten this precaution. Was it perhaps true, as the young ones thought, that she was getting a little slower in her movements, a little dulled in her thoughts?

CHAPTER XL.

John Tatham had in vain attempted to persuade Elinor to
come to his house, to dine there in comfort—he was going out
himself—so that at least in this time of excitement and trouble
she might have the careful service and admirable comfort of his
well-managed house. Elinor preferred her favourite lodgings and
a cup of tea to all the luxuries of Halkin Street. And she was fit
for no more consultations that night. She had many, many things
to think of, and some new which as yet she barely comprehended.
The rooms in Ebury Street were small, and they were more or less
dingy, as such rooms are; but they were comfortable enough, and
had as much of home to Elinor as repeated visits there with all
her belongings could give them. The room in which she slept was
next to that in which her boy had usually slept. That was enough
to make it no strange place. And I need not say that it became
the scene of many discussions during the few days that followed.
The papers by this time were full of the strange trial which was
coming on: the romance of commercial life and ruin—the guilty
man who had been absent so long, enjoying his ill-gotten gains,
and who now was dragged back into the light to give an account
of himself—and of other guilt perhaps less black than his own,
yet dreadful enough to hear of. The story of the destroyed books
was a most remarkable and picturesque incident in the narrative.
The leading papers looked up their own account of the facts
given at the time, and pointed out how evidently justified by the
new facts made known to the public was the theory they had
themselves given forth. As these theories, however, were very
different, and as all claimed to be right, perhaps the conclusion
was less certain than this announcement gave warrant to believe.

But each and all promised "revelations" of the most surprising kind—involving some of the highest aristocracy, the democratic papers said—bringing to light an exciting story of the private relations between husband and wife, said those of society, and revealing a piquant chapter of social history hushed up at the time. It was a modest print indeed that contented itself with the statement that its readers would find a romance of real life involved in the trial which was about to take place. Elinor did not, fortunately, see all these comments. The *Times* and the *Morning Post* were dignified and reticent, and she did not read, and was indeed scarcely cognisant of the existence of most of the others. But the faintest reference to the trial was enough, it need hardly be said, to make the blood boil in her veins.

It was a curious thing in her state of mind, and with the feelings she had towards her husband's family, that one of the first things she did on establishing herself in her Ebury Street rooms, was to look for an old "Peerage" which had lain for several years she remembered on a certain shelf. Genteel lodgings in Ebury Street which did not possess somewhere an old "Peerage" would be out of the world indeed. She found it in the same corner as of old, where she had noted it so often and avoided it as if it had been a serpent; but now the first thing she did, as soon as her tray was brought her, and all necessary explanations given, and the door shut, was to take the book furtively from its place, almost as if she were afraid of what she should see. What a list there was of sons of Lord St. Serf! some she had never known, who died young: and Reginald in India, and Hal, who was so kind—what a good laugh he had, she remembered, not a joyless cackle like Mariamne's, a good natural laugh, and a kind light in his eyes: and he had been kind. She could remember ever so many things, nothings, things that made a little difference in the dull, dull cloudy sky of a neglected wife. Poor Hal! and he too was gone, and St. Serf dying, and—— Pippo the heir!—Pippo was perhaps, for any thing she knew, Lord Lomond now.

To say that this did not startle Elinor, did not make her heart

387

beat, did not open new complications and vistas in life, would be a thing impossible. Pippo Lord Lomond! Pippo, whom she had feared to expose to his father's influence, whom she had kept apart, who did not know anything about himself except that he was her son—had she kept and guarded the boy thus in the very obscurity of life, in the stillest and most protected circumstances, only to plunge him suddenly at last, without preparation, without warning, into the fiery furnace of temptation, into a region where he might pardonably (perhaps) put himself beyond her influence, beyond her guidance? Poor Elinor! and yet she was not wholly to be pitied either. For her heart was fired by the thought of her boy's elevation in spite of herself. It did not occur to her that such an elevation for him meant something also for her. That view of the case she did not take into consideration for a moment. Nay, she did not think of it. But that Pippo should be Lord Lomond went through her like an arrow—like an arrow that gave a wound, acute and sharp, yet no pain, if such a thing could be said. That he should discover his father had been the danger before her all his life, but if he must find out that he had a father that was a way in which it might not be all pain. I do not pretend that she was very clear in all these thoughts. Indeed, she was not clear at all. John Tatham, knowing but one side, had begun to think vaguely of Elinor what Elinor thought of her mother, that her mind was not quite as of old, not so bright nor so vivid, not so clear in coming to a conclusion; had he known everything he might not have been so sure even on that point. But then had he known everything that Elinor knew, and been aware of what it was which Elinor had been summoned by all the force of old fidelity and the honour of her name to do, John would have been too much horrified to have been able to form an opinion. No, poor Elinor was not at all clear in her thoughts—less clear than ever after these revelations—the way before her seemed dark in whatever way she looked at it, complications were round her on every side. She had instinctively, without a word said, given up that idea of flight. Who was it that said the heir to a peerage could not be hid?

John had said it, she remembered, and John was always right. If she was to take him away to the uttermost end of the earth, they would seek him out and find him. And then there was— his father, who had known all the time, had known and never disturbed her——No wonder that poor Elinor's thoughts were mixed and complicated. She walked up and down the room, not thinking, but letting crowds and flights of thoughts like birds fly through her mind; no longer clear indeed as she had been wont to be, no longer coming to sudden, sharp conclusions, admitting possibilities of which Elinor once upon a time would never have thought.

And day by day as he saw her, John Tatham understood her less and less. He did not know what she meant, what she was going to do, what were her sentiments towards her husband, what were her intentions towards her son. He had found out a great deal about the case, merely as a case, and it began to be clear to him where Elinor's part came in. Elinor Compton could not have appeared on her husband's behalf, and whether there might not arise a question whether, being now his wife, her evidence could be taken on what had happened before she was his wife, was by no means sure—"Why didn't they call your mother?" John said, as Mrs. Dennistoun also had said—but he did not at all understand, how could he? the dismay that came over Elinor, and the "Not for the world," which came from her lips. He had come in to see her in the morning as he went down to his chambers, on the very morning when Pippo, quite unexpected and also not at all desired, was arriving at Euston Square.

"It would have been much better," he said, "in every way if they had called your mother—who of course must know exactly what you know, Elinor, in respect to this matter——"

"No," said Elinor with dry lips. "She knows nothing. She— calculates back by little incidents—she does not remember: I— do——"

"That's natural, I suppose," said John, with an impatient sigh and a half-angry look. "Still—my aunt——"

"Would do no good at all: you may believe me, John. Don't let us speak of this any more. I know what has to be done: my mother would twist herself up among her calculations—about Alick Hudson's examination and I know not what. Whereas I—there is nothing, nothing more to be said. I thought I could escape, and it is your doing if I now see that I cannot escape. I can but hope that Providence will protect my boy. He is at school, where they have little time for reading the papers. He may never even see—or at least if he does he may think it is another Compton—some one whom he never heard of——"

"And how if he becomes Lord Lomond, as I said, before the secret is out?"

"Oh, John," cried Elinor, wringing her hands—"don't, don't torment me with that idea now—let only this be past and then: Oh, I see, I see—I am not a fool—I perceive that I cannot hide him as you say if that happens. But oh, John, for pity's sake let this be over first! Let us not hurry everything on at the same time. He is at school. What do schoolboys care for the newspapers, especially for trials in the law courts? Oh, let this be over first! A boy at school—and he need never know——"

It was at this moment that a hansom drew up, and a rattling peal came at the door. Hansoms are not rare in Ebury Street, and how can one tell in these small houses if the peal is at one's door or the next? Elinor was not disturbed. She paid no attention. She expected no one, she was afraid of nothing new for the present. Surely, surely, as she said, there was enough for the present. It did not seem possible that any new incident should come now.

"I do not want to torment you, Elinor—you may imagine I would be the last—I would only save you if I could from what must be—— What! what? who's this?—PHILIP! the boy!"

The door had burst open with an eager, impatient hand upon it, and there stood upon the threshold, in all the mingled excitement and fatigue of his night journey, pale, sleep in his eyes, yet happy expectation, exultation, the certainty of open arms to receive him, and cries of delight—the boy. He stood for a second looking into the strange yet familiar room. John Tatham had sprung to his feet and stood startled, hesitating, while young Philip's eyes, noting him with a glance, flashed past him to the other more important, more beloved, the mother whom he had expected to rush towards him with an outcry of joy.

And Elinor sat still in her chair, struck dumb, grown pale like a ghost, her eyes wide open, her lips apart. The sight of the boy, her beloved child, her pride and delight, was as a horrible spectacle to Elinor. She stared at him like one horrified, and neither moved nor spoke.

"Elinor!" cried John, terrified, "there's nothing wrong. Don't you see it's Philip? Boy, what do you mean by giving her such a fright? She's fainting, I believe."

"I—give her a fright!" cried, half in anguish, half in indignation, the astonished boy.

"No, I'm not fainting. Pippo! there's nothing wrong—at home?" Elinor cried, holding out her hand to him—coming to herself, which meant only awakening to the horror of a danger far more present than she had ever dreamt, and to the sudden sight not of her boy, but of that Nemesis which she had so carefully prepared for herself, and which had been awaiting her for years. She was not afraid of anything wrong at home. It was the first shield she could find in the shock which had almost paralysed her, to conceal her terror and distress at the sight of him from the astonished, disappointed, mortified, and angry boy.

"I thought," he said, "you would have been glad to see me, mother! No, there's nothing wrong at home."

"Thank heaven for that!" cried Elinor, feeling herself more and more a hypocrite as she recovered from the shock. "Pippo, I was saying this moment that you were at school. The words were scarcely off my lips—and then to see you in a moment, standing there."

"I thought," he repeated again, trembling with the disappointment and mortification, wounded in his cheerful, confident affection, and in his young pride, the monarch of all

391

he surveyed—"I thought you would have been pleased to see me, mother!"

"Of course," said John, cheerfully, "your mother is glad to see you: and so am I, you impetuous boy, though you don't take the trouble of shaking hands with me. He wants to be kissed and coddled, Elinor, and I must be off to my chambers. But I should like to know first what's up, boy? You've got something to say."

"Pippo, what is it, my dearest? You did give me a great fright, and I am still nervous a little. Tell me, Pippo; something has brought you—your uncle John is right. I can see it in your eyes. You've got something to tell me!"

The tired and excited boy looked from one to another, two faces both full of a veiled but intense anxiety, looking at him as if what they expected was no good news. He burst out into a big, hoarse laugh, the only way to keep himself from crying. "You don't even seem to remember anything about it," he cried, flinging himself down in the nearest chair; "and for my part I don't care any longer whether any one knows or not."

And Elinor, whose thoughts were on such different things—whose whole mind was absorbed in the question of what he could have heard about the trial, about his father, about the new and strange future before him—gazed at him with eyes that seemed hollowed out all round with devouring anxiety. "What is it?" she said, "what is it? For God's sake tell me! What have you heard?"

It goes against all prejudices to imagine that John Tatham, a man who never had had a child, an old bachelor not too tolerant of youth, should have divined the boy better than his mother. But he did, perhaps because he was a lawyer, and accustomed to investigate the human countenance and eye. He saw that Philip was full of something of his own, immediately interesting to himself; and he cast about quickly in his mind what it could be. Not that the boy was heir to a peerage: he would never have come like *this* to announce *that*: but something that Philip was cruelly disappointed his mother did not remember. This passed through John's mind like a flash, though it takes a long time to describe.

"Ah," he said, "I begin to divine. Was not there something about a—scholarship?"

"Pippo!" cried Elinor, lighting up great lamps of relief, of sudden ease and quick coming joy, in her brightened eyes and face. "My boy! you've won your battle! You've got it, you've got it, Pippo! And your foolish, stupid mother that thought for a moment you could rush to her like this with anything but good news!"

It took a few moments to soothe Pippo down, and mend his wounded feelings. "I began to think nobody cared," he said, "and that made me that I didn't care myself. I'd rather Musgrave had got it, if it had not been to please you all. And you never seemed so much as to remember—only Uncle John!" he added after a moment, with a half scorn which made John laugh at the never-failing candour of youth.

"Only the least important of all," he said. "It was atrocious of the ladies, Philip. Shake hands, my boy, I owe you five pounds for the scholarship. And now I'll take myself off, which will please you most of all."

He went down-stairs laughing to himself all the way, but got suddenly quite grave as he stepped outside—whether because he remembered that it does not become a Q.C. and M.P. to laugh in the street, or for other causes, it does not become us to attempt to say.

And Elinor meanwhile made it up to her boy amply, and while her heart ached with the question what to do with him, how to dispose of him during those dreadful following days, behaved herself as if her head too was half turned with joy and exultation, only tempered by the regret that Musgrave, who had worked so hard, could not have got the scholarship too.

CHAPTER XLI.

Elinor made much of her boy during that day and the following days, to take away the sense of disappointment which even after the first great mortification was got over still haunted young Philip's mind. It surprised him beyond measure to find that she did not wish to go out with him, indeed in so far as was possible avoided it altogether, save for a hurried drive to a few places, during which she kept her veil down and sheltered herself with an umbrella in the most ridiculous way. "Are you afraid of your complexion, mother?" the boy asked of her with disdain. "It looks like it," she said, but with a laugh that was full of embarrassment, "though it is a little late in the day." Elinor was perhaps better aware than Pippo was that she had a complexion which a girl might have envied, and was still as fresh as a rose, notwithstanding that she was a year or two over forty; but I need not say it was not of her complexion she was thinking. She had been careful to choose her time on previous visits to London so as to risk as little as possible the chance of meeting her husband. But now there was no doubt that he was in town, and not the least that if he met her anywhere with Pippo, her secret, so far as it had ever been a secret, would be in his hands. Even when John took the boy out it was with a beating heart that his mother saw him go, for John was too well known to make any secret possible about his movements, or who it was who was with him. Perhaps it was for this reason that John desired to take him out, and even cut short his day's work on one or two occasions to act as cicerone to Philip. He took him to the House, to the great excitement and delight of the boy, who only wished that the entertainment could have been made complete by a speech from Uncle John, which was a point in which his guide, philosopher, and friend, though in every other way so complaisant, did not humour Pippo. On one occasion during the first week they had an encounter which made John's middle-aged pulses move a little quicker. When they were walking along through Hyde Park, having strolled that way in the fading of the May afternoon, when the carriages were still promenading up and down, before they returned to Halkin Street to dinner, where Elinor awaited them—it happened to Mr. Tatham to meet the roving eyes of Lady Mariamne, who lay back languidly in her carriage, wrapped in a fur cloak, and shivering in the chill of the evening. She was not particularly interested in anything or any person whom she had seen, and was a little cross and desirous of getting home. But when she saw John she roused up immediately, and gave a sign to Dolly, who sat by her, to pull the check-string. "Mr. Tatham!" she cried, in her shrill voice. Lady Mariamne was not one of the people who object to hear their voice in public or are reluctant to make their wishes known to everybody. She felt herself to be of the cast in which everybody is interested, and that the public liked to know whom she honoured with her acquaintance. "Mr. Tatham! are you going to carry your rudeness so far as not to seem to know me? Oh, come here this moment, you impertinent man!"

"Can I be of any use to you, Lady Mariamne?" said John, gravely, at the carriage door.

"Oh, dear no; you can't be of any use. What should I have those men for if I wanted you to be of use? Come and talk a moment, that's all; or get into the carriage and I'll take you anywhere. Dolly and I have driven round and round, and we have not seen a creature we cared to see. Yes! there was a darling, darling little Maltese terrier, with white silk curls hanging over his eyes, on an odious woman's lap; but I cannot expect you to find that angel for me. Mr. Tatham, who is that tall boy?"

"Pippo," said John, quickly (though probably he had never in his life before used that name, which he disapproved of angrily, as people often do of a childish name which does not please them), "go on. I'll come after you directly. The boy is a cousin of mine, Lady Mariamne, just from school."

"Mr. Tatham, I am quite sure it is Nell's boy. Call after him. What's his name? Bring him back! John Thomas, run after that young gentleman, and say with my compliments——"

"Nothing," said John, stopping the footman with a lifted hand and a still more emphatic look. "He is hastening home to—an engagement. And it's evident I had better go too—for your little friend there is showing his teeth."

"The darling!" said Lady Mariamne, "did it show its little pearls at the wicked man that will not do what its mummy says? Dolly, can't you jump down and run after that boy? I am sure it is your Uncle Philip's boy."

"He is out of sight, mother," said Miss Dolly, calmly.

"You are the most dreadful, wicked, unkind people, all of you. Show its little teeth, then, darling! Oo's the only one that has any feeling. Mr. Tatham, do tell me something about this trial. What is going to be done? Phil is mixed up in it. I know he is. Can they do anything to anybody—after all this time? They can't make you pay up, I know, after a certain time. Oh, couldn't it all be hushed up and stopped and kept out of the newspapers? I hate the newspapers, always chuckling over every new discovery. But this cannot be called a new discovery. If it's true it's old, as old as the old beginning of the world. Don't you think somebody could get at the newspaper men and have it hushed up?"

"I doubt if you could get hold of all of them, their name is legion," said John.

"Oh, I don't care what their name is. If you will help me, Mr. Tatham, we could get hold of most of them—won't you? You know, don't you, poor St. Serf is so bad; it may be over any day—and then only think what a complication! Dolly, turn your head the other way; look at that silly young Huntsfield capering about to catch your eye. I don't want you to hear what I have got to say."

"I don't in the least way want to hear what you have got to say, dear mamma," said Dolly.

"That would have made me listen to every word," said Lady Mariamne; "but girls are more queer nowadays than anything that ever was. Mr. Tatham"—she put her hand upon his, which was on the carriage door, and bent her perfumed, powdered face towards him—"for goodness' sake—think how awkward it would be—a man just succeeding to a title and that sort of thing put in all the papers about him. Do, do stop it, or try something to stop it, for goodness' sake!"

"I assure you," said John, "I can do nothing to stop it. I am as powerless as you are."

"Oh, I don't say that I am powerless," said Lady Mariamne, with her shrill laugh. "One has one's little ways of influence." Then she put her hand again upon John with a sudden grip. "Mr. Tatham," she said, "tell me, in confidence, was that Phil's boy?"

"I have told you, Lady Mariamne, it is a nephew of mine."

"A nephew—oh, I know what kind of a nephew—*à la mode de Bretagne!*"

She turned her head to the other side, where her daughter was gazing calmly in front of her.

"Dolly! I was sure of it," she cried, "don't you hear? Dolly, don't you hear?"

"Which, mamma?" said Dolly, gravely; "of course I could not help hearing it all. Which part was I to notice? about the newspapers or about the boy?"

Lady Mariamne appealed to earth and heaven with the loud cackle of her laugh. "He can't deny it," she said; "he as good as owns it. I am certain that's the boy that will be Lomond."

"Uncle St. Serf is not dead yet," said Dolly, reprovingly.

"Poor Serf!—but he's so very bad," said Lady Mariamne, "that it's almost the same thing. Mr. Tatham, can't we take you anywhere? I'm so glad I've seen Nell's boy. Can't we drive you home? Perhaps you've got Nell there too?"

John stood back from the carriage door, just in time to escape the start of the horses as the remorseless string was touched and the footman clambered up into his seat. Lady Mariamne's smile went off her face, and she had forgotten all about it, to judge from appearances, before he had got himself in motion again. And a little farther on, behind the next tree, he found young Philip waiting, full of curiosity and questions.

"Who was that lady, Uncle John? Was she asking about me? I thought I heard her call. I had half a mind to run back and say 'Here I am.'"

"It was much better that you didn't do anything of the kind. Never pay any attention when you think you hear a fine lady calling you, Philip. It is better not to hear the Siren's call."

"When they're elderly Sirens like that!" said the boy, with a laugh. "But I say, Uncle John, if you won't tell me who the lady is, who is the girl? She has a pair of eyes!—not like Sirens though—eyes that go through you—like—like a pair of lancets."

"A surgical operation in fact: and I shouldn't wonder if she meant to be a doctor," said John. "The mother has done nothing all her life, therefore the daughter means to do much. It is the natural reaction of the generations. But I never noticed that Miss Dolly had any eyes—to speak of," said the highly indifferent middle-aged man.

The boy flushed with a sense of indignation. "Perhaps you think the old lady's were finer?" he said.

"I never admired the old lady, as you call her," said John, shortly; and then he turned Philip's attention to something, possibly with the easily satisfied conviction of a spectator that the boy thought of it no more.

"We met my Lady Mariamne in the park," he said to Elinor when they sat at dinner an hour later at that bachelor table in Halkin Street, where everything was so exquisitely cared for. It was like Elinor, but most unlike the place in which she found herself, that she started so violently as to shake the whole table, crying out in a tone of consternation, "John!" as if he did not know very well what he might venture to say, or as if he had any intention of betraying her to her son.

"She was very anxious," he said, perhaps playing a little with her excitement, "to have Philip presented to her: but I sent him on—that is to say, I thought I sent him on. The fellow went no farther than to the next tree, where he stood and watched Miss Dolly, not feeling any interest in the old lady, as he said."

"Well, Uncle John—did you expect me to look at the old lady? You are not so fond of old ladies yourself."

"And who is Miss Dolly?" said Elinor, trying to conceal the beating of her heart and the quiver on her lips with a smile; and then she added, with a little catch of her breath, "Oh, yes, I remember there was a little girl."

"You will be surprised to hear that we are by way of being great friends. Her ladyship visits me in my chambers——"

Again Elinor uttered that startled cry, "John!" but she tried this time to cover it with a tremulous laugh. "Are you becoming a flirt in your old age?"

"It appears so," said John. And then he added, "That aphorism, which struck you as it struck me, Elinor, by its good sense—about the heir to a peerage—is really her production, and not mine."

"Miss Dolly's? And what was the aphorism, Uncle John?" cried Philip.

"No, it was not Miss Dolly's, my young man. It was the mother's, and so of course does not interest you any more."

It did not as a matter of fact: the old lady was supremely indifferent to Pippo; but as he looked up saying something else which did not bear upon the subject, it occurred to the boy, as it will sometimes occur by the merest chance to a young observer, to notice his mother. She caught his eye somehow in the most accidental way; and Pippo was too well acquainted with her looks not to perceive that there was a thrill in every line of her countenance, a slight nervous tremble in her hands and entire person, such as was in no way to be accounted for (he thought) by anything that had been said or done. There was nothing surely to disquiet her in dining at Uncle John's, the three alone, not even one other guest to fill up the vacant side of the table. Philip had himself thought that Uncle John might have asked some one to meet them. He should have remembered that he himself, Philip, was now of an age to dine out, and see a little society, and go into the world. But what in the name of all that was wonderful was there in this entertainment to agitate his mother? And John Tatham had a look—which Philip did not understand—the look of a man who was successful in argument, who was almost crushing an opponent. It was as if a duel had been going on between them, and the man was the victor, which, as was natural, immediately threw Philip violently on the other side.

"You're not well, mother," he said.

"Do you think not, Pippo? Well, perhaps you are right. London is too much for me. I am a country bird," said Elinor, with smiling yet trembling lips.

"You shall not go to the theatre if you are not up to it," said the boy in his imperious way.

She gave him an affectionate look, and then she looked across the table at John. What did that look mean? There was a faint smile in it: and there was a great deal which Philip did not understand, things understood by Uncle John—who was after all what you might call an outsider, no more—and not by him, her son! Could anything be so monstrous? Philip blazed up with sudden fire.

"No," said John Tatham; "I think Philip's right. We'll take her home to be coddled by her maid, and we'll go off, two wild young fellows, to the play by ourselves."

"No," said Philip, "I'll leave her to be coddled by no maid. I can take care of my mother myself."

"My dear boy," said Elinor, "I want no coddling. But I doubt whether I could stand the play. I like you to go with Uncle John."

And then it began to dawn upon Philip that his mother had never meant to be of the party, and that this was what had been settled all along. He was more angry; more wounded and hurt in his spirit than he had of course the least occasion to be. He was of opinion that his mother had never had any secrets from him, that she had taken him into her confidence since he was a small boy, even things that Granny did not know! And here all at once there was rising between them a cloud, a mist, which there was no reason for. If he had done anything to make him less worthy he would have understood; had there been a bad report from school, had he failed in his work and disappointed her, there might have been some reason for it. But he had done nothing of the kind! Never before had he been so deserving of confidence; he had got his scholarship, he had finished the first phase of his education in triumph, and fulfilled all her expectations. And now just at this point of all others, just when he was most fit to understand, most worthy of trust, she turned from him. His heart swelled as if it would burst, with anger first, almost too strong to be repressed, and with that sense of injured merit which is of all things the most hard to bear. It is hard enough even when one is aware one deserves no better. But to be conscious of your worth and to feel that you are not appreciated, that is indeed too much for any one. There was not even the satisfaction of giving up the play which he had looked forward to, making a sacrifice of it to his mother, in which there would have been a severe pleasure. But she did not want him! She preferred that he should leave her by herself to be coddled by her maid, as Uncle John (vulgarly) said. Or perhaps was there somebody else coming, some old friend whom he knew nothing of, somebody, some one or other like that old witch in the carriage whom Pippo was not meant to know?

It ended, however, in the carrying out of the plan settled beforehand by those old conspirators. The old conspirators do generally manage to carry out their plans for the management of rebellious youth, however injured the latter may feel. Pippo wound himself up in solemn dignity and silence when he understood that it was ordained that he should proceed to the play with John Tatham. And the pair had got half way to Drury Lane—or it may have been the Lyceum, or the Haymarket, or any of half-a-dozen other theatres, for here exact information fails—before he condescended to open his lips for more than Yes or No.

But Philip's gloom did not survive the raising of the curtain, and he had forgotten all offences and had taken his companion into favour again, and was talking to Uncle John between the acts with all the excitement of a country youth to whom a play still was the greatest of novelties and delights, when he suddenly saw a change come over John Tatham's countenance and a slight bow of recognition directed towards a box, which made Philip turn round and look too. And there was the old witch of the carriage, and, what was more interesting, the girl with the keen eyes, who looked out suddenly from the shade of the draperies, and fixed upon Philip—Philip himself—a look which startled that young hero much. Nor was this all; for later in the evening, after another act of the play, some one else appeared in the same box, and fixed the dark and impassive stare of a long pair of opera-glasses upon Philip. It amused him at first, and afterwards it half frightened him, and finally made him very angry. The gazer was a man, of whom, however, Philip could make nothing out but his white shirt front and his tall stature, and the long black tubes of the opera-glass. Was it at him the man was looking, or perhaps at Uncle John? But the boy thought it on the whole unlikely that anybody should stare in that way at anything so little out of the ordinary as Uncle John.

"I say," he said, in the next interval, "who is that fellow staring at us out of your old lady's box?"

"Staring at the ladies behind us, you mean," said John. "Pippo, do you think we could make a rush for it the moment the play's over? I've got something to look over when I get home. Are you game to be out the very first before the curtain's down?"

"Certainly I'm game," said Philip, delighted, "if you wish it, Uncle John."

"Yes, I wish it," said the other, and he put his hand on the boy's shoulder as the act finished and the characters of the piece drew together for the final tableau. And the pair managed it triumphantly, and were the very first to get out at the head of the crowd, to Philip's immense amusement and John Tatham's great relief. The elder hurried the younger into the first hansom, all in the twinkling of an eye: and then for the first time his gravity relaxed. Philip took it all for a great joke till they reached Ebury Street. But when his companion left him, and he had time to think of it, he began to ask himself why?

CHAPTER XLII.

I will not say that Philip's sleep was broken by this question, but it undoubtedly recurred to his mind the first thing in the morning when he jumped out of bed very late for breakfast, and the events of the past night and the lateness of the hour at which he got to rest came back upon him as excuses in the first place for his tardiness. And then, which was remarkable, it was not the scene in the play in which he had been most interested which came to his mind, but a vision of that box and the man standing in front of it staring at him through the black tubes of the opera-glass which came before Philip like a picture. Uncle John had said it was at the ladies behind, but the boy felt sure it was no lady behind, but himself, on whom that stare was fixed. Who would care to stare so at him? It faintly gleamed across his thoughts that it might be some one who had heard of the scholarship, but he dismissed that thought instantly with a blush. It also gleamed upon him with equal vagueness like a momentary but entirely futile light, consciously derived from story books, and of which he was much ashamed, that the inexplicable attention given to himself might have something to do with the girl who had such keen eyes. Philip blushed fiery red at this involuntary thought, and chased it from his mind like a mad dog; but he could not put away the picture of the box, the girl putting aside the curtain to look at him, and the opera-glass fixed upon his face. And then why was Uncle John in such a hurry to get away? It had seemed a capital joke at that moment, but when he came to think of it, it was rather strange that a man who might be Solicitor-General to-morrow if he liked, and probably Lord Chancellor in a few years, should make a schoolboy rush from the stalls of a theatre with the object of being first out. Philip disapproved of so undignified a step on the part of his elderly relation. And he saw now in the serious morning that Uncle John was very unlikely to have done it for fun. What, then, did it mean?

He came down full of these thoughts, and rather ashamed of being late, wondering whether his mother would have waited for him (which would have annoyed him), or if she would have finished her breakfast (which would have annoyed him still more). Happily for Elinor, she had hit the golden mean, and was pouring out for herself a second cup of coffee (but Philip was not aware it was the second) when the boy appeared. She was quite restored to her usual serenity and freshness, and as eager to know how he had enjoyed himself as she always was. He gave her a brief sketch of the play and of what pleased him in it as in duty bound. "But," he added, "what interested me almost more was that we had a sort of a—little play of our own."

"What?" she cried, with a startled look in her eyes. One thing that puzzled him was that she was so very easily startled, which it seemed to Philip had never been the case before.

"Well," he said, "the lady was there whom Uncle John met in the park—and the girl with her—and I believe the little dog. She made all sorts of signs to him, but he took scarcely any notice. But that's not all, mother——"

"It's a good deal, Pippo——"

"Is it? Why do you speak in that choked voice, mother? I suppose it is just one of his society acquaintances. But the thing was that before the last act somebody else came forward to the front of the box, and fixed—I was going to say his eyes, I mean his opera-glasses upon us."

Philip had meant to say upon me—but he had produced already so great an effect on his mother's face that he moderated instinctively the point of this description. "And stared at us," he added, "all the rest of the time, paying not the least attention to anything that was going on. It's a queer sensation," he went on, with a laugh, "to feel that black mysterious-looking thing like the eyes of some monster with no speculation in them, fixed upon you. Now, I want you to tell me—— What's the matter, mother?"

"Nothing, Pippo; nothing," said Elinor, faintly, stooping to lift up a book she had let fall. "Go on with your story. I am very much interested; and then, my dear?"

"Mother," cried Philip, "I don't know what has come over you, or over me. There's something going on I can't understand. You never used to have any secrets from me. I was always in your confidence—wasn't I, mother?"

It was not a book she had let fall, but a ring that she had dropped from her finger, and which had to be followed over the carpet. It made her red and flushed when she half raised her head to say, "Yes, Pippo—you know—I have always told you——"

Philip did not remark that what his mother said was nothing after all. He got up to help her to look for her ring, and put his arm round her waist as she knelt on the floor.

"Yes, mamma," he said, tenderly, protectingly, "I do know: but something's changed; either it's in me that makes you feel you can't trust me—or else it is in you. And I don't know which would be worst."

"There is no change," she said, after a moment, for she could not help the ring being found, and immediately when his quick, young eyes came to the search: but she did not look him in the face. "There is no change, dear. There is only some worrying business which involves a great many troubles of my old life before you were born. You shall hear—everything—in a little while: but I cannot enter into it all at this moment. It is full of complications and—secrets that belong to other people. Pippo, you must promise me to wait patiently, and to believe—to believe—always the best you can—of your mother."

The boy laughed as he raised her up, still holding her with his arm. "Believe the best I can! Well, I don't think that will be a great effort, mother. Only to think that you can't trust me as you always have done makes me wretched. We've been such friends, haven't we, mamma? I've always told you everything, or at least everything except just the nonsense at school: and you've told me everything. And if we are going to be different now——"

"You've told me everything!" the boy was as sure of it as that he was born. She had to hold by him to support herself, and it cost her a strong effort to restrain the shiver that ran through her. "We are not going to be different," she said, "as soon as we leave London—or before—you shall know everything about this business of mine, Pippo. Will that satisfy you? In the meantime it is not pleasant business, dear; and you must bear with me if I am abstracted sometimes, and occupied, and cross."

"But, mother," said Philip, bending over her with that young celestial foolish look of gravity and good advice with which a neophyte will sometimes address the much-experienced and heavily-laden pilgrim, "don't you think it would be easier if it was all open between us, and I took my share? If it is other people's secrets I would not betray them, you know that."

Unfortunately Elinor here murmured, scarcely knowing what words came from her lips, "That is what John says."

"John," said the boy, furious with the quick rage of injured tenderness and pride, "Uncle John! and you tell him more, him, an outsider, than you tell me!"

He let her go then, which was a great relief to Elinor, for she could command herself better when he was a little farther off, and could not feel the thrill that was in her, and the thumping of her heart.

"You must remember, Pippo," she said, "what I have told you, that my present very disagreeable, very painful business is about things that happened before you were born, which John knew everything about. He was my adviser then, as far as I would take any advice, which I am afraid never was much, Pippo," she said; "never, alas! all my life. Granny will tell you that. But John, always the kindest friend and the best brother in the world, did everything he could. And it would have been better for us all if I had taken his advice instead of always, I fear, always my own way."

Strangely enough this cheered Pippo and swept the cloud from his face. "I'm glad you didn't take anybody's advice, mother. I shouldn't have liked it. I've more faith in you than anybody. Well, then, now about this man. What man in the world—I really mean in the world, in what is called society, for that is the kind of people they were—could have such a curiosity about—me?"

She had resumed her seat, and her face was turned away from him. Also the exquisite tone of complacency and innocent self-appreciation with which Philip expressed this wonder helped her a little to surmount the situation. Elinor could have laughed had her heart been only a trifle less burdened. She said: "Are you sure it was at you?"

"Uncle John said something about ladies behind us, but I am sure it was no ladies behind. It might, of course," the boy added, cautiously, "have been *him*, you know. I suppose Uncle John's a personage, isn't he? But after all, you know, hang it, mother, it isn't easy to believe that a fellow like that would stare so at Uncle John."

"Poor John! It is true there is not much novelty about him," said Elinor, with a tremble in her voice, which, if it was half agitation, was yet a little laughter too: for there are scarcely any circumstances, however painful, in which those who are that way moved by nature are quite able to quench the unconquerable laugh. She added, with a falter in which there was no laughter, "and what—was the—fellow like?"

"All that I could see was that he was a tall man. I saw his large shirt-front and his black evening clothes, and something like grey hair above those two big, black goggles——"

"Grey hair!" Elinor said, with a low suppressed cry.

"He never took them away from his eyes for a moment, so of course I could not see his face, or anything much except that he was more than common tall—like myself," Pippo said, with a little air of pleased vanity in the comparison.

Like himself! She did not make any remark. It is very doubtful whether she could have done so. There came before her so many visions of the past, and such a vague, confused, bewildering future, of which she could form no definite idea what it would be. Was it with a pang that she foresaw that drawing towards another influence: that mingled instinct, curiosity, perhaps admiration and wonder, which already seemed to move her boy's unconscious mind? Elinor did not even know whether that would hurt her at all. Even now there seemed a curious pungent sense of half-pleasure in the pain. Like himself! So he was. And if it should be that it was his father, who for hours had stood there, not taking his eyes off the boy (for hours her imagination said, though Pippo had not said so), his father who had known where she was and never disturbed her, never interfered with her; the man who had summoned her to perform her martyrdom for him, never doubting—Phil, with grey hair! To say what mingled feelings swept through Elinor's mind, with all these elements in them, is beyond my power. She saw him with his face concealed, standing up unconscious of the crowded place and of the mimic life on the stage, his eyes fixed upon his son whom he had never seen before. Where was there any drama in which there was a scene like this? His son, his only child, the heir! Unconsciously even to herself that fact had some influence, no doubt, on Elinor's thoughts. And it would be impossible to say how much influence had that unexpected subduing touch of the grey hair: and the strange change in the scene altogether. The foolish, noisy, "fast" woman, with her *tourbillon* of men and dogs about her, turned into the old lady of Pippo's careless remark, with her daughter beside her far more important than she: and the tall figure in the front of the box, with grey hair——

Young Philip had not the faintest light or guidance in the discovery of his mother's thoughts. He was much more easy and comfortable now that there had been an explanation between them, though it was one of those explanations which explained nothing. He even forgave Uncle John for knowing more than he did, moved thereto by the consolatory thought that John's advice had never been taken, and that his mother had always followed her own way. This was an incalculable comfort to Pippo's mind, and gave him composure to wait calmly for the clearing up of the mystery, and the restoration of that perfect confidence between his mother and himself which he was so firmly convinced had existed all his life. He was a great deal happier after, and gave her an excellent account of the play, which he had managed to see quite satisfactorily, notwithstanding the other "little play of our own" which ran through everything. At Philip's age one can see two things at once well enough. I knew a boy who at one and the same moment got the benefit of (1st) his own story book, which he read lying at full length before the fire, half buried in the fur of a great rug; and (2nd) of the novel which was being read out over his head for the benefit of the other members of the family— or at least he strenuously asserted he did, and indeed proved himself acquainted with both. Philip in the same way had taken in everything in the play, even while his soul was intent upon the opera-glass in the box. He had not missed anything of either. He gave an account of the first, from which the drama might have been written down had fate destroyed it: and had noticed the *minauderies* of the heroine, and the eager determination not to be second to her in anything which distinguished the first gentleman, as if he had nothing else in his mind: while all the time he had been under the fascination of the two black eyeholes *braqués* upon him, the mysterious gaze as of a ghost from eyes which he never saw.

This occupied some part of the forenoon, and Philip was happy. But when he had completed his tale and began to feel the necessity of going out, and remembered that he had nowhere to go and nothing to do, the prospect was not alluring. He tried very hard to persuade his mother to go out with him, but this was a risk from which Elinor shrank. She shrank, too, from his proposal at last to go out to the park by himself.

"To the Row. I sha'n't know the people except those who are in *Punch* every week, and I shall envy the fellows riding—but at least it will be something to see."

"I wish you would not go to the Row, Pippo."

"Why, mother? Doesn't everybody go? And you never were here at this time of the year before."

"No," she said, with a long breath of despair. No; of all times of the year this was the one in which she had never risked him in London. And, oh! that he had been anywhere in the world except London now!

Philip, who had been watching her countenance with great interest, here patted her on the shoulder with condescending, almost paternal, kindness. "Don't you be frightened, mother. I'll not get into any mischief. I'll neither be rode over, nor robbed, nor run away. I'll take as great care of myself as if you had been there."

"I'm not afraid that you will be ridden over or robbed," she said, forcing a smile; "but there is one thing, Pippo. Don't talk to anybody whom you—don't know. Don't let yourself be drawn into—— If you should meet, for instance, that lady—who was in the theatre last night."

"Yes, mother?"

"Don't let her make acquaintance with you; don't speak to her, nor the girl, nor any one that may be with her. At the risk even of being uncivil——"

"Why, mother," he said, elevating his eyebrows, "how could I be uncivil to a lady?"

"Because I tell you," she cried, "because you must—because I shall sit here in terror counting every moment till you come back, if you don't promise me this."

He looked at her with the most wondering countenance, half disapproving, half pitying. Was she going mad? what was happening to her? was she after all, though his mother, no better than the jealous foolish women in books, who endeavoured at all costs to separate their children from every influence but their own? How could Pippo think such things of his mother? and yet what else could he think?

"I had better," he said, "if that is how you feel, mother, not go

411

to the Row at all."

"Much better, much better!" she cried. "I'll tell you what we'll do, Pippo—you have never been to see—the Tower." She had run over all the most far-off and unlikely places in her mind, and this occurred to her as the most impossible of all to attract any visitor of whom she could be afraid. "I have changed my mind," she added. "Well have a hansom, and I will go with you to see the Tower."

"So long as you go with me," said Pippo, "I don't care where I go."

And they set out almost joyfully as in their old happy expeditions of old, for that long drive through London in the hansom. And yet the boy was only lulled for the moment, and in his heart was more and more perplexed what his mother could mean.

CHAPTER XLIII.

Fortune was favourable to Elinor that day. At the Tower, where she duly went over everything that was to be seen with Pippo, conscious all the time of his keen observance of her through all that he was doing, and even through his interest in what he saw—and feeling for the first time in her life that there was between her boy and her something that he felt, something that was not explained by anything she had said, and that awaited the dreadful moment when everything would have to be told—at the Tower, as I say, they met some friends from the north, the rector of the parish, who had come up with his son to see town, and was naturally taking his boy, as Elinor took hers, to see all that was not town, in the usual sense of the word. They were going to Woolwich and Greenwich next day, and with a pang of mingled trouble and relief in her mind Elinor contrived to engage Pippo to accompany them. On the second day I think they were to go to St. Katherine's Docks, or the Isle of Dogs, or some other equally important and interesting sight—far better no doubt for the two youths than to frequent such places as the Row, and gaze at the stream of gaiety and luxury which they could not join. Pippo in ordinary circumstances would have been delighted to see Woolwich and the docks—but it was so evident to him that his mother was anxiously desirous to dispose of him so, that his satisfaction was much lessened. The boy, however, was magnanimous enough to consent without any appearance of reluctance. In the many thoughts which filled his mind Philip showed his fine nature, by having already come to consent to the possibility that his mother might have business of her own into which he had no right to enter unless at her own time and with her full consent. It cost him an effort, I allow, to come to that: but yet he did so, and resolved, a little pride helping him, to inquire no more, and if possible to wonder or be offended no more, but to wait the time she had promised, when the old rule of perfect confidence should be re-established between them. The old rule! if Pippo had but known! nothing yet had given Elinor such a sense of guilt as his conviction that she had told him everything, that there had been no secrets between them during all the happy life that was past.

How entirely relieved Elinor was when he started to join his friends next morning it would be impossible to put into words. She watched all his lingering movements before he went with eyes in which she tried to quench the impatience, and look only with the fond admiration and interest she felt upon all his little preparations, his dawning sense of what was becoming in apparel, the flower in his coat, the carefully rolled umbrella, the hat brushed to the most exquisite smoothness, the handkerchief just peeping from his breast-*pocket. It is always a revelation to a woman to find that these details occupy as much of a young man's attention as her own toilette occupies hers; and that he is as tremulously alive to "what is worn" in many small particulars that never catch her eye, as she is to details which entirely escape him. She smiles at him as he does at her, each in that conscious superiority to the other, which is on the whole an indulgent sentiment. Underneath all her anxiety to see him go, to get rid of him (was that the dreadful truth in this terrible crisis of her affairs?), she felt the amusement of the boy's little coquetries, and the mother's admiration of his fresh looks, his youthful brightness, his air of distinction; how different from the Rector's boy, who was a nice fellow enough, and a credit to his rectory, and whose mother, I do not doubt, felt in his ruddy good looks something much superior in robustness, and strength, and manhood to the too-tall and too-slight golden youth of the ladies at Lakeside! It even flitted across Elinor's mind to give him within herself the title that was to be his, everybody said—Lord Lomond! And then she asked herself indignantly what honour it could add to her spotless boy to have such a vain distinction; a name that had been soiled by so much ignoble use? Elinor had prided herself all her life on an indifference to, almost a contempt for, the distinctions of rank: and that it should occur to her to think of that title as an embellishment to Pippo—nay, to think furtively, without her own knowledge, so to speak, that Pippo looked every inch a lord and heir to a peerage, was an involuntary weakness almost incredible. She blushed for herself as she realised it:—a peerage which had meant so little that was excellent—a name connected with so many undesirable precedents: still I suppose when it is his own even the veriest democrat is conscious at least of the picturesqueness, the superiority, as a mode of distinguishing one man from another, of anything that can in the remotest sense be called a historical name.

When Pippo was out of sight Elinor turned from the window with a sigh, and came back to the dark chamber of her own life, full at this moment of all the gathered blackness of the past and of the future. She put her hands over her eyes, and sank down upon a seat, as if to shut out from herself all that was before her. But shut it out as she might, there it was—the horrible court with the judgment-seat, the rows of faces bent upon her, the silence through which her own voice must rise alone, saying—what? What was it she was called there to say? Oh, how little they knew who suggested that her mother should have been called instead of her, with all her minute old-fashioned calculations and exact memory, who even now, when all was over, would probably convict Elinor of a mistake! Even at that penalty what would not she give to have it over, the thing said, the event done with, whatever it might bring after it! And it could now be only a very short time till the moment of the ordeal would come, when she should stand up in the face of her country, before the solemn judge on his bench, before all the gaping, wondering people— before, oh! thought most dreadful of all, which we would not, could not, contemplate—before one who knew everything, and say—— She picked herself up trembling as it were, and uncovered her eyes, and protested to herself that she would say nothing that was not true. Nothing that was not true! She would tell her story—so well remembered, so often conned; that story that had been put into her lips twenty years ago which she had repeated then confused, not knowing how it was that what was a simple fact should nevertheless not be true. Alas! she knew that very well now, and yet would have to repeat it before God and the world. But thinking would make it no better—thinking could only make it worse. She sprang up again, and began to occupy herself with something she had to do: the less it was thought over the better: for now the trial had begun, and her ordeal would soon be done too. If only the boy could be occupied, kept away—if only she could be left alone to do what she had to do! That he should be there was the last aggravation of which her fate was capable; there in idleness, reading the papers in the morning, which was a thing she had so lately calculated a boy at school was unlikely to do; and what so likely as that his eye would be caught by his own name in the report of the trial, which would be an exciting trial and fully reported—a trial which interested society. The boy would see his own name: she could almost hear him cry out, looking up from his breakfast, "Hallo, mother! here's something about a Philip Compton!" And all the questions that would follow—"Is he the same Comptons that we are? What Comptons do we belong to? You never told me anything about my family. Is this man any relation, I wonder? Both surname and Christian name the same. It's strange if there is no connection!" She could almost hear the words he would say—all that and more—and what should she reply?

"I have only one thing to say, Elinor," said John, to whom in her desperation she turned again, as she always did, disturbing him, poor man, in his chambers as he was collecting his notes and his thoughts in the afternoon after his work was over: "it is the same as I have always said; even now make a clean breast of it to the boy. Tell him everything; better that he should hear it from your own lips than that it should burst upon him as a discovery. He has but to meet Lady Mariamne in the park, the most likely thing in the world——"

"No, John," cried Elinor, "no; the Marshalls are here, our Rector from Lakeside, and he is taking his boy to see all the sights. I have got Pippo to go with them. They are going to Woolwich to-day, and afterwards to quite a long list of things—oh, entirely out of everybody's way."

Her little look of uneasy triumph and satisfaction made John smile. She was not half so sure as she tried to look; but, all the same, had a little pride, a little pleasure in her own management, and in the happy chance of the Marshalls being in London, which was a thing that could not have been planned, an intervention of Providence. He could not refuse to smile—partly with her, partly at her simplicity—but, all the same, he shook his head.

"The only way in which there is any safety—the only chance of preserving him from a shock, a painful shock, Elinor, that may upset him for life——"

"How do you mean, upset him for life?"

"By showing him that his mother, whom he believes in like heaven, has deceived him since ever he was born."

She covered her face with her hands, and burst into a sobbing cry. "Oh, John, you don't know how true that is! He said to me only yesterday, 'You have always told me everything, mother. There has never been any secret between us.' Oh! John, John, only think of having that said to me, and knowing what I know!"

"Well, Elinor; believe me, my dear, there is but one thing to do. The boy is a good boy, full of love and kindness."

"Oh, isn't he, John? the best boy, the dearest——"

"And adores his mother, as a boy should," John got up from his chair and walked about the room for a little, and then he came behind her and put his hand on her shoulder. "Tell him, Elinor: my dear Nelly, as if I had never said a word on the subject before, I beseech you tell him, trust him fully, even now, at the eleventh hour."

417

She raised her head with a quivering, wistful smile. "The moment the trial is over, the moment it is over! I give you my word, John."

"Do not wait till it is over, do it now; to-night when he comes home."

She began to tremble so that John Tatham was alarmed—and kept looking at him with an imploring look, her lips quivering and every line in her countenance. "Oh, not to-night. Spare me to-night! After the trial; after my part of it. At least—after—after—oh, give me till to-morrow to think of it!"

"My dear Elinor, I count for nothing in it. I am not your judge; I am your partisan, you know, whatever you do. But I am sure it will be the better done, and even the easier done, the sooner you do it."

"I will—I will: at the very latest the day after I have done my part at the trial. Is not that enough to think of at one time, for a poor woman who has never stood up before the public in all her life, never had a question put to her? Oh, John! oh, John!"

"Elinor, Elinor! you are too sensible a woman to make a fuss about a simple duty like this."

"There speaks the man who has stood before the world all his life, and is not afraid of any public," she said, with a tremulous laugh. But she had won her moment's delay, and thus was victorious after a fashion, as it was her habit to be.

I do not know that young Philip much amused himself at Woolwich that day. He did and he did not. He could not help being interested in all he saw, and he liked the Marshalls well enough, and in ordinary circumstances would have entered very heartily into any sight-seeing. But he kept thinking all the time what his mother was doing, and wondering over the mysterious business which was to be explained to him sooner or later, and which he had so magnanimously promised to wait for the revelation of, and entertain no suspicions about in the meantime. The worst of such magnanimity is that it is subject to dreadful failings of the heart in its time of waiting—never giving in, indeed, but yet feeling the pressure whenever there is a moment to think. This matter mixed itself up so with all Philip saw that he never in after life saw a great cannon, or a pyramid of balls (which is not, to be sure, an every-day sight) without a vague sensation of trouble, as of something lying behind which was concealed from him, and which he would scarcely endure to have concealed. When he left his friends in the evening, however, it was with another engagement for to-morrow, and several to-morrows after, and great jubilation on the part of both father and son, as to their good luck in meeting, and having his companionship in their pleasures. And, in fact, these pleasures were carried on for several days, always with the faint bitter in them to Philip, of that consciousness that his mother was pleased to be rid of him, glad to see his back turned, the most novel, extraordinary sensation to the boy. And it must also be confessed that he kept a very keen eye on all the passing carriages, always hoping to see that one in which the witch, as he called her, and the girl with the keen eyes were—for he had not picked up the name of Lady Mariamne, keen as his young ears were, and though John had mentioned it in his presence, partly, perhaps, because it was so very unlikely a name. As for the man with the opera-glasses, he had not seen his face at all, and therefore could not hope to recognise him. And yet he felt a little thrill run through him when any tall man with grey hair passed in the street. He almost thought he could have known the tall slim figure with a certain swaying movement in it, which was not like anybody else. I need not say, however, that even had these indications been stronger, Woolwich and the Isle of Dogs were unlikely places in which to meet Lady Mariamne, or any gentleman likely to be in attendance on her. In Whitechapel, indeed, had he but known, he might have met Miss Dolly: but then in Whitechapel there were no sights which virtuous youth is led to see. And Philip's man with the opera-glass was, during these days, using that aid to vision in a very different place, and had neither leisure nor inclination to move vaguely about the world.

For three days this went on successfully enough: young Philip Compton and Ralph Marshall saw enough to last them all the rest of their lives, and there was no limit to the satisfaction of the good country clergyman, who felt that he never could have succeeded so completely in improving his son's mind, instead of delivering him over to the frivolous amusements of town, if it had not been for the companionship of Philip, who made Ralph feel that it was all right, and that he was not being victimised for nothing. But on the fourth day a hitch occurred. John Tatham had been made to give all sorts of orders and admissions for the party to see every nook and corner of the Temple, much to Elinor's alarm, who felt that place was too near to be safe; but she was herself in circumstances too urgent to permit her dwelling upon it. She had left the house on that particular morning long before Philip was ready, and every anxiety was dulled in her mind for the moment by the overwhelming sense of the crisis arrived. She went to his room before he had left it, and gave him a kiss, and told him that she might be detained for a long time; that she did know exactly at what hour she should return. She was very pale, paler than he had ever seen her, and her manner had a suppressed agitation in it which startled Philip; but she managed to smile as she assured him she was quite well, and that there was nothing troubling her. "Nothing, nothing that has to do with us—a little disturbed for a friend—but that will be all over," she said, "to-night, I hope." Philip made a leisurely breakfast after she was gone, and it happened to him that morning for the first time as he was alone to make a study of the papers. And the consequence was that he said to himself really those words which his mother in imagination had so often heard him say, "Hallo! Philip Compton, my name! I wonder if he is any relation. I wonder if we have anything to do with those St. Serf Comptons." Then he reflected, but vaguely, that he did not know to what Comptons he belonged, nor even what county he came from, to tell the truth. And then it was time to hurry over his breakfast, to swallow his cup of tea, to snatch up his hat and gloves, and to rush off to meet his friends. But on that day Philip was unlucky. When he got to the place of meeting he found nothing but a telegram from Ralph, announcing that his father was so knocked up with his previous exertions that they were obliged to take a quiet day. And thus Philip was left in the Temple, of all places in the world, on the day when his mother was to appear in the law-courts close by—on the day of all others when if she could have sent him for twenty-four hours to the end of the earth she would have done so—on the day when so terrible was the stress and strain upon herself that for once in the world even Pippo had gone as completely out of her mind as if he had not been.

The boy looked about him for awhile, and reflected what to do, and then he started out into the Strand, conscientiously waiting for the Marshalls before he should visit the Temple and all its historical ways; and then he was amused and excited by seeing a barrister or two in wig and gown pass by; and then he thought of the trial in the newspapers, in which somebody who, like himself, was called Philip Compton, was involved. Philip was still lingering, wondering if he could get into the court, a little shy of trying, but gradually growing eager, thinking at least that he would try and get a sight of the wonderful grand building, still so new, when he suddenly saw Simmons, his uncle John's clerk, passing through the quadrangle of the law-courts. Here was his chance. He rushed forward and caught the clerk by the arm, who was in a great hurry, as everybody seemed to be. "Oh, Simmons, can you get me into that Brown trial?" cried Philip. "Brown!" Simmons said. "Mr. Tatham is not on in that." "Oh, never mind about Mr. Tatham," said the boy. "Can't you get me in? I have never seen a trial, and I take an interest in that." "I advise you," said Simmons, "to wait for one that your uncle's in." "Can't you get me in?" said Philip, impatiently: and this touched the pride of Simmons, who had many friends, if not in high places, yet in low.

CHAPTER XLIV.

Philip had never been in a court of law before. I am almost as ignorant as he was, yet I cannot imagine anything more deeply interesting than to find one's self suddenly one of a crowded assembly trying more or less—for is not the public but a larger jury, sometimes contradicting the verdict of the other, and when it does so almost invariably winning the cause?—a fellow-creature, following out the traces of his crime or his innocence, looking on while a human drama is unrolled, often far more interesting than any dramatic representation of life. He was confused for the moment by the crowd, by the new and unusual spectacle, by the bewilderment of seeing for the first time what he had so often heard of, the judge on the bench, the wigged barristers below, the one who was speaking, so different from any other public speaker Philip had ever heard, addressing not the assembly, but the smaller circle round him, interrupted by other voices: the accused in his place and the witness—standing there more distinctly at the bar than the culprit was—bearing his testimony before earth and heaven, with the fate of another hanging on his words. The boy was so full of the novel sight—which yet he had heard of so often that he could identify every part of it, and soon perceived the scope of what was going on—that he did not at first listen, so full was he of the interest of what he saw. The imperturbable judge, grave, letting no emotion appear on his face; the jury, just the reverse, showing how this and that piece of evidence affected them; the barristers who were engaged, so keenly alive to everything, starting up now and then when the witness swerved from the subject, when the opposition proposed a leading question, or one that was irrelevant to the issue; the others who were not "in it," as Simmons said, so indifferent; and then the spectators who had places about or near the central interest. Philip saw, with a sudden leap of his heart, the ladies of the theatre and park, the witch and the girl with the keen eyes, in a conspicuous place; the old lady, as he called her, full of movement and gesture, making signs to others near her, keeping up an interrupted whispering, the girl at her side as impassive as the judge himself. And then Pippo's roving eye caught a figure seated among the barristers with an opera-glass, which made his heart jump still more. Was that the man? He had, at the moment Philip perceived him, his opera-glass in his hand: a tall man leaning back with a look of interest, very conspicuous among the wigged heads about him, with grey hair in a mass on his forehead as if it had grown thin and had been coaxed to cover some denuded place, and a face which it seemed to Philip he had seen before, a face worn—was it with study, was it with trouble? Pippo knew of no other ways in which the eyes could be so hollowed out, and the lines so deeply drawn. A man, perhaps, hard worn with life and labor and sorrow. A strange sympathy sprang up in the boy's mind: he was sure he knew the face. It was a face full of records, though young Philip could not read them— the face, he thought, of a man who had had much to bear. Was it the same man who had fixed so strange a gaze upon himself at the theatre? And what interest could this man have in the trial that was going on?

The accused at the bar was certainly not of a kind to arouse the interest which sprang into being at sight of this worn and noble hero. He had the air of a comfortable man of business, a man evidently well off, surprised at once and indignant to find himself there, sometimes bursting with eagerness to explain, sometimes leaning back with an air of affected contempt—not a good man in trouble, as Philip would have liked to think him, nor a criminal fully conscious of what might be awaiting him; but a man of the first respectability, indignant and incredulous that anything should be brought against him. Philip felt himself able to take no interest whatever in Mr. Brown.

It was not till he had gone through all these surprises and observations that he began to note what was being said. Philip was not learned in the procedure of the law, nor did he know anything about the case; but it became vaguely apparent to him after awhile that the immediate question concerned the destruction of the books of a joint-stock company, of which Brown was the manager, an important point which the prosecution had some difficulty in bringing home to him. After it had been proved that the books had been destroyed, and that so far as was known it was to Brown's interest alone to destroy them, the evidence as to what had been seen on the evening on which this took place suddenly took a new turn, and seemed to introduce a new actor on the scene. Some one had been seen to enter the office in the twilight who could not be identified with Brown; whom, indeed, even Philip, with his boyish interest in the novelty of the proceedings, vaguely perceived to be another man. The action of the piece, so to speak (for it was like a play to Philip), changed and wavered here—and he began to be sensible of the character of the different players in it. The counsel for the prosecution was a well-known and eminent barrister, one of the most noted of the time, a man before whom witnesses trembled, and even the Bench itself was sometimes known to quail. That this was the case on the present occasion Philip vaguely perceived. There were points continually arising which the opposing counsel made objections to, appealing to the judge; but it rarely failed that the stronger side, which was that of the prosecution, won the day. The imperious accuser, whose resources of precedent and argument seemed boundless, carried everything with a high hand. The boy, of course, was not aware of the weakness of the representative of the majesty of the law, nor the inferiority, in force and skill, of the defence; but he gradually came to a practical perception of how the matter stood.

Philip listened with growing interest, sometimes amused, sometimes indignant, as the remorseless prosecutor ploughed his way through the witnesses, whom he bullied into admissions that they were certain of nothing, and that in the dusk of that far-off evening, the man whom they had sworn at the time to be quite unlike him, might in reality have been Brown. Philip got greatly interested in this question. He took up the opposite side himself with much heat, feeling as sure as if he had been there that it was not Brown: and he was delighted in his excitement, when there stood up one man who would not be bullied, a man who had the air of a respectable clerk of the lower class, and who held his own. He had been an office boy, the son apparently of the housekeeper in charge of the premises referred to when the incident occurred, and the gist of his evidence was that the prisoner at the bar—so awful a personage once to the little office boy, so curtly discussed now as Brown—had left the office at four o'clock in the afternoon of the 6th of September, and had not appeared again.

"A different gentleman altogether came in the evening, a much taller man, with a large moustache."

"Where was it that you saw this man?"

"Slipping in at the side door of the office as if he didn't want to be seen."

"Was that a door which was generally open, or used by the public?"

"Never, sir; but none of the doors were used at that time of night."

"And how, then, could any one get admittance there?"

"Only those that had private keys; the directors had their private keys."

"Then your conclusion was that it was a director, and that he had a right to be there?"

"I knew it was a director, sir, because I knew the gentleman," the witness said.

"You say it was late in the evening of the 6th of September. Was it daylight at the time?"

"Oh, no, sir; nearly dark—a sort of a half light."

"Did the person you saw go in openly, or make any attempt at concealment?"

"He had a light coat on, like the coats gentlemen wear when they go to the theatre, and something muffled round his throat, and his hat pulled down over his face."

"Like a person who wished to conceal himself?"

"Yes, sir," said the witness.

"And how, then, if he was muffled about the throat, and his hat pulled over his face, in the half light late in the evening, could you see that he had a large moustache?"

The witness stood and stared with his mouth open, and made no reply.

The counsel, with a louder voice and those intonations of contemptuous insinuation which are calculated to make a man feel that he is convicted of the basest perjury, and is being held up to the reprobation of the world, repeated the question, "How could you see that he had a large moustache?"

"I saw it," said the witness, hotly, "because I knew the gentleman."

"And how did you know the gentleman? You thought you recognised the gentleman, and therefore, though you could not possibly perceive it, you saw his moustache? I fear that is not an answer that will satisfy the jury."

"I submit," said the counsel for the defence, "that it is very evident what the witness means. He recognised a man with whose appearance he was perfectly familiar."

"I saw him," said the witness, "as clear as I see you, sir."

"What! in the dark, late on a September night, with a coat collar up to his ears, and a hat pulled down over his face! You see my learned friend in broad daylight, and with the full advantage of standing opposite to him and studying his looks at your leisure. You might as well say because you know the gentleman that you could see his half was dark and abundant under his wig."

At this a laugh ran through the court, at which Philip, listening, was furiously indignant, as it interrupted the course

426

of the investigation. It was through the sound of this laugh that he heard the witness demand loudly, "How could I be mistaken, when I saw Mr. Compton every day?"

Mr. Compton! Philip's heart began to beat like the hammers of a steam-engine. Was this, then, the real issue? And who was Mr. Compton? He could not have told how it was that he somehow identified the man whom the witness had seen, or had not seen, with the man who had the opera-glass, and who had fixed a dreadful blank stare upon the other in the witness-box during a great part of this discussion. Was it he who was on his trial, and not Brown? And who was he? And where was it that Philip had known and grown familiar with that face, which, so far as he could remember, he had never seen before, but which belonged to the man who bore his own name?

When the counsel for the prosecution had turned the unfortunate witness outside in, and proved that he knew nothing and had seen nobody: and that, besides, he was a man totally unworthy of credit, who had lied from his cradle, and whose own mother and friends put no trust in him, the court adjourned for lunch. But Philip forgot that he required any lunch. His mind was filled with echoes of that name. He began to feel a strange certainty that it was the same man who had fixed him with the same gaze in the theatre. Who was Mr. Compton, and what was he? The question took the boy's breath away.

He sat through the interval, finding a place where he could see better, through the kind offices of the usher to whom Simmons had commended him, and waiting with impatience till the trial should be resumed. Nobody remarked the boy among the crowd of the ordinary public, many of whom remained, as he did, to see it out, Philip cared nothing about Brown: all that he wanted to know was about this namesake of his—this Compton, this other man, who was not Brown. If it was the man with the opera-glass, he was not so much excited as his young namesake, for he went to luncheon with the rest; while the boy remained counting the minutes, eager to begin the story, the drama, again. The impression left, however, on Philip's impartial mind was that the last witness, though driven and badgered out of what wits he had by the examination, had really seen a man whom he perfectly knew, his recognition of whom was not really affected either by the twilight or the disguise.

The thrill of interest which he felt running through all his veins as the court filled again was like, but stronger than, the interest with which he had ever seen the curtain rise in the theatre. His heart beat: he felt as if in some sort it was his own fate that was going to be decided: all his prepossessions were in favour of that other accused, yet not openly accused, person who was not Brown; and yet he felt almost as sure as if he had been there that the office boy of twenty years ago had seen that man stealing in at the side door.

Young Philip did not catch the name of the next witness who was called; such a thing will happen sometimes even with the quickest ear at a moment when every whisper is important. If he had heard he would probably have thought that he was deceived by his excitement, impossible as it was that such a name should have anything to do with this or any other trial. The shock therefore was unbroken when, watching with all the absorbed interest of a spectator at the most exciting play, the boy saw a lady come slowly forward into the witness-box. Philip had the same strange sense of knowing who it was that he had felt the previous witness to have in respect to the man whom he could not see, but yet had infallibly recognised: but he said to himself, No! it was not possible! No! it was not possible! She came forward slowly, put up the veil that had covered her face, and grasped the bar before her to support herself; and then the boy sprang to his feet, in the terrible shock which electrified him from head to feet! His movements, and the stifled cry he uttered, made a little commotion in the crowd, and called forth the cry of "Silence in the court." His neighbours around him hustled him back into his place, where he sank down incapable indeed of movement, knowing that he could not go and pluck her from that place—

could not rush to her side, could do nothing but sit there and gasp and gaze at his mother. His mother, in such a place! in such a case! with which—surely, surely—she could have nothing to do. Elinor Compton, at the time referred to Elinor Dennistoun, of Windyhill, in Surrey—there was no doubt about the name now. And Philip had time enough to identify everything, name and person, for there rose a vague surging of contention about the first questions put to her, which were not evidence, according to the counsel on the other side, which he felt with fury was done on purpose to prolong the agony. During this time she stood immovable, holding on by the rail before her, her eyes fixed upon it, perfectly pale, like marble, and as still. Among all the moving, rustling, palpitating crowd, and the sharp volleys of the lawyers' voices, and even the contradictory opinions elicited from the harassed judge himself—to look at that figure standing there, which scarcely seemed to breathe, had the most extraordinary effect. For a time Philip was like her, scarcely breathing, holding on in an unconscious sympathy to the back of the seat before him, his eyes wide open, fixed upon her. But as his nerves began to accustom themselves to that extraordinary, inconceivable sight, the other particulars of the scene came out of the mist, and grew apparent to him in a lurid light that did not seem the light of day. He saw the eager looks at her of the ladies in the privileged places, the whispers that were exchanged among them. He saw underneath the witness-box, almost within reach of her, John Tatham, with an anxious look on his face. And then he saw, what was the most extraordinary of all, the man—who had been the centre of his interest till now—the man whose name was Philip Compton, like his own; he who fixed the last witness with the stare of his opera-glass, who had kept it in perpetual use. He had put it down now on the table before him, his arms were folded on his breast, and his head bent. Philip thought he detected now and then a furtive look under his brows at the motionless witness awaiting through the storm of words the moment when her turn would come; but though he had leant forward all the time, following every point of the proceedings with interest, he now drew back, effaced himself, retired as it were from the scene. What was there between these two? Was there any link between them? What was the drama about to be played out before Pippo's innocent and ignorant eyes? At last the storm and wrangling seemed to come to an end, and there came out low but clear the sound of her voice. It seemed only now, when he heard his mother speak, that he was certified that so inconceivable a thing as that she should be here was a matter of fact: his mother here! Philip fixed his whole being upon her—eyes, thoughts, absorbed attention, he scarcely seemed to breathe except through her. Could she see him, he wondered, through all that crowd? But then he perceived that she saw nothing with those eyes that looked steadily in front of her, not turning a glance either to the right or left.

For some time Philip was baffled completely by the questions put, which were those to which the counsel on the other side objected as not evidence, and which seemed, even to the boy's inexperienced mind, to be mere play upon the subject, attempts to connect her in some way with the question as to Brown's guilt or innocence. Something in the appearance, at this stage, of a lady so unlike the other witnesses, seemed to exercise a certain strange effect, however, quickening everybody's interest, and when the examining counsel approached the question of the date which had already been shown to be so momentous, all interruptions were silenced, and the court in general, like Philip, held its breath. There were many there expecting what are called in the newspapers "revelations:" the defence was taken by surprise, and did not know what new piece of evidence was about to be produced: and even the examining counsel was, for such a man, subdued a little by the other complicating threads of the web among which he had to pick his way.

"You recollect," he said in his most soothing tones; "the evening of the 6th September, 1863?"

She bowed her head in reply. And then as if that was sparing herself too much, added a low "Yes."

"As I am instructed, you were not then married, but engaged to Mr. Philip Compton. Is that so?"

"Yes."

"One of the directors of the company of which the defendant was manager?"

"I believe so."

"I am sorry to have to enter upon matters so private: but there was some question, I believe, about an investment to be made of a portion of your fortune in the hands of this company?"

"Yes."

"You received a visit from Mr. Compton on the subject on the day I have mentioned."

The witness made a slight movement and pause: then answered as before, but more firmly, "Yes:" she added, "not on this subject," in a lower tone.

"You can recollect, more or less exactly, the time of his arrival?"

"Yes. It was in the evening, after dinner; in the darkening before the lamps were lit."

"Were you looking for him on that night?"

"No; it was an unexpected visit. He was going to Ireland, and paused on his way through town to come down to Windyhill."

"You have particular reasons for remembering the date, which make it impossible that there could be any mistake?"

"No; there could be no mistake."

"You will perhaps inform the court, Mrs. Compton, why your memory is so exact on this point."

Once more she hesitated for a moment, and then replied—

"It was exactly ten days before my marriage."

"I think that will do, Mrs. Compton. I will trouble you no further," the counsel said.

The hubbub which sprang up upon this seemed to Philip for the moment as if it were directed against his mother, which, of course, was not the case, but intended to express the indignant surprise of the defence at the elaborate examination of a witness

431

who had nothing to say on the main subject.

The leader on the other side, however, though taken by surprise, and denouncing the trick which his learned brother had played upon the court by producing evidence which had really nothing to do with the matter, announced his intention to put a further question or two to Mrs. Compton. Young Philip in the crowd started again from his seat with the feeling that he would like to fly at that man's throat.

"Twenty years is a long time," he said, "and it is difficult to be sure of any circumstance at such a distance. Perhaps the witness will kindly inform us what were the circumstances which fixed this, no doubt one of many visits, on her mind?"

Elinor turned for the first time to the side from which the question came with a little movement of that impatience which was habitual to her, which three persons in that crowd recognised in a moment as characteristic. One of these was John Tatham, who had brought her to the court, and kept near that she might feel that she was not alone; the other was her son, of whose presence there nobody knew; the third, sat with his eyes cast down, and his arms folded on his breast, not looking at her, yet seeing every movement she made.

"It was a very simple circumstance," she said with the added spirit of that impetuous impulse: but then the hasty movement failed her, and she came back to herself and to a consciousness of the scene in which she stood. A sort of tremulous shiver came into her voice. She paused and then resumed, "There was a calendar hanging in the hall; it caught Mr. Compton's eye, and he pointed it out to me. It marked the 6th. He said, 'Just ten days——'"

Here her voice stopped altogether. She could say no more. And there was an answering pause throughout the whole crowded court, a holding of the general breath, the response to a note of passion seldom struck in such a place. Even in the cross-examination there was a pause.

"Till when? What was the other date referred to?"

"The sixteenth of September," she said in a voice that was

scarcely audible to the crowd. She added still more low so that the judge curved his hand over his ear to hear her, "Our wedding-day."

"I regret to enter into private matters, Mrs. Compton, but I believe it is not a secret that your married life came to a—more rapid conclusion than could have been augured from such a beginning. May I ask what your reasons were for——"

But here the other counsel sprang to his feet, and the contention arose again. Such a question was not clearly permissible. And the prosecution was perfectly satisfied with the evidence. It narrowed the question by the production of this clear and unquestionable testimony—the gentleman whom it had been attempted to involve being thus placed out of the question, and all the statements of the previous witness about the moustache which he could not see, etc., set aside.

Philip, it may be supposed, paid little attention to this further discussion. His eyes and thoughts were fixed upon his mother, who for a minute or two stood motionless through it, as pale as ever, but with her head a little thrown back, facing, though not looking at, the circling lines of faces. Had she seen anything she must have seen the tall boy standing up as pale as she, following her movements with an unconscious repetition which was more than sympathy, never taking his gaze from her face.

And then presently her place was empty, and she was gone.

Philip was not aware how the discussion of the lawyers ended, but only that in a moment there was vacancy where his mother had been standing, and his gaze seemed thrown back to him by the blank where she had been. He was left in the midst of the crowd, which, after that one keen sensation, fell back upon the real trial with interest much less keen.

CHAPTER XLV.

Philip did not know how long he remained, almost paralysed, in the court, dazed in his mind, incapable of movement. He was in the centre of a long row of people, and to make his way out was difficult. He felt that the noise would call attention to him, and that he might be somehow identified—identified, as what? He did not know—his head was not clear enough to give any reason. When he came more to himself, and his eyes regained a little their power of vision, it seemed to him that everybody had stolen away. There was the judge, indeed, still sitting imperturbable, the jury restless in their box, the lawyers going on with their eternal quarrel over a bewildered witness, all puppets carrying on some unintelligible, wearisome, automaton process, contending, contending for ever about nothing. But all that had secured Philip's attention was gone. John Tatham's head was no longer visible under the witness-box; the ladies had disappeared from their elevated seats; the man with the opera-glass was gone. They were all gone, and the empty husks of a question which only concerned the comfort and life of the commonplace culprit in the dock were being turned over and over like chaff by the wind. And yet it was some time before poor young Pippo, shy of attracting attention, feeling some subtle change even in himself which he did not understand, afraid to have people look at him and divine him, knowing more of him perhaps than he himself knew, could make up his mind to move. He might have remained there till the court broke up but for the movement of some one beside him, who gathered up his hat and umbrella, and with some commotion pushed his way between the rows of seats. Philip followed, thankful of the opportunity, and, as it happened, the sensation of the day being over, many others followed too, and thus he got out into the curious, wondering daylight, which seemed to look him in the face, as if this Philip had never been seen by it before. That was the impression given him—that when he first came out the atmosphere quivered round him with a strange novelty, as if he were some other being, some one without a name, new to the world, new to himself. He did not seem sure that he would know his way home, and yet he did not call a passing hansom, as he would have done yesterday, with a schoolboy's pleasure in assuming a man's careless, easy ways. It is a long way from the Law Courts to Ebury Street, but it seemed a kind of satisfaction to be in motion, to walk on along the crowded streets. And, as a matter of fact, Philip did lose his way, and got himself entangled in a web of narrow streets and monotonous little openings, all so like each other that it took him a long time to extricate himself and find again the thread of a locality known to him. He did not know what he was to do when he got in. Should he find her there, in the little dingy drawing-room as usual, with the tea on the table? Would she receive him with her usual smile, and ask where he had been and what he had seen, and if the Musgraves had enjoyed it, exactly as if nothing had happened? Even this wonder was faint in Philip's mind, for the chief wonder to him was himself, and to find out how he had changed since the morning—what he was now, who he was? what were the relations to him of other people, of that other Philip Compton who had been seated in the court with the opera-glass, who had arrived at Windyhill to visit Elinor Dennistoun on the 6th of September, 1863, twenty years ago? Who was that man? and what was he, himself Philip Compton, of Lakeside, named Pippo, whom his mother had never once in all his life called by his real name?

To his great wonder, and yet almost relief, Philip found that his mother had not yet returned when he got to Ebury Street. "Mrs. Compton said as she would very likely be late. Can I get you some tea, sir? or, perhaps you haven't had your lunch? you're looking tired and worrited," said the landlady, who had known Pippo all his life. He consented to have tea, partly to fill up the time, and went up languidly to the deserted room, which looked so miserable and desert a place without her who put a soul into it and made it home. He did not know what to do with himself, poor boy, but sat down vacantly, and stared into empty space, seeing, wherever he turned, the rows of faces, the ladies making signs to each other, the red robes of the judge, the lawyers contending, and that motionless pale figure in the witness-box. He shut his eyes and saw the whole scene, then opened them again, and still saw it—the dingy walls disappearing, the greyness of the afternoon giving a depth and distance to the limited space. Should he always carry it about with him wherever he went, the vision of that court, the shock of that revelation? And yet he did not yet know what the revelation was; the confusion in his mind was too great, and the dust and mist that rose up about him as all the old building of his life crumbled and fell away.

"I'm sure as it's that nasty trial, sir, as has been turning your mamma all out of her usual ways," said the landlady, appearing with her tray.

"Oh, the trial! Did you know about the trial?" said Philip.

"Not, Mr. Pippo, as ever she mentioned it to me. Mrs. Compton is a lady as isn't that confidential, though always an affable lady, and not a bit proud; but when you've known folks for years and years, and take an interest, and put this and that together—— Dear, dear, I hope as you don't think it's taking a liberty. It's more kindness nor curiosity, and I hope as you won't mention it to your mamma."

Pippo shook his head and waved his hand, at once to satisfy the woman and dismiss her if possible; but this was not so easy to do.

"And Lord St. Serf so bad, sir," she said. "Lord, to think that before we know where we are there may be such changes, and new names, and no knowing what to say! But it's best not to talk of it till it comes to pass, for there's many a slip between the cup and the lip, and there's no saying what will happen with a man that's been a-dying for years and years."

What did the woman mean? He got rid of her at length, chiefly by dint of making no reply: and then, to tell the truth, Pippo's eye had been caught by the pile of sandwiches which the kind woman, pitying his tired looks, had brought up with the tea. He was ashamed of himself for being hungry in such a dreadful emergency as this, but he was so, and could not help it, though nothing would have made him confess so much, or even touch the sandwiches till she had gone away. He pretended to ignore them till the door was shut after her, but could not help vividly remembering that he had eaten nothing since the morning. The sandwiches did him a little good in his mind as well as in his body. He got rid of the vision of the faces and of the red figure on the bench. He began to believe that when he saw her she would tell him. Had she not said so? That after awhile he should hear everything, and that all should be as it was before? All as it was before—in the time when she told him everything, even things that Granny did not know. But she had never told him this, and the other day she had told him that it was other people's secrets, not her own, that she was keeping from him. "Other people's secrets"—the secrets of the man who was Philip Compton, who went to Windyhill on the 6th of September, ten days before Elinor Dennistoun's marriage day. "What Philip Compton? Who was he? What had he to do with her? What, oh, what," Pippo said to himself, "has he to do with me?" After all, that was the most tremendous question. The others, or anything that had happened twenty years ago, were nothing to that.

Meanwhile Elinor, of all places in the world, was in John Tatham's chambers, to which he had taken her to rest. I cannot tell how Mr. Tatham, a man so much occupied, managed to subtract from all he had to do almost a whole day to see his cousin through the trial, and stand by her, sparing her all the lesser annoyances which surround and exaggerate such a great fact. He had brought her out into the fresh air, feeling that movement was the best thing for her, and instead of taking her home in the carriage which was waiting, had made her walk with him, supported on his arm, on which she hung in a sort of suspended life, across the street to the Temple, hoping thus to bring her back, by the necessity of exertion, to herself. And indeed she was almost more restored to herself by this remedy than John Tatham had expected or hoped. For though he placed her in the great easy-chair, in which her slender person was engulfed and supported, expecting her to rest there and lie motionless, perhaps even to faint, as women are supposed to do when it is particularly inconvenient and uncomfortable, Elinor had not been there two minutes before she rose up again and began to walk about the room, with an aspect so unlike that of an exhausted and perhaps fainting woman, that even John, used as he was to her capricious ways, was confounded. Instead of being subdued and thankful that it was over, and this dreadful crisis in her life accomplished, Elinor walked up and down, wringing her hands, moaning and murmuring to herself; what was it she was saying? "God forgive me! God forgive me!" over and over and over, unconscious apparently that she was not alone, that any one heard or observed her. No doubt there is in all our actions, the very best, much for God to forgive; mingled motives, imperfect deeds, thoughts full of alloy and selfishness; but in what her conscience could accuse her now he could not understand. She might be to blame in respect to her husband, though he was very loth to allow the possibility; but in this act of her life, which had been so great a strain upon her, it was surely without any selfishness, for his interest only, not for her own. And yet John had never seen such a fervour of penitence, so strong a consciousness of evil done. He went up to her and laid his hand upon her arm.

"Elinor, you are worn out. You have done too much. Will you try and rest a little here, or shall I take you home?"

She started violently when he touched her. "What was I saying?" she said.

"It does not matter what you were saying. Sit down and rest. You will wear yourself out. Don't think any more. Take this and rest a little, and then I will take you home."

"It is easy to say so," she said, with a faint smile. "Don't think! Is it possible to stop thinking at one's pleasure?"

"Yes," said John, "quite possible; we must all do it or we should die. And now your trial's over, Nelly, for goodness' sake exert yourself and throw it off. You have done your duty."

"My duty! do you think that was my duty? Oh, John, there are so many ways to look at it."

"Only one way, when you have a man's safety in your hands."

"Only one way—when one has a man's safety—his honour, honour! Do you think a woman is justified in whatever she does, to save that?"

"I don't understand you, Elinor; in anything you have done, or could do, certainly you are justified. My dear Nelly, sit down and take this. And then I will take you home."

She took the wine from his hand and swallowed a little of it; and then looking up into his face with the faint smile which she put on when she expected to be blamed, and intended to deprecate and disarm him, as she had done so often: "I don't know," she said, "that I am so anxious to get home, John. You were to take Pippo to dine with you, and to the House to-night."

"So I was," he said. "We did not know what day you would be called. It is a great nuisance, but if you think the boy would be disappointed not to go——"

"He would be much, much disappointed. The first chance he has had of hearing a debate."

"He would be much better at home, taking care of you."

"As if I wanted taking care of! or as if the boy, who has always been the object of everybody's care himself, would be the proper person to do it! If he had been a girl, perhaps—but it is a little late at this time of day to wish for that now."

"You were to tell him everything to-night, Elinor."

"Oh, I was to tell him! Do you think I have not had enough for one day? enough to wear me out body and soul? You have just been telling me so, John."

He shook his head. "You know," he said, "and I know, that in any case you will have it your own way, Elinor; but you have promised to tell him."

"John, you are unkind. You take advantage of me being here, and so broken down, to say that I will have my own way. Has this been my own way at all? I would have fled if I could, and taken the boy far, far away from it all; but you would not let me. Yes, yes, I have promised. But I am tired to death. How could I look him in the face and tell him——" She hid her face suddenly in her hands with a moan.

"It will be in the papers to-morrow morning, Elinor."

"Well! I will tell him to-morrow morning," she said.

John shook his head again; but it was done behind her, where she could not see the movement. He had more pity of her than words could say. When she covered her face with her hands in that most pathetic of attitudes, there was nothing that he would not have forgiven her. What was to become of her now? Her position through all these years had never been so dangerous, in John's opinion, never so sad, as now. Philip Compton had been there looking on while she put his accusers to silence, at what cost to herself John only began dimly to guess—to divine, to forbid himself to inquire. The fellow had been there all the time. He had the grace not to look at her, not to distract her with the sight of him—probably for his own sake, John thought bitterly, that she might not risk breaking down. But he was there, and knew where she was to be found. And he had seen the boy, and had cared enough to fix his gaze upon him, that gaze which John had found intolerable at the theatre. And he was on the eve of becoming Lord St. Serf, and Pippo his heir. What was to be the issue of these complications? What was to happen to her who had hid the boy so long, who certainly could hide him no more?

He took her home to Ebury Street shortly after, where Philip, weary of waiting, and having made a meal he much wanted off the sandwiches, had gone out again in his restlessness and unhappiness. Elinor, who had become paler and paler as the carriage approached Ebury Street, and who by the time she reached the house looked really as if at last she must swoon, her heart choking her, her breathing quick and feverish, had taken hold of John to support herself, clutching at his arm, when she was told that Philip was out. She came to herself instantly on the strength of that news. "Tell him when he comes in to make haste," she said, "for Mr. Tatham is waiting for him. As for me I am fit for nothing but bed. I have had a very tiring day."

"You do look tired, ma'am," said the sympathetic landlady. "I'll run up and put your room ready, and then I'll make you a nice cup of tea."

John Tatham thought that, notwithstanding her exhaustion, her anxiety, all the realities of troubles present and to come that were in her mind and in her way, there was a flash something like triumph in Elinor's eyes. "Tell Pippo," she said, "he can come up and say good-night to me before he goes. I am good for nothing but my bed. If I can sleep I shall be able for all that is before me to-morrow." The triumph was quenched, however, if there had been triumph, when she gave him her hand, with a wistful smile, and a sigh that filled that to-morrow with the terror and the trouble that must be in it, did she do what she said. John went up to the little drawing-room to wait for Pippo, with a heavy heart. It seemed to him that never had Elinor been in so much danger. She had exposed herself to the chance of losing the allegiance of her son: she was at the mercy of her husband, that husband whom she had renounced, yet whom she had not refused to save, whose call she had obeyed to help him, though she had thrown off all the bonds of love and duty towards him. She had not had the strength either way to be consistent, to carry out one steady policy. It was cruel of John to say this, for but for him and his remonstrances Elinor would, or might have, fled, and avoided this last ordeal. But he had not done so, and now here she was in the middle of her life, her frail ship of safety driven about among

441

the rocks, dependent upon the magnanimity of the husband from whom she had fled, and the child whom she had deceived.

"Your mother is very tired, Philip," he said, when the boy appeared. "I was to tell you to go up and bid her good-night before you went out; for it will probably be late before you get back, if you think you are game to sit out the debate."

"I will sit it out," said Philip, with no laughter in his eye, with an almost solemn air, as if announcing a grave resolution. He went up-stairs, not three steps at a time, as was his wont, but soberly, as if his years had been forty instead of eighteen. And he showed no surprise to find the room darkened, though Elinor was a woman who loved the light. He gave his mother a kiss and smoothed her pillow with a tender touch of pity. "Is your head very bad?" he said.

"It is only that I am dreadfully tired, Pippo. I hope I shall sleep: and it will help me to think you are happy with Uncle John."

"Then I shall try to be happy with Uncle John," he said, with a sort of smile. "Good-night, mother; I hope you'll be better to-morrow."

"Oh, yes," she said. "To-morrow is always a new day."

He seemed in the half light to nod his head, and then to shake it, as one that assents, but doubts—having many troubled thoughts and questions in his mind. But Pippo did not at all expect to be happy with Uncle John.

CHAPTER XLVI.

It cannot be said that Uncle John was very happy with Philip, but that was a thing the others did not take into account. John Tatham was doing for the boy as much as a man could do. A great debate was expected that evening, in which many eminent persons were to speak, and Mr. Tatham gave Philip a hasty dinner in the House so that he should lose nothing, and he found him a corner in the distinguished strangers' gallery, telling him with a smile that he expected him hereafter to prove his title to such a place. But Philip's smile in return was very unlike the flush of pleasure that would have lighted it up only yesterday. John felt that the boy was not at all the delightful young companion, full of interest in everything, that he had been. Perhaps he was on his good behaviour, on his dignity, bent upon showing how much of a man he was and how little influenced by passing sentiments, as some boys do. Anyhow it was certain that he was much less agreeable in his self-subdued condition. But John was fortunately much interested in the discussion, in which, indeed, he took himself a slight part, and, save for a passing wonder and the disappointment of the moment, did not occupy himself so very much with Pippo. When he looked into the corner, however, in a lull of the debate, when one of those fools who rush in at unguarded moments, when the Speaker chances to look their way, had managed to get upon his foolish feet to the despair of all around, the experienced man of the world received a curious shock from the sight of young Philip's intense gravity, and the self-absorbed, unconscious look he wore. The boy had the look of hearing nothing, seeing nothing that was around him, of being lost in thoughts of his own, thoughts far too serious and troubled

443

for his age. Had he discovered something? What did he know? This was the instinctive question that rose in John's mind, and not an amused anticipation of Pippo's original boyish view of the question and the speakers, such as had delighted him on the boy's previous visits to the House. And indeed Philip's attention was little fixed upon the debate. He tried hard to bring it back, to keep it there, to get the question into his mind, but in spite of himself his thoughts flew back to the other public assembly in which he had sat unnoticed that day: till gradually the aspect of things changed to him, the Speaker became the judge, the wigged secretaries the pleaders, and he almost expected to see that sudden apparition, that sight that had plucked him out of his careless life of boyhood and trust, the sight of his mother standing before the world on trial for her life. Oh, no, no, not on trial at all! he was aware of that: a harmless witness, doing only good. The judge could have nothing but polite regard for her, the jury admiration and thanks for the clear testimony which took a weight from their shoulders. But before her son she was on her trial, her trial for more than life—and he who said with so much assurance that his mother had no secrets from him! until the moment arrived, without any warning, in the midst of his security, which proved that everything had been secret, and that all was mystery—all mystery! and nothing sure in life.

It crossed Philip's mind more than once to question John Tatham upon this dreadful discovery of his—John, who was a relation, who had been the universal referee of the household as long as he could remember, Uncle John must know. But there were two things which held him back: first, the recollection of his own disdainful offence at the suggestion that Uncle John, an outsider, could know more than he did of the family concerns; and partly from the proud determination to ask no questions, to seek no information that was not freely given to him. He made up his mind to this while he looked out from his corner upon the lighted House, seeing men move up and down, and voices going on, and the sound of restless members coming and going, while the business of the country went on. It was far more important than any private affairs that could be passing in an individual brain, and Philip knew with what high-handed certainty he would have put down the idea that to himself at his age there could be anything private half so exciting, half so full of interest, as a debate on the policy of the country which might carry with it the highest issues. But conviction comes readily on such subjects when the personal interest comes which carries every other away. It was while a minister was speaking, and everything hanging on his words, that the boy made up his mind finally that he would ask no questions. He would ignore that scene in the Law Courts, as if it had not been. He would say nothing, try to look as if nothing had passed, and wait to see if any explanation would come.

It was not, perhaps, then to be wondered at if John found him a much less interesting companion than ever before, as they walked home together in the small hours of the night. Mr. Tatham's own speech had been short, but he had the agreeable consciousness that it had been an effective one, and he was prepared to find the boy excited by it, and full of applause and satisfaction. But Philip did not say a word about the speech. He was only a boy, and it may be supposed that any applause from him would have had little importance for the famous lawyer— the highly-esteemed member who kept his independence, and whose speeches always secured the attention of the House, and carried weight as among the few utterances which concerned the real import of a question and not its mere party meaning. But John was hurt more than he could have thought possible by Philip's silence. He even tried to lead the conversation artfully to that point in the debate, thinking perhaps the boy was shy of speaking on the subject—but with no effect. It was exceedingly strange. Had he been deceived in Philip? had the boy really no interest in subjects of an elevated description? or was he ill? or what was the matter with him? It troubled John to let him go on alone from Halkin Street to his lodging, with a vague sense that something might happen. But that was, of course, too absurd. "Tell your mother I'll come round in the afternoon to-morrow, as soon as I am free," he said, holding Philip's hand. And then he added, paternally, still holding that hand, "Go to bed at once, boy. You've had a tiring day."

"Yes—I suppose so," said Philip, drawing his hand away.

"I hope you haven't done too much," said John, still lingering. "You're too young for politics—and to sit up so late. I was wrong to keep you out of bed."

"I hope I'm not such a child as that," said Philip, with a half-smile: and then he went away, and John Tatham, with an anxious heart, closed behind him his own door. If it were not for Elinor and her boy what a life free of anxiety John would have had! Never any need to think with solicitude of anything outside that peaceful door, no trouble with other people's feelings, with investigations what this or that look or word meant. But perhaps it was Elinor and her boy, after all (none of his! thinking of him as an outsider, having nothing to do with their most intimate circle of confidence and natural defence), who, by means of that very anxiety, kept alive the higher principles of humanity in John Tatham's heart.

Philip went home, walking quickly through the silent streets. They were very silent at that advanced hour, yet not so completely but that there was a woman who came up to the boy at the corner. Philip neither knew nor desired to know what she said. He thought nothing about her one way or another. He took a shilling out of his pocket and threw it to her as he passed—walking on with the quick, elastic step which the sudden acquaintance he had made with care had not been able to subdue. He saw that there was still a faint light in his mother's window when he reached the house, but he would not disturb her. How little would he have thought of disturbing her on any other occasion! "Are you asleep, mother?" he would have said, looking in; and the time had never been when Elinor was asleep. She had always heard him, always replied, always been delighted to hear the account of what he had been doing, and how he had enjoyed himself. But not to-night. With a heart full of longing, yet of a sick revolt against the sight of her, he went past her door to his room. He did not want to see her, and yet—oh, if she had only called to him, if she had but said a word!

Elinor for her part was not asleep. She had slept a little while she was sure that Philip was safely disposed of and herself secured from all interruption; but when the time came for his return she slept no longer, and had been lying for a long time holding her breath, listening to every sound, when she heard his key in the latch and his foot on the stair. Would he come in as he always did? or would he remember her complaint of being tired, a complaint she so seldom made? It was as a blow to Elinor when she heard his step go on past her door: and yet she was glad. Had he come in there was a desperate thought in her mind that she would call him to her bedside and in the dark, with his hand in hers, tell him—all that there was to tell. But it was again a relief when he passed on, and she felt that she was spared for an hour or two, spared for the new day, which perhaps would give her courage. It was an endless night, long hours of dark, and then longer hours of morning light, too early for anything, while still nobody in the house was stirring. She had scarcely slept at all during that long age of weary and terrible thought. For it was not as if she had but one thing to think of. When her mind turned, like her restless body, from one side to another, it was only to a change of pain. What was it she had said, standing up before earth and heaven, and calling God to witness that what she said was true? It had been true, and yet she knew that it was not, and that she had saved her husband's honour at the cost of her own. Oh, not in those serious and awful watches of the night can such a defence be accepted as that the letter of her testimony was true! She did not attempt to defend herself. She only tried to turn to another thought that might be less bitter: and then she was confronted by the confession that she must make to her boy. She must tell him that she had deceived him all his life, hid from him what he ought to have known, separated him from his father and his family, kept him in ignorance, despite all that had been said to her, despite every argument. And when Elinor in her misery fled from that thought, what was there else to think of? There was her husband, Pippo's father, from whom he could no longer be kept. If she had thought herself justified in stealing her child away out of fear of the influence that father might have upon him, how would it be now when they must be restored to each other, at an age much more dangerous for the boy than in childhood, and with all the attractions of mystery and novelty and the sense that his father had been wronged! When she escaped from that, the most terrible thought of all, feeling her brain whirl and her heart burn as she imagined her child turning from the mother who had deceived him to the father who had been deprived of him, her mind went off to that father himself, from whom she had fled, whom she had judged and condemned, but who had repaid her by no persecution, no interference, no pursuit, but an acceptance of her verdict, never molesting her, leaving her safe in the possession of her boy. Perhaps there were other ways in which Phil Compton's magnanimity have been looked at, in which it would have shown in less favourable colours. But Elinor was not ready to take that view. Her tower of justice and truth and honour had crumbled over her head. She was standing among her ruins, feeling that nothing was left to her, nothing upon which she could build herself a structure of self-defence. All was wrong; a series of mistakes and failures, to say no worse. She had driven on ever wilful all through, escaping from every pang she could avoid, throwing off every yoke that she did not choose to bear: until now here she stood to face all that she had fled from, unable to elude them more, meeting them as so many ghosts in her way. Oh, how true it was what John had said to her so long, so long ago—that she was not one who would bear, who if she were disappointed and wronged could endure and surmount her trouble by patience! Oh, no, no! She had been one who had put up with nothing, who had taken her own way.

And now she was surrounded on every side by the difficulties she had thrust away from her, but which now could be thrust away no more.

It may be imagined what the night was which Elinor spent sleepless, struggling one after another with these thoughts, finding no comfort anywhere wherever she turned. She had not been without many a struggle even in the most quiet of the years that had passed—in one long dream of peace as it seemed now; but never as now had she been met wherever she turned by another and another lion in the way. She got up very early, with a feeling that movement had something lulling and soothing in it, and that to lie there a prey to all these thoughts was like lying on the rack—to the great surprise of the kind landlady, who came stealing into her room with the inevitable cup of tea, and whose inquiry how the poor lady was, was taken out of her mouth by the unexpected apparition of the supposed invalid, fully dressed, moving about the room, with all the air of having been up for hours. Elinor asked, with a sudden precaution, that the newspapers might be brought up to her, not so much for her own satisfaction—for it made her heart sick to think of reading over in dreadful print, as would be done that morning at millions of breakfast-tables, her own words: perhaps with comments on herself and her history, which might fall into Pippo's hands, and be read by him before he knew: which was a sudden spur to herself and evidence of the dread necessity of letting him know that story from her own lips, which had not occurred to her before. She glanced over the report with a sickening sense that all the privacy of sheltered life and honourable silence was torn off from her, and that she was exposed as on a pillory to the stare and the remarks of the world, and crushed the paper away like a noxious thing into a drawer where the boy at least would never find it. Vain thought! as if there was but one paper in the world, as if he could not find it at every street corner, thrust into his hand even as he walked along; but at all events for the moment he would not see it, and she would have time—time to tell him before that revelation could come in his way. She went down-stairs, with what a tremor in her and sinking of her heart it would be impossible to say. To have to condemn herself to her only child; to humble herself before him, her boy, who thought there was no one like his mother; to let him know that he had been deceived all his life, he who thought she had always told him everything. Oh, poor mother! and oh, poor boy!

She was still sitting by the breakfast-table, waiting, in a chill fever, if such a thing can be, for Philip, when a thing occurred which no one could have thought of, and yet which was the most natural thing in the world—which came upon Elinor like a thunderbolt, shattering all her plans again just at the moment when, after so much shrinking and delay, she had at last made up her mind to the one thing that must be done at once. The sound of the driving up of a cab to the door made her go to the window to look out, without producing any expectation in her mind: for people were coming and going in Ebury Street all day long. She saw, however, a box which she recognised upon the cab, and then the door was opened and Mrs. Dennistoun stepped out. Her mother! the wonder was not that she came now, but that she had not come much sooner. No letters for several days, her child and her child's child in town, and trouble in the air! Mrs. Dennistoun had borne it as long as she could, but there had come a moment when she could bear it no longer, and she too had followed Pippo's example and taken the night mail. Elinor stood motionless at the window, and saw her mother arrive, and did not feel capable of going to meet her, or of telling whether it was some dreadful aggravation of evil, or an interposition of Providence to save her for another hour at least from the ordeal before her.

CHAPTER XLVII.

Mrs. Dennistoun had a great deal to say about herself and the motives which had at the last been too much for her, which had forced her to come after her children at a moment's notice, feeling that she could bear the uncertainty about them no longer; and it was a thing so unusual with her to have much to say about herself that there was certainly something apologetic, something self-defensive in this unaccustomed outburst. Perhaps she had begun to feel a little the unconscious criticism that gathers round the elder person in a house, the inclination involuntarily—which every one would repudiate, yet which nevertheless is true—to attribute to her a want of perception, perhaps—oh, not unkindly!—a little blunting of the faculties, a suggestion quite unintentional that she is not what she once was. She explained herself so distinctly that there was no doubt there was some self-defence in it. "I had not had a letter for three days."

And Elinor was far more humble than her wont. "I know, mother: I felt as if it were impossible to write—till it was over——"

"My darling! I thought at last I must come and stand by you. I felt that I ought to have seen that all the time—that you should have had your mother by your side to give you countenance."

"I had John with me, mother."

"Then it is over!" Mrs. Dennistoun cried.

And at that moment Pippo, very late, pale, and with eyes which were red with sleeplessness, and perhaps with tears, came in. Elinor gave her mother a quick look, almost of blame, and then turned to the boy. She did not mean it, and yet Mrs. Dennistoun felt as if the suggestion, "He might never have known had you not called out like that," was in her daughter's eyes.

"Pippo!" she said. "Why, Elinor! what have you been doing to the boy?"

"He does not look well," said Elinor, suddenly waking up to that anxiety which had been always so easily roused in respect to Pippo. "He was very late last night. He was at the House with John," she added, involuntarily, with an apology to her mother for the neglect which had extended to Pippo too.

"There is nothing the matter with me," he said, with a touch of sullenness in his tone.

The two women looked at each other with all the vague trouble in their eyes suddenly concentrated upon young Philip, but they said nothing more, as he sat down at table and began to play with the breakfast, for which he had evidently no appetite. No one had ever seen that sullen look in Pippo's face before. He bent his head over the table as if he were intent upon the food which choked him when he tried to eat, and which he loathed the very sight of—and did not say a word. They had certainly not been very light-hearted before, but the sight of the boy thus obscured and changed made all the misery more evident. There was always a possibility of over-riding the storm so long as all was well with Pippo: but his changed countenance veiled the very sun in the skies.

"You don't seem surprised to see me here," his grandmother said.

"Oh!—no, I am not surprised. I wonder you did not come sooner. Have you been travelling all night?" he said.

"Just as you did, Pippo. I drove into Penrith last night and caught the mail train. I was seized with a panic about you, and felt that I must see for myself."

"It is not the first time you have taken a panic about us, mother," said Elinor, forcing a smile.

"No; but it is almost the first time I have acted upon it," said Mrs. Dennistoun, with that faint instinct of self-defence; "but I think you must have needed me more than usual to keep you in order. You must have been going out too much, keeping late hours. You are pale enough, Elinor, but Pippo—Pippo has suffered still more."

"I tell you," said Philip, raising his shoulders and stooping his head over the table, "granny, that there is nothing the matter with me."

And he took no part in the conversation as they went on talking, of any subjects but those that were most near their hearts. They had, indeed, no thoughts at all to spare but those that were occupied with the situation, and with this new feature in it, Pippo's worn and troubled looks, yet had to talk of something, of nothing, while the meal went on, which was no meal at all for any of them. When it was over at last Pippo rose abruptly from the table.

"Are you going out?" Elinor said, alarmed, rising too. "Have you any engagement with the Marshalls for to-day?"

"I don't know," Philip said; "Mr. Marshall was ill yesterday. I didn't see them. I'm not going out. I am going to my room."

"You've got a headache, Pippo!"

"Nothing of the kind! I tell you there is nothing the matter with me. I'm only going to my room."

Elinor put her hands on his arm. "Pippo, I have something to say to you before you go out. Will you promise to let me know before you go out? I don't want to keep you back from anything, but I have something that I must say."

He did not ask with his usual interest what it was. He showed no curiosity; on the contrary, he drew his arm out of her hold almost rudely. "Of course," he said, "I will come in here before I go out. I have no intention of going out now."

And thus he left them, and went with a heavy step, oh, how different from Pippo's flying foot: so that they could count every step, up-stairs.

"What is the matter, what is the matter, Elinor?"

"I know nothing," she said; "nothing! He was like himself yesterday morning, full of life. Unless he is ill, I cannot understand it. But, mother, I have to tell him—everything to-day."

"God grant it may not be too late, Elinor!" Mrs. Dennistoun said.

"Too late? How can it be too late? Yes; perhaps you are right, John and you. He ought to have known from the beginning; he ought to have been told when he was a child. I acknowledge that I was wrong; but it is no use," she said, wiping away some fiery tears, "to go back upon that now."

"John could not have told him anything?" Mrs. Dennistoun said, doubtfully.

"John! my best friend, who has always stood by me. Oh, never, never. How little you know him, mother! He has been imploring me every day, almost upon his knees, to tell Pippo everything; and I promised to do it as soon as the time was come. And then last night I was so glad to think that he was engaged with John, and I so worn out, not fit for anything. And then this morning——"

"Then—this morning I arrived, just when I would have been better away!"

"Don't say that, mother. It is always, always well you should be with your children. And, oh, if I had but taken your advice years and years ago!"

How easy it is to wish this when fate overtakes us, when the thing so long postponed, so long pushed away from us, has to be done at last! There is, I fear, no repentance in it, only the intolerable sense that the painful act might have been over long ago, and the soul free now of a burden which is so terrible to bear.

Philip did not leave his room all the morning. His mother, overwhelmed now by the new anxiety about his health, which had no part in her thoughts before, went to his door and knocked several times, always with the intention of going in, of insisting upon the removal of all barriers, and of telling her story, the story which now was as fire in her veins and had to be told. But he had locked his door, and only answered from within that he was reading—getting up something that he had forgotten—and begged her to leave him undisturbed till lunch. Poor Elinor!

Her story was, as I have said, like fire in her veins; but when the moment came, and a little more delay, an hour, a morning was possible, she accepted it like a boon from heaven, though she knew very well all the same that it was but prolonging the agony, and that to get it accomplished—to get it over—was the only thing to desire. She tried to arrange her thoughts, to think how she was to tell it, in the hurrying yet flying minutes when she sat alone, listening now and then to Philip's movements over her head, for he was not still as a boy should be who was reading, but moved about his room, with a nervous restlessness that seemed almost equal to her own. Mrs. Dennistoun, to leave her daughter free for the conversation that ought to take place between Elinor and her son, had gone to lie down, and lay in Elinor's room, next door to the boy, listening to every sound, and hoping, hoping that they would get it over before she went down-stairs again. She did not believe that Philip would stand out against his mother, whom he loved. Oh, if they could but get it over, that explanation—if the boy but knew! But it was apparent enough, when she came down to luncheon, where Elinor awaited her, pale and anxious, and where Philip followed, so unlike himself, that no explanation had yet taken place between them. And the luncheon was as miserable a pretence at a meal as the breakfast had been—worse as a repetition, yet better in so far that poor Pippo, with his boyish wholesome appetite, was by this time too hungry to be restrained even by the unusual burden of his unhappiness, and ate heartily, although he was bitterly ashamed of so doing: which perhaps made him a little better, and certainly did a great deal of good to the ladies, who thus were convinced that whatever the matter might be, he was not ill at least. He was about to return up-stairs after luncheon was over, but Elinor caught him by the arm: "You are not going to your room again, Pippo?"

"I—have not finished my reading," he said.

"I have a claim before your reading. I have a great deal to say to you, and I cannot put it off any longer. It must be said——"

"As you please, mother," he replied, with an air of endurance.

And he opened the door for her and followed her up to the drawing-room, the three generations going one before the other, the anxious grandmother first, full of sympathy for both; the mother trembling in every limb, feeling the great crisis of her life before her; the boy with his heart seared, half bitter, half contemptuous of the explanation which he had forestalled, which came too late. Mrs. Dennistoun turned and kissed first one and then the other with quivering lips. "Oh, Pippo, be kind to your mother; she never will have such need of your kindness again in all your life." The boy could almost have struck her for this advice. It raised a kind of savage passion in him to be told to be kind to his mother—kind to her, when he had held her above all beings on the earth, and prided himself all his life upon his devotion to her! What Mrs. Dennistoun said to Elinor I cannot tell, but she clasped her hands and gave her an imploring look, which was almost as bitterly taken as her appeal to Philip. It besought her to tell everything, to hide nothing; and what was Elinor's meaning but to tell everything, to lay bare her heart?

But once more at this moment an interruption—the most wonderful and unthought-of of all interruptions—came. I suppose it must have been announced by the usual summons at the street-door, and that in their agitation they had not heard it. But all that I know is, that when Mrs. Dennistoun turned to leave the mother and son to their conversation, which was so full of fate, the door of the drawing-room opened almost upon her as she was about to go out, and with a little demonstration and pride, as of a name which it was a distinction even to be permitted to say, of a visitor whose arrival could not be but an honour and delightful surprise, the husband of the landlady—the man of the house, once a butler of the highest pretensions, now only condescending to serve his lodgers when the occasion was dignified—swept into the room, noiseless and solemn, holding open the door, and announced "Lord St. Serf." Mrs. Dennistoun fell back as if she had met a ghost; and Elinor, too, drew back a step, becoming as pale as if she had been the ghost her mother saw. The gasp of the long breath they both drew made a sound in the room where the very air seemed to tingle; and young Philip, raising his head, saw, coming in, the man whom he had seen in court—the man who had gazed at him in the theatre, the man of the opera-glass. But was this then not the Philip Compton for whom Elinor Dennistoun had stood forth, and borne witness before all the world?

He came in and stood without a word, waiting for a moment till the servant was gone and the door closed; and then he advanced with a step, the very assurance and quickness of which showed his hesitation and uncertainty. He did not hold out his hands—much less his arms—to her. "Nell?" he said, as if he had been asking a question, "Nell?"

She seemed to open her lips to speak, but brought forth no sound; and then Mrs. Dennistoun came in with the grave voice of every day, "Will you sit down?"

He looked round at her, perceiving her for the first time. "Ah," he said, "mamma! how good that you are here. It is a little droll though, don't you think, when a man comes into the bosom of his family after an absence of eighteen years, that the only thing that is said to him should be, 'Will you sit down?' Better that, however, a great deal, than 'Will you go away?'"

He sat down as she invited him, with a short laugh. He was perfectly composed in manner. Looking round him with curious eyes, "Was this one of the places," he said, "Nell, that we stayed in in the old times?"

She answered "No" under her breath, her paleness suddenly giving way to a hot flush of feverish agitation. And then she took refuge in a vacant chair, unable to support herself, and he sat too, and the party looked—but for that agitation in Elinor's face, which she could not master—as if the ladies were receiving and he paying a morning call. The other two, however, did not sit down. Young Philip, confused and excited, went away to the second room, the little back drawing-room of the little London house, which can never be made to look anything but

457

an anteroom—never a habitable place—and went to the window, and stood there as if he were looking out, though the window was of coloured glass, and there was nothing to be seen. Mrs. Dennistoun stood with her hand upon the back of a chair, her heart beating too, and yet the most collected of them all, waiting, with her eyes on Elinor, for a sign to know her will, whether she should go or stay. It was the visitor who was the first to speak.

"Let me beg you," he said, with a little impatience in his voice, "to sit down too. It is evident that Nell's reception of me is not likely to be so warm as to make it unpleasant for a third party. There was a fourth party in the room a minute ago, if my eyes did not deceive me. Ah!"—his glance went rapidly to where Philip's tall boyish figure, with his back turned, was visible against the further window—"that's all right," he said, "now I presume everybody's here."

"Had we expected your visit," said Mrs. Dennistoun, faltering, after a moment, as Elinor did not speak, "we should have been— better prepared to receive you, Mr. Compton."

"That's not spoken with your usual cleverness," he said, with a laugh. "You used to be a great deal too clever for me, you and Nell too. But if she did not expect to see me, I don't know what she thought I was made of—everything that is bad, I suppose: and yet you know I could have worried your life out of you if I had liked, Nell."

She turned to him for the first time, and, putting her hands together, said almost inaudibly, "I know—I know. I have thought of that, and I am not ungrateful."

"Grateful! Well, perhaps you have not much call for that, poor little woman. I don't doubt I behaved like a brute, and you were quite right in doing what you did; but you've taken it out of me since, Nell, all the same."

Then there was again a silence, broken only by the labouring, which she could not quite conceal, of her breath.

"You wouldn't believe me," he resumed after a moment, "if I were to set up a sentimental pose, like a sort of a disconsolate widower, eh, would you? Of course it was a position that was not without its advantages. I was not much made for a family man, and both in the way of expense and in—other ways, it suited me well enough. Nobody could expect me to marry them or their daughters, don't you see, when they knew I had a wife alive? So I was allowed my little amusements. You never went in for that kind of thing, Nell? Don't snap me up. You know I told you I never was against a little flirtation. It makes a woman more tolerant, in my opinion, just to know how to amuse herself a little. But Nell was never one of that kind——"

"I hope not, indeed," said Mrs. Dennistoun, to whom he had turned, with indignation.

"I don't see where the emphasis comes in. She was one that a man could be as sure of as of Westminster Abbey. The heart of her husband rests upon her—isn't that what the fellow in the Bible says, or words to that effect? Nell was always a kind of a Bible to me. And you may say that in that case to think of her amusing herself! But you will allow she always did take everything too much *au grand serieux*. No? to be sure, you'll allow nothing. But still that was the truth. However, I'll allow something if you won't. I'm past my first youth. Oh, you, not a bit of it! You're just as fresh and as pretty, by George! as ever you were. When I saw you stand up in that court yesterday looking as if—not a week had passed since I saw you last, by Jove! Nell—— And how you were hating it, poor old girl, and had come out straining your poor little conscience, and saying what you didn't want to say— for the sake of a worthless fellow like me——"

A sob came out of Elinor's breast, and something half inaudible besides, like a name.

"I can tell you this," he said, turning to Mrs. Dennistoun again, "I couldn't look at her. I'm an unlikely brute for that sort of thing, but if I had looked at her I should have cried. I daresay you don't believe me. Never mind, but it's true."

"I do believe you," said the mother, very low.

"Thank you," he said, with a laugh. "I have always said for a mother-in-law you were the least difficult to get on with I ever saw. Do you remember giving me that money to make ducks and drakes of? It was awfully silly of you. You didn't deserve to be trusted with money to throw it away like that, but still I have not forgotten it. Well! I came to thank you for yesterday, Nell. And there are things, you know, that we must talk over. You never gave up your name. That was like your pluck. But you will have to change it now. It was indecent of me to have myself announced like that and poor old St. Serf not in his grave yet. But I daresay you didn't pay any attention. You are Lady St. Serf now, my dear. You don't mind, I know, but it's a change not without importance. Well, who is that fellow behind there, standing in the window? I think you ought to present him to me. Or I'll present him to you instead. I saw him in the theatre, by Jove! with that fellow Tatham, that cousin John of yours that I never could bear, smirking and smiling at him as if it were *his* son! but *I* saw the boy then for the first time. Nell, I tell you there are some things in which you have taken it well out of me——"

"Mr. Compton," she said, labouring to speak. "Lord St. Serf. Oh, Phil, Phil!—--"

"Ah," he said, with a start, "do you remember at last? the garden at that poky old cottage with all the flowers, and the days when you looked out for wild Phil Compton that all the world warned you against? And here I am an old fogey, without either wife or child, and Tatham taking my boy about and Nell never looking me in the face."

Philip, at the window looking out at nothing through the hideous-coloured glass, had heard every word, with wonder, with horror, with consternation, with dreadful disappointment and sinking of the heart. For indeed he had a high ideal of a father, the highest, such as fatherless boys form in their ignorance. And every word made it more sure that this was his father, this man who had so caught his eyes and filled him with such a fever of interest. But to hear Phil Compton talk had brought the boy's soaring imagination down, down to the dust. He had not been prepared for anything like this. Some tragic rending asunder he could have believed in, some wild and strange mystery. But this man of careless speech, of chaff and slang, so little noble, so little serious, so far from tragic! The disappointment had been too sudden and dreadful to leave him with any ears for those tones that went to his mother's heart. He had no pity or sense of the pathos that was in them. He stood in his young absolutism disgusted, miserable. This man his father!—this man! so talking, so thinking. Young Philip stood with his back to the group, more miserable than words could say. He heard some movement behind, but he was too sick of heart to think what it was, until suddenly he felt a hand on his shoulder, and most unwillingly suffered himself to be turned round to meet his father's eyes. He gave one glance up at the face, which he did not now feel was worn with study and care—which now that he saw it near was full of lines and wrinkles which meant something else, and which even the emotion in it, emotion of a kind which Pippo did not understand, hidden by a laugh, did not make more prepossessing—and then he stood with his eyes cast down, not caring to see it again.

The elder Philip Compton had, I think, though he was, as he said, an unlikely subject for that mood, tears in his eyes—and he had no inclination to see anything that was painful in the face of his son, whose look he had never read, whose voice he had never heard, till now. He held the boy with his hands on his shoulders, with a grasp more full perhaps of the tender strain of love (though he did not know him) than ever he had laid upon any human form before. The boy's looks were not only satisfactory to him, but filled his own heart with an unaccustomed spring of pride and delight—his stature, his complexion, his features, making up as it were the most wonderful compliment, the utmost sweetness of flattery that he had ever known. For the boy was himself over again, not like his mother, like the unworthy father whom he had never seen. It took him some time to master the sudden rush of this emotion which almost overwhelmed him: and then he drew the boy's arm through his own and led him back to where the two ladies sat, Elinor still too much agitated for speech. "I said I'd present my son to you, Nell—if you wouldn't present him to me," he said, with a break in his voice which sounded like a chuckle to that son's angry ears. "I don't know what you call the fellow—but he's big enough to have a name of his own, and he's Lomond from this day."

Pippo did not know what was meant by those words: but he drew his arm from his father's and went and stood behind Elinor's chair, forgetting in a moment all grievances against her, taking her side with an energy impossible to put into words, clinging to his mother as he had done when he was a little child.

CHAPTER XLVIII.

It was while this conversation was going on that John Tatham, anxious and troubled about many things, knocked at the door in Ebury Street. He was anxious to know how the explanations had got accomplished, how the boy took it, how Elinor had borne the strain upon her of such a revelation. Well as he knew Elinor, he still thought, as is generally thought in circumstances so painful, that a great crisis, a great mental effort, would make her ill. He wanted to know how she was, he wanted to know how Pippo had borne it, what the boy thought. It had glanced across him that young Philip might be excited by so wonderful a new thing, and form some false impression of his father (whom doubtless she would represent under the best light, taking blame upon herself, not to destroy the boy's ideal), and be eager to know him—which was a thing, John felt, which would be very difficult to bear.

The door was opened to him not by good Mrs. Jones, the kind landlady, but by the magnificent Jones himself, who rarely appeared. John said "Mrs. Compton?" as a matter of course, and was about to pass in, in his usual familiar way. But something in the man's air made him pause. He looked at Jones again, who was bursting with importance. "Perhaps she's engaged?" he said.

"I think, sir," said John, "that her ladyship is engaged—his lordship is with her ladyship up-stairs."

"His—what?" John Tatham cried.

"His lordship, Mr. Tatham. I know, sir, as the title is not usually assumed till after the funeral; but in the very 'ouse where her ladyship is residing for the moment, there's allowances to be made. Naturally we're a little excited over it, being, if I may make so bold as to say so, a sort of 'umble friends, and long patronized by her ladyship, and young Lord Lomond too."

"Young Lord Lomond too!" John Tatham stood for a moment and stared at Mr. Jones; and then he laughed out, and turned his back and walked away.

Young Lord Lomond too! The boy! who had been more like John's boy than anything else, but now tricked out in a new name, a new position, his father's heir. Oh, yes, it was John himself who had insisted on that only a few days ago! "The heir to a peerage can't be hid." It was he that had quoted this as an aphorism worthy of a social sage. But when the moment came and the boy was taken from him, and introduced into that other sphere, by the side of that man who had once been the *dis*-Honourable Phil! Good heavens, what changes life is capable of! What wrongs, what cruelties, what cuttings-off, what twists and alterations of every sane thought and thing! John Tatham was a sensible man as well as an eminent lawyer, and knew that between Elinor's son, who was Phil Compton's son, and himself, there was no external link at all—nothing but affection and habit, and the ever-strengthening link that had been twisted closer and closer with the progress of these years; but nothing real, the merest shadow of relationship, a cousin, who could count how often removed? And it was he who had insisted, forced upon Elinor the necessity of making his father known to Philip, of informing him of his real position. Nobody had interfered in this respect but John. He had made himself a weariness to her by insisting, never giving over, blaming her hourly for her delay. And yet now, when the thing he had so worked for, so constantly urged, was done——!

He smiled grimly to himself as he walked away: they were all together, the lordship and the ladyship, young Lord Lomond too!—and Phil Compton, whitewashed, a peer of the realm, and still, the scoundrel! a handsome fellow enough: with an air about him, a man who might still dazzle a youngster unaccustomed to the world. He had re-entered the bosom of his family, and doubtless was weeping upon Philip's neck, and bandying about that name of "Nell" which had always seemed to John an insult—an insult to himself. And in that moment of bitterness John did not know how she would take it, what effect it would produce upon her. Perhaps the very sight of the fellow who had once won her heart, the lover of her youth, with whom John had never for a moment put himself in competition, notwithstanding the bitter wonder in his heart that Elinor—Elinor of all people!—could ever have loved such a man. Yet she had loved him, and the sight of him again after so many years, what effect might it not produce? As he walked away, it was the idea of a happy family that came into John Tatham's mind—mutual forgiveness, mutual return to the old traditions which are the most endearing of all; expansions, confessions, recollections, and lives of reunion. Something more than a prodigal's return, the return of a sinner bringing a coronet in his hand, bringing distinction, a place and position enough to dazzle any boy, enough to make a woman forgive. And was not this what John wished above all things, every advancement for the boy, and an assured place in the world, as well as every happiness that might be possible—happiness! yet it was possible she might think it so—for Elinor? Yes, this was what he had wished for, been ready to make any sacrifice to secure. In the sudden shock Mr. Tatham thought of the only other person who perhaps—yet only perhaps—might feel a little as he did—the mother, Mrs. Dennistoun, upon whom he thought all this would come like a thunder-clap, not knowing that she was up-stairs in the family party, among the lordships and the ladyship too.

He went home and into his handsome library, and shut the door upon himself, to have it out there—or rather to occupy himself in some more sensible way and shut this foolish subject out of his mind. It occurred to him, however, when he sat down that the best thing to do would be to write an account of it all to Mrs. Dennistoun, who doubtless in the excitement would have a long time to wait for news of this great change. He drew his blotting-book towards him with this object, and opened it, and dipped his pen in the ink, and wrote "My dear Aunt;" but he did not get much further. He raised his head, thinking how to introduce his narrative, for which she would in all likelihood be wholly unprepared, and in so doing looked round upon his book-cases, on one shelf of which the reflection of a ray of afternoon sunshine caught in the old Louis Treize mirror over the mantelpiece was throwing a shaft of light. He got up to make sure that it was only a reflection, nothing that would harm the binding of a particular volume upon which he set great store—though of course he knew very well that it could only be a reflection, no impertinent reality of sunshine being permitted to penetrate there. And then he paused a little to draw his hand lovingly over the line of choice books—very choice—worth a little fortune, which he laughed at himself a little for being proud of, fully knowing that what was inside them (which generally is the cream of a book, as of a letter, according to Tony Lumpkin) was in many cases worth nothing at all. And then John went and stood upon the hearth-rug, and looked round him upon this the heart of his domain. It was a noble library, any man might have been proud of it. He asked himself whether it did not suit him better, with all the comforts and luxuries beyond it, than if he had been like other men, with an entirely different centre of life up-stairs in the empty drawing-room, and the burden upon him of setting out children, boys and girls, upon the world.

When a man asks himself this question, however complacent may be the reply, it betrays perhaps a doubt whether the assurance he has is so very sure after all; and he returned to his letter to Mrs. Dennistoun, which would be quite easy to write if it were only once well begun. But he had not written above a few words, having spent some time in his previous reflections, when he paused again at the sound of a tumultuous summons at the street-door. As may be well supposed, his servant took more time than usual to answer it, resenting a noise so out of character with the house, during which John listened half-angrily, fearing, yet wishing for, a diversion. And then his own door burst open, not, I need not say, by any intervention of legitimate hands, but by the sudden rush of Philip, who seemed to come in in a whirl of long limbs and eager eyes, flinging himself into a chair and fixing his gaze across the corner of the table upon his astonished yet expectant friend. "Oh, Uncle John!" the boy cried, and had not breath to say any more.

John put forth his hand across the table, and grasped the young flexible warm hand that wanted something to hold. "Well, my boy," he said.

"I suppose you know," said Philip. "I have nothing to tell you, though it is all so strange to me."

"I know—nothing about what interests me most at present—yourself, Pippo, and what has happened to you."

John had always made a great stand against that particular name, but several times had used it of late, not knowing why.

"I don't know what you thought of me last night," said the boy, "I was so miserable. May I tell you everything, Uncle John?"

What balm that question was! He clasped Pippo's hand in his own, but scarcely could answer to bid him go on.

"It was unnecessary, all she wanted to tell me. I fought it off all the morning. I was there yesterday in the court and heard it all."

"In the court! At the trial?"

"I had no meaning in it," said Philip. "I went by chance, as people say, because the Marshalls had not turned up. I got Simmons to get me into the court. I had always wanted to see a trial. And there I saw my mother stand up—my mother, that I never could bear the wind to blow on, standing up there alone with all these people staring at her to be tried—for her life."

"Don't be a fool, Philip," said John Tatham, dropping his hand; "tried! she was only a witness. And she was not alone. I was there to take care of her."

"I saw you—but what was that? She was alone all the same; and for me, it was she who was on her trial. What did I know about any other? I heard it, every word."

"Poor boy!"

"So what was the use of making herself miserable to tell me? She tried to all this morning, and I fought it off. I was miserable enough. Why should I be made more miserable to hear her perhaps excusing herself to me? But at last she had driven me into a corner, angry as I was—Uncle John, I was angry, furious, with my mother—fancy! with my mother."

John did not say anything, but he nodded his head in assent. How well he understood it all!

"And just then, at that moment, he came. I am angry with her no more. I know whatever happened she was right. Angry with her, my poor dear, dearest mother! Whatever happened she was right. It was best that she should not tell me. I am on her side all through—all through! Do you hear me, Uncle John! I have seen you look as if you blamed her. Don't again while I am there. Whatever she has done it has been the right thing all through!"

"Pippo," said John, with a little quivering about the mouth, "give me your hand again, old fellow, you're my own boy."

"Nobody shall so much as look as if they blamed her," cried the boy, "while I am alive!"

Oh, how near he was to crying, and how resolute not to break down, though something got into his throat and almost choked him, and his eyes were so full that it was a miracle they did not brim over. Excitement, distress, pain, the first touch of human misery he had ever known almost overmastered Philip. He got up and walked about the room, and talked and talked. He who had never concealed anything, who had never had anything to conceal. And for four-and-twenty hours he had been silent with a great secret upon his soul. John was too wise to check the outpouring. He listened to everything, assented, soothed, imperceptibly led him to gentler thoughts.

"And what does he mean," cried the boy at last, "with his new name? I shall have no name but my own, the one my mother gave me. I am Philip Compton, and nothing else. What right has he, the first time he ever saw me, to put upon me another name?"

"What name?"

"He called me Lomond—or something like that," said young Philip: and then there came a sort of stillness over his excitement, a lull in the storm. Some vague idea what it meant came all at once into the boy's mind: and a thrill of curiosity, of another kind of excitement, of rising thoughts which he did not hardly understand, struggled up through the other zone of passion. He was half ashamed, having just poured forth all his feelings, to show that there was something else, something that was no longer indignation, nor anger, nor the shock of discovery, something that had a tremor perhaps of pleasure in it, behind. But John was far too experienced a man not to read the boy through and through. He liked him better in the first phase, but this was natural too.

"It happens very strangely," he said, "that all these things should come upon you at once: but it is well you should know now all about it. Lomond is the second title of the Comptons, Earls of St. Serf. Haven't I heard you ask what Comptons you belonged to, Philip? It has all happened within a day or two. Your father was only Philip Compton yesterday at the trial, and a poor man. Now he is Lord St. Serf, if not rich, at least no longer poor. Everything has changed for you—your position, your importance in the world. The last Lord Lomond bore the name creditably enough. I hope you will make it shine." He took the boy by the hand and grasped it heartily again. "I am thankful for it," said John. "I would rather you were Lord Lomond than——"

"What! Uncle John?"

"Steady, boy. I was going to say Philip Compton's son; but Lord St. Serf is another man."

There was a long pause in the room where John Tatham's life was centred among his books. He had so much to do with all this business, and yet so little. It would pass away with all its tumults, and he after being absorbed by it for a moment would be left alone to his own thoughts and his own unbroken line of existence. So much the better! It is not good for any man to be swept up and put down again at the will of others in matters in which he has no share. As for Philip, he was silent chiefly to realise this great thing that had come upon him. He, Lord Lomond, a peer's son, who was only Pippo of Lakeside like any other lad in the parish, and not half so important at school as Musgrave, who did not get that scholarship. What the school would say! the tempest that would arise! They would ask a holiday, and the head master would grant it. Compton a lord! Philip could hear the roar and rustle among the boys, the scornful incredulity, the asseverations of those who knew it was true. And a flush that was pleasure had come over his musing face. It would have been strange if in the wonder of it there had not been some pleasure too.

He had begun to tolerate his father before many days were over, to cease to be indignant and angry that he was not the ideal father of his dreams. That was not Lord St. Serf's fault, who was not at all aware of his son's dreams, and had never had an ideal in his life. But John Tatham was right in saying that Lord St. Serf was another man. The shock of a new responsibility, of a position to occupy and duties to fulfil, were things that might not have much moved the dis-Honourable Phil two years before. But he was fifty, and beginning to feel himself an old fogey, as he confessed. And his son overawed Lord St. Serf. His son, who was so like him, yet had the mother's quick, impetuous eyes, so rapid to see through everything, so disdainful of folly, so keen in perception. He was afraid to bring upon himself one of those lightning flashes from the eyes of his boy, and doubly afraid to introduce his son anywhere, to show him anything that might bring upon him the reproach of doing harm to Pippo. His house, which had been very decent and orderly in the late Lord St. Serf's time, became almost prim in the terror Phil had lest they should say that it was bad for the boy.

As for Lady St. Serf, it was popularly reported that the reason why she almost invariably lived in the country was her health, which kept her out of society—a report, I need not say, absolutely rejected by society itself, which knew all the circumstances better than you or I do: but which sufficed for the outsiders who knew nothing. When Elinor did appear upon great occasions, which she consented to do, her matured beauty gave the fullest contradiction to the pretext on which she continued to live her own life. But old Lord St. Serf, who got old so long before he need to have done, with perhaps the same sort of constitutional weakness which had carried off all his brothers before their time, or perhaps because he had too much abused a constitution which was not weak—grew more and more fond in his latter days of the country too, and kept appearing at Lakeside so often that at last the ladies removed much nearer town, to the country-house of the St. Serfs, which had not been occupied for ages, where they presented at last the appearance of a united family; and where "Lomond" (who would have thought it very strange now to be addressed by any other name) brought his friends, and was not ill-pleased to hear his father discourse, in a way which sometimes still offended the home-bred Pippo, but which the other young men found very amusing. It was not in the way of morals, however, that Lord St. Serf ever offended. The fear of Elinor kept him as blameless as any good-*natured preacher of the endless theme, that all is vanity, could do.

These family arrangements, however, and the modified happiness obtained by their means, were still all in the future, when John Tatham, a little afraid of the encounter, yet anxious to have it over, went to Ebury Street the day after these occurrences, to see Elinor for the first time under her new character as Lady St. Serf. He found her in a languor and exhaustion much unlike Elinor, doing nothing, not even a book near, lying back in her chair, fallen upon herself, as the French say. Some of those words that mean nothing passed between them, and then she said, "John, did Pippo tell you that he had been there?"

He nodded his head, finding nothing to say.

"Without any warning, to see his mother stand up before all the world to be tried—for her life."

"Elinor," said John, "you are as fantastic as the boy."

"I was—being tried for my life—before him as the judge. And

he has acquitted me; but, oh, I wonder, I wonder if he would have done so had he known all that I know?"

"I do so," said John, "perhaps a little more used to the laws of evidence than Pippo."

"Ah, you!" she said, giving him her hand, with a look which John did not know how to take, whether as the fullest expression of trust, or an affectionate disdain of the man in whose partial judgment no justice was. And then she asked a question which threw perhaps the greatest perplexity he had ever known into John Tatham's life. "When you tell a fact—that is true: with the intention to deceive: John, you that know the laws of evidence, is that a lie?"

THE END.

www.ingramcontent.com/pod-product-compliance
Lightning Source LLC
Chambersburg PA
CBHW022017050726
47499CB00004BA/1029